Sere from the Green

LAUREN JANKOWSKI

SERE FROM THE GREEN: Book One of the Shape
Shifter Chronicles
Copyright © 2017 by Lauren Jankowski.

Published by Snowy Wings Publishing
www.snowywingspublishing.com

Cover art by Najla Qamber Designs.

ISBN: 978-1-946202-44-4

To Sophia,

Thank you so much for making a difference in this author's life.

You rock!

DEDICATION

For anyone who has ever looked for a character they could
identify with and was left wanting.

All the best,

Lauren

Jankowski

CHAPTER ONE

On the outskirts of a quiet town, a plain red Camry that had seen better days was parked in an untouched stretch of field. Inside, a woman sat in the driver's seat. Her pale skin seemed to glow in the car's dark gray interior. An olive green camera case sat on the empty passenger's seat next to her; a worn copy of *Frankenstein* rested on top of it. Assorted books were tossed haphazardly in the backseat, buried under newspapers, magazines and different bags. There wasn't any trace of food or drink in the car. Being sensitive to different smells, she almost never ate or drank in her vehicle. She found the smell of old food revolting.

Normally very alert and aware of her surroundings, the woman hadn't noticed when night fell, nor the sweet smell of the grass that drifted in through the open windows. Holding a penlight in one hand and an open paperback in the other, she remained engrossed in her favorite novel: *The Strange Case of Dr. Jekyll and Mr. Hyde*. The book had been heavily worn from repeated readings and some of the thin tan pages were close to falling out. She was so lost in the story that the whole world could have ended around her and she wouldn't have noticed.

Isis groaned as she switched off the penlight, tossing it onto the seat next to her and resting her elbow on the open window. Her eyes were aching from the long hours of reading with nothing but a dim light to illuminate the tiny black print. She tossed the book to the cluttered backseat and ran her long slender fingers through her short dark brown hair, cursing the day she had decided to give photojournalism a try. Now she was stuck at a local paper in a town where practically nothing ever happened.

"I could be doing more productive things right now," Isis grumbled sullenly, glancing toward a small park that was barely visible in the distance. Her boss, in his infinite wisdom, had put her on crime duty. She got to take pictures of cats stuck up in trees or the outside of supposedly burglarized houses. Wherever there were cops, Isis had to be there taking pictures. But she was also under strict orders not to anger the police or antagonize them, something that seemed impossible for her. Isis always assumed it was the job of journalists to question authority, but her boss didn't seem to share that sentiment. When Isis had first started the job, she had questioned why the town even needed a police force. Until a few weeks ago, about ninety percent of the calls on her scanner had been false alarms from paranoid hipsters who freaked out if they saw a shadow. Then, a sudden crime spree had hit town, requiring Isis to work overtime. Now she wasn't sure which situation was preferable.

Isis' bright green eyes slowly traveled over to her trusty police scanner, which was quiet for the first time in more than a week. She couldn't even listen to music in case something really juicy came on. The temptation to turn it off was strong, but Isis did not want to be known as the woman who lost three jobs by the time she turned twenty-eight. That would undoubtedly look bad on her resume.

Turning her eyes back to the windshield, Isis toyed with the necklace at her throat as she watched the lights gradually go out in the town. The charm, an emerald shamrock, glimmered in the faded moonlight.

Isis let out a frustrated sigh and tossed her head back against the headrest, contemplating whether or not it was time for a move. Putting down roots wasn't something she had ever been interested in doing and she frequently needed changes of scenery. The only reason she stayed was because she did have a couple friends in town who she enjoyed being able to visit and hang out with on occasion. Still, she was bored and wondered if her boss was purposely punishing her. She did have an uncanny ability to get on people's bad sides, as her friends enjoyed reminding her. It was a trait she'd had throughout her life.

Somewhere nearby, a nightingale began to sing its warbling song and a dark shape darted across the sky, most likely a bat. Isis glanced at the clock and saw it was five minutes before two in the morning. As she looked up to the stars glistening in the navy-colored sky, Isis thought about the stories she had photographed over the past month: domestic disturbances, break-ins, a rave that had gotten completely out of control, a few robberies, and more incidents of violence than she cared to count. It was as if the town had gone on a hedonistic bender and was gradually descending into chaos. Only Isis and most of the police force still ventured out at night. In the past few weeks, Isis had a number of close calls and narrow escapes.

Just when she decided to call it a night, the police scanner suddenly crackled to life. Isis closed her eyes and massaged her brow as she listened to the report of gunfire at the old vacant factory on the outskirts of town, which was so close she could almost see it. It would take the police a while to reach it, even without traffic. *Okay, but maybe I didn't hear that,* Isis thought as she contemplated ignoring the report. It was late at night and her shift was supposed to have ended more than two hours ago…

But taking the job could also get her on her boss' good side for a change. After a moment, Isis shook her head and turned her eyes to the road, switching off the scanner before turning the key in the ignition. The car grumbled to life.

"Let's see. Warm bath or twenty minutes alone in a dark abandoned factory, rumored to be haunted, possibly containing an armed lunatic or dead bodies in the middle of an increase of violent crimes," Isis muttered as she turned onto the road, heading for the old factory. "Let's go with the creepy old building possibly harboring an unbalanced gun wielding individual. I mean, I have only been shot at four or five times over the past few weeks. Anything for a goddamn paycheck."

She floored the gas pedal, ignoring any speed limits.

~~*~*~*

The old factory was something of a local legend that had spawned countless tales. It was a gigantic crumbling brick structure, rumored to be haunted by a variety of unsavory types — depending on which legend was being told. Graffiti covered the outside and vandals had shattered the windows with rocks, but few dared to venture inside. It had been abandoned for more than twenty years and no one knew why it hadn't been torn down. Only the occasional ghost tour drove past the place, giving a different story every year.

Isis parked behind the building, knowing the arriving officers would park in front. She turned the car off and leaned over to the glove compartment, undoing the bungee cord that held it closed. Reaching in, Isis grabbed her driving gloves. She kept most of her law-bending tools in the glove compartment, everything from her lock-picking kit to a couple fake IDs, which came in handy more often than one would think. Pulling on the tight gloves, Isis moved aside scraps of paper with various scribbled notes and grabbed the small zippered pouch that held a diamond pick and tension wrench, among other things. She unzipped it, grabbed the two small tools, and shoved them into her right front pocket.

"Best investment I ever made," Isis mumbled to herself as she put the kit back, refastened the bungee cord, and unlocked the door. Isis used her shoulder to force the door open and stood out of the car, staring at the massive looming building for a moment. A small shiver went down her spine. It felt like the factory was looking at her. *Need to watch less horror movies,* Isis thought as she shook her head and reached back into the car for her camera case and pen light, sweeping a few stray papers out of the way and tossing the other book into the backseat. Out of the corner of her eye, Isis thought she saw a shadow standing across from the car, but when she straightened up, she saw nothing. Frowning, Isis closed the door and jerked around, feeling cold fingertips trail lightly across the back of her neck. She rubbed her neck and squinted as she peered through the darkness, but she saw nothing.

"Damn crime spree is getting to me," she muttered.

Isis carefully put her camera case on the hood and moved around to the back of her car, popping open the trunk. She glanced to her left when she heard the whisper of wind slithering through the overgrown grass. There was not a cricket or nocturnal bird to be heard and the night was lit only by the occasional dull flair of a firefly.

"Yeah, I've seen this movie before," she grumbled, talking for her own benefit. Despite the eerie atmosphere, Isis wasn't the least bit intimidated. She had always been fearless to a fault and loved an occasional adrenaline rush, which made her well-suited to her job. Reaching into the trunk, Isis grabbed the twenty-one inch expandable baton that she always had with her. It only weighed around twenty ounces, but it packed a mean punch and had saved her skin on more than a few occasions. It nestled comfortably in its polycarbonate scabbard, which she clipped to her left hip pocket. Isis smiled as she drew the baton, testing the grip a couple times before sliding it back into the sheath.

Isis closed the trunk and walked around to the front of the car again, grabbing her camera case without even stopping. She had a confident walk that became even bolder when she was carrying a weapon, as her good friend Steve had pointed out more than once. He was a respected detective in town — which was a perk for Isis, since most of the police force despised her. The feeling was more than mutual on her part.

Isis moved to the flimsy chain link fence surrounding the property, finding a large hole that she could easily get through, and headed for the freight entrance; the easiest way to get in. She shook her head when she saw the flimsy security on the large doors: rusted chains with an equally rusty old padlock, which didn't even need to be picked. Pushing one of the creaky wooden doors open as far as it would go, Isis slid her thin body through the narrow opening. She clenched her teeth as she carefully pulled the camera case through. The last thing Isis needed was to break a top of the line digital camera. She let out a breath of relief once the camera was through and stood up, turning to observe the inside of the old factory.

It was dark, illuminated only by the murky light that seeped in through the broken windows, and covered in what seemed like centuries of dust and cobwebs. The horrible stench of rot and decay hung in the air. It was freezing cold, in stark contrast to the sweltering summer night outside, and she could see her breath every time she exhaled. Every now and again, she could hear the faint screech of a bat, flapping about in the upper levels. *Flying little rabies machines, could my night get any better?* Isis thought with no small amount of snark, shivering a little.

Isis continued to make her way through the dark empty space, coughing at the dusty stale air that invaded her lungs. She moved around the few wooden boxes that had been left when the place was abandoned and soon spotted what appeared to be a body on the floor a few feet away. Pausing to look around, Isis stared again at the old boxes and then at the body. A strong wind howled through the numerous broken windows, rattling the freight doors Isis had entered through.

As she continued to creep forward, Isis' footsteps sounded abnormally loud in the silent warehouse. Her heart beat quicker and her senses became just a little sharper as she continued to make her way toward the shape.

"Oh god," Isis murmured, putting the back of her hand over her nose and mouth. It was a woman, not much older than Isis. Her face had been torn apart, probably from a high-powered firearm; Isis couldn't be sure. She didn't know much about guns. It was without a doubt the most gruesome scene Isis had ever come across and she hesitated.

Shaking her head and lowering her hand, Isis carefully pulled her camera from its case. She squatted down as she removed the lens cap, snapping a few shots. In her younger years, Isis had dreamed of making some kind of difference in the world by photographing wars, massacres, poverty, and other horrific realities. She possessed a strong stomach and had never really been afraid of anything, which she felt made her ideal for such an assignment. The fact that she'd often have an ocean between her and any sort of relations was merely an added bonus. As she looked at the dead woman, Isis questioned whether she would have been able to photograph that kind of violence day after day.

"So, was it a jealous Don Juan?" she asked the body. "Or did someone just *really* not like you? Of course, it could be that people in general are terrible."

Isis' head jerked up when she thought she heard a creaking hinge. Her body stiffened painfully and she winced. It was then she noticed a glistening spot on the far wall. Taking out her penlight again, Isis shone the dim beam on the spot.

"What the fuck?" she whispered as she stood up and made her way over to the still-wet symbol, carefully avoiding the blood splatters. It looked like a large backwards "P" with an elongated stem. In the center of the stem, two equally long lines were crossed in the shape of a long "X," but instead of straight lines, there were odd shapes. The entire thing was contained within a circle. Isis tilted her head as she looked at the congealing substance on the cement wall. It was dark red, almost black — most likely blood.

"Tom, I swear to fucking god, I draw the line at serial killers," Isis grumbled as she snapped a few shots of the symbol. "This shit is right out of a serial killer textbook and I want *no* part of that."

After a moment, Isis moved back to the body. She put the camera away, running a thumb over her bottom lip. Something felt...off. Isis glanced up toward where the front entrance was.

"He hides behind the boxes," she murmured to herself, one hand held up. "Shoots the woman as she approaches, and then sticks around to paint a symbol on the wall with her blood? Why? And what were you doing here in the first place?"

Hearing a scuffing sound behind her, Isis laid her hand on her baton. She carefully slid it out of its scabbard, resting her thumb on the button that would expand it to its full length. She knew she had been pressing her luck, especially with the month she had been having. If she was going to die Isis was determined to go down fighting.

When she heard the footsteps get close enough, Isis pressed the button and spun around as swiftly as she was able, throwing her momentum into the swing. There was a muffled whacking noise followed by a very colorful curse as the shadowy form behind her crashed to the unforgiving cement floor.

"The hell, Isis!?" a voice groaned as the form rocked back and forth on the floor.

"Steve?" Isis breathed in surprise as she pulled her penlight out and shone it toward the writhing shape. Steve was grimacing in pain and holding his throbbing leg. He winced away from the light, raising one hand to shield his eyes.

"It's not enough to break my leg, you have to burn my corneas too?" he asked, irritated. Isis rolled her eyes and switched off the penlight, slipping it back into her pocket.

"I didn't hit you that hard, wuss," she said as she stood up, offering her hand. Steve accepted it, but she could feel the venomous look he shot her as she helped him to his feet. Steve had the lean build of a runner and was on the lighter side, a physique he had effortlessly maintained throughout his life. Isis helped him brush the dust off his clothing and out of his shaggy dark hair.

"I could have you arrested for assaulting an officer with a weapon. Who said you could have one of those?" Steve practically interrogated her. Isis pressed the button on the baton again, pressing it on the ground to collapse the weapon, and slid it back into its scabbard.

"I'm a twenty-eight year old, single, queer woman. You think I'm *not* going to carry a weapon?" Isis replied. "Oh and I'm a photojournalist who apparently specializes in crime photography now. Yeah, walking around unarmed is right at the top of my list of priorities. Be thankful I'm not carrying a gun."

"And how many damn times do I have to tell you to wait for the police?" Steve continued, as he stepped between her and the body. "You know, the captain isn't exactly fond of you as it is. Neither is anyone else in the squad for that matter."

Isis frowned in the dark, looking to where she assumed Steve's soulful brown eyes would be if she could see them. He couldn't guilt her with the wounded puppy look, yet another advantage of the dark. Steve turned around, switching on his own flashlight and pointing it toward the body.

"And I care because…?" Isis responded with mock curiosity. Steve shook his head and Isis smiled, enjoying how much she vexed him.

"A little bird told me a rumor that the boys in blue use a photo of me for target practice. Any truth to it?"

"Not for shooting practice, but there is a dartboard in the office that your picture keeps finding its way onto," Steve replied, distracted. He kept the bright beam of his flashlight on the body.

Isis pouted. "Well that's a bit disappointing. What does a girl have to do to get her picture up in the shooting range?"

"I'm sure it'll happen eventually, knowing your talent for rubbing people the wrong way and your history of challenging any sort of authority."

Isis chuckled and looked over at her friend. He turned back toward her and pointed his flashlight in her direction, careful to keep the beam out of her eyes. She raised an eyebrow slightly, waiting for him to go into mom-friend mode.

"Isis, you of all people should know that it's not safe to be urban exploring at night, especially not now," Steve said. She shook her head and thought about just how predictable her friend was. There were times when it was reassuring, but mostly it was irritating.

"I need to make a living, Steve," Isis replied. "I can't just hide in my apartment because there have been a few break-ins."

"A few break-ins? A few—?" Steve paused and ran a hand over his face in exasperation. "Isis, in the past couple months, you've nearly been shot three separate times. Then there was the incident two weeks ago when you were almost hit by a car while photographing the scene of a robbery. Is your life really worth a paycheck?"

"Four times," Isis corrected. "You're forgetting the rave incident last week. And it was an SUV not a car and that *barely* counts as a close call. Those damn things are too bulky and slow. You're welcome for that clear picture of the license plate, by the way."

"Isis," Steve sighed as he shook his head, frowning when a thought came to him. "Wait a minute. Aren't you supposed to be off until next week?"

"Steve, check this out," Isis said, quickly changing

the subject. She wanted to avoid the topic of what had happened last week when she had been photographing a rave for a story on teenage subcultures. Someone had fired a gun into the crowd, which caused a panic that swiftly turned into pandemonium — leading to multiple injuries and a few fatalities. In the chaos, Isis had been knocked down and would have been trampled had it not been for Steve's timely appearance. He always seemed to be in the right place at the right time.

"Christ, Isis. The doctor said you had to take it easy," Steve protested, reaching down and rubbing his sore leg.

"A couple bruised ribs and a concussion and she expected me to lie around doing nothing for a month? I don't think so," Isis protested, waving her penlight at the wall. "Now will you please look at what I'm pointing to?"

"Two cracked ribs and a broken one," Steve corrected her as he stepped up beside her. He frequently gave up when arguing with her, unless she was doing something life-threatening. Isis was high-strung and extremely stubborn, which wasn't a good combination.

"What is this?" she asked, circling her beam of light around the blood. Steve pointed his own flashlight toward the symbol. She glanced over at Steve when he didn't respond right away, noticing he was squinting as he studied the strange markings.

"What's wrong?" she asked. He moved closer and she followed, twisting around when she thought she heard footsteps behind them. Shivering a little, Isis turned her attention back to the wall in front of them.

"Odd," Steve murmured as he continued to

examine the symbol, moving his flashlight over each part of the symbol.

"What?" she asked. Steve looked over at her with a half-smile.

"Off the record?" he asked, raising an eyebrow.

"I just take the pictures, Steve. I don't write the stories," Isis replied, wondering if her friend would ever figure out what her job did and did not entail. He still confused journalist and photojournalist, though Isis was sure he was sometimes trying to get a rise out of her. Steve snickered and looked back at the symbol.

"The main part of it seems to be a Chi Rho, an early christogram, one that was frequently stamped on money. Except the top of it…it's backwards. I've never seen that before. It's like a corruption or something. The markings on the stem resemble cuneiform script, one of the earliest forms of writing," he explained, highlighting the different parts with his flashlight beam.

"What does it say?" Isis asked, fascinated. Steve shrugged and shook his head.

"I know what cuneiform looks like, but I don't know how to read it or translate it," he replied. "My archeological and ancient linguistic knowledge is sadly quite limited."

"Well that's disappointing," Isis muttered, running a hand through her hair. "I've got to be honest, Steve. The fact that you know all that, it's a little scary."

"I read a lot," Steve replied as he looked back to the body. Isis kept looking at the symbol, surprised at how cleanly it was drawn. It didn't look like it had been created in a rush.

"About christograms?" Isis said under her breath

as she turned and followed him back to where she had left her camera.

"I'm a student of the world," Steve stated.

"Uh huh," Isis replied, disinterested. She pulled out her camera and took a couple quick shots of the symbol on the wall. She shivered again and rubbed her arm briefly, feeling the goosebumps on her flesh.

"You'd think some of the heat would've gotten in by now," she commented. Steve didn't seem to notice as he continued to study the body. He crouched down and rubbed his chin, keeping his light on the dead woman.

"Did you know her?" Isis asked as she put the camera away again, glancing over at her friend. Something about Steve's expression made her wonder if he recognized the body, although she didn't know how since the woman lacked a face and her clothing wasn't distinctive enough to identify her. The distant sound of police sirens interrupted whatever answer he might have given. Steve glanced up and then turned his attention back to Isis.

"Look, you got your shots. Could you at least give me until tomorrow afternoon to find out who she was and let me notify any relatives she might have?" Steve asked, tiredness seeping into his voice.

Isis nodded. "You know I will."

"Thank you," Steve said, gratitude apparent in his voice, and Isis shrugged in response. She wasn't heartless…at least, not most of the time. Not to people she considered friends. Steve gestured toward the back and she smirked mischievously.

"Can't I say hi to some of my old friends on the force?" she asked.

"Go," Steve ordered, emphatically pointing with

his flashlight. She raised her hands in surrender and hurried toward the back. She reached the freight doors and slid her camera bag out first, then slipped through the narrow opening, and hurried over to her car. Isis fished her keys out of her pocket as she approached the driver's door, glancing to where the red and blue lights were starting to become visible.

"Ooh, I didn't get shot. My luck might be looking up," Isis said as she sank into the car.

~~*~*~*

The newspaper offices were always bustling in the morning, the place coming alive shortly after seven. People ran around, their footsteps muted by dark gray carpeting. The air was filled with the sounds of rustling paper and ringing phones. Large cups of coffee were downed like shots of good tequila. The frantic sounds of computer keys clattered beneath all the other noises, adding to the neurotic atmosphere. Sunlight streamed in from the large windows on both ends of the building, illuminating the numerous desks spread across the floor as well as the large office toward the back.

Isis hurried through the door, almost cringing at the assault of noise. She purposely wore sneakers to avoid the annoying clicking sound heels made on the tile, a sound she absolutely hated. She rolled her eyes when she saw the dark-haired man with the headset, avoiding eye contact as she moved toward the double doors.

"ID, please," the bored voice stopped her in her tracks. Isis bit her bottom lip, clenched her fists briefly, and then forced a moderately pleasant expression on her face. Turning on the balls of her feet and approaching the desk, she laid her palms on the smooth gray surface, looking down at the receptionist. His feet were up on the desk and he was flipping through a magazine, sports related judging from the cover.

"Rick, we do this every damn day. Now, you know I work—"

"Please don't curse at me, ma'am," he replied without looking up at her, flipping another page in the magazine. Isis swallowed and cracked her neck. *I will not commit murder today,* she thought, repeating the mantra in her mind.

"You know I work here. I've been working here longer than you," she continued, forcing herself to be calm and polite. He wasn't going to get a rise out of her today.

"Still need to see your ID," Rick sighed, still looking at his magazine. Isis smiled and reached down into the dark green satchel that she had slung diagonally over one shoulder, fishing out her ID.

"You know what? Even *you* can't dampen my good mood today," she said as she showed the card to Rick. He glanced at it, shrugged, and gestured vaguely toward the double doors that led to the busy offices.

"Thanks, Satan," Isis grumbled under her breath as she reached the doors and pushed one open, entering the offices. As soon as the door swung shut behind her, her editor pounced.

"An hour and a half late, Isis," he chastised, pointing at the expensive watch on his bony wrist as he followed her. Isis glanced over her shoulder at him as they moved toward her desk. He was a scrawny man who looked as though he had avoided daylight from the day he was born. His mop of sandy-colored hair was noticeably thinning — most likely from stress — making him appear older than he was. He always reeked of cheap coffee and breath mints.

"I'm sorry, Tom. Trust me, when you see what I've got, you'll want to marry me," Isis replied as she reached her desk.

Tom responded with a skeptical look. Isis took off her satchel and placed it on the desk, opening it and reaching into one of the front pockets, retrieving her flash drive.

"You know the murder in the old factory last night?" she said, sinking into her seat. She switched on her computer. Tom stared at her, bewildered.

"What murder?" he asked.

"Oh come on. The story has to have broken by now," Isis said, leaning back in her tall computer chair. "A woman was killed in the old factory last night, shot at close range. Weird symbol painted in blood on the wall?"

Tom shook his head. "I'll ask Chris about it later. Just show me what you've got."

Isis frowned as she slid the flash drive into the USB port, waiting for the icon to show up on screen. She clicked it, ignoring her boss hovering over her. Isis' eyes widened as she stared at the thumbnail preview images that showed up, scrolling down as she tried to make sense of what she was seeing.

"No. That can't be right," she muttered, clicking on various shots. The pictures were of the old factory. Everything was exactly how she remembered it…except there was no body. There wasn't even a sign of a body. The symbol had also disappeared, leaving only a blank concrete wall.

"This isn't right, Tom. There was a woman's body, right there," Isis pointed at the screen. She was unnerved and trying her best not to show it.

Tom let out a long minty sigh. "Did you grab the wrong flash drive?"

"No. These are in the old factory," Isis replied, not turning away from the screen. "Where's the symbol? This doesn't make any sense."

Tom leaned down, speaking under his breath, "If you were drinking on the job—"

"I wasn't drinking on the job!" Isis shouted, drawing some curious looks over to her. "I wasn't under the influence of anything. There was a body, right there, and a symbol in blood on the wall. I saw it. The cops were there. Steve was there!"

"Isis, if there had been a murder last night, I think someone would've heard about it," a hint of irritation crept into the editor's voice.

"For Christ's sake," Isis scowled and stood up, grabbing her satchel. She ejected the flash drive and shut the computer down. The noise level had noticeably dropped as her coworkers turned to watch the unfolding drama.

"Where are you going?" Tom asked as she moved past him.

"Bodies don't just disappear into thin air," she replied, pulling the strap of her satchel over her head. She was through the doors before Tom had a chance to respond. He shook his head and headed back to his office. The noise continued once more as everyone went back to their jobs.

~~*~*~*

Isis pulled into the morgue parking lot, pulling off her sunglasses and squinting against the bright sun. It was a beautiful summer day, but she was too furious to appreciate it. She shifted into park with much more force than was necessary. Her satchel sat forgotten in the back seat, amid stacks of papers. She clipped her ID card onto the pocket of her jeans and undid another button on her dark green blouse to deal with the summer heat. Grabbing her black sunglasses, she slid them over her eyes again.

She unlocked her car door and kicked it a few times to open it, stepping out into the humid warmth. Slamming the door shut, Isis moved across the parking lot toward the front doors of the miniscule gray brick building. Isis had only been to the place a handful of times. She sometimes wondered if the medical examiners found the town as dull as she did.

Just before she reached the door, a movement caught Isis' eye. She glanced over to the small alleyway and noticed a scrawny black and tan tortoiseshell cat sitting atop the grimy dark blue dumpster. His bright golden eyes fixed on her and he let out a deep yowl, arching his back and rubbing against the wall the dumpster was next to. She smiled and stepped into the alley, avoiding the dirty puddles of what she hoped was water.

"Hello pretty," Isis cooed as she scratched the cat under his chin, surprised by how silky and clean the cat's fur felt. "What's your name, huh? What's your name?"

The cat purred and rubbed her hand affectionately with his head. Isis didn't get along with people, but animals were another story. She had never been bitten or stung in her life and animals, even feral and wild ones, seemed to relax in her presence. Looking over her shoulder, Isis saw another car pull into the parking lot.

"Talk about luck," she muttered as she continued to pet the stray cat. She watched as Steve stepped out of his blue Prius — possibly the ugliest car Isis had ever seen — and started toward the morgue. He stopped just before the doors and sighed, running a hand through his hair. Isis massaged the cat behind his ears one more time and stepped out of the alley.

"Well, if it isn't the Celia to my Rosalind," she said, causing her friend to visibly jump and spin around. "Though I'm sure some of your fellow detectives would refer to me as a more villainous character. If any of them actually picked up a book that is. But that would probably impede on their schedule of covering up incidents of excessive force and planting evidence."

"Isis? What are you doing here?" Steve asked, surprised.

"I was about to ask you the same thing," Isis replied, a smile splitting her lips. "Going in to identify a body?"

"I'm meeting someone," Steve replied, looking nervous when Isis leaned her weight against the door and pushed it open a little. She glanced over her shoulder, unbothered, and then back to him with a small grin.

"Steve, don't tell me you're still afraid of cadavers," she teased. "What's the name of that phobia?"

"Necrophobia or thanatophobia," Steve responded. "After the Greek personification—"

"For as long as I've known you, you've had a

weird thing about funerals, wakes, morgues, pretty much death in general," Isis interrupted, leaning against the door a little more. "You can't tell me that's not a phobia."

"I'm not *afraid* of cadavers," Steve insisted. "I just...I don't like the morgue."

Isis stared at him for a moment. "You're a detective."

"So?" Steve replied defensively. Isis pushed the door open wider.

"They're not going to jump up and bite you. I'll go in with you and protect you from all the spooky dead bodies," she coaxed.

"What are you doing here anyway? Some kind of human interest piece or something?" Steve asked, stalling. Isis frowned, resting her elbows up on the bar that was used to push the door open.

"I'm here for the same reason as you: the body in the old factory last night. Or was there another murder I'm unaware of?" she explained. Steve stared at her, frowning in a way that was meant to be confusion, but Isis saw right through the act. She and Steve had known each other for so long, they could read one another like a book.

"What body?" he asked. Isis ran her hands over her face, silently counting to ten.

"I certainly hope you're better at lying to Justin than me," she growled. "I'm not crazy. Why is everyone acting like nothing happened last night? What is so important about this woman?"

"Isis, what are you talking about?"

Isis glared at him, pushed the door open fully and disappeared inside the morgue.

~~*~*~*

"I don't know what to tell you. Nobody matching that description came in last night. We had maybe ten pick-ups this week, but none at the old factory."

Isis gritted her teeth and massaged her temples, getting more confused and irritated by the minute. "That's not possible. There was a body there last night. It was a woman, about my age, shot in the face."

The medical examiner, Redfield according to his nametag, shook his head as his eyes wandered down to her chest again. "Nope, sorry. Maybe an autopsy was against their religious beliefs?"

"It wouldn't matter if it was a murder—!" Isis snapped, stopping to rein in her temper. Redfield shrugged, uninterested in whatever she was saying.

"Look, could I just see last night's intake form?" Isis asked as politely as she could manage. She felt like decking the infuriating man, who looked as though he just graduated from high school and acted in the same way.

"Sure, as soon as I see some ID," Redfield replied, smiling in a way that was meant to be flirtatious. *Not if you were the last living thing on Earth, creep,* Isis thought as she unclipped her ID badge and pulled a couple twenties out of her pocket, placing them under the badge, which she then slid across the desk in a smooth motion. Redfield barely glanced at the badge as he handed over the clipboard and pocketed the cash.

"You didn't get this from me," he whispered, glancing around in a way that Isis assumed was meant to be suave. *Christ, men are easy,* she thought.

"My lips are sealed," Isis replied with a wink, watching as Redfield got up and strode back toward the room where the bodies were kept. Her smile vanished and she looked down to the blank form in front of her, her heart sinking.

I'm losing my mind, Isis thought as she shook her head and rubbed her eyes. The M.E. was right, no bodies from the old factory last night. There were no names in the black grid lines. Had the whole thing been a hallucination? But what about the pictures? The thought of not being able to trust her mind or perception was terrifying to her.

Isis suddenly felt claustrophobic and the smell of chemicals began to make her feel ill. She had to get out of the building, into fresh air. She wanted to breathe actual oxygen instead of whatever was recycled in the building. As she put the clipboard back on the sterile desktop, something caught her eye. Isis twisted her body and leaned down to get a closer look.

It was so faint, she could've been imagining it, but there appeared to be phantom pen marks on the page. It looked like someone had been writing something else on another sheet of paper just on top of the blank sheet. *Bryn Adams, 3 a.m.,* Isis mouthed, tilting her head a little to better make out the faint outlines. They seemed to be disappearing before her eyes.

The sound of a drawer slamming caused her to jump. Glancing toward the back, Isis hurried across the slick tiles toward the bright sunlight streaming in through the windows of the door.

Pulling the door open, Isis nearly walked into Steve as she stepped out into the revitalizing sunlight. Taking a few steps away from the door, she dropped her hands to her knees, almost doubling over. Her eyes were still stinging from the unnatural lighting inside the morgue and Isis wondered how the hell people could work in that place for extended periods of time.

"Did you find what you were looking for?" Steve asked. Isis turned her head, almost having forgotten her friend was there. What was he hiding from her and why?

"No," she replied, straightening up again. Steve frowned as he watched her.

"Isis, I'm not keeping anything from you," he said in his gentle voice, sounding hurt. She swallowed and looked to where her car was parked. Being as cynical as she was, Isis tended to keep everyone at arm's length, but Steve was one of the few people in her life who she allowed to be close to her and he had never given her a reason to mistrust him. The fact that he was lying hurt more than she was willing to let on.

"Neither am I," she responded, moving toward her car. She could practically feel Steve's sad eyes following her every step. Pausing when she was halfway across the lot, Isis let out a long sigh. *Dammit, I'm going to have to take the high road,* she realized. There weren't many people in her life and as much as she hated to admit it, Isis did need friends. She turned around and looked back to where he was still standing by the morgue door. A car pulled into a parking space nearby, just behind her.

"Look, I have to get back to work before I'm fired. Again," she called back to him. "I'll call you later tonight, all right?"

Steve nodded, a small grin playing across his face, and gave a short wave of parting. Isis turned back to continue on her way to her car and accidentally walked into the man who had just pulled into the parking space.

"Sorry," Isis mumbled the apology as she looked at the man, pausing. He looked mildly surprised with his hands held out, probably because she had just walked into him. He stood a little less than a head taller than her and had a full head of black hair. The man was clean-shaven and had the clearest blue-green eyes Isis had ever seen. There was something else though, something almost familiar…

The stranger nodded with a slight smile, accepting the apology, and stepped around her as he continued toward the morgue.

"Um, kind of a weird question," Isis began hesitantly, her voice stopping the stranger in his steps. He twisted a little so that he was looking at her again. "Have we met before?"

The stranger paused for a moment, then smiled amicably and shook his head. "No. I don't believe so."

Isis frowned, either in disappointment or confusion, she wasn't sure which. *I'm having a very strange day*, she thought.

"That's a pretty charm," the man commented, drawing her out of her thoughts. Isis looked up at him and he gestured to the emerald at her throat. "Looks very lucky."

She smiled, but it felt forced. "Thank you."

He nodded and watched as she turned back to her car. Isis was so bewildered by the odd chain of events that she didn't notice the man talking with Steve as she pulled out of the parking lot.

CHAPTER TWO

It was a typical quiet night for the small hospital in town. A heavy antiseptic smell hung in the air, the kind that burned the nostrils and lingered on the tongue. Shades of blue were scattered throughout the entire hospital and even the lights seemed to have a blue tint. Doctors and nurses rushed around through the unnaturally bright halls, blurs of blues and whites and pinks and greens. Every now and again, the intercom system would crackle to life, calling for a doctor or nurse to report to various destinations. The waiting area, normally filled with stone-faced people waiting for news of a loved one or patients in need of care, was now empty save for one man who paced the hall like a big cat in a cage.

Jet walked back and forth, running his hands through his thick black hair, messing it up beyond its usual untidiness. His dark-colored clothing stuck out in the brightly lit hallway. The walls had become a blur as he quickened his pacing, yet his powerful gait remained silent. The night's events raced through his mind and he would have given anything for his wife, Lilly, to be there with him. But she was needed elsewhere.

Jet pulled his cell phone out of his pocket, unable to wait anymore. He had to get answers and doing nothing was going to drive him mad. Dialing the number he knew by heart, Jet pressed send and waited as the phone rang. Tapping a knuckle against the wall, Jet struggled not to fidget too much.

"Jet?" Remington's soothing Irish brogue filtered through the receiver. For a moment, Jet was tempted to snap at him for taking so long to answer the phone. However, it had been a long night and Jet knew his nerves were frayed. Yelling at his long-time trainer wasn't going to help anybody.

"Any word on Jade?" Jet asked, glancing around to make sure he was alone. The hall was still empty, but he wasn't about to take any chances.

"Nothing yet, but I expect to be hearing from her in another few minutes. And before you ask, yes, Lilly is still with her," Remington replied, his tone compassionate. Jet sometimes wondered if the ancient shape shifter was telepathic. He always seemed to know what was on Jet's mind. Jet's father had once told him that Remington was the best protector when it came to reading people. It was a skill the trainer had taught to his adopted daughter, Alex.

"I need you to come down here," Jet said. "I haven't gotten word from Dr. Gavin yet, so I assume the bodies are still in transport to the hospital morgue. I just need you to wait here and make arrangements."

There was a brief pause and Jet could practically

hear Remington's puzzlement. "If you're already down there, why can't you take care of it?"

"Because there's something else I need to do," Jet replied, working out a script in his mind. He glanced behind him when he heard a quiet squeaking, noticing a janitor in a drab uniform roll a dirty yellow bucket with the handle of his mop. He kept his eyes on the floor as he put up yellow plastic warning signs. Glancing up, the man tipped his hat in Jet's direction. Jet gave him a half-nod, acknowledging the greeting.

"I don't suppose you'll tell me what this mysterious errand is." Remington's questions usually sounded like statements, especially when he saw right through a lie.

"I have to meet with someone who might have answers about what happened tonight," Jet replied, being vague. He kept his eyes on the janitor, watching the methodical motion of the mop as it slid across the floor.

"I see. This someone wouldn't happen to be a woman with unclear loyalties who delights in getting a rise out of you?" Remington asked with his typical dryness. If he hadn't been so worn out, Jet would've grimaced at the tone.

"Remington, will you please just come down here as soon as possible?" Jet requested, already exhausted. "Please don't make me order you to do so."

Remington sighed. "Very well. I'll have Alex leave Lilly a note."

"Thank you," Jet responded. He disconnected the call before Remington had a chance to follow up with any kind of "keep a level-head" type of caution. Jet stuck his hands in his pockets and moved toward the sliding glass doors that he had entered through.

It was a pain in the neck any time a shape shifter wound up in the hospital. They had to make sure they were in a safe zone, meaning at least one member of the staff knew about shape shifters or actually was one. Then there was concern about the various tests. It was even worse on the rare occasions that a shape shifter died and was taken to a hospital. It was extremely difficult for an ally to get the body released without an autopsy. However, it was of the utmost importance that the body was not brought to a morgue. Shape shifters, being immortal, had an instinctive dislike of death. Jet and Lilly had yet to find a shape shifter willing to work in the office of the medical examiner. Because of this, they lacked any contacts within the morgue, which was a disaster waiting to happen.

Jet slipped out into the cool night and glanced around. There were very few cars around, which wasn't unusual given the time, and everything was lit in strange shades of orange and black. The air was chilly and clouds drifted over the moon, making the night even darker. Jet shivered and hurried on his way, heading for a nearby forest.

When he got out of the glow of streetlights, he looked around once more to make sure he wasn't being watched. Once certain he was completely alone, the bones in his body began to change shape. His body lengthened while his limbs alternately grew and shrunk to keep up with the changing body. Within thirty seconds, a silver wolf stood in Jet's place. He shook himself and took off, loping toward the large forest that his elusive contact called home.

~~*~*~*

The night continued on and the forest was darker than the town. But it was also more tranquil, even peaceful. None of the noise of civilization touched the depths of the forest, which was exactly how Jet's contact liked it.

Jet sniffed the ground as he prowled through the enormous trees, anger making his vision flash red. He knew Sly was in the forest somewhere. She always was, lurking somewhere in the shadows.

Sly was a shape shifter and a good informant. The problem lay with her loyalties: she had always been on her own side, doing only what benefitted her. She was never seen unless she wanted to be, and very little was known about her. At one time she'd been a friend to Jet, but that had been many, many years ago. Times changed, and so did shape shifters. He didn't trust Sly anymore, despite some protectors' attempts to defend her to him. Sly didn't appreciate others attempting to speak for her anyway.

He continued on, still haunted by the night's events. A swishing noise in the treetops ripped him out of his thoughts. Looking up, he saw a large brown speckled owl watching him with enormous ring-shaped yellow eyes. Its beak clicked as it hooted before flapping its enormous wings and flying away; disappearing into the night. Jet shifted from wolf to human again and looked around. *I must be in the middle of the forest by now,* he thought

"Sly!" he called, not worrying about being overheard. "Sly, I know you're here. I know you know what happened. I'm not in the mood for games tonight!"

The ominous forest remained silent save for the

fading echo of Jet's voice. Minutes passed with no sign of the elusive Sly and Jet contemplated giving up. He didn't have the patience to wait for her to make an appearance.

"Must be your lucky night, protector. Normally I don't respond to grown men throwing temper tantrums," a quiet sultry voice came from behind him.

Jet turned around to familiar piercing emerald eyes. Sly casually leaned against a tree with her arms crossed over her chest, unbothered by his tone. Her soft black hair was streaked with moonlight. He could only see her face clearly in the shadows, dark clothing concealing the rest of her. Jet sometimes wondered where his mysterious informant acquired her apparel, since he only ever saw her in the forest and knew of her strong aversion toward humans. *Damn things are like irrational self-destructive cockroaches,* she had once told him.

Sly combined her beauty with intelligence and physical skill and used both to her advantage, having a well-deserved reputation for being as clever as she was lethal. Jet didn't like talking with her and he definitely wasn't in the mood to deal with her. He stormed over, making sure to step right into her personal space. Sly smiled up at him, though he could tell she wasn't thrilled with having him so close. It wasn't something he'd normally do, but after the night he'd had, he didn't feel like being toyed with.

"Temper, temper. Threats make me quiet, Jet. And with this sudden increase in violence...well, you don't know what I might be inspired to do," Sly cautioned, an underlying threat in her calm tone. She didn't show any traces of fear. Jet knew he was always at a disadvantage when talking to her; she knew him like the back of her hand and that he would never hurt her. Any threat he tried would be empty.

"Did you have anything to do with what happened tonight?" Jet hissed through his teeth, fists clenching at his sides.

Sly leaned forward slightly so that her face was inches from his, a small grin playing across her features. "Threats make me quiet."

Jet glared at her as he took a step back so he stood just outside her personal space, fully prepared to step back in it should she try to walk away. She continued to smile, her sleek body losing some of its tenseness.

"I'm not asking again," Jet warned. Sly glanced around, closing her eyes briefly and inhaled through her nose. Opening her eyes again, she turned back toward him.

"Were you swimming in rubbing alcohol? You reek," Sly said, grimacing in disgust.

"Sly," Jet warned, attempting not to raise his voice. Sly didn't like being yelled at and would walk away if he yelled.

"No," Sly answered, looking up to the moon, unbothered.

"No what?" he barked the question and she rolled her eyes back to him.

"I didn't have anything to do with what happened tonight, Jet, and even you're not dense enough to believe otherwise. Much as I dislike our human neighbors, I dislike separatists even more. Besides that, it's not in my best interest to wage war against the protectors," Sly responded in an uninterested tone. "Especially not when one of my lovers is counted among your people. How is Jade, by the way?"

"Last I heard, Jade was being treated by guardian healers," Jet answered.

"Figures," Sly said, glancing at her fingernails. "Any other questions you care to snarl at me tonight?"

"Who was behind the attack? And don't even try telling me you don't know because we both know that's unlikely," Jet said sharply, struggling to keep the images of that night's debacle at bay. He knew he would be sick if he remembered the blood, the sounds in his earpiece. It was too much for Jet at the moment.

"I saw what you did, Jet. Onyx appeared to be the responsible party. We're both aware of the rumors that someone is making a play for Adara's territory. Sending out Onyx to kill two protectors — fairly well-known ones at that — was a show of strength, a message not to mess with her," Sly responded as she moved to walk away. "Contrary to what you believe, assassins don't consult me about their politics and hierarchies. Have Jade call the Rebel Lair and leave a message with Alpha when she's all healed up and recovered."

Jet swiftly stepped around her, blocking her way, and she smirked at him. It was a risky move, since she was the more capable fighter. But Jet knew it wasn't in her best interests to get into a physical altercation with one of the leaders of the protectors.

"How did they know we'd be there?" Jet demanded, sick and tired of her games. Her thin smile remained as she crossed her arms over her chest again and tilted her head, studying him.

"Why do you come to me for answers even though you don't trust me?" she asked, her tone almost playful.

"I asked you a question," Jet said.

"And I answered your question, now I want an answer," Sly was quick to respond. "You don't trust me, yet you continue to come to me for answers and for the life of me, I can't figure out why."

"Because you're the only one who has them," Jet responded gruffly as he glanced out into the darkened forest. Sly shook her head once, amusement dancing across her face.

"Now we both know *that's* not true," she replied to Jet's lame answer. "And I know I'm not the protectors' favorite individual, so you also risk your reputation by coming to me for information, not to mention Lilly's. I want to know why."

"You're the most accurate," Jet answered, his tone telling Sly that was the only answer she'd get out of him. "Now, how did they know we were going to be there?"

Sly continued to stare at him, no emotion or answer evident on her face. Jet was getting frustrated, which was melting into anger.

"I gave you an answer," he snapped. She clicked her tongue and looked off into the woods, her gaze becoming distant.

"You've been so distracted by this recent increase in crime and the instability among the assassins that you never looked right in front of your nose," Sly murmured, thinking aloud. "I believe I warned you about that before you decided to follow up on this lead."

"What does that mean?"

Sly rolled her neck and turned her eyes back to him. "Think about it, Jet. Who's the missing body?"

"Gia, but it wasn't her. She's part of the Four," Jet replied as he began to think back on the night. He had lost contact with Gia shortly after Nat died. Her earpiece had just shorted out, but that didn't make sense. Jet and Remington had done a complete equipment check that day. They had known there was a possibility for danger — there always was, but they were usually prepared. There was no reason why Gia's earpiece should have just gone silent the way it did.

Sly chuckled, pulling Jet out of his thoughts.

"I'm guessing you don't do complete background checks on your assets," she stated, smiling craftily as she looked at Jet.

"Of course I do," he said, insulted at the suggestion he was careless.

"Not thoroughly enough. Had you listened to me before, this night could've been avoided," she stated in her typical cryptic manner.

"Spit it out, Sly," Jet growled. She would dance around the issue all night if only to annoy him.

"Young Gia's loyalty has always been to Adara," Sly stated matter-of-factly. "The woman basically raised her. Your supposed member of the Four was actually a turncoat, an assassin born and bred."

Jet felt a wave of nausea overtake him. Adara was one of the top assassins, prominent among the separatists, and a constant thorn in the protectors' side. Little was known about the small but extremely dangerous group of shape shifters that were assassins and even less was known about their leaders. Shortly before Jet and Lilly had become the leaders of the protectors, assassins had joined with the separatists; shape shifters that believed their species was superior to all others and therefore should wield the most power. The violent tactics of the separatists meant job security for assassins.

"No, that can't be right. You're lying," Jet repeated. Sly, who had been walking away, twisted back to look at him.

"And what exactly would I have to gain by lying?" Sly asked before turning again, calling over her shoulder, "In the future, you might want to consider looking at all the evidence with a clear head before confronting me, Jet. I might not be in such a good mood next time."

Jet leaned against a tree and looked up at the moon, the coolness of the soft glow calming him.

"Why didn't you tell me?" he asked. Sly turned around and leaned against a nearby tree, a few feet away from him.

"You don't ask, I don't tell. That's always been the rule," Sly answered as if it were the most obvious thing in the world.

"Two innocent protectors died tonight—"

"Protectors die every day. Not my problem, not really yours either," Sly interrupted. "And I still think you should revisit your interpretation of that prophecy."

Jet was quiet for a moment. "I don't know what that means."

"No news there," Sly said with a half-smile. "Read your copy of the prophecy carefully, Jet, every word. You really don't want to skim those things."

Jet gave her a look that was anything but amused. She held his gaze, her devil-may-care attitude never slipping.

"I don't suppose you're going to help me," Jet mumbled.

"I already have," she replied with a shrug. "Since you've had such a rough night, I'll give you a freebie but I want to reiterate that I still think prophecies are complete bullshit that make you lazy. Might as well read tea leaves or bird innards or whatever the hell humans do nowadays."

Jet almost rolled his eyes. "Yes, you've told me. Time and time again."

Sly cocked an eyebrow. "From what I understand about this particular prophecy, there's a line concerning one of royal and common blood."

"Yes?" Jet asked. Sly pulled herself up to a low branch on the tree, sprawling out over the rough bark. She resembled the Cheshire cat as she watched him, slowly swinging her legs back and forth behind her.

"Since the original prophecy is contained in the Book of Oracle — a guardian book — and they hold us in such *high* regard," Sly smirked when Jet rolled his eyes at her sarcasm. "Would it be fair to say that the phrase 'common blood' most likely refers to shape shifters?"

"I suppose," Jet answered, but he took the words with a grain of salt as he always did. It was of no matter to Sly. Either he took her advice or he didn't. She sat up and leaned back against the trunk, pulling one knee up to her chest.

"So, if we follow that logic, then 'royal blood' would probably refer to the guardians. A guardian and a shape shifter sleeping together, in defiance of the most sacred of Sacred Laws," Sly gasped overdramatically as her hand fluttered up to her chest. "*Scandalous.*"

Jet glared at her, which amused her even more.

"So, who do we know that has broken the most sacred of the Sacred Laws and remains a guardian to this day?" Sly asked, waiting for Jet to respond.

He closed his eyes and pinched the bridge of his nose. "I assume you're referring to Passion."

"Aw, give the boy a cookie. He got one right," Sly said. "To sum up, we agree that the prophecy is most likely referring to her daughter."

"Electra?" Jet asked skeptically.

Sly arched an eyebrow and hopped down from her branch, brushing the dirt off her pants.

"No, Jet. I don't think the prophecy is referring to Electra," Sly replied in her *God-you're-an-idiot* tone. "I'd recommend facing the truth soon, Jet. Something is going on and whatever it is, it's not good. You may not like her, but at least Adara is the devil you know. She keeps stability among the assassins in this area. If that goes, well, it will lead to all sorts of unpleasantness."

"I thought you didn't believe in prophecies," Jet pointed out. Sly turned from him, walking off into the shadows.

"I don't," she called back. "I trust in what I see, as should you."

She vanished into the night. Jet stared at the place where she had been standing, not bothering to call out. She had already told him everything he needed to know and he didn't have the patience for more of her games. The silver stars twinkled merrily in the sky, winking and glimmering. A million thoughts warred for control in his mind as he turned in the direction of home, wanting desperately to get into the nice comfortable bed he shared with his wife and sleep off the night's events. He brushed past plants, his jeans quietly whispering against the jagged green leaves. Jet was so lost in thought he didn't notice a pair of blue eyes watching him. As he continued on, the figure followed him, staying up in the trees.

The branches overhead rustled, drawing Jet's attention. He frowned as he squinted and looked into the branches, trying to find the origin of the quiet sound. After a moment, he kept walking, keeping a sharp ear open. Shape shifters had superior hearing and could often pick up sounds that humans missed. No one else would have heard the figure silently descend from the treetops and weightlessly land. Jet waited until both of its feet were on the ground before striking out with a roundhouse kick. The figure caught his foot and used his momentum to throw him to the ground so that he landed on his back. Jet started to get up but stopped when he felt the cool blade of a knife against his throat, dangerously near his jugular. The figure's face moved, the skin shimmering faintly in the moonlight.

"I thought that was guardian silver," Jet said with a smile.

"A girl's got to protect herself, especially in times like these," Passion replied with a casual shrug as she put her knife back in its simple sheath and helped him to his feet. She was an earth guardian, one of many who kept the earth running smoothly. It was her job to keep the emotion of passion under control. Passion was the granddaughter of Adonia, the queen of the guardian women, and her mother was Artemis, next in line to rule. Jet and Passion had been friends ever since his youth and had seen each other through many trials and tribulations. He thought of her as another one of his sisters and he was the little brother she never had or knew. Guardian men and women were raised separately and rarely saw each other.

"Lilly's worried. She told me that you wanted to kill Sly," Passion explained. Her throaty voice was like honey, warm and sweet to the ear.

"Everybody wants to kill Sly," Jet replied shortly, brushing past her. He heard her quicken her pace and she caught up to him, giving him a gentle bump with her shoulder.

"Come on, Jet. I'm supposed to be the impulsive one," Passion attempted to joke with her friend, sighing when her attempt fell flat. "Talk to me, please."

"You can relax, I didn't kill Sly. Protectors don't kill innocents," Jet paused and frowned as they continued walking. "Although, I don't think the term 'innocent' really applies to Sly."

"And to think, you and she used to be friends," Passion snickered before sobering and becoming serious. "Do you want to talk about it?"

"I was careless, the lead was bad, we were ambushed, end of story," Jet answered.

"I highly doubt it was that simple," Passion began as she brushed some wavy strands of hair behind her ear.

"No?" Jet asked sharply, stopping so that he could face Passion. "Aside from knowing that there has been unrest among the assassins lately, I somehow missed some important information. Gia is loyal to Adara and according to Sly, practically raised by her. I didn't see that and I should have. So please, explain to me how this isn't my fault."

Passion stared at him, unbothered by the accusatory tone. Jet turned and continued walking.

Passion was quick to follow him, holding her hands behind her.

"You're not all-knowing, my friend. We all make mistakes — miss things that seem so obvious in hindsight. Some things we're not meant to know until it's too late," she replied. "Trust me."

Jet looked over at her. Passion was wise and not many appreciated that about her. She had raven-colored hair, which she dyed the color of the sun and almost always kept tied up in some way. Her eyes were constantly changing color; an extremely rare guardian trait and one that hadn't been seen in a few generations.

"Sly also mentioned only Jade was part of the Four," he continued.

Passion looked at him; her pale blue eyes sparkling. She was wearing a bright red dress that had an asymmetrical cut and a plunging neckline. It wasn't the typical guardian attire, but Passion had never been one for following pointless rules and regulations. She was determined to be herself, no matter what the other guardians thought of her. Jet had always admired that about her and he knew Lilly felt the same.

"I suppose that's good news," she said as they kept walking. "Did she say anything else about who the others might be?"

Jet rubbed the back of his stiff neck and stopped walking, wishing he hadn't brought the subject up. Passion also stopped and looked to him expectantly and he knew he wouldn't be able to lie to her. She was going to find out, better sooner than later.

"She said one of them was your daughter," Jet spoke carefully.

Passion frowned. "Electra?"

Jet hesitated. "No."

Passion was quiet as she stared at him with an unreadable expression. Jet didn't want to be the first to break the suddenly uncomfortable silence, but he knew she wouldn't.

"I was hoping—" he began.

"I'm not bringing her into this life. Neither are you or anyone else," Passion stated with a finality that reminded Jet she was also a mother.

"It's not something that can be avoided indefinitely," Jet pointed out. Passion turned from him and began to walk away. He hurried to catch up with her.

"At some point, she's going to notice that she's not human," he argued. "Passion, you're going to have to face your past eventually."

Passion stopped and glared at him, incredulous. "Did you *actually* just say that to me? I'm reminded of my past every damn day. Every exchange I have with other guardians. Every conference I have with Aneurin and most of the guardian men. Every conversation I have with my daughter, I'm reminded of my past."

"I was only suggesting—"

"I know damn well what you were suggesting," Passion growled.

Jet shook his head. "Passion, it's not fair to hide the truth from them. They have a right to know."

Passion refused to meet his eyes. "I don't care. You're not bringing her into this life."

"Just because their father was an assassin doesn't mean they'll follow in his footsteps," Jet argued. "Electra's astute. She's going to find out sooner or later and if she finds out later she'll realize you kept it from her. What do you think her reaction is going to be? They're twenty-eight, Passion. You can't shelter them forever."

"I won't let them suffer for my past," Passion stated adamantly.

"They won't," Jet reassured her. Passion turned her angry eyes back to him.

"You're right, they won't. Because I forbid you to approach her, end of story."

Before Jet could respond, Passion disappeared in a flash of bright silver light. He stared at the empty spot she used to occupy. It was really quite annoying the way she could use the guardian ability of Appearing to get out of conversations she didn't want to have.

Jet ran a hand through his hair, overcome with frustration. He stood straight, his muscles and bones creaking as they changed form. Silvery black fur sprouted all over his body as he turned back into a wolf and loped through the dark forest, heading for home.

~~*~*~*

The protectors' mansion sat hidden behind a stretch of hills in the middle of a vast tract of land. Trees were scattered throughout the property, giving the place a forest-like appearance. There was even a small brook that ran along the gravel driveway leading up to the massive home, and there were numerous animals roaming the grounds at any given time. The entire estate had always been hidden from human eyes by guardian magic: even the road leading through the hills was concealed. It acted as a safe haven for protectors and their allies; those who were trusted enough to know the secret location.

The winding path that served as a driveway was long and ambling, weaving its way up through the hills to the enormous dwelling. Countless windows studded the façade, and there was always a light on in at least one, making it as warm and inviting throughout the night as it was during the day. The architecture evoked the French Renaissance style, with elements of Baroque and Gothic thrown in for good measure. The ancient chateaux had always belonged to the Monroe family — a gift from the guardians, and they made sure it never fell into any kind of disrepair, giving the place a timeless feeling.

The peaceful feeling of the land was lost on Jet as he strode up the long path, soon catching sight of the towers in the distance. The sounds of nocturnal birds cascaded down from the trees. Jet kept his eyes on the ground and his hands in the pockets of his jeans as he continued on his way. In the back of his mind, he wondered whether or not anyone was still awake. At least one of his children undoubtedly, but would Lilly or Jade or Remington be up waiting for him? The grief was starting to crash down on him and Jet just wanted to sleep. He didn't have the energy to even begin processing all that had happened.

Looking up from his feet, Jet saw the vast chateaux in the distance. The light was on in one of the main rooms, indicating someone was awake. Jet's eyes turned back to the path and he kicked at a large stick. In his mind, he was planning out three different conversations: one for Lilly, one for Remington, and one for Jade. He glanced to the side when he heard the roar of a motorcycle somewhere on the estate, probably one of his daughters. Jet scrubbed a hand over his face, wanting more than anything to get out of the tomb that the night had become. He wistfully thought of a long hot shower and climbing into bed, but knew it was unlikely sleep would come easy. It wasn't every night that he screwed up as badly as he had this night. Looking up toward the mansion, it didn't seem any closer. Was the path growing?

When he finally reached the front of the towering chateaux, Jet abruptly changed his path and headed for the back, walking alongside the wall. He needed just a little more time to organize his thoughts. Jet could picture the look of disapproval on Remington's face and distracted himself by fishing his keys out of his pocket. The rough teeth scraped against his finger, causing him to curse under his breath. Pulling the keys out, Jet angrily sorted through them, searching for the one to the kitchen door. He found it right as he entered the dull pool of light above the door. Jet carefully wrapped his fingers around the other keys so they wouldn't jingle and began to work on the locks. He clenched his teeth as he finally finished and pushed the quiet door open. *I've been reduced to creeping into my own home like a burglar,* he thought with a mix of irritation and embarrassment.

Jet closed the door behind him and locked it again, stuffing the keys back in his pocket. The kitchen was silent except for the soft hum of the appliances and the only light came from the long hallway. Jet continued his trek through the dark kitchens, which was the liveliest area during the daytime hours. He stepped into the hallway, glancing down at the large squares of black and white tiles. He knew the halls like the back of his hand, having called the mansion home since he was a child. Jet had been born within the chateaux' walls and spent the greater portion of his formative years in the enormous dwelling. He'd always felt safe here, and Jet noticed some of the tension in his shoulders loosening a little as he wandered through the arches.

There were few portraits on the towering walls of the first floor; the majority of the mansion's art was on the second and third floors. The walls on the first floor had tapestries that told stories of great shape shifters, mostly protectors, throughout time. There were weavings of shape shifters in battle, side by side with mostly unsuspecting humans.

Jet glanced up at the stories surrounding him, wondering what his would look like. All these leaders had been valiant shape shifters with well-honed battle skills, knowledgeable in diplomacy and politics. Though he came from the same lines as most of them, Jet frequently questioned if he could match their valor. Could he achieve the impossible if called upon to do so? Tonight was certainly a reason to doubt his abilities.

He stopped at a particular tapestry — his favorite. A radiant woman stood proud and tall, clothed in a shimmering dress of silver and black, splattered with blood. She was unaffected by the battle raging around her and the bodies of her fallen enemies lay at her bare feet. She wielded a pair of elegantly crafted knives and a glowing aura shimmered about her, giving her an almost otherworldly appearance. There was both rage and grief in her bright silver blue eyes. Selene, the beloved guardian of stars, was truly a vision of magnificence. It was said that she brightened whatever place she entered and she was thought to have been the most beautiful being to ever walk the Earth or the Meadows. No one — human, guardian, or shape shifter — had yet matched her beauty or her bravery. Passion's daughter, Electra, was said to look similar to her, and as Jet studied the tapestry he could see why.

Jet sighed after a moment, his shoulders slumping as he scrubbed his hand over his eyes. Selene had disappeared long ago, never to be seen again. At least, that was how the legend went. Both shape shifters and guardians searched high and low for Selene, but it was as if she had just vanished. Jet couldn't help but wonder if that was one of the reasons Passion was reluctant to let her other daughter enter the life she was destined for.

"If you can hear me, Selene, I could really use some advice right now," Jet murmured to the picture. It was an age-old tradition shared among guardians and protectors: in times of strife or doubt, they would ask Selene for guidance. Selene's blank eyes just continued to stare straight ahead. Jet didn't usually talk to the pictures — he believed it to be utterly ridiculous and completely pointless, but he didn't know whom else to turn to.

"I'm pretty sure she would tell you that talking to tapestry won't do much good," a familiar voice came from behind him. Jet smiled and turned, looking in the direction of the voice.

Jade was reclining on the stairs, watching him with her sultry brown eyes. Her dark wavy hair was down, something she rarely did. She was wearing a dark blue nightshirt that just skimmed her thighs, leaving her long legs bare.

"I didn't see you there," Jet mentioned as he

approached the winding stairway. She nodded, glancing off to the side.

"Kinda figured that when you came into the hall with your back toward me," Jade replied with a hint of teasing.

"Are you all right? I didn't know if—"

"I'm fine, Jet. Good as new, guardian healers know how to do their jobs," she interrupted, her dark eyes turning back to him. "Were you able to retrieve the others?"

"Remington isn't back yet?"

"I haven't seen him. Why? What's wrong?"

Odd. I would've thought he'd be back by now, Jet thought as he scratched the back of his head. Jade watched him, resting her weight on one elbow.

"I heard you talked to Sly," she mentioned, interrupting his thoughts. "Jet, did you kill my lover?"

"No. I knew if I did, I'd have to answer to you," Jet quipped and Jade snickered.

"Fairly certain Alpha would beat me to the punch," Jade corrected with a weak smile that didn't quite reach her eyes. Jet chuckled and dropped his gaze again, unsure what else to say.

"It's not over, is it?" she asked, but it sounded more like a statement. Jade was much older than she looked and quite experienced. She rarely asked questions and when she did, they sounded more like statements.

Jet shook his head. "I'm afraid not. Sly is right about one thing: as much as I dislike Adara and her line of work, she does keep things stable among the assassins. I prefer to deal with an evil I know rather than one I don't."

Jade brushed some hair behind her ear,

swallowing.

"What do you need me to do?" she asked after a moment. Jet stared at her in surprise; her loyalty never ceased to amaze him.

"You still trust me, even after what happened tonight?" Jet said, trying to keep the astonishment out of his voice. Jade shrugged and spread her hands as if to say *obviously*.

"Not like you pulled the trigger," she replied. "We knew the danger going in. Blaming you for something that wasn't your fault isn't a productive use of my time. So, what do you need me to do?"

"It can wait until tomorrow," Jet answered with a small smile. "Get some rest."

Jade nodded and rose to her feet. "Lilly's upstairs, by the way. She's probably asleep by now."

"Thank you," Jet replied, his tone implying that he meant for more than the relayed information. Jade smiled, a thin melancholy gesture, and continued up the stairs, disappearing around a bend in the hall on the next floor.

Jet glanced down the main hall. Everything could wait until tomorrow. It had been a long night and he was exhausted. He climbed up the winding stairs that Jade had been resting on, moving up to the second floor and proceeded down the dimly lit hallways until he reached the door to the master bedroom. As quietly as he could, Jet pushed down the handle and opened the door.

The room was dark and the windows were open, letting in the cool night air. Jet looked to the left and could just barely make out his wife's slender form on the bed. Lilly was laying with her back to the door, her golden hair shimmering like gossamer in the pale moonlight. Jet closed the door behind him and moved to the bed. After emptying his pockets and putting the contents on the small table next to the bed, he carefully sat on the edge of the mattress, reached down, and began to untie his shoes.

"Do you want to talk?" Lilly's soft voice brushed against his ear. Jet kicked off his shoes and got under the thin covers, wrapping an arm around her waist as she curled up against his chest. He breathed in her sweet scent as he kissed her forehead.

"Tomorrow," he whispered. He felt her nod against him and closed his eyes, hoping that sleep would not elude him. Lilly began to hum a quiet tune and Jet soon fell into a peaceful sleep.

~~*~*~*

Jet groaned when the shrill ring of a phone broke through his sleep. He turned over and groaned again when the harsh sunlight beat against his eyelids. His hand fumbled around the smooth wooden surface of his night table, clumsily searching for the source of the ringing. He knocked over the lamp before finally finding the phone. Jet picked up the thin device and resisted the strong urge to throw it across the room. He squinted as he brought the phone to his ear, glancing over at the numbers of his clock. It was six-thirty in the morning. He'd been asleep for less than three hours.

"Wha?" Jet managed groggily as he tried to force his eyes to remain open.

"We've got a problem," Remington's voice filtered through. *It's too damn early for someone to be that awake,* Jet thought as he rolled onto his back. He still couldn't understand how his wife could get up almost every morning to watch the sun rise. Jet had never been a day person and the concept baffled him.

"Mmhm," he mumbled, running a hand over his sleep-mussed hair.

"Wake up, Jet," Remington ordered in his stern voice. Jet rubbed his eyes, restraining himself from making the smart aleck remark that he wanted to.

"M'awake," he argued, trying to force the sleep from his rough voice. "Wha's the problem?"

"Bryn's body isn't here. It's at the morgue."

Jet's eyes snapped open and he sat straight up, all traces of sleep leaving him in an instant. "What? How?"

"I—"

"Never mind. I'll meet you at the morgue in an hour," Jet responded as he swung his legs over the end of the bed. He disconnected the call and quickly set about putting his shoes on, mentally swearing the entire time. Of all the things that could've happened, this was the worst. Jet only hoped they would be able to remedy the situation before any permanent harm was done.

CHAPTER THREE

Isis sat alone in her small apartment, staring at her open laptop. The only illumination was the blue pendant light above her head. Slowly scrolling through the empty pictures, Isis squinted as she pulled one up. A single spiral filled with hastily scribbled notes sat off to the side, forgotten for the moment. It had been a few days since the incident at the warehouse and she still hadn't found any answers about what had happened.

Isis leaned back and rubbed her neck with one hand, closing her stinging eyes. Another dead end; everything was just countless dead ends. She had tried searching the name Bryn Adams, but that had yielded absolutely nothing useful. Isis wasn't prone to believing in conspiracy theories. However, the whole situation was just so bizarre.

She glanced up when a flash of lightning lit up the sky outside. Shortly afterward, there was a distant rumble of thunder. It had been a stormy overcast day — which hadn't done wonders for her already bad mood. Shaking her head, Isis turned her attention back to the bright laptop screen.

"What am I missing?" she softly asked herself as she ran her fingers through her hair. "What am I missing? What am I missing?"

She clicked on another photograph and stared at it for a moment. Frowning, she leaned closer to the screen, squinting. Isis had already ruled out some kind of camera malfunction; that wouldn't cause only one or two things to vanish entirely. Besides, it didn't explain the disappearing body, and she was certain that had not been some kind of hallucination. Isis leaned back again and tilted her chair, running her hands over her face and through her hair.

"I'm going insane," she muttered. "I am actually losing my damn mind."

A sudden knocking on the door yanked her out of her racing thoughts. She looked over her shoulder. Another knock sounded and Isis cautiously got to her feet. She was not expecting anybody. Isis reached over to the counter, where she had placed a baseball bat.

Moving through the dark apartment, Isis stepped around whatever little furniture she had. She had always had good night vision and rarely ever bumped into something, even when her surroundings were completely dark. The few times she had been dragged into haunted houses — usually by her annoyingly upbeat cousin, Shae — Isis had always been able to see perfectly in her darkened surroundings and could usually see where the next scare was going to come from. Isis rolled her eyes when she remembered that she had not called Shae since the incident at the rave, which landed her in the emergency room. *That's going to cost me,* she thought as she raised the baseball bat into a two-handed clutch and prepared to swing should the person at the door decide to try kicking it in.

"Who is it?" she called. There was quiet for a moment.

"Put down whatever weapon you're holding, Isis," Steve's weary voice filtered through the door. Isis frowned and lowered the bat, holding it in a one-handed grip again.

"Steve? Aren't you working a double shift?" Isis asked, tightening her grip on the bat and looking around for any indication of the time. She had been so absorbed in the pictures that she had lost track of everything else.

"What are you—?" The disbelief in Steve's voice almost made her smile. "Isis, that's tomorrow."

Isis moved to the door, peering out through the peephole. Steve was standing there with his hands in his pocket, looking completely worn out. The increase in work was obviously taking its toll. She removed the chain from the door, twisted the deadbolt, and pulled the door open. Blinking rapidly, Isis raised a hand before her eyes and grimaced at the assault of the bright hallway lights.

"Before you say anything, I'm sorry," Steve said before she had a chance to speak. Isis frowned and opened her mouth to ask what he meant when Shae stepped into view from where she had been leaning against the wall, next to the door. Her auburn hair shimmered in the light and she smiled widely. Isis struggled not to roll her eyes, not really in the mood to deal with a hopeless optimist.

"Hey Ice Queen, heard you got canned...again,"

Shae greeted in her typical friendly manner, craning her neck as she peered over Isis' shoulder. "Uh oh. Are you in your dark place? Are we going to have to take shifts?"

She moved around Isis and stepped inside before her cousin could protest, flipping on the light switch and illuminating most of the main area of the apartment. Isis turned furious green eyes on Steve and shook the baseball bat at him. He spread his hands, the guilty expression never leaving his face. She nodded over her shoulder and he scurried inside. Isis closed the door behind them and twisted the deadbolt again, sliding the chain back into place. Shae pulled out a small compact from her purse, and began applying a rose-colored lipstick.

"What is it with you and locks?" Shae asked, not looking up from the mirror as she smacked her painted lips, closing the compact again. "Honestly Isis, have you ever been in an unlocked room for any measurable amount of time?"

Isis leaned the bat against the door and turned to face her cousin, who was putting the lipstick and mirror back in her small purse. "Shae, it's been a really bad week. Could we maybe not do this?"

Shae smiled as she placed her purse on the small coffee table and flopped on the couch, kicking off her fashionable shoes. "Yeah, Steve filled me in on the way up. I swear, Isis, you're the only photojournalist who could get fired in the middle of a crime spree. What is this, your fourth job?"

"My third and I'm only suspended. It's not even my fault," Isis replied as she moved to a nearby chair.

"Neither were the other incidents," Shae pointed out, causing Isis to glare at her.

"To be fair, the reasons given for her firing at the second job were rather shady," Steve mentioned. "However, this time was kind of your fault, Isis."

"Bodies don't just disappear into thin air! And I didn't appreciate the editor being a patronizing ass!" Isis snapped, feeling defensive.

Shae whistled and shook her head. "Sweetie, when are you going to learn? You have to get along with people, or at least make an effort to do so."

Isis flopped into the chair next to the couch and put a hand over her eyes, uninterested in participating in an argument. Raising her hand, she studied Shae, noticing her moderately fancy clothing. Her cousin had always had great fashion sense, but she looked even more dressed up than usual.

"Going to some high society function or are you just doing that weird thing where you dress up for absolutely no reason?" Isis asked.

"Planning on going out to a club later on," Shae replied with a wicked smile. "I don't feel like going to bed alone tonight."

"Well, happy hunting, I guess," Isis said as she reclined back in the chair and stretched her arms over her head. Shae laughed as she got up from the couch and wandered over toward the kitchen table, leaning down to look at the still open laptop.

"What's this?" she asked curiously as she scrolled through the pictures, enlarging one.

"The reason why I was fired." Isis suddenly snapped her fingers and sat up. "Shae, you're into all that supernatural bullshit. Would you know of anything that could make a body vanish without a trace?"

"Okay, first of all, I'm not *into* all that supernatural

bullshit as you so eloquently put it," Shae began without looking away from the picture. "Second, no, I don't know of anything that would make a body disappear. Is that what this whole thing is about?"

Isis looked over at Steve, who was leaning his elbows on the counter and looking toward the laptop. As if sensing her eyes on him, Steve looked to her and met her gaze. He spread his hands again and turned his attention back to the table, drawing Shae's attention.

"I'm sorry, Isis," he said. Shae looked from him to Isis, her interest piqued.

"What am I missing?" she asked with a half-smile.

Isis got out of the chair and approached her cousin. "There were a bunch of cops at the old factory that night, including our dear Steve here. However, none of them remember a damn thing. Or so they claim. I tend to take the word of the police with a grain of salt, as you know."

"Whoa, that's creepy," Shae said as she turned her eyes back to the pictures. *Creepy doesn't even begin to describe it,* Isis thought as she followed Shae's gaze to the strange pictures. All the empty pictures, where there should've been a body. Lightning flashed again and Steve looked toward the windows, his brow furrowing.

"So, did you two stop by just to lecture me about my antisocial ways?" Isis asked, placing her hands on her hips.

"No," Shae replied, turning her back to the laptop and leaning against the table. "I was coming to yell at you for not calling to tell me you had recently been in the hospital."

"It wasn't a big deal, Shae. They didn't even keep

me overnight," Isis shot back, glancing over to Steve when he moved toward the windows. *Damn Steve. He's worse than a high school cheerleader,* she thought.

"Only because there weren't enough available beds," Steve countered, distracted. "And your cousin was being stubborn and demanding to be released. It was basically against the advice of the doctors."

"I was lucky enough to catch Steve on his way in," Shae explained, glancing behind her to Steve before looking back to Isis. "Got any wine?"

I wish, Isis thought as she shook her head. Shae looked disappointed as she wandered back into the main room. Isis ran her fingers through her smooth hair, her attention wandering to where Steve was peering out of the blinds. Isis looked around the apartment, wondering who had chosen the impossibly light shade of blue that coated the walls. It was so bland — it reminded her of the walls in the emergency room. She preferred more dramatic colors and would have repainted had she planned on remaining in the place for an extended amount of time.

"Photography, art, photography, mythology, hmm these are new," Shae's voice drew her attention over to where she was looking through Isis' few books. Isis had gone out after getting suspended and purchased a few mythology and paranormal books, none of which provided any help with her quandary. Isis turned her attention back to where Steve was still looking out the window.

"Steve, what the hell are you looking at?" she asked, irritated. Steve was quiet for a moment, his eyes glued to the night.

"I think there's something out there," he spoke in

a soft tone of voice. Shae looked up and Isis moved over to where Steve was standing. She gently pushed him to the side as she peered out the small window, observing the quiet night.

"Wow, you're right. Look at all those trees and light posts," she said with no small amount of sarcasm. "The increase in work is making you paranoid, detective."

Steve gave her a very dry look and peered out the blinds one final time to the empty street outside.

~~*~*~*

Jet turned up the collar of his long coat, his eyes fixed on the building across the street. He was watching one window in particular, which had become illuminated a few minutes ago. It was on the fourth floor and, from what he could see, the occupant had drawn the blinds. Crossing his arms over his chest, he tapped one gloved finger on his arm. Minutes passed and soon he felt a drop of rain hit his head. The protector looked up to the sky, sniffing the air. Another drop slapped his forehead, trailing down his temple.

"Perfect," he muttered as he rolled his neck, listening to the deep cracks and resumed his watching. Jet shrank back in the shadows when the blinds were disturbed. Someone was looking out the window, but Jet was far enough away to avoid detection. It began drizzling and Jet regretted not taking a hat. Thunder rumbled overhead, but he disregarded it, having more important things on his mind. Mostly, he was wondering how much the young photographer had figured out. Jet had been surprised at how much she looked like her mother and he couldn't help but smile at the thought.

"Stooping to voyeurism, I see," a quiet but angry voice came from his right, startling him. "Quite the leader you are, Jet."

"Dammit, Passion!" he growled, his heart in his throat. Glancing to the side, he saw her a few feet away, looking nothing short of furious. She had always had the unnerving ability to sneak up on people with her eerily silent way of moving. Passion had tied her hair up in an elegant bun and she showed no sign of being affected by the rain. Her arms were crossed tightly and he could see she was digging her nails into her upper arm. She watched him and his mind raced through possible excuses, none of which would work.

"I take it you're here on unofficial business," Jet said. He had every right to be here. Passion, on the other hand, did not. She narrowed her eyes at him. *If looks could kill,* Jet thought as he kept her gaze.

"It's really this easy for you, isn't it?" she asked, her tone astonished. "You could just walk in there and ruin her life without thinking twice, couldn't you?"

Jet's mouth dropped open as he stared at her in disbelief. "I can't believe you're asking me that, Passion. You think this is *easy* for me?"

"I think you care more about a prophecy than innocent people," she growled.

Jet shook his head and turned his attention back to the window. "I won't even dignify that with a response."

"I won't let you do this, Jet. You'll have to go through me to get to her."

"Okay, Passion," Jet said as he turned to face his friend, uncrossing his arms and sliding his hands into his coat pockets. "Say I leave her alone, like you ask. How long do you think she's going to stay hidden? She's been asking *a lot* of questions about what happened at the old factory. That's going to raise a hell of a lot of red flags, if it hasn't already. With the current chaos, it wouldn't be difficult for one person to disappear. Any experienced assassin could easily take advantage of this situation. You know there's currently a power struggle of some sort happening among assassins, right? A half-guardian would be a very tempting mark."

Passion went quiet for a moment, her expression reflecting hesitance. The rain picked up, soaking them both. The wind howled through the trees, lifting a few loose strands of Passion's hair.

"She has protection," she argued, shaking her head.

"Not enough," Jet replied, fidgeting when he felt rain drops crawling down the back of his neck.

"Get her more," Passion snapped.

Jet let out a frustrated laugh and dragged his hands down his face. "You still don't get it. She's a hybrid, something that hasn't happened for centuries. Her bloodline alone means she will always be in danger and if she doesn't learn to defend herself, she won't survive long."

Passion was quiet for a long while as the storm continued to intensify.

"Leave," she finally spoke calmly. "Don't let me catch you around here again."

Jet opened his mouth to reply, then thought better of it and closed it. He shook his head in defeat, stepped around her and vanished into the night. Passion closed her eyes and inhaled, holding her breath for a moment before exhaling. Allowing her eyes to flutter open, she looked up to the window that Jet had been watching. A sudden melancholy overtook her and her eyes changed from green to blue. She hated arguing with her friend, but her priorities were clear. The cold rain continued to pour down her bare shoulders and her red dress clung to her body. After a moment, Passion stepped back into the darkness and disappeared in a flash of silver.

~~*~*~*

"You could've gone with her."

Steve looked over at Isis, who was stretched across the couch with her legs resting on Steve's lap. She always liked to sprawl across furniture like a cat whereas Steve preferred just sitting and taking up as little space as possible. Shae had left more than an hour ago to go clubbing. She loved to be around people and often went out at night, usually in the nearest city. Isis had gone once and decided to never do it again. Shae and Steve were quick to agree with her. Large crowds of people and Isis just didn't mix.

Steve shook his head. "Maybe if I didn't just work a full shift or if I didn't have to work a double tomorrow. I have enough of a headache without listening to blasting techno noise for hours on end. The club scene is more Justin's area than mine. He's more the extrovert."

"How is your boyfriend anyway?" Isis asked, feeling a little guilty for not asking earlier. Isis almost never got along with her friends' partners — Justin being the very rare exception. He was very similar to Steve, calm and level-headed. When they had first met, Isis had been impressed with his patience and unflappable demeanor. Justin eventually won her over when she saw how happy he and Steve were together.

"Partner," Steve corrected, making Isis grin. "He's good, just out there saving the world. When we last spoke, he was working in Guinea, but he was going to be moving soon. We're going to Skype in a couple days, if you want to say hi."

Isis shrugged and rested her wrists on her forehead, her eyes closed as she thought back to their school years. She had become friends with Steve in elementary school and they had attended the same middle and high school together. They had separated only when Steve went to the academy and Isis had gone to study photography. She had a knack for it and even had a few shows in the beginning of her career. Her advisor had called her the next Diane Arbus, although most of her work had been of nature. Her need to make a living had forced Isis to give up her passion and settle for photojournalism, which she didn't particularly care for even though she was good at it.

"Do you ever feel like you're meant for something more?" she asked, as she opened her eyes again and focused on the ceiling.

"I'm sure everyone does at one time or another," Steve replied as he looked over at her. "Why do you ask?"

She was quiet for a moment, thinking over her words. "I don't know. I've always felt out of place, like I'm in the wrong life or something. If that makes any sense."

"Sounds kind of ominous."

Isis shrugged. "I don't know what to do, Steve. I know I saw that body. I'm not going to stop until I figure out what happened. I just wish I knew where the hell to actually look."

Steve smiled at her sympathetically, gently rubbing her shin.

"You're going to be fine," he reassured her. "You'll figure everything out. You're too damn stubborn to give up."

Isis grinned, quirking an eyebrow. "I seem to remember you saying something similar in high school."

Steve laughed and shook his head. Isis had always been headstrong, something that didn't go over well with most teachers. Steve was a born goody two-shoes, but after befriending her, he frequently found himself in the principal's office or sitting in detention on a fairly regular basis. Then there had been the times Isis had nearly gotten into physical altercations when other students made the mistake of attempting to bully the few friends she had. Isis never knew how she managed to avoid suspensions.

"Hey Steve?" a thoughtful frown crossed her face. "How many sports have you played?"

Steve brightened up and twisted his body a little, whistling as he thought about the question. "Let's see, I've been in some form of track since the first grade. I tried baseball for two years, played basketball throughout high school. I tried soccer for one season, didn't really care for it. I always play football at family get-togethers. You and I took those self-defense courses together, but I'm not sure if that's a sport."

Isis propped up her upper body with her elbows.

"Have you ever been injured?"

"Um," Steve shut his eyes, shaking his head after a moment. "No, not that I can recall."

Isis was quiet for a while, studying him. "That doesn't strike you as…unusual?"

Steve stared at her. "Do you want me to get hurt, Isis?"

She shook her head. "No."

An uncomfortable silence fell between them. Isis flopped down again, covering her eyes with the backs of her hands.

"I'm losing my mind, Steve."

Steve snorted. "That's assuming you were ever sane to begin with."

Isis gently kicked him and smiled. Steve winced a little with a quiet hiss and she tilted her head, lifting her hands up so she could peer at him.

"I twisted the wrong way, might have pulled a muscle in my leg," he explained. She nodded, unconvinced. For a while, they just sat there, not saying anything. Then Steve stretched his arms above his head, dropping them back at his sides.

"You good to stay alone tonight or do you want me to sleep on the couch?" he asked. Isis shook her head.

"No. I'll be fine," she said, swinging her legs off the couch so Steve could stand up. Isis glanced at the small digital clock on the bookcase. It was eleven o'clock.

"I'm right downstairs if you need me," Steve reminded his friend as they moved toward the door. Throughout their lives, they had been neighbors.

Isis unlocked the door and opened it. "My ever-vigilant protector."

"What would you do without me?" Steve replied with a charming grin.

"Goodnight," she said.

"Night," Steve said, pointing at her. "No all-nighter. You have to sleep."

Isis laughed and nodded, watching as Steve strode down the hall toward the stairs. He never took elevators if he could avoid them, preferring stairs whenever he could. She closed the door again and locked it, leaning her back against the cool wood. She closed her eyes and rested her head against the door, her mind wandering back to when she had first met Steve. Her life was certainly better with him in it and Isis knew she wasn't the easiest person to get along with. Throughout her life, Shae and Steve were often her only friends. While she and Shae clashed on occasion, she almost never fought with Steve. It was pleasant, having a friend that she could always turn to and trust not to be judgmental.

Isis opened her eyes and stepped away from the door. She moved into the kitchen and toward the windows, peering out the blinds. With two fingers, she lifted the blinds a little and looked out into the night. The storm hadn't lasted very long, maybe half an hour. The water glistened on the leaves of the trees and the tan pavement. The streets were bare, nobody in sight. No strange shadows or unusual shapes. Everything was just…quiet.

Isis dropped the blinds again, muttering under her breath, "Ridiculous."

She moved out of the kitchen and through the apartment to her small bedroom, switching off the lights as she went. When she entered her bedroom, Isis moved to the small table beside the bed, switching on the lamp and opening the single drawer in the table, pulling out the expandable baton she always kept in there. She held it for a minute, staring at the short black instrument, something tugging at her mind. After a moment, Isis shook her head and placed it on the table, turning her attention to the bed. She pulled aside the soft blankets and sat down, swinging her long legs up and under the covers. Once she was comfortable, she reached up and switched off the lamp.

Isis lay with her head on the soft pillow for a while, simply staring at nothing as she replayed the incident in the warehouse in her head. *I know I didn't imagine that whole thing,* she thought as she slowly drifted off to sleep.

~~*~*~*

Isis wandered through the crumbling ruins of what had once been a magnificent castle of stone. Her feet were bare and she was wearing a crimson dress that fastened behind her neck. The dress had an uneven hemline, much like a dancer's dress. The material was smooth and sleek and felt absolutely wonderful against her flesh. She looked up to the sky, watching as clouds raced overhead.

A sudden fire lit within her and she felt the desire to run, to be free. She began to run forward, unbothered by the rough stone underfoot. The air was so clean and sweet. She shivered with pleasure as she continued to move through the strange land. A sudden growling brought her attention to the left, where she spotted a sleek black leopard stretched out beneath a massive tree. The large cat's golden eyes met hers and Isis felt a strange connection with the enormous animal.

Her skin was sparkling, as if it held all the stars in the sky. It should have been a strange sight, but she was unbothered. The vastness of the land, its call was too strong to ignore. Yet she didn't know how to answer it. She wanted to, needed to, but she had absolutely no idea how. Isis stared up at the higher pillars that were still standing. Cats of all shapes and sizes, wild and domesticated, were perched up on the tops, all watching her. Everywhere she looked, there were animals of all shapes and sizes. She ran her slender hands up her neck and into her hair, her pulse beating just a little faster. Her temperature rose a little and she could feel the heat rising from her skin.

Her eyes snapped open when she heard a distant howl. For a split second, her vision was heat sensitive. She blinked and it went back to normal, though all her senses remained sharper. The mysterious call felt as though it were already a part of her.

After a few more steps, she came upon a short flight of stairs. Isis stepped up on the first step, twisting around when she heard the whisper of paw pads against stone. A coyote stood a few feet behind her. They looked at each other for a moment. Isis knelt down and the animal approached her without hesitation. He had sandy brown fur and his back was mottled with silver. He tucked his bushy tail between his legs and licked the bottom of her face and neck, whining affectionately and wagging his tail. Isis smiled and stroked his soft fur. For a split second, she saw herself through the coyote's eyes. She looked almost ethereal, like a goddess towering above the animal.

She stroked the coyote's head again. The animal turned and looked deeper into the ruins, his ears flattening against his head and a rumbling growl vibrating in his throat. She tried to soothe the frightened animal as he slowly backed up until he was almost cowering behind her. Straightening up again, Isis felt the wind blow her dark hair back.

There was a square-shaped opening in front of her, a doorway of some kind. Tendrils of milky white reached out, *fluttering weightlessly in the wind. They seemed to reach for her, beckoning her to come inside. She instantly became wary, bending her knees and stiffening her posture. Her eyes darted around, searching for some other way to enter the ruins. She glanced down when she heard the coyote start yipping. He loped forward to one of the walls, leapt up on the stone and looked back to her.*

Instinct took over as Isis ran forward and leapt up onto the stone, landing on two feet instead of four. She hopped off the stones, landing in a crouching position on the other side of the wall. Isis continued wandering, her senses alert for even the smallest change in her surroundings. Glancing back briefly to where the coyote still stood on the wall, she saw him sitting on his haunches, watching her every move.

Isis turned and continued forward, but slowed her pace so that she was walking. Stone changed to soft grass and suddenly she was coming to the edge of a cliff. She cautiously peered down to the rushing water below. Isis couldn't believe her eyes when she saw the steep drop. She could barely make out the dark blue water below that crashed upon the shore. The wind blew at her back, her hair reaching forward. Turning back, Isis noticed a strange tan and white shape to her right. Isis frowned and walked along the cliff edge to investigate, uneasiness growing with every step. As she neared it, Isis heard a sudden crunch. The ground had become dry and rough beneath her feet. Isis looked down and took a step back.

There was a large circle of dead withered grass just in front of whatever the shape was. When she stepped onto the dead grass, the air suddenly took on an artificial quality. It was as though it had been recycled and sterilized. The color of her dress even seemed to dull. Isis turned her attention to the strange shape a few feet away from her, in the center of the circle of dead grass.

It was a remarkably realistic sculpture of a man, an old

man with snowy white hair who was on the shorter side. He was wearing a nice caramel-colored suit with shiny expensive shoes. Everything about his appearance was neat and tidy, completely non-threatening, but something about him frightened Isis. There was only one unusual thing about the man: around his eyes was a black blindfold. Isis circled the sculpture, amazed by how extraordinarily life-like it was. She stopped when she was standing in front of it again, wondering what the point and purpose of the blindfold was. It wasn't even a blindfold. It looked like it was an actual physical part of his visage. She tilted her head, looking the statue up and down.

One of the statue's arms suddenly shot out and latched onto her arm, jerking her forward and pulling her off balance. Isis let out a cry of pain, feeling like her skin was burning and blistering under his grip. The muscles and bones in her arm felt like they were being compressed and an uncomfortable coldness started to spread throughout her body.

"I'll find you!" a voice bellowed.

Isis gasped as she jerked awake and crashed to the floor. She fought against the grip that held her, banging into the table. Behind her, the lamp smashed against the ground but Isis ignored it, only focusing on getting away from the blindfolded old man.

When she finally got loose, Isis scrambled backwards, colliding with the wall next to the door. She was breathing harshly and could hear nothing but her heart hammering in her chest. Isis looked around the room and her wide eyes fell on a pile of sheets on the ground. It finally dawned on her that the grip of the old man was just the blankets from her bed. She must have been tossing and turning and gotten tangled up. Isis let out a breathless laugh at her stupidity, running a shaking hand over her sweaty face.

Noticing the sharp shards of glass from the broken light bulb, Isis groaned and raised her eyes to the ceiling. She got to her feet, taking a minute to allow her legs to stop shaking, and then opened the door to her room. Making her way to the kitchen, she could see the sunlight peeking through the blinds. Isis retrieved the broom and dustpan from where she kept them, pausing for a moment when something caught her eye.

"Son of a bitch," she muttered in disbelief as she looked at her upper arm. There were five noticeable red welts ringing around her upper arm, as if someone had scratched her. A shiver crept down her spine, settling in the pit of her stomach. Isis shook it off, chalking it up to paranoia, probably due to all the recent weirdness she had experienced. There were a million rational explanations for the welts. She had always been a violent sleeper and often woke up with small bruises on her legs and arms.

Isis went back to her room and swept up the shards of glass. Once she tossed them in the trash, she moved back into the kitchen and put away the broom and dustpan. As she washed her hands, her gaze wandered toward the windows. Drying her hands with a towel, Isis moved across the space and pulled up the blinds. Outside, she saw two older women speed-walking in colorful clothing. Across the street, a middle-aged man was walking a huge yellow lab that paused to lift a leg on every street lamp. A few empty cars sat in front of the curbs. It was just another average, ordinary day.

Isis turned away from the window and shook her head, chuckling at her overactive imagination. *Get a grip, Isis. It was just a damn dream,* she thought as she headed back to her bedroom.

But she couldn't shake the cold feeling that settled in the back of her mind.

~~*~*~*

Jet started up his car and checked his mirrors for other cars, deciding that it would be unwise to approach the young woman today. He didn't even know what he'd say. Anything he thought of made him sound like a lunatic. She was safe...for the time being. He couldn't wait for much longer though.

He pulled out of the parking space and headed for the mansion.

CHAPTER FOUR

It was always peaceful in the lands of the Meadows, home of the guardians; god-like beings who watched over the Earth and kept things running smoothly. The only way to enter the lands was through Appearing, an ability possessed only by the guardians and a few select shape shifter families.

The Meadows were divided into two main territories and each guardian chose at a young age which one they would call home. The two regions were separated by an enormous span of mountains. Each territory was further divided into smaller realms, corresponding to the different elements.

Jet's clear blue eyes traced over the mountains on the map that currently held his attention. He was in the Pearl Castle, home to the royal line of guardian women. The ancient map was enormous, covering almost an entire wall. It was a detailed image of the lands of the guardian women, as recorded by the first guardians. Vast fields of golden grass surrounded the Pearl Castle, which stood in the exact center of the women's territories. To the east were the realms of the guardians of fire, day, and light, which were symbolized with plenty of warm and bright colors. To the south there was an endless span of blue water, branching off in many different directions and traveling through almost all the lands. That was the aquatic home of the water guardians. To the north of the castle were the lush green lands of the plant and nature guardians. Jet's eyes wandered next to the gentle slope of dark hills, home of the night guardians.

He turned around, glancing down the quiet marble halls. The Meadows had always been a second home to Jet. Most shape shifters were intimidated by the guardians and part of Jet and Lilly's job was to act as a liaison between the guardians and the protectors. Jet had been introduced to the guardians at a very young age and so was accustomed to their ways. Many of them were like a second family to him, including the women of the royal line.

Jet twisted a little when he thought he heard footsteps behind him, letting out a breath of relief when he saw it was only a messenger. The chaotic sounds of the first floor drifted up to the third, where the living quarters of the royal line were located. The first and second floors were used for a variety of reasons — such as meetings or just when the guardians wanted to mingle with each other. For the most part, they communicated using messengers. The messengers rarely ever spoke, only doing so in dire emergencies. It was their job to care for the plant and animal life in the Meadows, as well as the guardians. They gathered and prepared food and drink, tended the lands, cleaned and decorated the castles, and did various other everyday things. They wore the colors of whatever land they were from, but only in pastel or muted shades. The bright dramatic shades were only for official guardians and their apprentices and heirs to wear. When he was younger, Jet had been frightened of the messengers. He found their silence rather spooky.

This is absolutely ridiculous, Jet thought, frustrated. He had come to the Pearl Castle to see Passion's daughter, Electra, but he couldn't bring himself to knock on her door. He wasn't even in the right hallway yet. Dropping his hands to his hips, Jet mentally berated himself for being such a coward. There was no turning back at this point. He had to do this, whether he wanted to or not. *Once, just once, would it kill her to not be so damn obstinate?* Jet thought as he remembered the exchange he'd had with Passion outside the apartment building.

"Jet!"

Jet turned just in time to have Electra leap into his arms, embracing him. Though she was slender and a couple inches shorter than him, she still almost knocked Jet over in her enthusiasm. He smiled as he hugged her, brushing some of her flowing dark hair behind her shoulder. Electra was nothing short of lovely and had a charming personality. At twenty-eight, she had already received plenty of offers for courtship from younger guardian men and a few women. Usually that didn't start until guardians reached at least their seventies. Electra had not accepted any offers, but she had already taken a few lovers. Older guardians would have frowned upon a young guardian having sex outside of official courtships and unions, but Electra knew how to keep her personal life private. It was a useful skill that Passion had taught her long ago and Electra herself had taught it to many of the guardians who were her age.

Electra was still smiling as she pulled back from the embrace, although Jet could see something akin to worry deep in her sparkling hazel eyes. Her eyes were very expressive and often changed color, a rare trait she had inherited from her mother. She had gotten most of her looks from Passion, as well.

"Where have you been? I haven't seen you in *ages*," Electra stated, her tone happy and upbeat. She was more of an optimist than her mother, but she was still young.

"I know. I'm sorry," Jet apologized, frowning as he studied her. "Are you all right? You look a little flushed."

He had known Electra her entire life, had even been present at her birth, and over the years he had developed a familial attachment to her. As he looked at her, Jet couldn't believe how fast the years had gone by. It seemed like only yesterday he held a tiny infant in his arms and now she was a fully grown adult woman, with the makings of a great guardian.

Electra smiled in a mischievous way and brushed some hair behind her ear. "I was just...working out."

Jet chuckled. "I see."

Electra glanced over at the map he had been looking at moments earlier. "I've always loved this. It's really amazing that we still have such beautiful relics from our ancestors. To think, Betha actually helped create this map when the Meadows first came into being."

Jet swallowed and looked around again. "Is your

mother here?"

"Not in the castle," Electra replied. "She's swimming in the aquatic realm. My guess is she won't be back for some time. Would you like me to send a messenger for her?"

"Ah no, no that won't be necessary," Jet said, thanking his lucky stars for the break. "Would you like to go for a walk, Electra? There are some important matters that I need to discuss with you and I know you hate being stationary for too long."

Electra nodded and followed him toward the main stairway. "Jet, you're being really mysterious. Should I be concerned?"

Jet swallowed and continued to lead the way down the stairs, pretending as though he hadn't heard her. He wanted to avoid talking until they got outside. The last thing he needed was to be the cause of a scene in the Pearl Castle.

It seemed to take forever, but Jet and Electra finally reached the outer gardens of the Pearl Castle. Once they were outside, Electra skipped forward so that she was standing on Jet's left and kept pace with him.

"Where's Lilly?" Electra asked, looking around for her. It was very rare for the two to be separated, especially when they visited the Meadows. Lilly was co-leader of the protectors and she always attended meetings with Jet and accompanied him on any trips they had to take. Jet had asked her to come with him, but she told him it was something he had to do on his own, whether or not he realized it.

"She's at home, dealing with some matters that required attention," Jet answered as he looked down the winding path that led out of the gardens. "I needed to speak with you privately and it couldn't wait."

"Well, I certainly hope you're not here to ask me to be your mistress. Many still haven't forgiven you for corrupting the youngest and loveliest daughter of Viridia," Electra teased, reaching down and grabbing a small red flower that had fallen off one of the many plants in the vast gardens. She placed it behind her ear and continued to keep up with Jet. They strode past a few stone benches and a couple messengers who were working in the gardens.

Jet laughed at the jest and glanced over at some Siroi lilies that grew nearby. They were his favorite flower and one that his wife used to watch over back when she had been a guardian.

"I really wish you'd just tell me what's on your mind," Electra commented, pulling Jet out of his thoughts.

"I will," Jet promised as they continued down the path that led away from the Pearl Castle. Once they had exited the castle grounds, Jet let Electra choose which path to go down. He already knew which direction she would pick: the one that led to the woodland realm, the realm she loved most apart from her home.

Walking down the path, the air had a sweet woodsy scent as they approached the vast forests. Jet looked over at Electra, still thinking about what exactly to say. The thought of hurting her broke his heart and he knew she would be hurt by what he revealed. Birds merrily chirped about them as a soft breeze rustled through the tree limbs. The bright afternoon sun shone down from above, glistening in Electra's dark brown hair. A green glint caught Jet's eye and he noticed she still wore the shamrock necklace the guardian Emerald had given her on the day of her birth.

"Electra, what do you know about the Four?" Jet finally asked. Electra shrugged as they continued down the path, grabbing a hanging twig and fiddling with it.

"Only what you and Mom have told me," she responded. "There are supposedly four shape shifter women who will save the guardians and other innocents from some unknown threat. Why do you ask?"

"It's part of the reason why I came here to see you," Jet explained, holding his hands behind his back. "I need your help to retrieve one of the Four, possibly the most important one."

Electra frowned, confused. "Why would you need my help approaching a protector?"

Jet swallowed and stopped walking. Electra took a few steps more before turning back to look at him, a questioning look on her face.

"Electra, there's something you have to know about this particular shape shifter," Jet began, feeling more unsure than he had in quite a while. Electra turned her whole body so that she was facing him fully and crossed her arms over her chest, waiting patiently.

"Yes?" she said after a moment when Jet didn't continue. A breeze suddenly swept through the grasses, brushing through her silky hair. Jet looked at her for a moment, rubbing the back of his head. Her kind eyes were almost painful to look at.

"The shape shifter — she's part guardian," Jet explained. Electra scrunched up her nose a little, obviously not believing him.

"Jet, that's not possible," Electra replied with a laugh. "Sacred law forbids romantic relationships between shape shifters and guardians. There hasn't been a hybrid in ages."

Jet nodded. "That's true, which is why this particular shape shifter has no idea of her heritage or that we even exist."

"That is ludicrous. *How* could she not know what she is?" Electra asked, picking at the twig she still held.

"Part of her mother's punishment for breaking one of the Sacred Laws was that one of her two daughters had to be given up to be raised as a human," Jet answered as he turned his gaze out over the beautiful fields of golden grass. His sharp ears could faintly pick up the distant sounds of water.

"Okay, so why not ask for the help of her mother or her…" Electra trailed off and Jet looked back to her. For a few moments, she was silent as she stared at him, her face unreadable. Then she began shaking her head slowly. Jet took a step forward, pausing when she stepped back and held up a hand. He waited for her to speak, knowing that there was nothing more he could say at the moment.

"Wait, this doesn't make sense. She would've said something," Electra started, her brow creasing as she tried to figure out what he was telling her. Jet watched her sympathetically, wishing he could prepare her for the next blow.

"It's not an easy time for her to remember," he said. She looked at him, her expression reflecting the conflicted feelings she was experiencing.

"Is it you?" she asked. Jet tilted his head, unsure

what she meant, and it suddenly dawned on him what she was asking.

"Is it…? Oh, no. No, I'm not your father," he replied with a small shake of his head. Electra frowned and shifted her weight a little. He could tell that she didn't know how to feel about his answer.

"Do you know who he is?" she asked, meeting his gaze again. Jet nodded, looking off into the forest.

"I do," he said. She watched him, waiting for him to elaborate. He gathered his nerve and turned his gaze back to her.

"Electra, I need your word that you'll let me explain after I tell you," Jet stated. He knew he was treading on dangerous ground and wished more than anything that Passion had heard him out. Going behind her back was killing him, but he had to do it. Electra seemed to glow against the dark brown tree trunks behind her. Though her face remained unreadable, Jet could see fear hidden within her eyes even as she nodded in agreement. Her slender fingers drifted up to her chest and she began to toy with the charm at her throat.

"Fine," she replied, her voice steely.

Jet hesitated for a moment. "His name was Roan Deverell."

The color drained from Electra's face and she took a step back, shaking her head. "Jet, it can't be. Please, tell me that it isn't."

Jet stepped closer to her, wishing he could offer some comfort to the young guardian. Electra shook her head and looked as though she were going to be sick.

"How could she?" Electra murmured, sounding lost and confused. Every guardian and shape shifter knew the story of Roan Deverell. The Deverells were one of the most respected protector families in the world; many of them were recalled in legends as great heroes. Roan was different, going against the Deverell lineage to become one of the most feared assassins ever. They knew he was responsible for at least fifteen deaths and undoubtedly many, many more. Most protectors still refused to speak his name and he had become their equivalent to the humans' boogieman. He had disappeared long ago, leaving a legacy of blood and pain in his wake. A legacy the rest of the Deverells were still trying to clean up.

"She didn't know, Electra," Jet replied as he leaned against the tree next to her. "She had run away from the Meadows and met him in a park. From what I understand, she fell in love and was prepared to stay on Earth with him. But then, she realized what he was, witnessed his cruelty, and she returned to the Meadows."

Electra slid down the tree so that she was sitting on the ground and brought her knees up to her chest. Like all guardians, Electra knew about the power of words. However, she probably never thought that her entire life could be altered with nothing more than a few sentences. As she ran her hands down her face, Jet sat next to her, waiting for her to speak again.

"What does that make me?" she asked, looking at her hands as she began slowly rubbing them together in a circular motion.

"Pardon?" Jet turned his eyes to her.

"I've always thought I was a guardian, but that's not entirely true, is it?" Electra stated, iciness creeping into her tone. Jet looked off to the Pearl Castle in the distance. It was made of white brick with subtle hints of gold, which made it glisten like something out of a fairytale.

"You're half shape shifter and half guardian. That doesn't make you any less guardian, you're still considered full-blooded," he answered.

"So good to know," Electra grumbled, rising to her feet. "My entire life has been a lie, you only thought to tell me now, and I have a twin sister out there somewhere who has no idea what she is."

Jet winced at her tone. "It isn't that simple, Electra."

"Why didn't you tell me sooner?" Electra demanded, turning accusing eyes on him. "Or is this just one of those situations where you waited until you needed something from me?"

"He didn't tell you because the High Council forbade him from doing so," a wise feminine voice came from behind Electra. She twisted to look behind her as Jet stood up again.

Adonia stood a short distance behind Electra, looking nothing short of radiant. The queen of the guardians had long red hair and vibrant moss green eyes that seemed to pierce straight through whomever she was looking at. She held herself with an air of confidence that wasn't haughty or pretentious. Her skin sparkled in the sunlight; the same subtle gleam that lit the skin of all guardians. She wore an orchid-colored dress with a gauzy net that resembled mist. Adonia smiled compassionately at her great-granddaughter, unbothered by Electra's irate glare. Her smooth hands were pressed together in front of her and she nodded in greeting at Jet, who bowed in respect.

"I hope you don't mind, Jet, but I followed the

two of you," she spoke in her melodic voice.

"Not at all," he replied, glad for the support.

Electra stormed off, stepping around her great-grandmother, not saying another word to either of them. Jet moved to follow her, but was stopped from doing so by Adonia's hand on his shoulder.

"Give her some space. Let her process what she has learned," she spoke, glancing in the direction Electra had gone. "I have faith that my great-granddaughter will make the right decision."

Jet turned to face the regal woman. "I really need her help, Adonia."

She nodded in understanding, smiling. "I know. I've been watching her sister as well and I know that soon she will need to enter the life she is destined to have. Do not worry. Electra is strong and she is also curious. She has a lot to think about and it is best to let her work through it on her own."

Jet glanced down the path, longing to go after the young guardian. He wanted to offer some kind of comfort to the young woman he had come to love as a niece or even another daughter, but knew that was most likely impossible. He turned back to Adonia, a small sad smile playing across his face.

"Passion will never forgive me for this. I crossed a line and betrayed her trust," he stated. She reached forward and placed a palm on his cheek.

"You have other things to worry about now," she said. "You shouldn't dwell on the things that you have no control over. Go home, Jet. You've done all you can here."

Jet nodded and she dropped her hand, allowing him to pass by her. She turned her head a little to call over her shoulder.

"Make sure you have a room prepared at the mansion for a guest," she suggested in a cryptic tone. Jet paused and glanced back to her. Adonia sometimes made strange predictions that he never really understood until they happened. All guardians had a mysterious way about them and Jet had learned long ago not to question it. He nodded once and then vanished in a flash of dark blue light.

~~*~*~*

The southern lands of the Meadows were filled with different bodies of water. There were rivers, lakes, springs, and a vast ocean that stretched as far as the eye could see. There were also large circular pools of water where the women could enjoy a nice soak whenever they had a moment to spare.

Passion sat in one of the smaller pools, the warm clean water washing over her nude flesh, relaxing her. Her eyes were closed and her face was turned toward the sunlight. Normally, she had a lover accompany her to the water lands, but today was one of the rare times when Passion desired solitude. Raising one hand, she listened to the delicate splash of the droplets rejoining the larger body of water. She ran her fingers through her wet hair, enjoying the fresh smell of the trees that surrounded her. Ocean's lands were the only place the guardians were allowed to be naked outside of their own rooms. Passion smiled, recalling the clothing rule as one of the many she'd delighted in breaking during her younger days. She used to enjoy strolling nude down the halls of the Pearl Castle or in other lands. In her mind, the body was nothing to be ashamed of. After Electra had been born, she had curbed some of her wilder ways.

Passion glanced over her left shoulder when she glimpsed pale powder blue, noticing one of the water messengers standing nearby. The woman had light brown hair, which was tightly braided and held in a neat bun. She stood near a tree trunk that served as a table, prepared to approach with a silver decanter of water if called for. Passion sighed and turned her eyes forward again. It was nearly impossible to get any kind of privacy outside of her room. Messengers were everywhere, waiting on the guardians hand and foot. It became annoying after a while, though Passion was sure she was in the minority feeling that way.

After another moment in the water, Passion stood up and stepped back onto solid ground. The messenger hurried over with a towel, slipping it over her shoulders.

"Thank you," Passion murmured, offering a friendly smile when the messenger nodded and stepped back. Passion ran the soft fabric up and down her body, allowing it to soak up any excess liquid. When she was done, the messenger was right there with the scarlet dress she had been wearing prior to getting in the water. Once again, Passion thanked her as she slipped on the dress. She pulled her wet hair back in a messy ponytail as she walked down the path that would take her back to the Pearl Castle.

Passion smiled when she recognized Phoenix, the youngest daughter of the head fire guardian, walking down the path toward her. Phoenix was about a year younger than Electra and had a similar rebellious nature. The two women had bonded while growing up in the Meadows. Phoenix had flowing dark red hair and golden eyes, looking every inch a daughter of the lands of fire. The younger guardian frowned when she neared Passion, nodding in greeting and pausing when they met on the path.

"What are you doing here?" Phoenix asked. Passion looked around at the fields of golden grass, before turning her gaze back to Phoenix.

"Last time I checked, I lived here," she replied with gentle teasing. "Aneurin hasn't gotten his way yet."

"No. I mean, I saw Jet and Electra walking a few minutes ago and I just assumed you were going to meet up with them," Phoenix replied, gesturing over her shoulder. Passion froze, her heart pumping faster.

"Jet was here? Talking to Electra?" she asked, doing her best to mask the fear in her suddenly small voice. Phoenix shrugged, a cool wind brushing through her long hair.

"Yeah, he left a few…" she trailed off when Passion suddenly ran past her, sprinting toward the castle.

~~*~*~*

The first level of the Pearl Castle was always bustling with activity. There was a sea of pastel colors as messengers rushed around, delivering important letters and other documents from one guardian to another. There was usually a guardian or two waiting for a meeting with Adonia or Artemis. The guardians — being polite and dignified by nature — rarely ever fought and always managed to avoid hindering another's business. Even though there was constant movement on the castle's lower level, it didn't affect the overall serene atmosphere.

Passion stormed through the large doors, hurrying through the multitude of messengers. She reached the marble steps and began running up them, heading for the third level. Messengers and other guardians swiftly stepped out of the way when she passed them, recognizing by the look on her face that the guardian of passion was not happy.

"Passion?" an austere voice called from somewhere behind her. Passion knew who it was, but ignored her. There was only one guardian she knew with that voice and she was someone whom Passion did not want to talk to at the moment.

"Passion, I know you can hear me. We have to—"

"Not now, Calliope!" Passion snapped as she spun around to face the muse. The muses worked under her and most of them disliked her, mainly because she was much younger and less experienced than they were. Calliope was the head muse and thought Passion was an irresponsible screw-up. When Passion had been growing up, Calliope had been her tutor. The eldest muse found it demeaning to work for someone she had once taught and had no qualms making her feelings known.

Calliope took a step back at Passion's sharp tone. It was rare that the guardian directed anger at her. They didn't care for each other, but like all guardians, they respected each other and treated one another with civility. If Passion barked at her, it was a sign to back off for the time being. Calliope turned back, making her way down the steps. Passion watched her until she disappeared down the first flight of steps before continuing her mad dash.

Once Passion set foot on the third floor, she

began to run down the hall toward Electra's room. The detailed tapestries and paintings on the walls became a blur as Passion dashed by, keeping her focus on her destination. The daylight took on an almost soft blue glow on the upper levels, giving the space a dream-like appearance. Passion reached the tall wooden door and knocked on it, waiting for her daughter to respond.

"Electra?" she called, reaching for the curvy gold lever. She pushed it down and opened the door, stepping into her daughter's room and searching for the young guardian. Passion swallowed as she moved to the desk, looking for a note or anything that would tell her where Electra was.

"She's gone," a stern voice came from behind her. Passion gritted her teeth and turned back to the door, keeping a hand on the desk. Her mother, Artemis, stood in the doorway with her arms crossed over her chest. Though she was slender, Artemis still had an intimidating presence. Her short raven-colored hair was neatly brushed away from her face and her dark blue eyes had a serious look to them, as they always did.

"Where is she?" Passion asked, not attempting to hide the anger in her voice.

"I don't think she would want me to tell you," Artemis replied, unbothered by her daughter's tone.

"I am not in the mood for this, Mother," Passion warned. "What did he tell her?"

"What you should have told her a long time ago," Artemis answered, her tone remaining even. Passion let out a half-laugh, nodding.

"Never miss an opportunity to preach to me, do you?" she said.

"Maybe if you had more respect for the rules of your people, I wouldn't have to. You certainly wouldn't be in this situation if you had listened to me twenty-eight years ago."

"Wow, just wow. You're still holding that against me. You're *still* dwelling on what happened over twenty years ago," Passion snapped.

"You had two daughters by a shape shifter, Passion. Not just a shape shifter, an assassin. A murderer. I think I'm allowed to chalk that up to reckless behavior on your part."

Passion glared at her mother before turning her attention back to the room, walking around as she continued to look for any sort of note. She and her mother had always had a shaky relationship, turbulent even before the incident with Roan. After Roan, the only time they could muster the strength to act civil toward one another was when Electra was around. When Electra had reached her teenage years, she had witnessed a few clashes that took place between Passion and Artemis. The daughter of Passion always managed to remain neutral. She loved them both and so stayed out of their arguments.

"You have to start taking responsibility for your actions—"

"Because you did *so* much better as a mother," Passion shot back as she spun around and faced her mother again, relishing in the brief stunned expression that crossed Artemis' face. Passion rarely went low, but when she needed to, she made sure her words struck hard.

"You got off easy, Passion," Artemis said, a hint of anger lacing her voice. "You are lucky you weren't banished."

"You're not exactly blameless in my so-called indiscretions, mother," Passion shot back.

"What's that supposed to mean?" Artemis asked, almost daring her daughter to respond.

"You smothered me! You never let me make any decisions! You were so terrified of me becoming another disgraced guardian that you turned my life into a prison!"

Passion was close to tears. She needed to find Electra and explain…everything. She ran a hand through her hair as she started to pace, feeling close to panicked. Her emotions were running wild and her mother wasn't helping matters.

"I was right about Roan wasn't I?" Artemis asked coolly.

Passion let out a sob of laughter. "Yes, mother, you certainly were. Congratulations."

Passion ran her hands over her face as she turned away from her mother and sank down on the bed, swallowing her tears. She would not let her mother see her cry.

"You're still in love with him, aren't you?" Artemis suddenly spoke again. Passion could feel her eyes slowly change red as she turned her furious gaze back to her mother, who now stood above her.

"Get. Out," she growled.

"Don't you—" Artemis began.

"Get out!" Passion roared. Artemis fumed but turned and strode from the room, clenching her teeth when Passion slammed the door behind her. The loud bang echoed down the relatively quiet hall. Leaning her back against the wall, Passion tried to calm herself by breathing in and out, counting slowly to one hundred. Behind the door, she heard a quiet conversation between her mother and grandmother.

"What happened?"

"Passion threw another one of her tantrums," Artemis replied, anger still apparent in her voice.

"Artemis, you cannot change the past. Passion is hurting. Please do not bait her into a fight."

"She is hurting because of something that is partly her own fault," Artemis replied. For a moment, there was quiet.

"Let her be for now," Adonia spoke softly, her voice suggesting that it wasn't a request. As Passion sank to the floor, drawing her knees up to her chest, she heard a soft knocking on the door.

"Passion?" Adonia's kind voice filtered through the door and she paused for a moment, waiting for Passion to respond. "If you want to talk, I'm going to be in my office."

Passion listened to her footsteps move down the hallway, not wanting to talk to her grandmother. She didn't want to speak with anyone but her daughter. As soon as she couldn't hear the footsteps anymore, Passion buried her face in her knees and wept.

~~*~*~*

"Have you managed to get a hold of the Deverells yet?"

Jade rolled her neck so that she was looking at Jet. The two were sitting in his study, where Jet and Lilly did most of their work. He sat behind a large desk, fidgeting as he had been ever since returning from the Meadows. The sun had set a little more than an hour ago and the study was filled with a warm glow from the few lamps set up around the room.

Jade nodded and folded her arms over her chest. "Yeah, I spoke to Ajax this afternoon. Jensen's taking it pretty hard, which is to be expected. He doesn't want to talk to me."

"Maybe I should call again," Jet murmured, thinking out loud but Jade shook her head.

"I wouldn't recommend that. He doesn't want to talk to anyone. Nero was lucky to get two words out of him," she replied, turning her eyes to the ceiling. "Jet, would you please let me go talk to her? Electra's not going to show up, not tonight anyway."

Jet glanced at the clock, noticing it was after nine. "Just…give her a few more minutes."

"Okay, but I still think this is a really bad idea," Jade commented. No sooner had she finished speaking than there was a knock on the door. Jade sat up while Jet called for whomever it was to come in. The door opened and Lilly stepped inside, a small smile dancing on her lips.

"Electra is here," she stated in her pleasant voice.

"Send her in," Jet replied, turning to Jade. "I told you she'd come through."

Jade shook her head and lay back down across the chair, muttering, "I still hold to my earlier assessment that it's a bad idea."

CHAPTER FIVE

Isis lay on the couch in her cozy apartment, enjoying the pleasant evening after a tiring week of researching mythology and the occult. Having nothing better to do, she had decided to watch a movie. The DVD was one of her favorite movies: *Suspiria*. Isis had an affinity for horror films, one that Steve had been forced to share. She could not count the number of times he complained to her about suffering from nightmares.

The lights were off, but the vivid colors of the movie illuminated the dark room in blues and yellows and reds. Isis watched as the main character cautiously strode into her friend's empty room, her wide eyes searching the space. She frowned and watched as the girl looked for any sign of the former occupant. Isis slowly sat up, remembering this part in the movie. She jumped at the quiet but stern voice of the eerie schoolmistress as she inquired about whether Suzy was looking for Sara. An unsettling feeling of déjà vu crept over Isis as Suzy insisted that it was simply impossible that her friend would disappear and was ignored. *Exactly! Exactly! People don't just disappear. Don't let them get away with that shit,* Isis thought as she shuddered. Out of the corner of her eye, she noticed the drapes rise in a breeze, fluttering and falling back into place.

The DVD skipped and Suzy was creeping down a dark hallway with golden leaves painted on the walls. Isis frowned and looked around for the remote control. The few DVDs she owned were in good condition and never had one skipped on her before. The murky blue light made visibility nonexistent. She jolted at the sound of a gasp, shaking her head when she realized it was only the movie. A crash of lightning and another sharp gasp had her looking for any kind of remote so she could lower the volume. Her TV had suddenly become louder and the last thing Isis needed was to be evicted for fighting with angry neighbors. *Where is that damn thing? Don't tell me it disappeared too,* she thought as she got on her hands and knees and felt around under the couch. She could hear ragged breathing from the TV behind her, the volume making it sound much closer. Isis could almost feel the breath on the nape of her neck.

"Who is it!? Who's there!?" an unpleasant rough voice demanded, causing Isis to jerk up. Her insides clenched up and she gripped the sofa, letting out her breath when she realized it was only the movie.

"Get a grip, Isis," she chastised herself. "You're acting like a child."

As she stood up and approached the TV, the witch began to cackle in sadistic amusement. Isis reached down to lower the volume. The room was briefly illuminated in red and then blue again.

"Now death is coming for you!" the witch cackled as Isis tried to turn the volume down and the television suddenly blinked off. Isis looked at the TV and then the DVD player. Both were black, indicating that the power had gone out.

"Dammit," she grumbled in annoyance, looking toward the kitchen. The clock on the microwave was also dark. Isis groaned and ran her hands over her face, wondering if her week could possibly get any worse.

Moving to the kitchen, her bare feet soon touched smooth linoleum and she went over to the refrigerator, reaching for the small cabinet overhead where she kept matches and a flashlight. Isis paused when she saw a glow out of the corner of her eye, noticing the light was on in the hall. How could the power be out in just one apartment? She was up to date on her bills so...

Before another thought could form in her mind, a coil of steel wrapped around her throat and cinched to completely cut off her oxygen. Isis gagged as her hands flew up to the sharp metal about her neck. Lifting up both feet, she pushed off the fridge, hoping to knock her assailant off balance. She succeeded in knocking the mysterious person back a couple steps, enough to collide with the counter, but the coil remained tight. The attacker spun her around and began dragging her out of the kitchen. Isis, using her free hand, desperately searched for any kind of weapon. Her thrashing knocked everything off the counter.

Her assailant suddenly fell backward and the two crashed to the ground. Isis gagged, fighting for air, as she dug her elbow into the attacker's ribs and clawed at their face. A thin line of hot blood welled up beneath the coil as Isis tried slamming her head against her unknown assailant. In desperation, she began to kick her legs around.

Dark spots started to form in her vision and moving became more and more difficult as her breath slowly ran out. Above her, the drapes once again fluttered about in the cool night breeze.

~~*~*~*

Jade stood in the elevator next to Electra, who was drumming her fingers impatiently. She had not said two words since telling Jet and Lilly that she would help them and her ire was almost tangible. Jade glanced at the floors as they lit up, wondering what had happened to the music that used to play in elevators. It had been annoying as hell, but a situation such as the one she found herself in warranted it. Jade wasn't a fan of stony silences. Of course, she wasn't a fan of inane blather either.

"I don't suppose anyone has given *any* thought about what we should say to her," Electra growled. Jade looked over to her, surprised she had broken the quiet first.

"What were you thinking of saying?" she asked.

"Hi, I'm your identical twin sister. Welcome to your new life, everyone will lie to you until it benefits them to tell the truth and you'll be treated as little more than a pawn," Electra replied icily. Jade studied her for a moment, biting the inside of her cheek as she looked back to the floors lighting up.

"Maybe I should do the talking," Jade mentioned. The gold door finally slid open on the fourth floor and the two women stepped out into a clean hallway. It was quiet and their footsteps seemed strangely silent on the hardwood floor. Whatever faint sounds they heard were peculiar, more muted than was natural. Jade frowned as she looked around them, sensing something wasn't right. It felt exactly like the warehouse had, right before all hell broke loose. She was distantly aware of Electra continuing to speak, but paid no attention. Jade reached for the gun she was concealing in the back of her pants, carefully pulling it out and holding it in a two-handed grip.

"Jade?" Electra asked, noticing the firearm for the first time. Guardians were forbidden from using guns and their laws prohibited violence. Protectors led more dangerous lives than the guardians and so their use of weapons was allowed.

"Probably nothing," Jade replied, but she picked up her pace a little and jogged down the hall. They reached the door and Jade immediately noticed that the lights were out. She tilted her head, listening for any noise inside the apartment. When she heard nothing, she glanced over her shoulder down the hall she and Electra had just come down, noticing faint traces of light under all the other doors.

"Maybe she's not home," Electra offered as she leaned against the wall behind her. Jade shook her head as she reached for the knob.

"Our source says she will be in all night," she said, trying the knob and finding it locked. Jade swore under her breath as she pointed the muzzle of her gun toward the ground.

"Stand back," she warned Electra.

"Wouldn't picking the lock be a better, less destructive solution?" Electra suggested as she stayed leaning against the opposite wall.

"Takes too long," Jade replied as she raised her long leg and kicked at the doorjamb. It took two strong kicks, but Jade managed to splinter the doorframe. The door swung open as the chain snapped and rattled against the wood.

The apartment was dark and silent. In her peripheral vision, Jade saw the drapes flutter in the breeze. Jade swiftly, but cautiously, moved inside the apartment. Her dark brown eyes did a sweep of her shadowy surroundings. Nervousness coiled in her stomach, but years of experience allowed her to ignore the unpleasant feeling as she moved around the apartment. She didn't like the vibe she was getting in the apartment. It was too similar to what had happened last week. Everything was unnaturally cold and still. The darkness had an abnormal heaviness to it and it almost seemed to be breathing. Tiny droplets of sweat began to bead on Jade's forehead as she continued to look around.

A sudden shriek behind her and a burst of blue light caused her to spin around, gun drawn. Jade let out a breath of relief when she saw it was only the TV, which had suddenly burst to life. The image of a once beautiful woman, now grotesquely deformed by barbed wire, filled the screen. Jade spun back when she heard coughing and was startled when a dark form bolted past her. The protector didn't have time to wonder about it as she narrowly dodged a club of some kind coming down toward her head. Jade was able to maneuver her skull out of the way, but the blunt weapon managed to clip her wrist and caused her to lose her grip on her gun. Jade let out a cry of pain and was thrown across the room by a phantom force. She collided with the wall, bringing a picture down with her as she crashed to the floor, hearing the glass on the picture shatter next to her. Jade's eyes fell on a bat within reaching distance and she lunged for it, grabbing it and rising to her feet again, prepared to take on whatever the mystery form was. She was shocked to find the apartment empty. Her eyes darted about the room as she held onto the bat, doing a mental check of her injuries. Her wrist was at the very least sprained, more likely fractured, and her ribs hurt every time she inhaled, probably from her collision with the wall. The sound of ragged breathing and high-pitched screaming brought her attention back to the television. In the movie, small trinkets began to explode and an empty chair slid across the room. Jade approached it, her walk a little stiffer than normal, and turned it off, her eyes still traveling about the apartment.

Her gaze landed on the open window and, for a moment, Jade could have sworn she heard the rattle of the fire escape outside. The sound was so faint, she was unsure whether or not she had just imagined it. *Better safe than sorry,* she thought as she took a step toward the open window.

"Jade!" Electra's winded voice came from the hall, making Jade hesitate. She had completely forgotten she was with a guardian and therefore responsible for her safety. As a protector, her loyalty to the guardians always came first.

"Dammit," Jade cursed as she hurried to retrieve her gun, before running out into the hall. Electra was pushing herself up from a sitting position, looking dazed.

"She kicked me," she stated, sounding indignant.

The kick had obviously been well-aimed because it had knocked the wind out of the young guardian.

"Which way did she go?" Jade asked, looking down the hall. They had to get out of there fast. There was a chance a tenant had called the police and dealing with cops was not something Jade particularly enjoyed doing.

"After she kicked me?" Electra asked, nodding down the opposite way they had come. "Down that way and she took the stairs."

"Go back to the car and stay there until I get back," Jade ordered as she tossed Electra her keys before dashing down the hall, the cream-colored doors becoming a blur. She reached the door to the stairs and threw it open, running to the railing and looking down. It wasn't long before Jade caught a glimpse of someone two flights below, running down the stairs. She turned and began making her way down the first flight, allowing her body to melt into another form as she continued her pursuit. The muscles and bones expanded and contracted as she shrunk down to all fours, a long tail growing out behind her. Fur sprouted from her flesh and within seconds, she was an adult snow leopard, her personal favorite form. Growing up in Brazil, Jade had heard stories of such majestic creatures and never lost her fascination with them. To her, there was something almost magical about snow and the animals found in colder climates.

Her body easily wove down the stairs as she made use of the leopard's natural agility. She leapt up onto one railing and soared across to another, hopping down entire flights that way. Finally, she caught up to the woman and moved in front of her, turning on her heel and getting up on two legs. Using her two front paws, Jade pinned the woman against the wall. The woman let out a yell, her eyes widening, and without thinking, Jade allowed her body to shift back into its usual human form. Her muzzle shrank back into a human nose and mouth, the fur disappeared and her joints straightened out again. Jade shook her head as her ears returned to their normal form and she rotated her shoulders a bit.

For a moment, the two women stood staring at each other. Both were breathless from the chase and Jade could see the other woman's entire body was shaking. She was taken aback by how similar the woman looked to Electra. It was uncanny, right down to the charm she wore at her throat. The younger twin wore her hair shorter than the guardian, but other than that, she was her sister's mirror image.

"I take it you're Isis?" Jade asked, arching an elegant dark eyebrow. The woman stared at her in complete disbelief, still shaking.

"You just…you just…What the fuck!?" she stammered, on the verge of a panic attack. *Definitely a bad idea,* Jade thought as she removed one hand from the wall and picked up the emerald shamrock from where it rested on the woman's chest. She flipped it over and read the inscription on the back, nodding once.

"Yep, you're her," she said, dropping it again and looking back to the frightened woman. "Look, I know that was kind of…shocking and probably a lot for you take in. I apologize for that. I fear I was a little careless."

Jade winced in sympathy as her long fingers drifted over to Isis' throat where there was a thin line of blood. Isis jerked her head away from the touch, raising one hand defensively. Jade dropped her hand and lowered her other hand, not offended by the woman's suspicion. If she'd had the life Isis had, she would probably be wary of strangers too. Especially strangers that could turn into animals, a feat that should have been impossible. *It was stupid and impulsive to shift in front of her,* Jade thought, annoyed with her carelessness. It was something she frequently chastised younger protectors for: relying too much on shifting and getting sloppy about it.

"You've had a very long night and probably have a lot of questions. Come on, there's a car waiting," Jade offered as she turned and started moving toward the next flight of stairs. She was halfway down when she realized Isis wasn't following her. Turning, Jade placed her hands on the black railings, moving back up a couple steps.

"Somebody tried to kill you. Chances are they're not the type to just give up. Next time, I won't be around," Jade pointed out as she looked to the woman who still stood with her back pressed against the wall.

"I have no idea who you are," Isis replied, suspicion reflected on her face.

Jade smiled and offered her hand. "Name's Jade and I just saved your life. Please come with me."

Isis didn't move, causing Jade to sigh and drop her hand. She climbed back up the stairs and leaned against the banister at the top.

"You want evidence that I'm on your side, all right. I know about the body, Bryn Adams," Jade said, deciding to try a different tact. *Bingo,* she thought as Isis' eyes widened again and she straightened up from the wall. The younger woman swallowed and took a careful step toward her, unable to hide her curiosity.

"That wasn't a hallucination?" she asked, but it sounded more like a statement of vindication. Jade shook her head once.

"No. I was there," she replied, looking down the steps. As much as Jade didn't want to think about that night, she knew she had to if only to coax Isis into coming with her.

"So, what happened? Where's the body?" Isis demanded, now within reaching distance. Jade turned her dark brown eyes back to her.

"I said I knew *about* the body, not what *happened* to it," she clarified, starting down the stairs. "If you want to help solve that mystery, come with me."

It took a moment, but Jade finally heard Isis' footsteps trailing hers as they moved down the stairs and toward the lower floor. She smiled a little, pleased that she had accomplished what she had set out to do.

~~*~*~*

Isis sat in the back seat of Jade's Mustang, which was currently doing eighty by her estimate. Isis clutched her seat every time Jade took a sharp turn, which felt like every other minute. In the front seat were Jade and Isis' twin sister, Electra. Isis had only known her sister less than an hour and had already managed to royally piss her off. Her uncanny ability to get on people's bad sides was still going strong. Though Isis knew she wouldn't have enjoyed getting kicked in the diaphragm.

"Ow! Quit elbowing me," Electra snapped at Jade,

shifting in her seat so she was a little further away from the driver.

"Say something to her," Jade said under her breath.

"Like what?" Electra asked, not even attempting to be quiet.

"Um, I can hear you," Isis said from the back, wondering if they had forgotten about her. She wasn't sure she should draw attention to herself, but there was an uncomfortable tension in the car and she was still incredibly nervous. Raising a hand to massage her aching throat, Isis grimaced a little at the sting.

"Look, it's not her fault that the High Council thought it best to lie to both of you," Jade replied, ignoring her passenger in the backseat. Electra sat back in a huff and it became uncomfortably silent once again. Isis leaned forward, resting her arms on the backs of their seats.

"Are you with the FBI?" she asked.

"No," Jade replied.

"CIA?"

"No," Electra responded, staring out the window.

"MI-5?"

"No," Electra and Jade responded simultaneously in obvious exasperation. Isis frowned, thinking of other organizations that employed covert agents. Deciding that was a fruitless line of questioning for the moment, Isis turned her attention to Jade.

"So, can I turn into a snow leopard? Or is it some sort of virus, like transferred through a bite or sex or something?" she asked. Electra let out a huff that sounded like a laugh and shook her head, massaging her brow.

"It's hereditary and you'll be able to shift once

you're trained," Jade answered.

"How much longer before we get to wherever we're going?" Isis asked, glancing out the window when a car shot by with its brights on. The buildings became sparser as they traveled further from the town.

"It'll be a while yet," Jade replied, glancing over at Electra when she shifted her weight. The young guardian glanced over at her sister before turning her eyes to the clean windshield.

"Great. Then you two will have no problem explaining to me just what the hell is going on," Isis stated as she crossed her arms over her chest. "Because last time I checked, wereleopards didn't exist."

Electra snorted while Jade screeched to a halt at a red light. The sleek car jerked a little at the sudden stop.

"I'm not a wereleopard," Jade protested, sounding offended. "Electra, please explain to your sister just who and what we are."

"Fine," Electra said and twisted in her seat so that she was facing the back and looking at Isis. It was weird to suddenly have a sibling, especially one who happened to be her identical twin. *I'm even weirder than most people assume,* Isis thought, waiting for the woman to speak.

"You and I are hybrids, the only two in existence," she began, a hint of bitterness in her voice. "Part shape shifter and part guardian. I'll start with the guardians, because I know more about them. I was raised as a guardian and didn't know I was only half until a few hours ago."

Jade cleared her throat loudly as she pressed on

the gas pedal again, the interior of the car illuminated by green light. Electra glared at her with the most impressive side-eye Isis had ever seen before turning back to the conversation.

"Guardians are similar to the deities you've undoubtedly read about in assorted mythologies, only less omnipotent and powerful. We're...they're not gods. They watch over things on Earth and keep it running as smoothly as possible."

"Like God?"

Jade snorted. "Nobody is infallible. That concept was created by humans, best we can tell."

"Jade's right," Electra put in. "There is no omnipotent creator, as far as we know."

"Why don't people worship you?" Isis asked, leaning forward, intrigued.

"Because they don't know about us and again, guardians aren't gods," Electra replied. "Guardians can only guide. All life forms have free will. The guardians gave them a nudge when it came to sciences and the arts. Humans created religions, charities, and different sorts of government."

"Mortality is a powerful motivator, makes people come up with all kinds of things, whether for good or ill," Jade added, a hint of weariness in her voice. Isis looked between them, feeling more and more confused by the minute. Electra glanced at Jade, who kept her eyes on the road.

"Anyway, there are not only elemental guardians but emotion guardians as well," she continued. "Like the elements, there's a guardian for every emotion."

Isis frowned. "Why?"

"Well, if one emotion got out of control, it would be disastrous. For bigger things like water and plants there are many guardians, but almost every emotion only has one guardian. Keeping the Earth running smoothly is as dangerous as it is complicated. There are many who would love to get control of the Meadows and all her inhabitants because to do so would mean complete control of all the worlds out there. Good protects good, that's the way it has always been. There are shape shifters whose job it is to protect the guardians, as well as the innocent on Earth."

"And that's what," Isis had to rack her brain to remember the woman's name, "Jade is?"

"Yes," Electra replied. "Shape shifters are beings that are mostly human. The only thing different is that they can change into any animal at will."

"Like in the legends of the Sioux?"

Jade twisted her hand a couple times and scrunched up her nose. "Not really."

Electra smiled and shook her head. "Shape shifters are found in many cultures and mythologies — every story is a little different, but shape shifters such as Jade are their own people and culture. They are not the beings found in myths."

Isis looked between the two of them, frowning. She was still having trouble believing what they were telling her despite having seen it firsthand. Glancing out the window, she wished Steve was with her. *Really wish I had my fucking phone,* she thought as she flopped back.

"The shape shifters known as protectors do an amazing job," Electra continued, glancing once more at Jade before turning her attention to Isis again. "They protect the guardians as well as innocents here on Earth at any cost. They have fought in many wars alongside humans, without humans even knowing, and some still do to this day. They put their lives on the line without a second thought every day, practically every moment they live."

"And how does this pertain to my supposedly being able to do this…shape shifting?" Isis asked, the words sounding strange in her mouth. She tried to figure out exactly when her life had become one giant conspiracy theory. The world was almost certainly fucking with her at this point.

"I'm getting there," Electra responded, arching an eyebrow. "Has anyone ever told you you're extremely impatient?"

"Call it a character flaw," Isis replied. Jade chuckled as she braked smoothly at a stop sign and then made a right turn onto a quiet unlit street. Isis straightened up, not recognizing the area anymore. In the distance, she could see hills and it seemed like that was where Jade was heading. *Hills are a perfect place to hide a body. Great,* Isis thought.

"The guardians have a book called The Book of Oracle," Electra continued, frowning. "Jade, this isn't the right—"

"I'm taking a scenic route. Go on, continue your story," Jade said as she leaned back in her seat. "The Book of Oracle."

"Oh-kay," Electra said, her tone suggesting she was a little unsure about the new route. After a moment she turned her eyes back to Isis. "Anyway, the Book of Oracle contains prophecies, mostly things that may happen in the future. Several months after we were born, a prophecy appeared telling of what protectors refer to as the Four. Four shape shifter women who will save the Meadows, home of the guardians, and all the other worlds out there from a threat we don't yet have a name for. Basically they're going to change the future, hopefully for the better. We found three of the four and according to the leaders of the protectors, you're the fourth."

"Protectors are one faction of shape shifters," Jade put in. "The others you'll learn about later."

Isis was silent for a moment, considering all that she had just heard.

"Did Steve or Shae put you two up to this?" she asked, certain her friends were pranking her. Though that wouldn't explain the near-death experience she'd had.

"Who?" Electra asked, looking over at Jade. Isis ran her hands over her face. *This is absolute lunacy. I've just entered the goddamn Twilight Zone,* she thought.

"I've never turned into an animal before," she insisted.

"Neither has your sister," Jade countered. "You haven't been trained properly. I'm sure you've seen signs though. Animals relax around you. Sometimes it almost feels like you know what they're thinking. A longing to run free. One hell of a libido. Am I getting warm?"

"Wrong on the libido thing. I'm on the ace spectrum, been Gray-A my whole life," Isis stated, crossing her arms over her chest. "Very, *very* low libido. Pretty much non-existent."

"No shit?" Jade looked up at the rearview mirror, interest and amusement reflecting in her eyes. "You're just all kinds of unique."

"What's that supposed to mean?" Isis asked, feeling more than a little defensive.

"Asexuality is almost unheard of in shape shifters.

It's even rarer than it is among humans," Jade explained, snickering as though she were remembering a joke. "Two members of the Four are ace spectrum, how very odd. It's certainly going to raise a few eyebrows at the very least."

"Great," Isis grumbled as she turned her gaze out the window, trying to see through the shadows. The road was starting to become curvy and she couldn't see any houses or other buildings that would give an indication of where they were.

"Jade said shape shifting is hereditary?" Isis mentioned, not directing the question to anyone in particular.

"It is," Electra responded. "Our father was a shape shifter. Our mother is part of the royal line and she's the guardian of passion."

"Hence her name: Passion," Jade added with a half-smile.

"Where exactly are the guardians?" Isis asked, glancing around, half-expecting to see one flying next to the car.

"As I mentioned earlier, they live in the Meadows," Electra answered, leaning sideways against her seat. "You can only get there by Appearing."

"Appearing?" Isis was more skeptical than ever. *Getting in this car was definitely not the wisest decision I've ever made*, she thought as she toyed with the lock on the door.

"It's similar to what humans call teleporting," Jade explained, shrugging when Electra looked at her. Judging from her mannerisms, Isis wondered whether her twin spent very much time on Earth.

"You mentioned our father. Is he in the Meadows?" Isis asked, a little uneasy when the two women exchanged a look that was not at all reassuring.

"No. Shape shifters don't live in the Meadows and it's against our Sacred Laws for them to court guardians or enter into any sort of romantic relationship," Electra answered. Isis raised an eyebrow at the vague response.

"So what, Passion and...?" she paused, waiting for a name. Electra looked to Jade again.

"Roan," Jade answered, squinting at the inky night just outside the windshield. After a moment, she turned the steering wheel and rather than running off the road, Isis was surprised to find the road continued on. Glancing out the window, she noticed she couldn't see a road ahead or behind her at all.

"Are they like Romeo and Juliet only alive or something like that?" Isis asked.

"No," Electra responded darkly, but Jade started chuckling, obviously finding the question rather funny.

"I really like her," Jade told Electra, smiling at Isis in the rearview mirror. Isis looked between the two women, picking up on the returning tension

"Okay, what is the deal with this guy?"

"He's a murdering bastard," Electra snapped, and Jade ran a hand over her face. Isis' eyes widened again and she looked between the two, waiting for one of them to expand upon the statement.

"It's not quite so simple. Remember those factions of shape shifters I mentioned earlier? Roan came from a family called the Deverells, one of the most decorated and respected protector lineages. But every family has its black sheep and Roan didn't follow in his family's footsteps. He was an assassin, the worst that we've ever known, perhaps the worst there ever has been. He murdered at least fifteen people and disappeared before the two of you were born. Jet and Lilly — they're the leaders of the protectors — are still trying to find him but it is doubtful anyone will ever see him again. Your mother had no idea that he was a killer when they met," Jade explained.

"How did she find out? Did he try to kill her?" Isis asked in complete disbelief. Aside from getting on people's bad sides, Isis was convinced that she was flypaper for dysfunction.

"No, she saw him kill a mark," Jade responded, her tone calm and collected. Isis went quiet again, shocked by the answer and the casual manner in which it had been delivered. After a moment, she swallowed and leaned forward.

"If all you're saying is true, why the hell was I never aware of any of this?" she asked after a moment. Jade glanced over at Electra, who was now leaning her elbow against the door and running her long fingers through her hair.

"The guardians are run by a High Council. It is comprised of all the leaders of the major lands: nature, fire, light, day, water, night, and the royal line. Your mother, Passion, broke one of the most important Sacred Laws. It was decided that part of her punishment would be that she would have to give up one of her daughters to be raised as human. Since you were born second, you were the one to be given up."

Isis closed her eyes. "So, who left me at the door of the agency?"

Electra glanced over at Jade, appearing to be curious about the question herself. Jade kept her eyes forward.

"Jet," she answered.

"I assume that's who we're going to see now," Isis said. Jade nodded once in response and Electra turned her gaze back out the window, mesmerized by the night. She rested her forehead against the window and closed her eyes.

"Do shape shifter bodies vanish into thin air often?" Isis asked, noticing Jade stiffened and gripped the steering wheel a little tighter. Electra opened her eyes and turned her head, looking over to Jade.

"Not often," Jade responded. "But it does happen and it has happened for quite some time — throughout history in fact. Jet and Lilly hope the Four can figure out that mystery. Personally, I don't see how it's possible seeing as how it has been happening almost as long as we've existed. Even the guardians have no clue what happens to them."

Jade turned onto the side street that Isis hadn't even seen, steering the car up a winding path. Isis looked out the window but couldn't see anything in the night; no indication of where they were.

"We're currently traveling through the hills," Jade explained when she noticed the questioning look on Isis' face. "There's a road hidden by guardian magic, one only protector eyes can see. The guardians created a special haven for the Monroe family, the protectors most loyal to them. Humans can't find it, neither can most other shape shifters. Only the Monroes can teach shape shifters how to see it and even then, it takes a bit of time. Ah, there's home."

Isis glanced out the window and did a double take, her jaw dropping as she stared at the sight that greeted her. An enormous mansion — more like a castle — could be seen in the distance. The architecture resembled some sort of Renaissance style and it was the biggest structure Isis had ever seen. It was surrounded by trees, bushes, and all sorts of plant life. There was a vast amount of land stretching out as far as the eye could see in every direction. There were more windows than she could count and a couple towers could be seen. Several lights illuminated the exterior of the building.

"You live *here*?" Isis asked, her voice squeaky. She was still marveling at how large and beautiful the enormous home was. It was like something out of a history book or fairy tale. *I don't have my camera either! Shit*, she thought.

"Where did you think we lived? A den?" Jade replied, a hint of teasing in her tone. She pulled up to a pair of elegant black gates, rolled down her window and flipped open the top of a nearby box, revealing a dark blue button and a handprint scanner. Jade pushed the button and pressed her palm against the scanner when it lit up. After a moment, there was a beep and then the gates swung open. Jade pulled the car in, checking the rearview mirror once again. Isis turned around, watching as the gates swung shut. *No turning back now*, she thought.

~~*~*~*

Isis glanced around the room that Electra and Jade had brought her to, which appeared to be a library or study. Bookshelves lined the walls; books with many different colored bindings sat in neat rows on the shelves. Toward the back of the room was a large wooden desk. A globe was to the left of the desk and in the front center of the desk was a bronze carving of a wolf. Behind the desk there was a large ornate red chair and behind the chair was a gigantic window that stretched from the floor almost to the ceiling, through which moonlight spilled. Outside the window was a large oak tree, coated in the night shadows. A few simple lamps sat on the small tables, making the room glow with warm light.

In front of the desk, there were two chairs and a crimson chaise lounge was set behind them. Jade was stretched out on it and Electra stood nearby, examining the rows of books on one of the shelves. Isis decided to remain standing, though she leaned on one of the bookshelves. She figured she had a better chance of escaping if she were on her feet. *Really wish I would have thought to stop at my car so I could have grabbed my other baton,* she thought. Isis didn't care what Steve said; she would have felt better if she'd had a weapon.

Her body went rigid when the door lever was pressed down, but the two other women didn't react. The wooden door swung open and a clean-shaven dark-haired man stepped into the room. He was wearing a dark green shirt and jeans that looked as though they'd been bought that day. Everything about his appearance was neat and orderly and he had a very confident stride. The man smiled at Isis and she couldn't help but stare at his blue-green eyes. She was certain that she knew him from somewhere…

"Isis, it is good to properly meet you," the man greeted warmly as he strode toward her. "My name is Jet and I'm sure Jade or Electra has already told you about me. My wife, Lilly, will join us shortly."

"The morgue," Isis exclaimed, snapping her fingers. Jet frowned as he stared at her, not understanding what she was talking about. Jade and Electra looked over at her, confused by the random statement.

"I bumped into you in the morgue parking lot," Isis clarified.

"Oh, yes. You did," he replied with a quiet laugh. The amusement melted from his face when he noticed her neck. Isis turned her head, trying to hide the thin red marks from where the wire had cut her flesh. Jet glanced over at Jade, who raised an eyebrow.

"It's late," Jet said as he stepped around her and toward the desk. "A room has already been prepared for you—"

"Excuse me?" Isis said, not liking his assumption that she had any intention of staying. Jet looked over at her from where he stood behind the desk.

"I assumed that you already knew you had to stay here," he said, looking toward Jade, who shrugged and spread her hands.

Jet turned his attention back to Isis. "I'm sorry, Isis, but I really must insist that you stay here. At least until you have completed your training."

Isis sighed and shrugged in defeat, already thinking of possible ways to escape. *I should really get a hold of Steve,* she thought, wondering where she could find a phone.

"We shall talk more in the morning. Lilly will show you to your room," Jet finished, gesturing behind her. Isis frowned and turned, nearly jumping a foot in the air when she saw a woman standing a few feet behind her.

"Jesus!" she yelled, putting a hand to her chest. She hadn't heard anyone else enter the room. Lilly smiled pleasantly, unbothered by the outburst, and gestured to the open door. Isis glanced around the study once more.

"Lead the way," Isis said, following the blonde woman out of the room. As they stepped into the large quiet hallway, Isis couldn't help but admire the gorgeous architecture. Visiting old houses and castles was one of her favorite things to do. Unfortunately, she couldn't entirely enjoy the beautiful mansion since she was surrounded by strange people and had no idea whether or not they meant her harm.

Turning her attention to Lilly, Isis studied her for a moment. There was something ethereal about the quiet woman and she seemed more goddess than human. *Or shape shifter, I guess,* Isis thought. Lilly wore a modest dress that was the color of a rainforest. Her hair was the color of the sun. It touched the small of her back in a braid and her kind eyes were the color of sapphires. Her stride was graceful and silent, hinting at some hidden inner power.

"You don't have to worry. You will come to no harm here," Lilly reassured her as they began to climb a twisting staircase.

"Sure," Isis said, glancing around. She had yet to see another individual and it was starting to make her nervous. Lilly glanced back at her with a kind smile before turning her eyes forward again.

"So, are you a shape shifter or a guardian?" Isis asked, wondering if that was an offensive thing to ask. Lilly's faint smile grew a little as she glanced at Isis again.

"I was born a guardian, but gave up the title and position when I married Jet and became leader of the protectors," she answered. Isis noticed a small golden lily at her throat. They reached the second floor and

Lilly led her down another long hallway. It was dimmer than the halls on the first floor and the walls were covered with magnificent portraits and paintings. There was also the occasional sculpture on a pedestal.

"Are these all your ancestors or something?" Isis asked as they passed by a portrait of a stern-faced man. She noticed that the men were mostly clean-shaven. She would have thought it would be the opposite for shape shifters.

"Some are, others are just great figures from our history," Lilly replied. "The animal sculptures and pictures represent all the forms shape shifters are capable of shifting into."

"Who makes them?" Isis toyed with the emerald at her throat as she looked at a sculpture of a fox.

"Some are made by shape shifter artists and others are gifts from the guardians," Lilly explained, glancing over at Isis and pausing for a moment. "Your necklace was made by a gem guardian named Emerald. The chain is pure guardian silver, which is unbreakable. The charm comes from the mineral caves in the Meadows."

Isis stared at the necklace. "Huh. Good thing I never had it appraised."

Lilly laughed, a melodic sound that reminded Isis of small delicate bells. She continued down the hallway and Isis followed.

"There's an animal in almost every picture," Isis mentioned as she continued to look at the paintings they walked by.

"It's the particular shape shifter's favorite form," Lilly responded. "I should warn you that some shape shifters are more comfortable in animal form. It's not uncommon to see a leopard or wolf roaming the hallways. My children are also fond of playing tricks on guests. Don't be frightened if you run into a bear or other large animal in the morning."

"How many people live here?" Isis asked, unable to conceal the shock in her voice. She chose to put the warning in the back of her mind for the moment.

"Right now?" Lilly paused as though tallying up the number of inhabitants. "Twelve, including you. Thirteen by tomorrow, not counting the romantic consorts who frequently stay or the staff, who mostly choose to stay in their own homes on the property."

"Romantic consorts?"

Lilly smiled and nodded. "Shape shifters are very open and many desire companionship, whether romantic or platonic. Many choose to live with multiple lovers."

"Jade mentioned something about libidos," Isis muttered.

"We are similar to humans in some ways and very different in others," Lilly replied.

"Makes sense," Isis said. Lilly stopped in front of a large arched door. She opened it, stepped inside, and switched on the light.

"Whoa," Isis breathed as she stepped into the huge room. She could feel her jaw drop again as she took in her new decadent surroundings. The large ornate bed looked extremely expensive, possibly an antique. Orchid-colored nightclothes were neatly folded on the bed. There was a short hallway leading to a back section of the room.

"I think this might be bigger than my apartment," Isis said as she looked over to the wooden dresser against the wall. There was a large, elaborate wardrobe across the room.

"The bathroom is in the back. If you need anything at all, the intercom is here next to the light switch," Lilly said as she gestured toward a metal plate with a couple buttons on the wall next to the light switches. "Just press the tan button and someone will answer. Breakfast is usually around eight or nine, but there's always someone in the kitchen. Electra is in the room across from yours and I'm sure Jade will take you to your apartment tomorrow to pick up some things. Have a good night, Isis."

Isis mustered a polite smile and Lilly left the room, closing the door behind her. Isis waited for a few minutes before approaching the door again. She opened it, looking up and down the hall. When she saw it was empty, Isis closed and locked the door. Striding across the room, she opened the doors that led out to the balcony and crossed the small space to the large stone balustrade, resting her hands on the rough stone as she leaned over and looked down. A cool breeze blew through her short hair. She clenched her teeth when she saw the distance to the ground, realizing there was no way she could walk away from the drop unscathed.

Isis turned to face the room again, drumming her fingers on the stone. Her eyes drifted over to the bed and she pursed her lips as an idea began to form in her mind. Crossing the balcony again and closing the doors, Isis turned her attention to the bed. She stripped the sheets off the mattress and set about separating them. No one was going to hold her prisoner.

CHAPTER SIX

Moonlight illuminated the three who remained in the study. The beams of light bounced off the gold writing and designs on the bindings of the books that lined the east and west walls from floor to ceiling.

After Lilly and Isis left, Electra turned around and leaned her weight against the bookcase that she had been studying since they arrived. Jade remained stretched out on the lounge, waiting for Jet to talk. Jet was playing with an ornate blue fountain pen, spinning it between his fingers. Electra watched him, enthralled by the motion of the pen. She shifted her weight, crossing her left leg over her right.

"What happened?" Jet finally asked, looking to Jade. She sat up and scratched the back of her head, squinting as she thought for a moment.

"I have no idea," Jade replied with a shake of her head. "Best I can tell, someone was strangling her when we arrived. There have been a couple of robberies in the area, but to me, this looked like the work of a professional. There was no sign of forced entry and I'm sure they didn't leave any kind of evidence behind. They used a garrote, which indicates an experienced assassin, meaning it could have been another attempt to show strength by Adara. If that's what it was, she came uncomfortably close. Had we been a moment later, Isis would've been dead."

Jade sighed and leaned forward, dropping her wrists to her knees. "That place, her apartment — there was a heaviness to the air. It was the same thing I felt when we entered the old factory."

"It just doesn't make sense. The guardians should have been alerted the second someone dangerous entered that apartment. They've had a protection spell on it since Isis moved in," Jet thought aloud, frowning when he noticed that Jade wasn't looking directly at him. "What are you leaving out?"

Jade looked a little uncomfortable as she began to rub her palms together, glancing over at Electra. "I have reason to believe that whoever was in that apartment had telekinetic ability."

Electra twisted around, looking toward Jade. "That's impossible. Telekinesis is a guardian ability and one that's forbidden to be used on Earth."

"Whoever it was threw me across the room with barely any physical contact and from what I could tell, they were shorter than me," Jade explained. Jet rubbed his eyes with his free hand.

"What kind of trouble has she attracted?" he muttered to himself.

"We should've approached her the moment she came into contact with Bryn's body," Jade mentioned as she leaned back against the smooth fabric of the lounge, stretching her arms across the back.

"Perhaps, but we cannot change the past," Jet

responded as he watched Electra approach the old globe. He could tell that she was still angry with him, maybe not as much as she was with her mother, but he had picked up on the iciness in her voice. Electra spun the old tan sphere, her fingers trailing across the continents, the bumpy mountains causing them to rise every now and again.

"We have to focus on the present and whatever threat we're facing," Jet continued as he leaned back in his chair. He steepled his fingers and rested them against his upper lip. His blue-green eyes were dark as he thought about what Jade had told him. The wooden clock that rested on one of the bookshelves chimed, drawing Electra's attention away from the globe.

"Why do you insist on keeping clocks? Is time really so important?" Electra asked Jet, her tone amused. She made her way over to the clock, studying the thin black minute and hour hands. There were almost no clocks in the Meadows. Most guardians had no need for them and only the guardians of time kept clocks.

Jet looked over to her and shrugged. "I like them. There is something soothing about a well-made clock."

"You can be such a sentimental fool sometimes," Electra chuckled as she ran her fingers over the smooth cherry wood of the clock.

"To each his own," Jet replied with a smile, before sobering. "Electra, you know you're always welcome here, but how long do you plan on staying? Your mother is going to be worried sick—"

"My mother worries about no one but herself," Electra growled, her gaze drifting to the books on the shelves. Jade exchanged a look with Jet, her eyes holding a clear warning to stop talking. He was treading on dangerous ground at the moment.

"You've had a long day. We can talk more in the morning," Jet said, not having the energy for an argument. Electra shook her head and stormed across the room, exiting the study and slamming the door behind her. Jade winced at the loud bang that echoed in the room.

"I think she may be a little miffed at me," Jet mentioned, thanking his lucky stars that Sly wasn't there. She delighted in pointing out his every misstep.

"Electra has a lot to deal with right now," Jade responded. "Give her some time before you sink into a woe-is-me routine."

Jet made a noncommittal sound as he looked back to the surface of the desk, studying his reflection. He was worried about being in the center of a three-way fight. Passion was undoubtedly furious at him and apparently so was Electra.

"When do you plan on speaking with Passion?" Jade asked. Jet gave her a wry look in response, to which she just shrugged. He glanced up when he heard a soft knocking on the door, which opened to reveal Lilly.

"I think she's settled in," Lilly reported as she crossed her hands in front of her. Jet smiled at her, nodding gratefully. He was about to suggest calling it a night when a bright gold light started to form next to him. Jet swallowed and turned his chair toward the glow as Passion materialized next to him. Her eyes were red-rimmed, most likely from crying, and she glared at Jet with a fury that had never been directed at him before. She was wearing a fiery red dress with a plunging neckline that seemed to enhance the rage in her eyes. Passion stood stiffly, as if she was made of granite, and her fists were clenched so tightly her knuckles were white.

"Can I talk to you?" she asked with a chilling calm. Jet glanced at the lamps as they suddenly became brighter and began to buzz, threatening to burst. The irate guardian's fury was charging all forms of energy around them. The study became bathed in a harsh bone white glow, making it appear as though it was daytime in the single room. Jade was staring at him; so was Lilly. He gestured for them to leave. Jade got up and walked out, glancing back at Jet once before disappearing in the hall.

"Lilly, would you mind closing the door behind you?" Jet requested. Lilly smiled at him and made her way out of the room, closing the door behind her. Jet hesitated for a moment and then turned to face his friend, who was still glaring at him.

"Passion, I didn't have a—"

He was cut off when Passion slapped him, which took him by surprise. She had never struck him before. Yelled at him plenty of times, but never physically hit him. He swallowed and gently touched his stinging lip, unsurprised when the tips of his fingers came back bloody.

"Don't you dare try to use that excuse with me, Jet. There is always a choice," she said, her voice soft and restrained. Jet looked back to her, not sure how to respond. Passion turned away from him and looked out the large window.

"Electra's here," Jet offered after a moment. "In case you didn't know."

Passion didn't respond, but gripped her upper

arms tighter. Jet gingerly probed his bloody lip, contemplating his next words.

"I won't apologize for what I did," Jet began as he looked down to his bloody fingertips again. She twisted her body toward him, surprise replacing fury in her eyes. The lights dimmed ever so slightly.

"I made you a promise when your daughters were born. Do you remember?" Jet explained. "I told you that I would protect them until my dying breath. Isis was in danger and I protected her the only way I could. I am sorry that it involved going behind your back, but if I had to do it again, I would. I made the right decision, Passion."

"She had a life, Jet. One that you destroyed," she stated as she turned back to the window. "Was some damn vague prophecy really worth ruining her life?"

Jet looked down, wringing his hands. If he was being completely honest, he still questioned whether he had gone about the situation in the right way. His friend needed to burn off steam, understandably, and Jet was more than willing to let her. He glanced up again when she let out a bark of laughter that sounded more like a sob. His heart nearly broke when he saw tears welling up in her eyes.

"You know what the really pathetic thing is?" Passion asked, her voice trembling with tears that were threatening to fall. "I was stupid enough to trust you. Did I know you could go behind my back to my daughter? Of course I did, but I never thought you actually would."

She turned away from the window, facing him again. "I never want to see you again, Jet. As far as I'm concerned, from this moment on, we're strangers."

"Before you leave," Jet said, drawing her attention back to him. "Will you do me one last favor? There was an attempt on Isis' life tonight, which thankfully Jade managed to stop. Would you ask your mother or grandmother how that was able to happen when there was supposed to be a protection spell on whatever living space Isis inhabited?"

He could see the hesitance in the guardian's expression, as though she didn't know whether or not to believe him. Jet ran his hands over the armrests, feeling his heart twist painfully in his chest. It was possible this was the last time he would see her. Passion was one of his best friends. She had always been an important part of his and Lilly's lives and the thought of losing that bond was physically painful.

"I don't care whether or not you give me the answer," he continued. "Send a messenger if you must. I just...I really want to know what happened tonight and you deserve to know as well. I want to make sure Isis is as safe as she can be."

Passion didn't say another word as she dematerialized in a brilliant flash of golden light, disappearing back to the Meadows. The second she was gone, the lamps dimmed again and Jet was left alone in a dark room. He rested his elbows on his knees and dragged his hands down his face, hoping he had made the right choice. The sound of the study door opening again made Jet straighten up.

"What happened to you?" a young feminine voice asked. Jet looked at his youngest daughter, who was leaning against the open door. Hunter smiled at him, taking in her father's appearance. While most of Jet and Lilly's daughters took after their mother in appearance, Hunter looked more like her father. She had the same dark hair, which she kept very short, barely long enough to touch the nape of her neck, and his caring blue-green eyes. Unlike him, she was a rebel. Ever since she was a child, Hunter questioned authority and tested boundaries.

Jet took in her attire as she walked toward the desk, wondering if she would ever grow out of her punk phase. She towered over him with her favorite knee-high black boots, which were splattered with some kind of florescent paint. He often wondered how she walked in those things; they had what looked to be a ten-inch heel. Smiling at his daughter, Jet realized he hadn't seen much of his family the past couple weeks and he'd missed them.

"Is that the current fashion trend or were you in another brawl?" he asked, gesturing to her ripped jeans and clothing.

"Fashion," she answered with a devil-may-care smile as she hopped up on the desk. "If I had been in a brawl, I'm fairly certain I'd have some blood on me. And then I'd be in a mood because blood is a pain in the ass to get out of clothing."

"I'm certain you'd manage," Jet replied. "I take it you disregarded my request that you not go out late night clubbing for a while, at least until your mother and I find the cause of all this chaos and the strife among assassins settles or resolves itself."

"I took it under consideration. But I figured carrying a Taser and mace was enough of a deterrent for any seedy types," Hunter said with a dismissive shrug. Jet sat back and twisted his chair a little so that he could look out the window.

"Who split your lip?" Hunter asked, as she leaned back on the desk.

"Passion," Jet answered, looking back to his daughter. Hunter scrunched up her face a little, obviously confused.

"You two never fight," she said. "What happened?"

"I had to tell Electra who her father was and I went behind Passion's back in order to do so," Jet explained, rubbing the bridge of his nose. Hunter stared at him, her mouth dropping open in shock.

"Dad, how could you do that to her?"

Jet shrugged. "I didn't have a choice, Hunter. Her other daughter was in danger and Passion wanted to keep Isis in the dark in the hopes that she could have a normal life."

"Why couldn't you just put her under protection?" Hunter asked as she picked up a pen and began spinning it around in her fingers. "Or get her more or something?"

Jet was quiet for a moment, watching the shadow of the pen as it twirled about his daughter's fingers. "Because I have reason to believe she's part of the Four."

Hunter dropped the pen and stared at him. "Part of the what now?"

Jet shook his head. "I just hope I'm right this time."

Hunter was quiet for a long time. "Me too."

~~*~*~*

The sun rose, casting Isis' room in warm light. She was testing the sturdiness of the furniture in the room. Climbing up on the mattress, she examined the large post at the end of the bed, which was made of thick and heavy wood. *That'll do,* she thought as she grabbed one end of the sheets she had been working on all night. Isis had spent hours tying knots in the fabric. Her dexterous fingers worked swiftly as she tied her makeshift rope to the heavy post, double-checking to make sure it was secure. She gathered up the coiled sheets and made her way over to the balcony doors, opening one and tossing the rope out onto the balcony. *Never thought all those rock-climbing classes with Steve would come in handy one day,* Isis thought as she walked across the balcony and checked to make sure she didn't have any unwanted company lurking about.

When she was satisfied there were no witnesses around, Isis picked up the rope again and threw it over the balustrade. The rope was longer than she had expected, reaching all the way to the ground. Isis swallowed, feeling mild vertigo as she looked down to the stone walkway below. The ground seemed to plummet even further down and she got a little lightheaded. Isis looked up and across the lands, her resolve returning. *I've done worse. This is just a little climb down a rope. The worst that could happen is a broken bone and that Jet guy undoubtedly has good insurance,* she reassured herself. Isis carefully took a hold of the smooth sheet with one hand, placing her other on the rough stone as she swung her long slender legs over the balustrade. She placed her feet between the balusters and took a hold of the knotted sheet in her hands.

"Okay, don't look down," she whispered to herself. Somewhere nearby, a robin chirped and a gentle wind brushed against her back, causing her to grit her teeth. Isis began to carefully descend, going as fast as she dared. The rope swayed a little in the occasional breeze, but her grip never loosened. Her arms shook with the weight of her body and the muscles twitched. It had been a long time since she had been climbing, mainly because Steve's schedule no longer allowed for the random adventure trip. Neither did hers, but Isis had never been one to let her job get in the way of something she wanted to do.

After what seemed like years, Isis' feet finally touched solid ground. She smiled in victory as she turned around to make her way to the gates, her smile falling when she saw Jade sitting on a stone bench nearby. The woman held a knife in one hand and a partially eaten peach in the other. She smiled and placed another peach slice in her mouth, waving with the hand that held the round fruit. Isis felt her shoulders drop as she stared at Jade, shocked that she hadn't noticed her earlier. Jade was the picture of relaxation with one of her long legs folded under her while the other swung back and forth. Her dark hair was loosely held back from her face with a butterfly-shaped hair slide.

"How?" Isis asked when she found her voice again. Jade chuckled, looking down to her peach.

"When you've lived as long as I have, you tend to notice certain…tells," she replied as she sliced into the juicy peach again. "For example, when a grown woman who has been raised by humans just accepts a story as fantastic as the one you were told last night, chances are she's planning something."

Jade paused as she slid another slice of peach in her mouth, gesturing with her knife at the makeshift rope as she chewed. "Nice try though. My compliments on your climbing ability."

Isis frowned as she cautiously approached the bench, studying the other woman. Jade smiled at her, unbothered by the scrutinizing look, and she cut another slice from the peach. The juice spilled over her hand, but she didn't pay it any heed.

"You don't look that much older than me," Isis commented, unable to hide her confusion. Jade raised the slice to her mouth, pausing for a moment and then laughing. She shook her head, closing her eyes and lifting her face toward the sun.

"I guess we forgot to mention that shape shifters and guardians are immortal," Jade said as she opened her eyes again and focused on the ripe fruit in her hand, slipping the peach slice in her mouth and chewing. She swallowed and licked the excess juice off her fingertips, her brown eyes traveling to Isis' face.

"Yeah, shape shifters and guardians don't die of 'natural causes' and we aren't affected by human ailments and maladies," she explained as she began to cut another slice from the peach. "The only way we die is if we're murdered or die in an accident or something like that."

"I have to sit down," Isis said after a moment, suddenly feeling dizzy. Jade scooted over and gestured to the stone bench. She offered the slice that she cut from the peach and Isis was barely able to shake her head. Jade shrugged and slipped it into her mouth. Isis swallowed and looked over at Jade, studying her features. As best she could tell, Jade was Latina, or perhaps Native American. She looked to be Isis' age, but if she were immortal...

"How old are you?" she asked, curiosity getting the better of her. Jade shrugged and looked off across the lands of the mansion.

"We generally don't keep track of our ages," she answered, her face scrunching a little as though she were thinking. "I was born in 1622, deep in the rainforests of Brazil."

"You're over three-hundred years old!?" Isis exclaimed in shock. Jade frowned and thoughtfully chewed on another peach slice. She swallowed and smiled in amusement.

"I suppose I am," she chuckled. "And here I thought I was a younger protector."

Isis felt almost panicked as she looked back to the ground. "I'm not years older than I think I am, am I?"

Jade shook her head as she licked her pinky finger. "Nope. You're twenty-eight. The guardians are capable of many things, but altering time isn't one of them. To interfere with free will and perception is a violation of their sacred laws."

Isis couldn't think of anything to say so she looked at the bright green grass in front of the stone pathway that wound around the enormous mansion. There were so many thoughts racing through her mind, warring for control. She wanted more answers, but there were just too many questions.

"Are you always up this early?" she asked the first question that popped into her head. Jade finished the last slice of her peach and placed the pit and knife aside, rubbing her mildly sticky hands together.

"Not always, but often enough. I enjoy sleeping in whenever I have a chance, usually when I have a lover or two keeping me warm," she said with a smile that was both suggestive and kind. Isis found it odd that she had known the woman less than twenty-four hours and already Jade was treating her like they had known each other a lifetime.

"You're very honest," Isis remarked. Jade laughed as she stood up and stretched her lean body.

"Shape shifters are very open," she said. "I mentioned the libido thing before, but you should know that our views of pretty much everything, including sexuality, is probably very different from what you are used to."

Isis snorted. "Except for the whole asexuality thing, right?"

Jade gave a half-smile. "Admittedly, we're not perfect. Unfortunately, we also have various prejudices. While they may be somewhat different from humans', they are prejudices nonetheless."

Isis leaned back a little. "So, what about you, Jade? What do you think of me?"

Jade was quiet for a moment, studying Isis. "If you're wondering whether or not I'm bothered by your being Gray-A, the answer is no. I will be proud to fight alongside you, as I am with any other protector. You're my teammate, that's what's important to me. If you're asking in a more general sense, I think you're unique."

Jade got up and stretched her arms over her head. "That's not to say other protectors will share my sentiments, frankly I doubt they will. But I get the distinct impression you're not overly concerned with what others think."

Isis stared at the older woman, suspicious. She was very leery when people offered unconditional acceptance so easily and without strings attached. Jade's words sounded genuine and sincere, but Isis didn't know her and therefore didn't trust her completely.

"So, the guardians, do they share your philosophy of acceptance?" Isis asked. Jade shrugged.

"Not entirely, many of them can be rather strict and reserved — one might even say repressed — though I don't believe that term is an accurate description," Jade answered. "Passion is an exception. She believes everyone should be allowed to pursue what makes them happiest in life and unfortunately, that makes her a favorite target of the more traditionalist guardians. Most of the High Council is very austere and more concerned with following and enforcing the Sacred Laws."

"Like the whole no sex with shape shifters?" Isis asked, leaning forward so that her arms were resting on her legs. She pressed her palms together, feeling curiosity ignite within her. Jade glanced back at her, nodding.

"They don't allow sex before courtship," she explained. "They also arrange courtship and they all wear proper dress. Though admittedly, those rules aren't exactly strictly enforced. There are always loopholes."

"Proper dress?"

Jade's attention was drawn over to a bee buzzing nearby, watching as it landed on the petals of a yellow tulip nearby. "The women wear dresses and the men wear something similar to a tunic. It will likely appear very dated to you."

"Ah," Isis said, smirking a little despite herself.

"However, the guardians don't force their ways on us for the most part," Jade said reassuringly, sitting on the bench again. "They merely ask for respect from protectors, which we give them. You should keep in mind that their safety always comes first. Our priority is protecting the guardians. It is our duty and we take that duty very seriously.

"The thing you have to remember, Isis, is that despite how we look, we are not human. We may share some similarities with them, but the guardians and the shape shifters are different species. The guardians have a different culture than us. And that is in no way meant to be a judgmental statement. We are no better or worse than any other culture, just different."

"Jade!" Electra's panicked voice interrupted their conversation. Both women looked to the side where the door was. A moment later Electra came into view, looking nothing short of flustered. She spotted Isis and let out a breath of relief, stepping out onto the walkway. As Electra approached them, she noticed the sheets hanging down from the balcony. She looked to the two of them, confused.

"She's inherited the family ingenuity," Jade answered the young guardian's unasked question, gesturing at the rope. "And the tendency toward flight too, apparently."

Electra frowned at Jade and placed her hands on her hips. She was wearing a blue shirt with a white shirt under it and a pair of stonewash jeans. To Isis, she looked just like an average ordinary human, certainly not a deity or deity-like being.

"Well it's a good thing she didn't get to the gate," Electra mentioned, turning her eyes to Isis. "You should know that as long as you're on this property, you're under the protection of the guardians. But once you step out there, past that gate we came through, that protection starts to gradually dissipate the closer you get to the street."

Isis stared at her for a moment, feeling a little uneasy. "Um, okay."

Jade snapped her fingers as though something had just dawned on her and Isis looked over at her, happy for the distraction.

"By the way, Isis, the first time you Appear, you'll notice afterwards that your skin will glisten a little in moonlight. Don't worry about it, it's due to your being half guardian," Jade explained, looking back to Electra. "I think I've covered just about everything she needs to know. Now you get to help me train her."

Electra stared at her, dropping her hands from her hips. "I'm not a teacher. I don't even know where I'd begin."

Jade smiled as she approached the young guardian, wrapping an arm around her shoulders. "That's why you have me and Remington to help you."

Electra gave her a very dry, mildly irritated look, before turning her attention to Isis. "Have you had breakfast?"

Isis shook her head. "Not really hungry."

It was a small lie. She could have eaten, but she really didn't trust these people to feed her. She still felt apprehensive of them and their motives. Electra maneuvered out from under Jade's arm in one smooth movement.

"Fine," Electra sighed, turning to Jade. "Lilly said we should take her back to her apartment so that she can pick up some things."

"All right, you both head over to the garage. I'll meet you there after I grab a bite to eat," Jade replied, smiling and winking at Isis. She turned on her heel and headed in the direction Electra had come from.

Electra turned to Isis and nodded over her shoulder, gesturing for her to follow. Isis got up and followed her twin, a new idea already starting to form in her mind.

~~*~*~*

Isis was quiet as she stood behind Jade and Electra in the elevator. She stared straight ahead at the dirty gold doors, not willing to break the tense quiet. Electra was looking up at the numbers while Jade leaned against one of the walls. The ride over had been completely silent except for the throaty voice of Shirley Manson and the throbbing beats of the Garbage playlist that Jade had blasted through the speakers.

"So, if this prophecy hadn't appeared, how much longer would it have been before someone told me about my heritage?" Electra suddenly asked, drawing both Isis and Jade's attention. Isis had sensed a palpable tension between Electra and Jet and that anger seemed to be directed at Jade to a certain extent. Electra looked over at Jade, who merely shrugged in response, her relaxed posture not changing.

"I really don't know, Electra," she answered. "Jet or Lilly would be better to ask."

Electra scowled and turned her attention back to the numbers until the door shuddered open. She all but stormed out, followed by Jade and then Isis. Isis' attention was drawn to the corner where a small decorative tree sat. The landlord had an affinity for plants, trees in particular. He cared for them like they were children and as much as Isis hated to admit it they did provide an almost warm feeling from an aesthetic point of view. There were a few on each floor, usually near the elevators. She frowned when she saw the plant was wilting and almost dead. *He's not going to be happy when he comes back from vacation,* she thought as she turned her attention down the hall.

It was ten o'clock in the morning, so the wall sconces were off and the light came from the brilliant summer sun. They had chosen to come when most of the tenants would be at work, much to Isis' chagrin. She had been hoping to catch Steve on his way out. While she absolutely abhorred asking for help, Isis was smart enough to recognize when she could use it. Had she bumped into Steve, she would have been able to let him know that she was in a bad situation without alerting the two strange women. They had known each other long enough to be able to read between the lines and he had always been good when it came to reading people. *Oh well, I'll just have to go to plan B,* she thought as they stopped in front of her apartment.

Isis stared at the door, amazed that it seemed to have already been repaired. She looked over to Jade, who was wearing a regular green camouflage top and ragged jean shorts. Small circular green sunglasses shielded her eyes and she was wearing a tan baseball cap. Noticing Isis staring at her, puzzled, Jade offered the younger woman a small smile.

"We've got many resourceful allies," she said cryptically. Isis couldn't help but roll her eyes at that.

"Really could have used you in the winter when the heating was on the fritz and it took several calls to even get the landlord up here," she grumbled, hesitating. "Should we be here? What if whoever it

141

was last night is back?"

"I asked Jet and Lilly the same thing, but they assured me the danger is likely to be minimal. According to them, your assailant won't be back, not in the daytime anyway," Electra responded, leaning back against the wall behind her. "I wouldn't eat or drink anything, just to be on the safe side."

"No. Poison is much too impersonal for whomever was here. I wouldn't be surprised if they didn't even own a gun," Jade observed.

"That's comforting," Isis muttered, unable to hide her sarcasm, as she reached for the knob. She turned it, unsurprised to find it open. Jade had done a number on the door last night. She was about to step in when Jade put a hand on her arm.

"Better safe than sorry," Jade explained as she stepped into the apartment. "You and Electra stay out here for a minute. I'm going to do a quick sweep."

Isis moved back and leaned against the wall across from the door. She glanced over at Electra, who stood with her arms crossed over her chest. Electra's outfit today was dark denim jeans with just a hint of a sparkle and a burgundy tank top, which made her emerald necklace stand out. She glanced over at Isis when she felt her gaze, her olive green eyes expectant. For one of the first times in her life, Isis wished she was better at connecting with people. If Electra were her sister, and based on appearance that seemed very likely, Isis felt she should at least try to have a conversation with the woman.

"Jade told me guardians had to wear dresses," Isis mentioned, deciding that was probably the safest topic at the moment.

Electra scoffed and ran her fingers through her

ponytail. "If we're being observed, yes. I don't really care for dresses and neither does my...*our* mother. Well, she does, but not the kind that meets the guidelines."

"Oh," Isis said, turning her eyes back to the open door and suppressing her anxiety. After a moment, she turned back to Electra, who had fixed her eyes on the open door again.

"My eyes," Isis said, drawing the woman's attention back to her. "They change color sometimes. I've got pictures where they look blue and others where they look green. At first, I chalked that up to them being hazel, but they don't just absorb color. They actually change color."

Electra nodded. "You get that from Mother. It's an extremely rare guardian trait. As far as Adonia knows, Mom and I are the only current guardians who have it. I guess you're the third."

"Adonia?" Isis asked.

"She's our great grandmother and queen of the guardian women," Electra said. It was obvious she was still getting used to Isis. She said "our" as if the word felt strange in her mouth. They were spared any further awkward small talk when Jade appeared back in the doorway.

"All clear," she reported. Electra gestured for Isis to go in, which she swiftly did. She moved right for the bedroom, listening for whether Electra or Jade was following her. When she was satisfied that they weren't, she went to the closet and grabbed a duffle bag. She swiftly threw some clothes inside, along with a couple of her expandable batons. Her eyes fell on her dresser, where her cell phone was. Looking toward the hallway, Isis could hear someone flipping through a book and muted conversation. She reached forward and snatched the phone off the dresser, slipping it into her pocket. Moving back to the bed and zipping the duffle bag shut, Isis grabbed the tough woven handles and made her way back to the main part of the room.

Electra was standing at the bookcase, thumbing through one of her books on mythology. Jade was on the couch, her arms stretched out across the back and her fingers drumming on the fabric. She glanced over at Isis.

"Ready to go?" she asked.

"I'm going to use the bathroom first," Isis replied. Jade shrugged and Isis made her way to the bathroom, moving casually. She entered the bathroom and locked the door behind her. Pulling out her cell phone and turning it on, Isis felt her shoulders slump when the low battery warning flashed across the screen.

You need to charge this thing once in a while, Isis, Steve's words echoed in her mind. She always forgot to charge the damn thing, which was part of the reason she lost her first job come to think of it. Isis tried to dial Steve's number, almost flinging the phone across the bathroom when the screen blinked and went dead.

"Fuck," she hissed in frustration, dragging her fingers through her short hair. She put her hands on the sink and leaned forward, her mind racing. Isis thought of a number of plans, each more ludicrous than the one before. Looking at the mirror, Isis considered breaking it and using the glass to draw some blood. But she wasn't sure whether or not Steve would find it before these crazy people dismembered her and buried her who knew where.

Biting her lip, Isis reached up to the cabinet above the sink and pulled it open. Moving some items around on the narrow shelves, Isis' fingers brushed over something smooth. She grabbed a hold of it and found it was a Sharpie. Isis stared at it, wondering why the hell it was there in the first place. She did have a strange habit of leaving pens in weird places.

Isis felt her eyes widen as a thought came to her and she quickly looked around the bathroom, searching for something to write on. She had to find somewhere that Steve would see it, but that involved a certain amount of risk. Thinking quickly, Isis flushed the toilet and turned on the cold water tap. She uncapped the pen with her teeth and began to scribble words on the mirror: *HELP! SOS, I got in over my head! Massive castle at the edge of the road, hidden somewhere in the hills, easy to miss. Track my phone or something.*

Isis put the cap back on the Sharpie and placed it in the toothbrush holder. Now all she could do was hope that her friend noticed her absence and investigated. *He's a detective. It's his goddamn job,* she thought as she grabbed a few assorted toiletries and moved back out into the main area of the apartment, where the two women were waiting for her.

"All right, let's go," she said as she opened the duffle bag and tossed the toiletries inside, moving toward the front door. Isis suppressed a breath of relief when neither Jade nor Electra asked to use the bathroom. It was a small bit of luck, but she would take whatever she could get.

~~*~*~*

Isis was in a somewhat better mood when they returned to the mansion. She even looked out the window to enjoy the scenery. It was a lovely summer day. The air was sweet and the sun was shining. It was a little easier to see the road that went through the hills, though Isis only noticed it once they were on it. As Jade drove up the long driveway, Isis looked at all the different trees that were scattered throughout the land.

Jade pulled up in front of the mansion and shifted into park. "I'm going to let the two of you off here and pull into the garage. I'll meet you inside."

Electra got out of the car and Isis followed close behind. She listened to the crunch of their footsteps on the fine mineral underfoot. Isis considered attempting to have a conversation again, but decided against it. Electra didn't seem to be much of a conversationalist, at least not presently.

They walked down the long path across the reddish gravel toward the towering wooden front doors. Electra reached up to the lion's head, grasping the bronze ring it held in its mouth, and knocked it against the door twice. Then she stepped back and put her hands in her pockets, looking off toward the trees. Isis twisted her body to look behind her, wondering just how much land these people owned. The enormous mansion was impressive, but the vastness of their land was what really took Isis' breath away.

She heard the door being pulled open and turned back, letting out a shout of surprise at the familiar face that greeted her.

CHAPTER SEVEN

"Shae!?" Isis yelled. Her shout echoed off the surrounding trees and walls, causing Electra to jolt and stare at the two women, both of whom were almost too shocked to speak. The guardian looked between the two of them, waiting for one of them to fill her in.

"Isis!?" her cousin exclaimed, stunned. Shae had obviously been working out. Her auburn hair was slick with sweat and she wore a dark blue athletic top with tight black pants. A strong wind brushed against Isis' back as she continued to stare at her cousin, not believing her eyes. Electra cleared her throat and they both looked over at her, almost forgetting they weren't alone.

"You two know each other?" she asked. Shae looked at her before turning her gaze back to Isis, a small smile dancing across her lips. Isis finally spoke first.

"Are you...do you know these people?" she demanded, feeling anger flare within her. If Shae was behind this lunacy, Isis resolved to never to speak to her again. And she was definitely moving, preferably out of the country, and changing her identity.

"*You're* Passion's daughter? Oh my fucking god, that is brilliant. Oh, oh, I love my life *so* much right now. Thank you, world!" Shae shouted up to the sky before dissolving into giggles. Electra stared at her as though the woman had lost her mind, glancing over at Isis again.

"You're part of this? And why are you laughing?" Isis hissed, stress creeping into her voice. Shae snickered and shook her head, holding up a hand to prevent her cousin from having a conniption fit. She turned her sparkling green eyes to Electra.

"We grew up together, as cousins," Shae explained, studying Electra. "Wow, Jet mentioned you were identical, but this is just freaky. Hopefully you're better with people than Isis is. At least one of you should have some diplomatic skills."

"Isis, you're here," a tall man came up the hallway behind Shae. He had sky-blue eyes and thick black hair. His voice was smooth with a hint of an Irish brogue and held the subtle intelligence that academics often spoke with. His eyes turned to Electra and he bowed respectfully.

"Electra," he stated by way of welcoming.

She rolled her eyes. "You really don't need to bow. It's not like I'm full guardian."

"Excuse me, who the hell are you?" Isis demanded, looking the new stranger up and down as he straightened to his full height again. His bright blue eyes held a wisdom that contradicted how old he looked.

"Oh, I do beg your pardon. My name is

Remington and I'll be your trainer," Remington replied with a warm smile as he turned his gaze back to her and offered his hand, which she hesitantly took. She managed a polite smile as they shook hands, but inside she was screaming. *Ow, ow, ow, ow! How the fuck did he get a grip like that?* Isis thought, barely able to repress a sigh of relief when Remington released her hand from the almost bone-crushing grip he had held it in. Electra stepped past the three shape shifters and into the mansion without another word. Remington stepped forward and shut the door, his eyes turning to the two women still standing nearby.

"We call him Remy," Shae told Isis with a mischievous wink. Remington glared at Shae, his expression reflecting obvious annoyance. She just smiled and shoulder checked him playfully. Isis stared at her cousin, wondering if there was anyone Shae didn't like.

"You know you love me, Remy," Shae teased, beaming up at the trainer.

"Yes, Shae," he humored her before whapping the back of her head and smiling at the look of irritation she shot him. "My daughter, Alex, is already downstairs. Shae will take you and I'm sure Jade will join you soon. I need to have a quick word with Jet and Lilly."

Remington turned and walked in the direction of the study, down the long main hallway. When he was out of sight, Isis grabbed Shae's arm.

"Ow, hey!" Shae protested against the rough treatment. "Jesus Isis, you need to trim your damn nails or get a manicure or something, ow! You don't need to grip me that hard. You're worse than Remington."

149

"Shae, I swear to god, if this is one of your stupid pranks, I won't speak to you again! If it's true, why the hell was I never informed that our family could shape shift?" Isis growled, tightening her grip despite the yelp of pain from her cousin. "Is this another one of their let's-fuck-with-Isis'-head-for-sport games?"

"Honestly, you are *such* a drama queen at times. You were never told because they don't even know. The last shape shifter in our family died centuries ago. The bloodline was dormant until I was born," Shae answered, yanking her arm out of Isis' grip and glaring at her. "Both my parents have a dormant shape shifting gene. And I assure you, this is very real. Even I'm not this creative."

Isis wasn't sure whether she should be angry, happy, or both. She shook her head as the two traveled partway down the elegant hall until they reached a wooden door with a golden plaque that read *Training Room* in engraved letters. Shae opened the door and motioned for Isis to travel down the grayish blue stairs, which Isis promptly did. The staircase curved around a bend, various old weapons lining the brick walls — the railings keeping travelers a safe distance away from the gleaming blades.

Isis and Shae reached the bottom of the staircase almost at the same time. Isis looked around the large room, once again finding herself awestruck at the sheer size of the mansion. Each room seemed to be twice the size of any place she had ever lived or visited. And yet, despite its massive size, it still had a very home-like feel to it.

Different weapons and equipment lined the walls of the training room. The ceilings were high. There was a wooden door in the back marked with a black sign that said "opponent course" in raised letters. There was a boxing ring in the middle of the room. Punching bags and gymnastics equipment were in various places. The room was painted gray and blue mats covered most of the floor. The lights were located up in the ceiling and beamed down, illuminating every square inch of the room with a bright light.

A woman Isis had never seen before was kicking a punching bag. The whack of flesh against the rough red vinyl was the only sound in the basement. The woman was slender yet fit, with long black hair that was held back from her face. She wore red and black workout clothes that were similar to Shae's. Her hands were wrapped tightly in white tape and she held them in tight fists in front of her, protectively. She was sweating, but not as much as Shae. The cylindrical bag rattled violently on its chain every time the woman's powerful leg made contact with it.

"So, what about Remington?" Isis asked. Though they had just been fighting, it was quickly forgotten. She had never been able to stay mad at her cousin for very long.

"Old Remy? He's okay. He can be tough but it's all an act. He's a big softy," Shae replied, glancing over at Isis. "Although, you have always had a downright *impressive* ability to get on even the most patient peoples' bad sides."

Isis rolled her eyes over to Shae, not appreciating the jab. The lights above them buzzed, unnoticed by the women in the training room.

"Remington actually reminds me of James Bond weirdly enough," Isis mentioned, as she studied the large training room. She moved over to the nearest wall, examining the different blades.

Shae snickered as she followed her cousin to the weapons wall. "I know. He really looks like him and he's got the accent and everything."

"Bond was written to be British, Remington's accent is Irish," Isis pointed out, touching the hilt of a dagger. "Are we actually going to *use* these?"

"Yeah, probably," Shae responded as she looked over her shoulder and then back at Isis. "How do you do that?"

"Do what?" Isis asked, frowning as she reached out and ran her fingers over the hilt of a sword. It looked old, maybe an antique, but the metal still shone as if it were newly forged. All the weapons were well cared for and shone in the lights. Briefly, Isis considered attempting to lift one of the blades to keep on her in case she needed to make a fast escape. She decided against it, since she didn't have any experience fighting with a knife.

"Identify accents like Remington's," Shae clarified, drawing Isis' attention back to her. "You've always been able to do that. It's really weird."

"I don't know," Isis replied with a shrug. "I just can. Guess it's another one of my strange talents. I seem to have quite a few of those."

Shae laughed and twisted around when she heard footsteps coming down the stairs. Jade soon came into view, dressed in a green camouflage tank top and dark pants.

"Took you long enough," Shae teased.

"What's the matter, sweetheart? Miss me much?" Jade said with a flirtatious raised eyebrow. "Have you introduced Isis to Alex yet?"

"We were too busy talking about accents," Shae

explained, which made Jade roll her eyes and mutter something Isis didn't catch.

"Alex, come over here and join us," Jade called. The rattling of the chain stopped as Alex turned her eyes over to where the three were standing, studying them for a moment. Eventually, she strode away from the bag and toward the small group. Jade waited patiently until Alex reached them. Isis couldn't help but stare at Alex, who looked nothing like Remington.

"Isis, this is Alex. Alex the aro-ace, meet Isis the Gray-A," Jade introduced the two with a hint of teasing. Alex furrowed her brow a little as she turned her brown eyes to Jade, her expression reflecting surprise.

"Two members of the Four on the ace spectrum? That's unexpected," Alex said and Jade smiled, shrugging. The woman turned her attention back to Isis, looking her up and down, raising her eyebrows.

"She smells human," Alex stated. Isis rolled her eyes. *I'm sure that was meant to be an insult,* she thought.

"Be nice, Alex," Jade warned. Alex shrugged and turned her attention back to Isis.

"I meant no offense and I apologize if I caused any," Alex said. "You really had no idea about your heritage?"

Isis shook her head and spread her hands, unsure if Alex was looking for some kind of explanation. Next to her, Isis heard Shae scoff and recognized it as a sign that her cousin was annoyed. *Oh god, Shae, please don't start shit,* Isis thought, thinking about the weapons wall behind her.

"Last time I checked, neither did you, Alex," Shae commented, drawing a look from Alex that was nothing short of murderous.

"Sorry to interrupt," Isis began, hoping to prevent any further ugliness. "You're Remington's daughter? The guy I just met upstairs?"

"His adopted daughter. Yes, even we uncivilized shape shifters have adoption," Alex replied, not bothering to hide the hostility in her voice. Isis raised her hands in surrender and stepped back, unwilling to interfere any further. She definitely didn't want to start a fight with someone who likely had much more combat experience.

"Let's not resort to pettiness," Jade reprimanded as she stepped between the two as a kind of mediator. Alex glanced at Isis, but didn't say anything further.

"Jade is right. You four are supposed to work together as a team, not bicker like ill-mannered children."

Isis turned around, surprised to see Remington standing behind her on the bottom step. He had his arms crossed over his chest and was watching them with a passive expression. From the way he held himself, Isis estimated that he was just over six feet tall.

"We have a long few months ahead of us, so I suggest we get started," Remington continued as he crossed the training room, his voice loud enough that they could hear him clearly. He moved over to the boxing ring and removed a clipboard from the chalky white floor.

"Today is just a beginning run-through so I can see how your skills measure up against one another," he explained, his eyes traveling over to them. "Isis, you'll be working with your sister for a while. She wants you to meet her outside near the Koi pond."

Isis looked over to Shae, not thrilled with the prospect of leaving familiarity to spend time with a complete stranger. She wasn't comfortable with Electra, who seemed to be angry at the world. Shae shrugged and gave her an apologetic look. Isis sighed and turned, heading for the stairs.

"Isis, please tell Electra that I will be out later to see how you are progressing," Remington's voice made her hesitate for a minute. When she was sure he wasn't going to add anything more, Isis jogged up the stairs and out of the training room.

~~*~*~*

It was a picturesque summer afternoon. The mansion's lands were bathed in the golden light of the sun. A cool breeze prevented the temperature from becoming stifling. The air was alive with the songs of various birds and the babbling brook complimented their symphony.

Isis was soaking in the serenity of the lands as she meandered in the general direction of the Koi pond. In the kitchen, she had run into a man who introduced himself as Cassidy Monroe. The pleasant exchange had been a little uncomfortable due to the fact that Cassidy had been wearing nothing other than a pair of socks.

She finally spotted the large Koi pond and her sister. Electra was perched atop one of the smooth red stones that surrounded the body of water. Her eyes were down as she gazed into the clean pool. Isis approached, leaning forward a little once she reached the pond, admiring the large colorful fish. Almost every color of the rainbow was captured in their beautiful scales. Her eyes were drawn to one in particular, though she wasn't sure why. It was a solid-colored fish, an orange one. It didn't move differently or look different from the other fish, but it stood out to her for some reason.

"There are close to a hundred Koi in here," Electra said as she shifted her weight so that she could dangle her bare feet just above the water. "Pick the shape shifter out."

"Huh?" Isis asked, frowning as she looked up to her sister. Electra turned her gaze up from the pond to Isis.

"Pick the shape shifter," she repeated in a patient tone. It was the first time since meeting Electra that Isis didn't detect any anger or annoyance in her voice. Isis looked back into the Koi pond. She pointed to the orange fish.

"That one would be my guess, but don't ask me why," Isis replied as she looked up to Electra again. She leaned back, putting her hands behind her to prop herself up.

"Jay, you can come out now," Electra called out, watching the pool. The orange Koi that Isis had pointed out swam away to the other end of the pool, jumped out of the water, and landed on the stones. Instead of flopping about like a fish normally would, the scales melted into clothing and flesh. The body expanded and formed appendages. The face rounded out, becoming human in form and soon, a dark-haired man sat on the stone in place of the fish. The entire transformation had taken less than a minute.

Isis stared at him. "I'm *never* going to get used to that."

"Always trust your instincts," Electra said, turning

to the man who had been a fish a few seconds ago. "Thank you for your help, Jay."

Jay stood up and nodded to both women before turning and walking back the way Isis had come from, scrubbing a hand through his wet hair. Isis twisted to watch him go.

"That's Jet and Lilly's adopted son. He doesn't say much, which is why I decided to ask for his help," Electra explained as she stood up. "I'm going to help you tap into your power, which will make your training progress quicker."

Isis was quiet, looking off toward the trees in the distance. "How long is this training going to take?"

"Tapping into your abilities shouldn't take more than a month or two," Electra replied with a shrug. "As for the rest, you'll be training throughout your life."

Isis stared at her, but Electra had already hopped off the stone and was walking toward a small grove of trees.

"The rest of my life?" Isis asked. "You people do realize that I have a life outside of whatever kind of shenanigans you want to involve me in."

"Uh huh," Electra replied, uninterested. "Are you going to listen or are you going to make this even more difficult by fighting me on everything?"

Isis ran her hands over her face, aggravated by the way everyone seemed to be making her decisions for her. "Fine, teach away, oh wise demigod or whatever the hell you are."

Electra responded with one of the most impressive side eyed glares Isis had ever seen. For a moment, Isis thought the woman might punch her.

"I'm *not* a demigod. Do I really have to reiterate

that guardians aren't gods?" Electra asked as she sat down in a lotus position on the ground, gesturing for Isis to do the same.

"No," Isis grumbled as she sat on the ground, folding her legs under her. Contrary to her manner, Isis found she was curious about what Electra would teach her.

"There are a number of guardian powers that you are capable of and an equal amount of shape shifter abilities," she began. "The main ability of shape shifters is, of course, to change form."

"Can I change into people?" Isis asked, not believing what she was asking. Electra shook her head.

"No, the only human form you possess is that which you are in now. Before you ask, no, you can't shift into inanimate objects either. You're also unable to shift into extinct creatures," she explained. A rabbit hopped away nearby, rustling the grass as he bounded out of sight. Electra glanced over her shoulder.

"The guardian abilities are a bit trickier due to their complex nature," Electra continued, looking back to Isis. "Every guardian has different abilities, though we do share many. Since we're of the royal line, we really only have the basics."

"Such as?" Isis asked, folding a knee up so that she could wrap her arm around it.

"Appearing, communing with nature, telekinesis," Electra listed. "Those are probably the most difficult. Most of the others are just minor abilities that will gradually become apparent in time. They can't really be taught."

"Quick question: these guardian abilities, do they include dreams?" Isis asked. Electra stared at her, puzzled.

"Dreams?" she asked, waiting for some kind of clarification.

"Yeah, like any kind of," Isis rotated her wrist a few times, "premonitory dreams or anything like that?"

"No," Electra replied, her face scrunching up a little as if she didn't understand the point of the question. "Those don't run in our family. Why?"

"Just curious," Isis said with a casual shrug. "How do we go about unlocking these abilities?"

"There is no *we* in this process," Electra stated. "I can only guide you. *You're* the one who has to do all the real work."

"Is this the part where you tell me to clear my mind?" Isis asked, her snarky tendencies returning. Electra rubbed her eyes in frustration, mumbling something about the family stubborn streak.

"Let's start with telekinesis, since that's one of the more important ones. And we'll see how far we get," she finally said, looking up again and blinking a few times. Isis could tell she had already annoyed her twin.

"What about shape shifting? Why aren't we starting with that?" Isis asked. If she really could change into an animal, she definitely wanted to try that out.

"Because you're not ready," Electra answered in a tone that said the matter wasn't up for discussion. She reached behind her head and removed one of the fiery red glass sticks from the neat bun she had tied her hair in. She held it just over her other outstretched palm. Isis leaned forward, intrigued, watching in amazement as Electra carefully opened her thumb and index finger. The stick remained hovering vertically above her palm. Isis' mouth dropped partly open in awe. Electra removed her other hand, staring at the hovering stick. After a moment, it began to spin.

"And you think I can do *that?*" Isis asked, waving her hand over and around the stick, searching for any hidden wires. When she could find none, she sat back and looked around for any other kind of trick that might explain the hovering stick.

"No, I know you can do that," Electra replied as she plucked the decorative stick out of midair. She turned her bright eyes, now blue, to her sister.

"Do you know how to center yourself?" she asked.

Isis shrugged. "I've meditated before, if that's what you mean."

"It's a start," Electra said, biting her lip as she tapped the stick against her palm. "You have to be completely still and fully open your mind. And don't close your eyes."

"Why not?"

"Just don't," Electra ordered. Isis looked at her and then turned her attention to the hair stick. The grass was soft against her hands and the wind was cool on her exposed skin. She stared at some distant point over Electra's shoulder, allowing the scenery and sounds to wash over her. Gradually, Isis began to feel the world expand around her until she was nothing more than an insignificant dot in a gigantic planet. There were so many sounds that the sheer amount threatened to overwhelm her. The birds alone were like a hundred orchestras. Electra watched her for a few minutes, though it could have been hours for all Isis knew. She held the hair stick out again, right in between the two of them.

"Just picture it floating in the air," Electra instructed, her soft voice sounding far away. "It is an inanimate object. You have complete control over it. It will do whatever you want."

Isis stared at it, her surroundings dissolving into nothingness. She and the stick were all that remained. She stared at it, imagining it floating in midair. Her eyes slowly slipped shut of their own volition.

"Isis!"

The shout drew her out of the empty space and her eyes snapped open. Isis lunged backward with a cry when she saw the pointed end of the hair stick inches away from her left eye. She glanced up again, noticing Electra was leaning forward and grasping the stick. Her twin looked exasperated.

"You're lucky I have quick reflexes," Electra chastised as she sat back, twirling the hair stick between her fingers. "*That's* why you never close your eyes. Try it again."

Isis looked around at their peaceful surroundings before turning her eyes back to Electra. "Uh, no. I don't think so."

"You have to learn this, Isis," Electra replied, tension creeping into her tone.

"No, I need to keep both my eyes," Isis protested, straightening up again. "Look, you've got the wrong person. There's nothing special about me. I don't have any superpowers, or whatever the hell this is. Sorry."

Electra glared at her, her nostrils flaring and her fists clenching.

"Even you don't believe that. Look at us, Isis, we're very obviously twins. I have powers, which means you do as well. It's in your blood. Like it or not, this is your life now. I'm not always going to be around to save you and neither is Jade. If you follow my instructions and Remington's, you will be able to defend yourself and do some good in the world. However, if you keep being a stubborn ass and let fear control your actions and decisions, you won't last a day. Now get up and try again."

Isis scowled, but did as her sister said. As she cleared her mind, she tried something different. She focused on her surroundings and on her anger at the ridiculous situation she found herself in. A strange tingling raced through her veins and Isis could feel her temperature go up a couple degrees. Still, she kept her eyes on the stick that Electra held in front of her.

Electra couldn't suppress the jolt of surprise that went through her when the stick was yanked from her grasp. It sped toward Isis again, only this time she caught it. For a moment, she looked stunned as she stared at the thin glass stick in her hand. Isis swallowed, studying the stick as though it were an alien object. Electra leaned forward and took it from Isis' grasp.

"Better," she said, clearing her throat. "We'll make a shape shifter guardian hybrid out of you yet. Now, try holding it in the air, no movement."

Electra held the stick out again, though her mind was elsewhere. Telekinesis should have taken at least a couple days for Isis to tap into, more likely a week. Electra remembered that she herself had tapped into her abilities much quicker than the other guardians. As she watched her sister, she couldn't help but wonder about their father. All that she really knew about him were the numerous stories painting him as the most ruthless of assassins, a monster who hid in the shadows and pounced on unfortunate victims who crossed his path. She knew his brothers much better, having seen them often throughout her childhood. Nothing had been overly extraordinary about them, at least nothing she knew of.

Electra slowly drew her hand away from the stick. It remained hovering in place, just like she had demonstrated.

CHAPTER EIGHT

A peaceful night fell on the mansion. The sky was a soft midnight blue with thousands of silver stars twinkling in the darkness and a crescent moon shining down on the land below. It was a warm night so most of the windows were open, allowing in the occasional breeze. Almost everyone was either asleep or out for the night, leaving the large home quiet.

Jet and Remington were in the library. Remington was sitting in a large ornate chair, his long legs stretched out in front of him. He was the very picture of relaxed in his reclined position. Jet stood near one of the windows, gazing out at the night. He had asked Remington to meet him in the library to discuss the Four's progress. The library was Jet's favorite place in the whole mansion. The architecture of the enormous space was beautiful and the large shelves housed at least a thousand books, probably more. It was the books that had always drawn Jet to the room. He loved the smell of books, a comforting scent he could recall all the way back to his childhood. When he was younger, he spent many hours in the library, reading with his sisters and brothers.

"Penny for your thoughts?" Remington called over his shoulder. Jet twisted to look at the chair where the trainer was sitting. He turned around and approached the fireplace Remington sat in front of. In colder months, there was usually a decent-sized fire going. Jet sat in the lounge near the chair, resting an elbow on the armrest. He supported his head with his thumb and index finger. In front of them was a sturdy wooden table, upon which rested a serving tray. There was a large glass decanter in the center of the silver tray and two tulip-shaped glasses sat in front of it. The decanter was filled with a fine tawny port, aged to perfection. Remington had already poured a glass for himself and now sat back, holding the glass between his middle and ring finger, twisting it methodically.

"How are they doing?" Jet asked, not needing to clarify whom he was speaking about. Remington ran the glass under his nose, closing his eyes as he took in the aroma of the port.

"Ahead of schedule. Hardly surprising," he finally answered, offering Jet a small smile.

"And how is she?" Jet asked, again feeling no need to specify whom he was speaking about. Remington chuckled, shaking his head once.

"She is her mother's daughter," he responded, a hint of mirth in his voice. He sipped the port, his brows knitting as he lowered the glass again.

"There is something," he paused for a moment, thinking of the right word, "unusual about how quickly she learns."

"How so?" Jet asked.

"Well," Remington leaned forward to place his glass on the table. "It's been a few months now and already she is at Alex's level as far as fighting ability, not to mention she has already tapped into almost all her abilities, both guardian and shape shifter."

"Oh." It was Jet's turn to frown. "Could it possibly be because of her guardian blood?"

"It could be," Remington responded with a half nod. "Although…"

"Yes?"

"I was just thinking. Electra was also more advanced than other guardians her age, wasn't she? If I recall correctly, she had fully tapped into all of her abilities a year before any of the other guardians her age," Remington replied, drumming his thumb on the armrest.

Jet thought for a moment. "You know, I think you're right. Could it just be a coincidence?"

Remington shrugged and took another sip of his port. Jet steepled his hands in front of his mouth and stared at the empty fireplace. He dropped his hands after a moment so that they pointed straight ahead.

"The Deverells have always been known for their intelligence and their loyalty — as well as their ability to get into and out of sticky situations — but I don't recall anything particularly extraordinary in the bloodline. Do you?" he asked, glancing over at his former mentor.

Remington was quiet as he thought. "There were plenty of stories of guardians taking early Deverells as lovers, but the same is said about many of the noble protector families. The only more recent thing that comes to mind was Roan's hunting ability. Some shape shifters used to refer to him as the lion. It wasn't so much his cold-bloodedness that frightened shape shifters as his ability to zero in on his...prey, for lack of a better term."

Jet let out a bitter laugh. "He certainly had a killer's instincts, nobody would argue that."

Remington shook his head. "It was more than that, Jet. It would be foolish to just think of him as a monster. Roan was a very complicated shape shifter. Very complicated and very smart; two qualities that make for a dangerous adversary."

"Well, thankfully we no longer have to worry about him," Jet replied, turning his eyes to Remington again. "Aside from training, how is Isis adjusting?"

Remington shrugged. "As well as can be expected in the circumstances. She has her good and bad days. She is letting go of the 'normal world' that she was accustomed to, which is a good thing."

"No more escape attempts?" Jet asked, only half-joking.

Remington chuckled again and gave a small shake of his head. "No, no. I believe she is done with that. Though, with a daughter of Passion, you can never be sure I suppose. She is not the most trusting protector I've ever trained, but that's to be expected."

"Of course," Jet responded, letting out a quiet laugh. "Can you even imagine being raised by humans?"

"Odd, how we're so close and yet so removed," Remington observed with a contemplative smile. It was strange, living among those who had no idea they even existed. They encountered each other every day, worked alongside each other, and a few even settled down and started families together.

"Any news from our informants concerning the

Key or the possible assassin power struggle? Are we still working under the impression the Key is a flashdrive?" Remington asked and Jet shrugged.

"We have never known exactly what the Key is, aside from it being a destructive force. The way the prophecy is worded suggests it evolves with the world, so chances are it's linked with technology in some way. We've seen magic evolving to affect and even interact with modern technology," Jet explained, stopping when Remington raised a hand.

"I know your reasoning, my friend. You have explained it many a time," he laughed.

"Oh right," Jet said, smiling despite the unease he felt. "Then no, I haven't heard anything new or different from our informants or allies. The sudden lull in crime leads me to believe it might have been dropped somewhere. But that's just a theory. Ugh, Remington, why can't we ever be faced with simple quandaries? The kind that can be solved in an afternoon preferably."

Jet groaned as he sank down on the lounge, glancing over at Remington, who offered him a sympathetic smile.

"The path of a protector has never been an easy one nor shall it ever be," Remington replied, pausing to sip his port. "Still no idea about who created the Key or their purpose for doing so?"

"I figured we'd worry about that once we retrieved the damn thing, whatever it may be," Jet answered. Remington nodded, but Jet could see he didn't agree with the dismissal.

"I can only worry about so much, Remington," he protested. Remington leaned forward and placed his glass on the table.

"It just strikes me as interesting that we find Isis and then there's a sudden lull," he said. "Even the assassins seem to have gone quiet, which you wouldn't expect if someone was challenging Adara's position."

Jet stared at him, confused. "Are you implying that Isis is somehow connected to the Key?"

"I'm just pointing out that some events have been quite convenient, which is why I believe you shouldn't just dismiss the origins of the Key or the possibility of there being a connection to the unrest among assassins and even to Isis," Remington replied in his usual calm and patient manner as he sat back, a thoughtful expression crossing his features.

"Point taken," Jet said after a moment, his gaze returning to the empty fireplace. A comfortable silence fell over them. Remington's eyes traveled back to Jet.

"Jet?" Remington's quiet tone suggested that he was going to bring up a sensitive topic. Jet turned his gaze back to his mentor.

"Have you spoken to her at all?" Remington asked, watching his former student to gauge his response. Jet swallowed, shaking his head.

"After what I did, I figured it best to give her space," he explained, turning his face up toward the ceiling and shutting his eyes. "I certainly have more than enough to keep me busy."

"You didn't have a choice," Remington reminded him gently.

"Why Rem, if I didn't know better, I'd say you were on my side," Jet commented with an almost playful tone. He could tell by the old trainer's expression that he had surprised him. Jet had

169

expected it: he hadn't used that tone since he had been an impatient young protector, eager to make his parents and Remington proud.

"This is not a situation with sides," Remington replied. "Though I never did agree with the High Council's decision."

"They were too harsh," Jet agreed. "It bordered on cruel, not only to Passion but to Isis and Electra as well."

"They have their reasons, no matter how baseless they sometimes appear."

"Oh, come on Remington," Jet said, rising to his feet and striding back to the windows. "Passion represents change and the old-fashioned guardians, particularly the men, have always despised that. They were just looking for an excuse to make an example of her."

"What's done is done, Jet. We can't go back and change the past," Remington stated, turning his head to the side. "We have to focus on the present and the future."

"He's right, my love," a feminine voice came from the doorway. Both men turned to see Lilly standing there, framed by the warm glow from the hallway wall sconces. She was wearing a silky pine green dress that glistened in the low light. Lilly smiled at both of them, but her eyes turned to Jet.

"Passion is impulsive and hot-tempered, but she won't cut us out of her life. Give her some time and she will forgive you. You'll see," she reassured.

"I don't know, Lilly," he said, tiredness seeping into his voice as he turned his gaze back to the dark summer night. "I've never betrayed her trust like this before."

"I believe I will retire for the evening," Remington said as he rose from his chair. "We can talk more in the morning, Jet, but please think over what I said."

He nodded to Lilly as he strode past her. "My lady."

Lilly gave him a gracious smile and nodded her head as well before turning back to her husband, who now stared out the clean panes of glass. She approached him and stood at his side, following his gaze into the tranquil night. Every now and again, a shadow would move about in the numerous trees on the property.

"Remington seems to think that the flashdrive, or whatever the Key is, has something to do with Isis and also the unrest among the assassins," Jet mentioned. "He does have a point. The timing is awfully convenient. The flashdrive surfaced shortly before the factory, which was located close to a known assassin base, and then it disappeared when Isis arrived here. What it means, I haven't the foggiest idea."

Lilly lowered her slender body so that she was resting her weight on the window bench and facing Jet. The moonlight gleamed in her golden hair, creating a halo about her head.

"All the more reason we should try to find and retrieve it before it falls into the wrong hands. We should consider sending the Four out to find some leads," she mentioned. Jet glanced down to her sapphire eyes, which were fixed on him. He looked back out the window and shook his head once.

"I don't know if that's wise, Lilly," he replied. After the disaster with Gia, Bryn, and Nat, he was hesitant to send out another team. It was a dangerous world out there, more so than most would ever know. Silence fell over the library, broken only by the soft ticking of the grandfather clock in the hall outside.

Lilly watched her husband, understanding the fear he kept buried deep within his heart. Jet was incredibly compassionate and empathetic, and losing the three women originally thought to be part of the Four had wounded him deeply. It was something that he would probably never get over entirely. Now that Isis was in the picture, Jet would be even more cautious. Though Passion had ended their friendship, Jet was still loyal to her and would protect her daughter with his life.

"It would be unwise to wait longer," Lilly said as she gazed out into the night again. "Every night the Key is out there is one night too long. Trust them, Jet."

Jet sank down next to her. "I do, Lilly."

"You're not ready," she observed, easily reading the emotions that crossed Jet's face. She reached over and stroked his cheek with the backs of her fingers. He leaned into her touch, closing his eyes.

"No, I'm not. People are killing for this thing and the assassins are more active than they have been in quite some time. I don't even want to think about what would happen if an assassin managed to get ahold of it. And if it has something to do with Isis…" he trailed off and shook his head. Lilly studied her husband in the pale light, which highlighted his weary appearance. He hadn't been sleeping much lately and it showed. Dark rings had started to form under his eyes and everything about him seemed dull, almost lifeless. Stress was beginning to take its toll.

"All the more reason to act now, while there's a

lull in crime," Lilly pointed out. "If we can retrieve it, we'll know more."

"I don't even know where to begin, Lilly," Jet replied, running his hands over his face. "It doesn't make sense that someone would just lose it, a tool that powerful. It had to have been dropped, but it could've been dropped anywhere."

"We won't find the answers tonight. You need rest. Are you coming up to bed?" Lilly asked, running her fingers through her husband's thick hair and gently kissing his cheek.

"Eventually," Jet replied, turning his head and meeting his wife's lips in a kiss. "I just want to spend a few more minutes down here."

Lilly nodded as she stood up and began walking toward the entrance of the library. She paused when she heard Jet call her name, twisting to look back at him.

"Thank you."

She smiled before turning again and continuing to the hallway. Jet watched her go before turning his eyes out to the star-filled sky. His eyes easily found the brightest star in the sky, one that he remembered from his childhood. Sirius.

~~*~*~*

Early in the morning, the throbbing beat of fast-paced music pounded through the basement where the Four were working out. Shae was hanging upside down on one of the bars in the far wall, doing curl-ups. Alex was stretching on a mat just behind the boxing ring. Jade and Isis were in the boxing ring. Jade was twisting a water bottle back and forth, watching Isis with a sly grin on her face. Isis was standing on the opposite side of the ring, resting her arms on the ropes behind her.

"Tigress," Jade suddenly said. In a little less than a minute, Isis had shifted into a large orange tigress. She licked her enormous chops and turned her gold eyes to Jade, who twisted the cap off her water bottle.

"African wild dog," she said before taking a swig of her water. Another few seconds and the tigress had shifted into a long-legged dog with a brown, black, tan, and white mottled coat. She tilted her head, awaiting Jade's next command. Jade was quiet, watching the animal in front of her.

"Polar bear," she commanded. It took a few more seconds, but the wild dog became an enormous off-white bear. The bear stood on its hind legs before dropping down to all fours again.

"Red fox."

A small orange fox with a bushy white-tipped tail soon took the place of the gigantic bear.

"Cat."

A black cat with piercing green eyes took the place of the fox. Jade took another swig of water and pointed up, twisting her finger in a circle. Soon the cat melted back into human form. Isis watched her as she capped the water again. Jade purposely took a long time putting the bottle down and then straightening up. She looked at Isis, an impressed grin dancing across her lips.

"You still take a little longer shifting from different sizes, but it's something that's corrected with experience," Jade reported. "Otherwise, you're doing great."

"Why don't we ever practice shifting into insects?"

Isis asked as she leaned against the ropes again. "Wouldn't that make the most sense for spying and infiltrating places?"

"Yeah, if you're willing to spend a week in utter agony," Alex commented from where she stretched on the mat. Isis glanced over her shoulder at her. Of all her teammates, Alex was probably the one she knew the least about. She knew that Remington had taken her in when she was very young, but that was about it. Alex kept to herself, almost as much as Isis did, and wasn't naturally chatty. She was a bookworm and Isis often saw her with her nose buried in a book from the mansion's library.

"Alex is right," Jade commented, drawing Isis' attention back to her. "The smaller the form, the more taxing it is on the body. Insect forms cause the muscles to burn for weeks. Plus, smaller sizes make for serious disadvantages. Something that small is very easy to kill or damage. As a general rule, we never go too small."

"Oh," Isis said. All three glanced over at Shae when she let out a long groan.

"I'm *so* bored," she moaned as she grabbed the bar and flipped her legs over her head. She let go of the metal bar and easily landed on her feet. When she straightened up, Shae put her hands on her hips.

"Let's go out," she suggested.

"No," Jade answered immediately. Shae rolled her eyes.

"Jade, we've been training non-stop for months," she protested. "I think we can handle ourselves on one little outing. We'll be together so we'll have each other's backs and we'll be in public, meaning lots and lots of witnesses. I haven't been dancing for *so* long.

Please."

Isis smiled and shook her head at Shae's pleading look. She could manipulate anyone with those green eyes of hers. Isis was still trying to figure out how she could make them appear so innocent. Her cousin could express everything through her eyes.

"Shae, no," Jade repeated just as firmly. Shae moved over to where the sound system was and turned up the volume dial, cupping a hand behind her ear. Isis winced and pinched the bridge of her nose, not enjoying the loud music.

"What, Jade? I can't hear you," she yelled. Jade turned back to Isis, who shook her head without looking up. Mercifully, Shae turned the music off.

"Come *on*," she continued. "When was the last time you let loose and had some fun? I say we've earned at least one night off."

Jade ran her hands over her face. The sound of peeling brought Isis' attention over to the supply table where Alex was focused on removing the tape from her hands. Alex met Jade's eyes and shrugged.

"I'll go alone if I have to," Shae threatened.

"No, you won't," Isis mentioned. "You'll drag me out with you and wind up getting both of us into trouble."

Jade looked over to Isis, who waved a hand dismissively. She could hear Alex snicker behind her.

"Experience," Isis explained, looking back at Shae. "I grew up with her."

Shae got up on her knees on the edge of the ring. "Isis can tell you that we don't give up easily."

The lights buzzed above them, illuminating everything with unnatural brightness. It was unusually quiet as all three looked to Jade, awaiting her answer.

She glanced over to where Alex was standing nearby.

"What do you think?" she called over to her.

Alex gave a small half-shrug. "It could be a learning experience or it could go horribly wrong. I have no strong feelings either way."

Jade turned back to look at Isis and Isis could tell she was debating her response. Isis wasn't sure which she preferred. They had been constantly warned about the dangers outside, but the mansion had begun to feel stifling and she had started craving a change of scenery. There was a thin line between being safe and being unreasonable. Isis suspected they were getting close to the latter.

"Fine, but two hours tops," Jade finally agreed, sounding resigned. Shae let out a happy laugh and jumped into the ring, hugging Jade, who didn't look thrilled with her decision.

"Don't worry, Jade. I'm going to show the three of you a great time," Shae promised. Isis raised an eyebrow at that statement, wondering if Shae remembered the last "great time" she had shown Isis. That evening had concluded with them almost ending up in jail.

"It's six o'clock now," Shae said, looking at the dark blue watch on her wrist. "We'll meet in the garage at seven sharp and arrive at the club around seven-thirty, eight o'clock."

She clapped her hands and bounced on her heels in excitement. "We're going to have so much fun."

Isis rolled her eyes, knowing that those words inevitably led to trouble. Still, she was eager to escape this world. Even if it was only for an hour or two.

~~*~*~*

Passion was in the gym in the Meadows, striking a punching bag. She was wearing her normal black and red workout clothes. Her midsection was bare as were her arms, something that would have probably annoyed her mother had she been there. The sound of Passion's fists hitting the bag echoed softly in the empty room. The light from the guardians of day and fire entered through the window and cascaded down to the floor of the room. Sweat ran down Passion's neck and back. It was rare for a guardian to sweat, but Passion had been punching and kicking the bag for hours on end, releasing every emotion she was feeling on the apparatus. She was so focused she didn't hear Adonia enter.

Adonia stood behind her granddaughter and crossed her arms over her chest, her silky orchid dress moving with her slender limbs.

"Destroying that isn't going to change what happened," Adonia commented. Passion froze for a moment, her entire body becoming rigid. She shook her head and turned her attention back to the punching bag, striking it even harder.

"I'm not trying to change anything. I'm pissed off and hitting something makes me feel better," Passion growled tersely as she began kicking the bag, enjoying the satisfying thwack of her foot hitting the smooth material.

"Who are you angry with?" Adonia inquired, though she already knew the answer. Passion let out a bark of laughter at the question.

"Well, let's see. Off the top of my head," Passion stopped kicking and faced her grandmother but did not make eye contact as she listed names on her fingers, "Artemis, Jet, you, the list goes on and on and," Passion paused as she spun around and kicked the bag again, causing it to swing back and forth. "On."

"I understand your anger and it is justified, but Passion, I know you're smart enough to realize Jet did what he had to do," Adonia explained. "His actions were not malicious."

Passion glared at her, her blue eyes flickering red for the briefest of moments. Her grandmother was always right and Passion hated that. She turned around and kicked the bag one more time, wishing she had something to stab it with. Behind her, she heard Adonia turn and start to make her way out of the large room. *Dammit, Jet,* Passion thought when she remembered the protector's request when she last saw him. At the time, Passion had been too furious to even consider asking his question. She stopped her violent workout for a moment.

"Before you leave, Grandmother," she said and turned around. "I do have a question."

Adonia paused and waited for Passion's question. The younger guardian studied her for a moment, chewing on her lower lip as she thought over how to ask it. Sometimes she had to pick her words carefully to get a clear answer. Unlike her mother and grandmother, Passion didn't have much experience in politics and preferred to be straightforward.

"I was told that an attempt was made on Isis' life, the night she was brought to the protector mansion. Now I was under the distinct impression that as a daughter of the Meadows, whether she knew it or not, she was entitled to protection. Was I misled in that belief?" Passion asked. Adonia crossed her arms over her chest.

"You were not. Isis did have protection throughout her life, both in the form of protectors and through guardian magic."

"Ah, guardian magic," Passion repeated. "I assume that means some kind of spell meant to alert the guards of any menace or threat."

"Yes, you're correct," Adonia affirmed.

"Then perhaps you can explain to me, Grandmother, how no one was aware of the assassin who made an attempt on Isis' life."

Adonia opened her mouth to respond, but closed it again. Her brow creased and Passion could tell her grandmother was thinking over her question. After a moment, Adonia shook her head, an apologetic expression crossing her features.

"I'm afraid I don't have an answer for you, Passion. We should have been aware of that and I do not know why we were not," she said, dropping her arms again. "I shall bring it up the next time the High Council convenes. If you desire an answer, I shall try and find one."

Passion let out an angry laugh. "Yes, because they have always been so forthright and honest with their answers. The damage has already been done. See that it doesn't happen again."

She stepped past her grandmother and retrieved her towel from where she had laid it on a bench, dabbing at her face and chest. Passion then moved to leave the workout room. She reached the door, put her hand on the door handle and was about to leave when Adonia's voice stopped her.

"Jet misses you too."

Passion paused but didn't turn around.

"Trying times are coming, Passion. I've seen it and so has Sibyl. Do not be so quick to discard so meaningful and powerful a bond as the one you share with Jet and Lilly."

Passion opened the door and walked out of the room, letting the heavy wooden door shut behind her.

As she walked down the long hallway to the main stairway, Passion smiled politely in greeting at the few guardians who passed her by. The gym was located on the second floor in the castle. Guardians only came down to train and workout when they had a spare moment, which was rarely ever. Passion loved the room because it was almost guaranteed that she would get some much needed peace and quiet if she went at the right time.

Passion stopped when she heard footsteps behind her. Turning around, she was surprised to see Electra standing in the middle of the hall a few feet away. She turned her eyes to the side, then back to Electra. *She doesn't look angry. Hopefully she's not looking for a fight,* Passion thought, suddenly feeling weary. There were no guardians in the hall anymore, but the sounds of rushing feet could be heard from the busier halls and floors. The lifeless eyes of the portraits on the walls stared down at them. The sunlight from the lands of day danced about their bodies, highlighting the guardian glisten in Passion's skin.

"Haven't seen you in a while," Passion began, studying her daughter. "Where have you been?"

"The mansion, where else?" Electra replied with a casual shrug. "Following in your footsteps, I guess."

Passion smiled, glancing down to her feet. "If you've come for a fight, I'll have to take a rain check. I just came from working out and I'm tired."

"I haven't come to argue," Electra said, her tone somewhat defensive. "Though I feel I would be justified if that were my purpose, seeing as how I was the one who was lied to my entire life."

"What did you come for then?"

Electra hesitated and Passion recognized the thoughtful look on her face. Her daughter was carefully considering her words.

"I have been helping Isis tap into her abilities, but I haven't taught her how to Appear yet. I wanted to ask your advice on whether or not I should," Electra answered after a moment, flipping her hair over her shoulder with a shake of her head.

"That's good for your sister. You're an excellent teacher," Passion said. While she wasn't exactly thrilled with the idea of her daughter being a protector, Passion was at least glad that her daughters had met each other and perhaps would now have the opportunity to be sisters.

Electra shrugged. "Jade helped a lot, but she's a good student and very clever. You haven't answered my question."

Passion was quiet for a moment, watching her daughter. "Is she as angry with me as you are?"

"I'm not angry at you, Mother."

"You are. But you have every right to be," Passion replied.

"I'm not dwelling on it. There are bigger things in life. Besides, Roan is dead."

Passion frowned at Electra's uncharacteristically hesitant behavior. "You know you aren't evil. Who your father was is no reflection on you."

Electra looked down at the floor. Passion walked up to Electra and held her in her arms, swallowing back tears.

"You are your own person, sweetheart. Blood is not everything," she whispered.

"I am the daughter of an assassin. That is a legacy of pain and death and a heavy burden to bear," Electra murmured, slumping a little in her mother's arms. Passion held her daughter tighter, wishing she could somehow shield her from all the cruelty in the world.

"It doesn't work that way. We forge our own path in life," Passion said with a shake of her head, a crafty smile dancing on her lips. "And give your mother some credit. I think my genes are a little stronger than any of the Deverells, and I know they are much stronger than Roan's."

Electra laughed softly. Passion held her at arm's length and looked into Electra's eyes.

"You teach your sister to Appear if you think it is the right time. I trust your judgement."

Electra went quiet for a moment, thinking it over. "I'll teach her to Appear when you talk to Jet again."

Passion dropped her arms, turned around, and continued down the hall, disappearing from her daughter's view. Electra shook her head and rolled her eyes, already feeling at home again.

"Impossible, she is just impossible," Electra muttered in frustration as she walked in the opposite direction toward the stairs that were closest to her bedroom.

~~*~*~*

At seven o'clock, Shae led the way to the garage. She walked over to the security system and played around with the wires until the buttons turned from red to green, a little trick she had learned from the youngest Monroe, Hunter. She walked into the garage and flipped on the light. The florescent glow brought out the color in the vast selection of cars and motorcycles.

Shae reached into her pocket and produced a set of keys as the other three entered the brightly lit garage. She jingled the keys.

"I hope no one objects to a black BMW," she said with a wide grin.

"Dare I ask how you got those?" Alex asked in a dry tone that sounded frighteningly like Remington without the accent.

"Alex, you are sucking all the fun right out of this," Shae responded as she bounced down the two steps. She was wearing a short grayish blue dress. It tied behind her neck and, like everything else Shae owned, it made her look spectacular.

Alex followed Shae down the rows of cars toward the BMW. She had chosen to wear blue jeans and an almost see-through black tank top that revealed a hint of her toned stomach. Jade wore a simple spaghetti-strapped top that left her shoulders and arms completely bare. She had on tight dark blue jeans that had just a hint of glitter and a belt of small gold discs wound around her waist. Isis had chosen to go with a backless black halter-top and dark slacks — which was as fancy and dressed up as she got.

They reached the car and Shae ducked into the driver's seat. Alex and Jade climbed into the backseat, while Isis sat in the empty passenger seat, running a hand through her soft wispy hair.

"Aw, Ice Queen, don't look so troubled," Shae

said as she started the car. "It's a chance for you to work on those people skills we talked about."

Isis gave her cousin a withering look, not amused by the joke. Shae smiled devilishly and shifted into gear, easing out of the parking space and heading toward the open garage door.

~~*~*~*

Jet stood outside and watched the large amber sun sink into a deep purple sky. He closed his eyes and breathed in the fresh air. The air carried a scent of jasmine with the faint hint of other flowers and pine from the nearby trees. The soft grass tickled his bare feet and the cool temperatures of the vanishing day pierced his cerulean shirt.

Whenever Jet had something on his mind, he would stand outside and let the fresh air relax him. It was a habit from his youth. Usually Passion or Lilly would be there to help him sort out his thoughts, but he wanted solitude at the moment. His mind was flooded with memories of Passion. He remembered playing in the Meadows with her when he was only a child, smiling as he thought about the races in crystal clear lakes in the water lands. She always beat him, mainly because Jet hated swimming and tended to avoid water at all costs. He had first met Passion when she had saved him from drowning while he was visiting the Meadows.

"I'm still the faster swimmer," a soft voice came from behind him. Jet's eyes snapped open and he twisted around. Passion stood there, gazing at the sunset. She glanced at him and then looked back to the horizon, not speaking further.

"You're not going to hurl me into the sun, are you?" Jet asked, only half-kidding. Passion raised an eyebrow, not responding right away.

"Maybe another day," Passion finally answered with a thin smile. For a moment, they stood and watched the setting sun, neither speaking a word. Jet debated whether or not he should apologize. He wasn't sure it was what his friend wanted to hear.

"I've missed you," Jet said, turning his eyes back to the sunset.

"I know," Passion sighed and walked over to his side. "I asked Adonia about the protection Isis should have had. My grandmother had no answers, but she will ask about it the next time the High Council meets."

Passion frowned and turned her eyes to her feet for a moment. "I…Jet, my daughter was left vulnerable and it nearly resulted in her losing her life. I know it probably sounds incredibly paranoid, but what if someone purposely weakened the protection spells?"

Jet shook his head. "I don't think that sounds paranoid. It is something Lilly and I spoke about briefly. But there is not much we can do, especially since we have no evidence. We must tread very carefully, Passion."

Passion nodded, meeting his gaze again. "I can't ever forgive you for what you did. But I can't lose our friendship either."

"I understand," Jet said with a sad smile. They stood together in a comfortable silence for a moment, enjoying the pleasant night.

"I'll do everything in my power to make sure no harm comes to Isis," Jet vowed. "I mean it, Passion.

Lilly and I will make sure she can defend herself against any threat, no matter where it might come from."

Passion raised an elegant eyebrow. "Are you implying you'll teach her how to kill a corrupt guardian?"

"Maybe just incapacitate them," Jet replied with a wink, smiling when his friend laughed.

Screeching tires and a slamming gate interrupted the moment between the two friends. Passion's face froze; she was either annoyed or worried or both. Jet closed his eyes and put his hands behind his head, already knowing without looking what had just happened. It was just his luck. *Right after I swear to protect her, that's just wonderful,* he thought. Dusk's gray light settled about them as stars began to twinkle in the sky and the moon began to glow.

"They stole a car, didn't they?" he asked Passion. Passion nodded as she continued watching the direction of the road. Jet groaned in exasperation, rubbing his eyes.

"I'll send out Hunter and Cassidy to make sure nothing happens to them," Jet reassured her. *Or my car,* he thought, deciding not to try and joke with Passion at the moment.

Passion nodded and smiled, her eyes telling Jet that she trusted him. Jet turned toward the house and when he looked back, she was gone.

~~*~*~*

Shae pulled up to the club's entrance, glancing at the long line outside the door. She smiled, obviously happy to be back in her kind of environment. She opened the driver's side door, not bothering to look back and check if the others were following, and tossed the keys to the valet who moved to do his job.

"Here she is," she declared, gesturing at the large building in front of them. Isis glanced up to the neon purple sign.

"Dionysia? Really, Shae?"

"Hey, you're the one who's half-god. I thought you'd appreciate it," Shae replied.

"They're not gods," Jade and Alex corrected simultaneously and Shae responded with a carefree wave of her hand. She approached the large bouncer who stood at the door. His stone-like face split into a very large grin when he saw Shae and he immediately pushed the door open, waving them in with one large meaty hand. Shae grinned and trailed her slender fingers across his broad chest as she passed him by.

"Friend of yours?" Isis asked as she followed Shae through the door. Her cousin just winked in reply and they entered the club.

House music blasted over the speakers, making the floor shake a bit. Tables and chairs were strewn about the edges, some occupied and some not. Most of the club patrons blended together in their nicely colored clothing. The people who worked in the club walked around wearing glow sticks about their necks, heads, and wrists. Some of the people on the dance floor held glow sticks in their hands. A strange neon blue glow seemed to light up the entire club.

Isis' attention was drawn to the side, to a man about her age who was sitting in the shadows. As she studied him, the club seemed to become deathly quiet. His long legs were resting on an empty chair sitting in front of him and his eyes were hidden behind a pair of designer sunglasses, which was quite odd since the club was so dark. A tan baseball cap covered his head but Isis could tell that he had dark hair. He was wearing a plain dark-colored t-shirt and jeans. There were a number of people sitting around him, including a woman in a pink dress who leaned against him, but he still stood out. His attention was focused on the people dancing on the floor, but he immediately looked in her direction when he felt her eyes on him. The two stared at each other, as though they were each surprised that they had been seen by the other.

"Isis!" Shae called. The pounding music was suddenly blasting again as Isis looked over at her cousin, blinking a few times. For a split second, she felt disoriented and a little dizzy.

"Bar's this way," Shae yelled over the noise. Isis glanced back to where the man was sitting, but he was gone. The sudden feeling of someone touching her arm caused her to start violently. She twisted toward the grasp, raising a hand to fend off an attack, and almost sighed in relief when she saw it was only Jade.

"You okay?" Jade shouted. "You look a little pale. Well, paler than usual."

Isis nodded, but the troubled feeling didn't leave her. She didn't know what was more disturbing: feeling uneasy or not knowing why. Isis followed Jade toward the bar where Shae was already flirting with the bartender. Isis noticed a man attempting to hit on Alex and smiled when her teammate rolled her eyes.

"Phil, I want you to meet some of my good friends," Isis could hear Shae say. "That's Alex and Jade and the one on the end there is my cousin, Isis. This here is my wonderful bartender who recently manned up and proposed to his lovely partner."

Isis stared at Shae, wondering if she knew everybody in the city on a first name basis. It never ceased to amaze her how sociable and extroverted Shae was.

"Well, the night is young and we have plenty of dancing to do," Shae said as she hopped off her seat. "Shall we?"

"God yes," Alex said, moving away from the would-be pickup artist, who seemed rather disappointed as he slunk away to try his luck with another woman.

"You three go ahead," Isis said. "I'm just going to hang out here for a bit."

Shae looked a little disappointed, but shrugged. "All right. Phil, be a dear and take good care of Isis here."

"Will do, Ms. Miller," Phil replied warmly, smiling as he watched her go off into the crowd. He turned his eyes to Isis.

"Can I get you anything?"

She shook her head and he turned back to his other customers. Isis stared at the dance floor, thinking about how much she hated clubs. The people and the noise — it was just too much. She preferred a quiet library or an arboretum, somewhere as far removed from large crowds as possible. Her next thought was whether or not that was the guardian in her.

"I always love to see a woman lost in thought," a gentle voice came over the noise of the club. "To me, that's when they're most beautiful."

Isis rolled her eyes and looked over toward the voice. An attractive man stood in front of her. He had short dark brown hair and a cleanly shaven face. His eyes were hidden behind sunglasses, much like the man Isis had seen when they first walked in. Dark clothing covered his fit body and he stood confidently but not arrogantly.

"Not interested, buddy," Isis said as she turned her attention back to the dance floor.

"Was that too aggressive or was the delivery wrong?" the man asked. The question didn't sound like flirtation but rather a genuine inquiry, as if he didn't know what he had done wrong.

"I'm just not interested," she repeated. The mystery man shrugged and put his hands behind his back, clearing his throat.

"Name's Mark Cooper, but everyone calls me Coop."

Isis shook her head. "Nope."

"I noticed you came with others," Coop mentioned. Isis raised an eyebrow but didn't look at the odd man. He certainly was determined, she'd give him that.

"Yeah, they're around here somewhere," Isis said and pointed toward the dance floor. "There they are."

Coop looked in the direction that she was pointing. "I see."

"Look, I have no idea how much clearer I could be about you not having a chance. So why are you still here? Just for the fascinating one-sided conversation?" Isis asked, keeping her eyes on the other three.

"No, actually. I have something to tell you, but I'd prefer to do it some place a little less," Coop hesitated for a moment, his eyebrows knitting together, "public."

"Oh my freaking god, are you actually serious?"

Isis looked over at Coop, having run out of patience. Now he was getting much too creepy for her liking, though oddly, she didn't feel threatened. Coop opened his mouth to clarify, but was interrupted when a man appeared out of nowhere and bumped into him, spilling his drink all over Coop. Isis jumped a little while Coop took a step back with his hands raised, obviously taken off guard. Isis looked at the guy who spilled his drink on Coop, recognizing him as the man she had seen earlier.

"Oh dude, I am so sorry," the man in the hat moaned, slurring as he brushed at the alcohol staining Coop's shirt. "I didn't see you there. I gotta lay off the Jägermeister, know what I mean?"

"Yeah," Coop grumbled as the man stumbled off. He brushed his hands down the front of his sopping shirt, which glistened in the dim light.

"You two know each other?" Isis asked.

"No," Coop responded, a little too quickly. Isis raised an eyebrow and turned her attention back to the dance floor. Coop stepped forward, right into Isis' personal space.

"Okay, you *really* need to back up. Right now," Isis warned, tensing up and preparing to kick the mysterious man where it counted. "Seriously, dude, I'm not going to tell you again."

"I know you're a shape shifter," Coop whispered. "You're in danger, Isis. There are people watching you that not even Jet, Lilly, nor the guardians know about."

Coop suddenly turned his head, glancing over his right shoulder. "Look over my shoulder. There's a woman in brown leather on the second floor, light cowboy hat. She's watching your friends."

Isis frowned and looked in the direction Coop had a few moments earlier, spotting the woman almost instantly. She was wearing a western outfit, but didn't stand out.

"So?" she asked, annoyed.

"She's an assassin by the name of Onyx, a very formidable one," Coop murmured, glancing to the left and the right. "Watch her right hip; you'll see what I'm talking about. Be careful, make sure she doesn't see you."

Isis sighed and looked back, leaning to the side to see around Coop. The woman turned and Isis saw the gleam of a large firearm for the briefest of moments. *Well shit,* Isis thought as she leaned back to look up at Coop again.

"In the past, her allegiance has been with the assassins and with Adara in particular. But recent whispers suggest that may have changed. Adara won't have control of this territory's assassins much longer," Coop murmured, glancing behind him. "Go. I'll make sure she doesn't follow you."

Isis looked at Coop once more, wondering whether or not to trust him, before hurrying through the pulsating crowd to inform the other three so they could leave. She definitely didn't want to be in a club with an armed individual.

~~*~*~*

The man watched as the Four left the club, leaning down so that his elbows rested on the hand railing in front of him. Coop must have alerted them to the presence of the assassin with the old west obsession who was out for their blood. Glancing at his watch, the man estimated he had fifteen more minutes until his absence was discovered. He closed his eyes, attempting to soothe his throbbing head. The damn music was making his ears bleed, and soon that would be a literal statement.

"What are you doing here, Dane?"

Dane opened his eyes and turned toward Coop, a smirk crossing his lips. "Hello to you too, L-series. Did I hear right? You're still going by Coop?"

"I am."

He snorted, gesturing at the other man's shirt. "Sorry about the drink, but you were kind of asking for it. Some place less public? That was *painful* to watch. What were you thinking?"

Coop glanced up at the assassin. "I'm not used to this kind of…assignment."

"That's because we weren't modified for it."

"You haven't answered my question. Why are you here?"

Dane looked around at all the attractive people. "For the night life. I enjoy the occasional opportunity to soak up all the delicious blissful ignorance."

"Still acting impulsively, I see," Coop grumbled as he leaned on the steel railing.

"Chill out, Coop. This is a completely informal trip. Carding doesn't know I'm out. A couple of the good ole security boys are covering for me," Dane said as he leaned on the railing next to Coop. "That's what you get for not having a poker-face."

"Or for playing with a known cheat," Coop added.

"We do what we have to in order to survive. I cheat. You live a life of servitude. Like a domesticated pet," Dane replied easily.

"Better than a Corporation puppet," he shot back. Dane lunged and grabbed Coop's shirt, jerking the man forward so that they were inches apart. Coop broke his hold and shoved Dane back. The two stood stiffly, waiting for the other to lash out. People around them quickly moved to avoid the two men who looked as if they were about to beat the living hell out of each other.

"Whatever he has planned, it won't work," Coop stated with conviction. Dane raised an eyebrow but didn't relax his position at all.

"Coop, we can't change things. You're deluding yourself if you think otherwise. They'll depose the head assassin in this state and put their shill in her place. If Grenich wants that hybrid, they'll have that hybrid. And believe me, they want her."

Coop glanced back up to where Onyx was standing. If she had seen Coop and Dane, she didn't give them a second glance. Dane followed his gaze.

"That the assassin who's after her?" he asked, smirking and shaking his head when Coop nodded. "Using shape shifters to hunt other shape shifters. You gotta hand it to Grenich. They really take twisted to a whole new level. And soon they'll have control over the assassins — have to admire their initiative."

Coop just grunted in response as he leaned down on the railing. For a moment, the two men stood in silence.

"Dane, you could come back with me. He can protect you," Coop began, but stopped when Dane shook his head and chuckled bitterly. It was odd. Dane couldn't even mimic a good smile when he laughed. Neither of them could really.

"Things are different there, Coop. Ever since the

break-out when you escaped," Dane said. "You think you're free, but you're not. I'd rather live like a zombie than a fugitive. Zombies meet better ends."

Dane straightened up, knowing he had stayed long enough. It was time to go back to the hellish prison he belonged to.

"Dane," he turned back when he heard Coop's voice. "Take care of yourself, okay?"

"I always do," Dane responded as he swaggered down the stairs and disappeared in the sea of pulsating bodies.

CHAPTER NINE

On the outskirts of town there was an old valley that no one dared venture to. To go there meant traversing through a barbed wire fence with large wooden signs declaring in large red letters *NO TRESPASSERS*. Once past the sharp barbs, there was a twisted forest of dead and dying trees and overgrown grass. The air smelled of burnt wood and decay. If an explorer did not get lost in the labyrinth, they would soon come upon a gradually sloping hill covered in brown grass and dried out dirt. In the center of the old valley was a large manor, the cold exterior warning strangers that they were not welcome. It shone like obsidian in the sun, glimmering in the pure rays. It looked neither new nor decrepit.

Once through the double doors, there was a long marble hallway. The inside of the manor was as menacing and cold as the outside, resembling a mausoleum more than a home. Icy light spilled from the many fixtures. It was impossible to walk quietly through the halls and the hollow sound of footsteps often echoed through the large, empty halls. Portraits sat on the gray walls, looming over the manor's occupants.

Gia stretched across her mother's large chair, bobbing her leg as she focused on filing her perfect nails. She glanced at the door to her mother's office. Adara had closed the door after receiving a call, but Gia could still make out her mother's side of the exchange.

"No, no, we haven't been able to retrieve it yet," she said, sounding more confident than she was. Gia knew that the man on the other line made her mother nervous, more nervous than Gia had ever seen her before. The young shape shifter didn't care. She was happy to while away the hours doing whatever she wished.

"I sent my best operative out last night and word has it the protectors have found the one you spoke of," Adara reported before going silent again as the person on the other end spoke. Gia glanced up at the sound of a distinctive clicking. Onyx was striding down the vast hallway in her alligator skin boots. A suede cowboy hat sat on top of her long dishwater blonde hair. She wore a sleeveless tan shirt with a bucking bronco design on it and low rise, dark stonewash jeans. She had holsters on her hips, which she frequently rested her hands on. Onyx had never quite left the Old West, and still fancied herself an old-fashioned gunslinger. She kept her look updated just enough so that she would never stand out in a crowd and only wore her guns visibly when around fellow assassins.

"Yee-haw," Gia commented, knowing it would get

under Onyx's skin. Sure enough, Onyx glared at her and tapped the butt of one of her guns. Gia smirked and went back to filing her nails. She preferred the modern socialite fashion — pinks and flesh tones and plenty of bare skin.

"Ooh, someone's in a mood. Must not have been a good night," Gia taunted, balancing the small pink nail file between her two index fingers.

"I cannot wait until this territory is under new management. Less deadweight," Onyx mused. "Is your mother around?"

"She's on the phone," Gia replied, pausing as she looked back to her file. "With our mysterious new client."

Onyx smiled and Gia studied her, knowing the assassin had more information about the client than she did. It bugged her to no end. Running her thumb over her bottom lip, Onyx shifted her weight a little.

"Poor little Gia. I fear your days are numbered," she spoke as though thinking out loud. Gia glanced at her, swallowing, which made Onyx's feral smile grow. The younger shape shifter opened her mouth to reply when a slamming door interrupted her. Adara stormed out of her office, striding across the hall to her chair.

"You, off," she ordered Gia. Gia rolled her eyes and swung her legs off the chair, standing aside so her mother could take her place. Adara stepped up to the chair, but didn't sit, turning her eyes to Onyx.

"I take it your new client isn't pleased with your lack of progress on the job," Onyx commented, crossing her arms over her chest.

"Choose your words carefully, Onyx," Adara warned and Onyx merely raised an eyebrow at the response.

"He doesn't have an endless store of patience, Adara," Onyx continued. "You worry about starting a war with the protectors, but you should be much more concerned with leaving your client dissatisfied. He has more power and sway than the protectors could ever dream of."

"I don't need you to tell me how to do my job or what to be concerned about."

"Well, apparently you do, seeing as how you're the one who brought this cancer upon us in the first place," Onyx was quick to point out.

"And here I thought you fearless," Adara replied. "Cowardice is not advisable in this line of work, Onyx."

Onyx chuckled, sticking her tongue against the inside of her cheek. "Neither is arrogance. I have enough sense to recognize a danger. Were it up to me, I wouldn't have gotten involved with the Grenich Corporation in the first place. But since he's already wormed his way into this territory, I'm sure as hell going to make sure I remain on his good side. I would advise you to do the same."

Gia scoffed. "He's a fool if he challenges an assassin leader."

Onyx pointed at Gia. "That right there, that's going to get both of you killed."

"Be silent unless you're asked to speak," Adara hissed at Gia, who rolled her eyes again and leaned back against the wall.

"He has informed me that the Key will be at the museum tonight," Adara explained. "I want the two of you to retrieve it."

"Is that what he requested?" Onyx asked,

furrowing her brow suspiciously.

"That is what *I'm* requesting," Adara stated in a tone that suggested the matter wasn't up for discussion. "Need I remind you that your loyalty is to me, not him?"

Onyx half-smiled and shook her head. "And you want me to drag your daughter along for what? Punishment?"

Gia looked back to her nails, bored. "Don't blame me for your parents not breeding outside the immediate family."

"Careful, child. Killing you would be the highlight of an otherwise lackluster week," Onyx threatened.

"You wouldn't dare," Gia replied with a smirk.

"Enough!" Adara's shout echoed throughout the halls, causing the windows to shudder in their frames. Both women turned their attention back to her and Onyx shifted her weight a little. The sunlight that beamed in through the many windows captured the dancing dust particles as they drifted about in space. Adara glared at them once more before turning on her heel and storming back into her office.

"You two will do this and if you question me again, you'll need to find a new territory to work in," she threatened without turning around. She slammed the door behind her. Onyx turned and walked back down the long hallway, disappearing out the front door.

Gia shrugged and sauntered in the opposite direction. Her hollowed steps echoed through the hall until she reached her room and entered it. The manor fell silent once again as she closed her door.

~~*~*~*

"What were you thinking?"

Isis opened her mouth to respond to Jet's demand.

"Don't answer that."

Her mouth snapped shut again as she watched him. He was so rigid that he was almost shaking with anger. The morning sun beamed down on them, creating a halo around Jet. He paced behind his desk while Isis sat in the plain black chair across from him, her long legs crossed at the knee. Ever since the trip to Dionysia the previous night, he had been positively livid with the Four. He had already spoken to the other three and now it was Isis' turn in the hot seat. She ran a hand through her brown hair, waiting for his next words.

"I would *really* like to know what was running through your head," Jet continued. "Do you have some kind of death wish?"

"In my defense, it wasn't my idea. In case you hadn't noticed, I'm not exactly a fan of crowds…or people in general," Isis replied. "And in Shae's defense, we have been training for over two months and I think we all needed a change of scenery. Plus, there were four of us."

"Outnumbering isn't always the best strategy. Remington has taught you that," Jet pointed out, the anger never ebbing from his voice. Isis ran her tongue over her teeth, doing her best not to lose her temper.

"Look, you're the one who uprooted me from my life and dragged me into all this insanity because of some prophecy," Isis countered. "If anyone in this room should be pissed, it should be me."

She had decided not to mention Coop to Jet or the other three. It would just cause them unnecessary worry and probably more interrogation. Jet stared at her for a moment, a myriad of emotions crossing his face.

"If you pull another stunt like that there will be repercussions," Jet warned, his stern voice telling her that he was not playing around. He sat down and looked at the file on the desk.

"Fine," she grumbled. "Can I go now?"

Jet waved his hand, gesturing that she could leave. She uncrossed her legs and left the study without another word.

Jet glanced up and watched her leave. She was getting very bold, much like her mother and sister. Jet shook his head, looking back down at the file in front of him. Her stride was so graceful, especially when she sauntered. The more skills she acquired, the more like a shape shifter she became. *The grace of a guardian, the tenacity of a shape shifter, and the stubbornness of her mother,* Jet thought with a quiet sigh.

At that moment, Lilly Appeared beside Jet in a bright flash of golden light. The air sparkled for a moment after her appearance.

"She is so much like Passion. It's going to get her into trouble," Jet observed as he sat back. Lilly sat on the arm rest of the computer chair, wrapping one arm around his shoulders as she traced his jaw line with the back of her free hand. The sunlight danced about their heads, illuminating everything within the medium-sized room.

"I don't know. She seems to be able to handle herself," Lilly replied with a small smile.

"I'm sending them to the museum ball tonight to look around," Jet said, reading the question in his wife's eyes

"For the flashdrive?" Lilly asked.

Jet nodded in response. "I spoke with Sly earlier. She has it on good authority that the Key will be somewhere in the museum, in something that looks ancient."

"This is according to her sources?" Lilly asked.

Jet nodded. "She may be a pain to deal with, but as you've pointed out, her information is usually accurate. Most of what we know about this thing is because of her."

"Yet you're still troubled," Lilly observed. Jet leaned forward, resting his elbows on the desk. He rubbed his hands together.

"I've been thinking about what Remington told me and the more I think about the flashdrive theory, the less sense it makes," he thought out loud. Lilly stood from the chair and sat on the desk instead, looking to her troubled husband.

"How so?"

"Supposedly it overrides any program, deciphers any language or code, and slips past any security program. Working on that theory, it can access any computer in the world and it turns up here? Why not some big city? Certainly it would be more useful there," Jet explained and leaned back, twisting the chair back and forth. "And why is Adara only concerned about it now?"

"You think the flashdrive is part of something bigger?" Lilly asked.

"I think the damn thing might be some kind of diversion," Jet responded. "And I think it's being used to stir up unrest among the assassins and direct our actions to a certain extent."

"It's not outside the realm of possibility," Lilly

agreed. "I still feel we should try to retrieve the flashdrive, if only to ensure it not be used for more nefarious purposes."

Jet nodded. "I agree. The flashdrive is still a powerful tool, one that we cannot allow to fall in the wrong hands. And I'm not comfortable with the possibility of an assassin coup. As reprehensible as Adara is, she is the devil we know. She brings a certain amount of stability to the assassins and she doesn't want a war with the protectors or other shape shifter factions."

Lilly was quiet for a moment. "I am concerned about the possibility of this being another trap or a setup."

Jet shook his head. "I considered that, but there are just too many witnesses. I think that this flashdrive has served its purpose and whoever created it probably wants to retrieve it. This could be a chance to catch a glimpse of whoever is behind all of this."

"You're sure about this?"

"As sure as I can be," he replied as he sorted through some papers on his desk. He picked up the phone and pressed the intercom button.

"Remington?"

"Yes, Jet," Remington's clear brogue came from the other end.

"Send them in."

"Right away, sir."

Two minutes later the four women were in his study. Isis looked the least thrilled to already be back inside the room. He pretended not to notice as he opened a file in front of him.

"Okay, I assume you have all been briefed on this

flashdrive," Jet began. "According to some reliable sources, it's been dropped at the museum and is hidden in something very old. The four of you are going to retrieve it before anyone else can. You'll be attending the annual fundraising ball tonight; dress formally. We have contacts working in the museum, so you will be able to move about freely but be sure to exercise caution all the same. You will be in constant communication with these," he explained as he set four ear coms on the desk.

"You're not going to turn into a mouse, are you?" Shae teased. "I could just carry you around in a fancy handbag."

"Shae, this isn't a joke," he stated. "Be on your guard. Onyx and possibly Gia could be there as well. There is still unrest among the assassins."

Jade brushed some dark hair behind her ear at the mention of Gia and Jet could tell from the small motion that she did not like the idea of running into her former ally.

"Where exactly is it? You only said that it is hidden in something very old. We're going to be in a museum. Practically everything in that place is ancient," Jade put in after being silent for a moment.

"You'll have to look for something that doesn't belong, which I realize will probably be difficult. I wish I could give you more to go on," Jet said. "According to our contacts, the museum just acquired some new artifacts recently, which they're in the process of preparing for display. I recommend looking through those first."

"The source is Sly, isn't it?" Jade said, looking up from the file she had picked up off the desk.

"Could you three excuse us for a minute?" Jet

asked. Isis and Shae were the first two out of the room. Jet could already hear Shae teasing Isis about dressing formally. He glanced over to Lilly, who was studying Jade.

Jade tilted the chair back and stuck her thumbs in her brown pants. She was wearing an olive-colored top with a tree of life design on it. She looked to them expectantly with her dark eyes. Jet moved around the desk so that he was across from her and next to Lilly. He rested his weight on the sturdy surface and folded his arms over his chest.

"We need to know that you're all right to go on this mission," Jet began. "We know Gia was your teammate and we know how you feel about betrayal."

"You two don't need to worry. I'm fine. Really," Jade replied. "I've been doing this a long time and I know what comes with the territory."

"Jade, are you absolutely certain?" Lilly asked. "If you wanted to hang back, we would understand."

"Nah, someone has to keep those three in line and out of trouble," Jade said with a small grin. Lilly exchanged a look with Jet, smiling. There were few shape shifters as dependable as Jade and the two were beyond grateful that she was part of the Four.

~~*~*~*

Jade and Shae walked in the front door of the ball at eight-thirty, Jade wore black pants and a white top with a tasteful draping neckline. Shae wore something similar, but her top was gold. Alex and Isis went in through the loading dock, let in by a flustered-looking woman in a nice business suit.

"Elevator to the second floor is this way," Alex

muttered under her breath, gesturing for Isis to follow her. As she followed her teammate, Isis glanced over at Alex, wondering if she should try to strike up a conversation. The only thing the two of them had in common was that they were both people of few words who had a love for books. Alex was much more into history and historical accounts than Isis, who preferred novels.

"Visual sweep confirms what the contacts suggested: security's pretty tight up front and in back, but it's weak on the side," Shae's voice crackled through the static in their earpieces.

"Typical," said Alex as they paused in front of the elevator. She pressed the button and glanced over at Isis. "You know the plan, right? No sightseeing, we need to be as quick as possible."

"Uh huh," Isis replied as she waited for the elevator car to arrive. The door slid open and the two women stepped inside. Alex pressed the button and the door closed again. As the car started to ascend, Isis turned her eyes to her feet and shifted her weight a little.

"You don't need to be nervous. Jet and Lilly's sources are solid," Alex commented. "This will likely be a boring mission."

"Yeah, I'm new to the whole world of espionage or whatever the hell you call this," Isis replied. "You've probably been on hundreds of missions before. I bet this is routine for you."

"Actually, it's my first time in the field."

Isis looked over at her teammate, surprised. "What? Really?"

Alex scoffed. "No!"

The door slid open and the two women stepped

out onto the darkened second floor. There were a few pools of light, illuminating various artifacts and it was eerily desolate.

Isis looked around, never having been in a museum after hours. There was no room for error on this "trip," but she felt woefully unqualified and unprepared for such an expedition. Isis noticed she was in the Egyptian wing of the museum.

"I'll look left, you take right," Alex whispered as she moved off in the opposite direction. Isis swallowed and let out her breath, heading deeper into the shadows. Everything smelled old and it was quiet throughout the upper floor. Soft pale light spilled over the various artifacts that sat behind glass. The artifacts stared with dead eyes at whoever passed their exhibit. There were many kinds of intricate urns and exquisite sarcophagi recreations. Out of the corner of her eye, Isis thought she saw a figure but when she turned, there was nothing. She let out her breath, suppressing a shudder. This place was giving her the creeps.

"Found your namesake yet?" Alex's humorless voice crackled in her ear.

"Fairly certain the guardians would take offense to that," Isis muttered. "I haven't found anything. Nothing stands out and I don't see anything that could contain a flashdrive."

"Me neither," Alex replied, falling silent for a moment. "Neither did Jade or Shae. Looks like this outing might be a bust."

A thought struck Isis as she looked down at her feet. "What if we're looking in the wrong place?"

"What?" Alex asked.

"It's kept where ancient things are but doesn't

belong, or something like that, right?" Isis thought out loud. She stopped moving in front of a photograph of archeologists with pyramids in the background.

"Yeah, and…?" Alex replied, the static crackling even more.

"What do they keep in the basement?" Isis asked after a moment, glancing behind her. She really didn't like this place, it reminded her too much of the night she had almost been killed.

"It's for storage mostly. And I think there are some restoration rooms down there," Alex replied. "Might be worth a look."

"I'm on it," Isis quickly volunteered as she began moving toward where the stairs were, thankful to get out of the shadowy surroundings.

"Just be careful and make sure you don't attract attention," Alex sighed and Isis almost smiled at the resignation in her tone.

Isis crept to the stairs that would lead to the first floor of the museum, using every skill Electra had taught her about remaining invisible to unwanted attention. She was most worried about the guard who would probably be positioned on the stairwell. When she reached the stairs, Isis peered over the banister, shocked by whom she saw.

Coop, the man from the club, was standing at the bottom of the stairwell. He was wearing a red security uniform. He really looked the part; he even had a walkie-talkie. Isis didn't know what to do. Running into him was a little too convenient to merely be a coincidence. Suddenly, he looked up to where she was and nodded his head, beckoning her to come down. Isis had the unsettling feeling that he had known what was happening on the second floor all along. She swallowed and made her way down the stairs, never taking her eyes off Coop. There was no point in hiding if he already knew she was there. If she went down, there was the possibility of fighting her way past him. It was risky, but it was the only option open to her.

"Are you stalking me?" Isis demanded when she reached the bottom of the stairs, glancing around to make sure nobody had seen her. Luckily for her, the people were too busy talking about themselves to care about her or the security guard.

"Why would you think that?" the man asked, his gaze glued to the crowd of people.

"Because you turn up everywhere I go—"

"You could be stalking me," he was quick to counter as his eyes scanned the well-dressed crowd.

"*And* you appear to know an awful lot about me, whereas I know next to nothing about you," Isis finished, smiling and nodding at a few random people who walked past them.

"Believe me, Ms. Benson, I'm not stalking you," Coop answered, suddenly tilting his head down as if he were hiding from somebody. Isis frowned at his strange behavior, ignoring Alex's constant inquiring about her position.

"What are you doing?" Isis asked. Coop glanced up, became very rigid, and turned his gaze away again.

"I can't talk right now," he whispered. "But there is much you need to be informed of. I'll call you when I can. Be careful on this mission, Ms. Benson. You're not the only one looking for the flashdrive."

"You don't have my…" Isis trailed off when Coop hurried away, vanishing from her sight, "number.

OK."

She glanced back toward the crowd where he had been looking and noticed a very chicly dressed and obviously very wealthy man look away. A few people walked hurriedly past her, but Isis didn't pay them any heed. She had a mission to complete and didn't feel like staying in the museum one minute longer than she had to.

"Isis, I'm going to lift an ID badge off one of the employees," Jade's voice filtered through her earpiece. "There are a few in attendance tonight. I'll pass it to you before you reach the door."

Isis swallowed and started making her way through the crowd, doing her best to remain inconspicuous. She slipped by people, careful not to bump into anybody. The tiled floor was slick and Isis mentally swore about a million times on her way toward the entrance to the basement. Spotting Jade out of the corner of her eye, Isis continued moving toward a darker hallway. Jade was moving confidently through the crowd, a flute of champagne in her right hand. Isis swallowed as the older protector got closer until she passed in front of Isis and the younger woman felt a slick card pressed into her palm. Both women continued moving in separate directions.

Isis looked over her shoulder to make sure no one was watching before she stepped over a thick rope and moved into an unlit hall of exhibitions. The door to the lower levels was tucked away where two different halls met. Isis found the door and swiped the badge through the slot, watching as the light went from red to green and the door clicked open. Isis pushed the heavy door and slipped inside, freezing when the hallway automatically lit up.

"Please tell me I didn't just set off an alarm," Isis hissed into her earpiece, not moving from where she stood in front of the door.

"No, you're still clear. The lights in the lower levels are automatic, but security is fairly lax," Alex reassured her. "The more advanced systems are on the first and second floors. They're trying to get funding to install a better security system. Try to stay out of the artifact storage section. I know there are a couple security cameras in there and we don't have the resources with us to get around them."

Isis let out a breath of relief and started to make her way down the bright hallway. There were few smells in the air — just chemicals and hints of dust. She coughed, not enjoying the overly sterile environment, and she almost wished she were back at the mansion.

Isis entered a bright room with window walls. Inside there was an enormous table with a light built into it. Some artifacts were laid around the table, obviously being worked on, judging from the small tools and bottles on the table. Isis was instantly suspicious of the scene, which was a little too perfect. Moving to the windowed door, she rolled her eyes when she found an obstacle.

"Don't suppose anyone knows the code for the restoration room?" she grumbled into her earpiece, massaging her brow.

"Try 07-04-17-76," Jade's voice answered. Isis tilted her head and allowed herself a half-smile as she entered in the code.

"Ooh, I smell a story," Shae's eager voice filtered through the earpiece.

"Dated a restoration expert who works here a

while back," Jade replied. "Lovely woman, very underappreciated in her job."

"Well, I hope we don't get her in trouble," Isis mentioned as the number pad switched to green and the door unlocked. She pulled on the door, her eyes widening a little in surprise at how heavy it was.

"Nah, the museum is small and everyone has the same codes. Alex wasn't lying about the poor state of security in the lower levels. Thieves *love* this place."

Isis entered the room and leaned down, removing her shoes, which she placed in the door to keep it ajar. She glanced around the enormous room, her heart sinking a little when she saw just how many objects there were on the table. *Well this fucking sucks,* she thought as she approached the brightly lit table and rested her gloved hands on the edge. Her eyes wandered over the objects as she tried to rule out various possibilities, drumming her fingers as she considered what to do. A gleam in her peripheral vision drew her attention to the right.

A large tome was placed on one of the shelves off to the side, behind glass. Isis moved over to it and pulled open the door, reaching in and taking the book from its pedestal. There were words etched into the cover in a language Isis didn't recognize. She brought it over to the table, placing it under a lighted magnifying glass, which she switched on.

"So, guys, what are the rules about damaging a potentially priceless artifact?" Isis asked as she examined the tome.

"Um, try not to do that," Jade replied. *Might not have a choice,* Isis thought as she raised her eyebrows. Looking around the room, she noticed a set of cabinets nearby. Approaching it, Isis started opening drawers and soon found a set of scalpels. Pulling one out, Isis went back to the table and turned her attention to the book, carefully running the scalpel's sharp blade around the edge of the thick cover. Peeling the aged page back, Isis felt her face fall when she found nothing. Spinning the scalpel around in her fingers, she carefully turned the heavy book over and examined the back cover. Repeating the same action, she peeled the page away from the cover. Nestled in the center of the thick cover was a tiny flashdrive, smaller than any Isis had ever encountered.

Isis pulled the flashdrive out and examined it, wondering how the hell someone had managed to conceal it so well and why. Something about the flashdrive itself was strange, though she couldn't quite put her finger on what. It was just a feeling. Twisting it around to look at the back, Isis froze and felt her blood go cold at what she saw.

Etched into the top was the same symbol she had seen in the warehouse, drawn in a murdered woman's blood. *No. No freaking way,* Isis thought as she examined the small flashdrive under the light. Palming the flashdrive, Isis slipped it into a small pocket in her pants.

A sudden grip on the back of her neck and one on her wrist pulled Isis out of her thoughts and her face was slammed into the table. Before she had a chance to recover, Isis was tossed against the bookshelves. She had never been hit so hard before and for a moment, Isis was dazed.

She was barely able to dodge out of the way of the fist speeding toward her face. Isis wound up behind her attacker and lashed out with the scalpel that was still in her hand. The person moved faster than her and managed to avoid the slash, leaning forward and striking back with a kick that knocked Isis against the table again. Isis ducked under another kick and backed up a few steps, holding the scalpel in a defensive position. Blood was crawling down the side of her face from a cut on her brow and Isis swiped at it with her free hand.

Isis felt her eyes widen a little when she recognized the woman Coop had pointed out at the club: Onyx. *Well shit,* Isis thought as she tried to figure out how the hell she managed to attract so much trouble. If she managed to survive this, there was no doubt in her mind that Shae would never let her hear the end of it. It was then Isis noticed Onyx was holding her earpiece, which she closed her fist around and crushed.

"You're quick on your feet, baby protector," Onyx complimented, running her fingers along the edge of the table as she approached Isis. "I must admit, I'm a little disappointed. I thought one with guardian blood would be taller. Perhaps a little more sparkly."

"Yeah well, I thought such a feared assassin would be decked out in leather or have an eyepatch or something," Isis responded, making sure to keep space between them as she continued backing up. "Life's full of disappointments."

Onyx smirked and then bolted forward, pulling herself up on the table and sliding across it, striking at Isis with a strong kick. Isis barely managed to leap out of the way, but was struck by the follow-up kick, which sent her crashing into a wheeling table. Isis grabbed a tray off the table and hurled it at Onyx, who slapped it away. She leapt off the table and ran at Isis, striking at her with a strong punch. Isis leaned away and pushed the punch past her, attempting to kick the assassin away. Onyx raised a knee, successfully blocking the kick, and pushed off the wall, striking Isis with a strong elbow.

Isis soon found herself on the table with Onyx's strong hand wrapped around her throat, strangling her. Isis clawed at Onyx's arm, trying to break the solid grip.

"This isn't personal, you know," Onyx growled from behind gritted teeth. "I don't like destroying unique things, but unfortunately, someone is paying good money for the Key's retrieval."

Isis gagged as she continued trying to break the tight grip, kicking at the woman's legs. She couldn't believe that she was actually going to die like this.

Just when Isis was sure she would pass out, Onyx's head was violently yanked back and Isis saw the gleam of a blade pressed against her throat.

"Let her go," a smoky voice ordered, pulling her head back further. "Now."

To Isis' shock, Onyx's grip on her throat slowly loosened and then disappeared. She rolled to the side, coughing and gasping as she struggled to get her breath back. Her vision was still hazy and for a moment, Isis worried she would lose consciousness. She raised her eyes and watched as the tall figure, concealed by a gray hoodie, dragged Onyx to the door and shoved her against the wall.

"Run along back to whatever master you serve, unless you wish for me to color the walls with your blood," the figure growled. Onyx glared at the figure for a moment, her yellow eyes flashing with rage.

"Do not test me, child," the figure threatened, rotating the knife around a few times with a fast wrist movement. Onyx smirked, her gaze sliding back to Isis.

"Until we meet again, baby protector," she called to her. Then she turned and disappeared down the hall. The figure turned back to Isis, who was still coughing and gagging as she attempted to get her breath back. In a few long strides, he was standing in front of her. Grabbing her hair, he pulled her head back and she almost fell over again. Grimacing in pain, Isis glared into his cold green eyes. Though the hood was up and the bottom part of his face was hidden behind some kind of mask, she could see he had reddish hair and a medium build. Doing her best to pick out distinguishing features, Isis continued holding his gaze.

"Where is it?" he demanded, pressing the sharp blade against her throat.

"Bit counterintuitive, isn't it? To save me only to kill me?" she managed to gasp out.

The man's eyes seemed to light up a little before he plunged the knife's sharp blade down between two of her fingers, causing her to flinch.

"You seem to be operating under the assumption that I care whether you live or die. I can assure you that I do not," he explained. "The flashdrive now. I won't ask again."

Isis remained silent and made no move to comply with his demands. Inside she felt a little frightened, but she was determined not to back down. The man shook his head as he pulled the knife out of the table, swiping the blade over her leg. Isis flinched when she heard the fabric tear and out of the corner of her eye, she saw the man hold out his hand and catch the flashdrive when it dropped out of the tear.

"Hey!" she snapped.

"You're brave, I'll give you that," he remarked as he slipped the flashdrive into a pocket in his hoodie. "But bravery is sometimes synonymous with foolishness."

"I'm not alone and I will personally hunt you to the ends of the Earth to get that flashdrive back," Isis swore, mentally kicking herself for the lame threat.

"I'll be sure to watch my back," the man replied in a tone that suggested he wasn't all that worried about her warning. He was about to leave, but paused and squinted at her. Using the blade of his knife, the mysterious man pulled Isis' charm out of her shirt and brought it closer to his face so that he could see it better. For a moment, Isis was scared he would demand she hand it over, but then he let it drop again and moved to the door of the room. Isis watched as he shifted into a black fox and then dashed off down the hall. Intending to give chase, Isis hopped off the table only to fall to the ground when her legs refused to support her.

Hearing Shae call her name, Isis groaned and rested her back against one of the windowed walls. She had a feeling she was going to get an earful for this incident.

~~*~*~*

Jet looked around the woods. The trees shot up toward the clear afternoon sky, dappling the sunlight on the dirt ground. Somewhere nearby, Jet could hear a babbling brook. He snarled to himself as he continued to look around, ignoring his peaceful surroundings. He was looking for Sly and he was beyond furious.

"Sly!" he yelled. His voice bounced off the trees and echoed back to him, startling any woodland creature that heard it. Jet continued looking around until he found her. She was sitting high up in a tree looking out over the forest. The sun fell on her, bringing out the sparkle of the dark blue backless top she wore. One denim-covered leg was pulled up so that it rested beneath her chin. Her other leg dangled off the branch, swaying back and forth, a clear indication that she was deep in thought. Her sleek black hair fell about her face, concealing it from him. Her expressive green eyes were blank as they fixed on the horizon.

"Do I even need to ask?" Jet called up to her. She glanced down to him, grinning.

"I do love hearing about the shenanigans you assume I get into," she retorted, a little displeased with her peace and quiet being interrupted.

Jet scowled. "Where is it?"

Sly stretched out so that she lay on her stomach on the thick branch, letting out a relaxed sigh as she ran her fingers over the bark.

"Say please," she taunted.

"Dammit, Sly!"

Sly got to her feet and leapt out of the tree, landing weightlessly on the dirt ground in a crouch, absorbing the impact in her knees. If a human had jumped from the height she had, they would have broken their legs.

"I don't have it," Sly answered as she straightened up and smoothed her jeans.

"Really?" Jet replied, not believing her for a second. Sly looked up at him, fury flashing in her eyes. Jet didn't often get a reaction out of her, but she would not tolerate being called a liar.

"Believe what you want, but in case you hadn't noticed, we're in a forest. There aren't a lot of outlets out here. Why the hell would I want a flashdrive?" she said, pointing out the obvious. "Especially one that assassins have such a keen interest in?"

Money or power, Jet thought before responding, "Who took it then?"

"Ah, now you believe me. Interesting." Sly arched an eyebrow as she began to walk deeper into the forest, touching each tree she passed. Jet knew he had offended her, and as a result she would be even more difficult. *If that's even possible,* he thought.

"Sly," Jet warned as he followed her.

"I don't know. I didn't see them," Sly answered as she hopped over a large log.

"You didn't see them?" Jet repeated, already knowing Sly had followed the Four to the museum. The mysterious woman seemed to be everywhere, hiding in the shadows. Jet couldn't think of one human contact who had ever seen Sly. It wouldn't surprise him if no human had ever seen her. She didn't trust humans and avoided them as much as possible.

"It was a very dark night and whoever it was obviously knew what they were doing," Sly answered with a hint of annoyance, not happy that someone had escaped even her attention.

"I'm not joking, Sly," Jet warned.

Sly turned to face him, her eyes serious. "Neither am I."

They stared at each other for another beat, and then Sly shifted into a leopard. Her muscles stretched and contracted, her pale flesh swiftly changed into beautifully spotted fur. Her expressive green eyes changed into round yellow ones. Her hands and feet expanded and formed into gigantic paws. The transformation took about thirty seconds and then she jogged off with a quiet growl, disappearing into the depths of the forest she called home.

~~*~*~*

"Are you absolutely sure that's all you could see?"

Isis sat on the desk, her back to Jet. He had already asked that question at least a hundred times. Even Jade shook her head and put her face in her hand.

"Yes, for the millionth time," Isis answered. "He was wearing a mask on the bottom of his face. I only saw his eyes and a bit of his hair, everything else was covered."

"Her throat was pretty badly bruised, Jet," Jade put in. "She had been in quite a scuffle."

Jet shook his head, troubled. "It just doesn't make sense. I don't know of any new assassins in this territory, certainly none with that particular modus operandi. It definitely wasn't one of you. Sly claims it wasn't her. Anyone else would have used the flashdrive by now."

"Is it possible that humans could have found out about it? They've been known to act irrationally when trying to acquire more power," Alex commented nonchalantly, but there was a hint of bitterness in her voice. Isis looked over to her, surprised by the rare sign of emotion from her normally reserved teammate.

"No," Jet answered, but he was beginning to wonder whether or not people did actually know about the flashdrive.

"Sly probably knows more than she's letting on. I'll talk with her when I next see her, maybe get some more information," Jade offered. Isis leaned back a little, interested in the mysterious source. Whenever her name came up, it was usually accompanied by irritation or exasperation. *She must have some damn valuable information,* Isis thought, more curious than ever about the elusive Sly.

Jet sat with his hands clasped together, touching his mouth in thought. They had lost the flashdrive the previous night and he had just returned from meeting with Sly. The air in the corner of the study began to shimmer and Electra Appeared, looking around the room.

"I take it things didn't go as planned," she observed.

"Yes, that's why I called on Adonia," Jet responded. "Do the guardians know what happened?"

Electra shrugged. "I've been told that we're as stumped as you."

"Is it possible that one of the guardians is against us?" Alex asked. Isis looked over to Shae, who was tossing a blue racquetball up in the air and catching it. She was unusually quiet.

"I doubt it. Our guards can sense evil intentions. A traitor would be in the dungeons before they knew what grabbed them," Electra responded as she leaned against the wall behind her and lifted one foot up to rest on it.

"Could the guardians even use it?" Isis asked her twin.

"We could, but I don't think we would. Guardians

are not really into technology in the Meadows," Electra replied as she brushed a hand through her hair.

"Why did this mystery person tie up Onyx but not Isis?"

Everyone looked up as Lilly entered the room.

"It was probably someone who had a grudge against Onyx, or maybe even Adara. They're both assassins after all. Both have their fair share of enemies," Jet replied. "Whoever it was, he probably didn't see Isis as a threat."

"Gee thanks," Isis muttered. Shae snickered as she continued to toss the ball up and down.

"Yes, but why not kill her?" Lilly pointed out. "I don't think we should overlook that he did technically save her, even though he did also steal the flashdrive. I can't think of any assassin who would do that. If he were an assassin, letting Onyx kill Isis would be an easier way of getting the flashdrive."

"If he were so concerned about my safety, he shouldn't have threatened to kill me," Isis stated bitterly as she hopped off the desk. She walked over to one of the shelves in the office and ran her slender fingers over the blue bindings of the books.

"Does it really count as a threat if you were already half-dead, ice queen?" Shae chuckled, laughing even more at the withering glare Isis gave her.

Jet got up and moved to the door. He walked down the large hall, heading for the library. Lilly exited behind him, following him into the first floor of the gigantic library, and watched him for a moment as he examined one of the bookshelves.

"Jet, is it possible that he's back?"

He frowned and looked over at her. "Who?"

"Roan," Lilly answered, glancing over her shoulder. "You must admit, Isis' description did sound rather similar to him. And he would be bold enough to challenge Adara's leadership. After all, this territory originally belonged to him."

Jet turned his gaze back to the books in front of him. "Anything is possible, but I very much doubt it. If it had been Roan, he would have killed Onyx *and* Isis. Mercy wasn't exactly something he was known for."

Lilly moved over to an elegant red chair and sat, resting her arms upon the curved arm rests. The sun beamed down upon them from the windows, casting light throughout the library. Jet turned to face his wife, noticing the concerned expression on her beautiful face.

"Lilly, it's all right," Jet reassured her, wishing he believed his own words.

~~*~*~*

Electra and Isis watched Shae and Jade practice sparring in the boxing ring. Alex sat off to the side, listening to her iPod while flipping through a large book about sword fighting techniques. Her head was bobbing as hard rock music thundered in her ears.

"Isis, would you like learn to Appear?" Electra asked, turning to face her sister.

Isis shrugged in response. "I guess. Does Passion want to meet me or something?"

"She does, but she won't admit it."

Isis' ringing cell phone interrupted their conversation. She frowned, not recognizing the number displayed on the screen. After a moment of debate, Isis answered the call, holding the phone to her ear. Shae had taken her to get a new one a couple weeks ago, insisting that her cousin have at least some form of modern communication.

"Whoever this is, I'm not interested in whatever you're selling," Isis answered.

"Hello Ms. Benson. I'm not selling anything," a masculine voice came from the other end of the line. Isis squinted, trying to place where she knew the voice from. The caller had a weird way of speaking, as if words didn't feel natural in his mouth. There was nothing but silence in the background, leading Isis to believe that the caller was in a room in his home or a very quiet office.

"Who the hell is this?" she asked, giving up trying to identify the voice.

"It's Coop from the club—"

"Oh Christ, you have *got* to be kidding me," Isis grumbled as she ran a hand over her face. She was definitely not in the mood to deal with him.

There was a short pause before Coop finished, "And at the museum last night. Apologies, have I upset you?"

"You somehow managed to get a hold of a relatively new number, so yeah. It's a bit concerning, seeing as how I'm fairly certain you've strayed into stalking territory at this point."

Electra looked at her twin, frowning. Isis waved her hand, indicating that she would explain the strange conversation later.

Coop was quiet again for a moment. "I see. I'm afraid I do not know how to remedy the situation."

Isis leaned back a little. "You can drop the man of mystery act and just tell me why you keep approaching me. Or you could leave me alone. Either option works for me."

"Right. Well, the information I have, which would interest you, is not exactly something that should be discussed over the phone. However, I know you would be unlikely to agree to an in-person meeting due to the high rate of assault and murder of women who meet with strangers, particularly men."

Isis took the phone away from her ear and stared at it for a moment. "You don't talk to a lot of women, do you?"

"Interacting with people in general isn't something I often do," he admitted and she heard a sound like a foot scuffing the floor. Isis raised an eyebrow, somewhat intrigued. She wasn't about to agree to a meeting with the man, but there was something about him that made her think there was a story behind his strange mannerisms. *Maybe he's a Martian,* she thought.

"Coop, unless—"

"The symbol you've seen, on the flashdrive and at the warehouse — you won't find it in any book," he stated. Isis instantly straightened up.

"What? What do you know about—?"

"I have to go. I'll contact you again if I can."

"No, Coop, don't you dare," Isis swore loudly when the call disconnected, tossing the phone to the side. "God dammit!"

She ran her hands over her short hair, closing her eyes and exhaling through her nose. Isis was frustrated with the lack of answers about the simple symbol. It was a damn symbol, an explanation of it shouldn't have been so difficult to find. Opening her eyes again, she noticed Electra was staring at her, concerned.

"Who was that?" she asked, her tone cautious.

"Some guy I've run into a couple times, who is very strange," Isis answered. "He might have had an answer about that symbol I keep encountering, but he's fucking weird and overdramatic and hung up before giving me any kind of concrete answer."

Isis noticed Electra's eyes were practically bugging out of her head and dismissively waved her hand to assuage her concern. "Don't worry. I have no plans to meet with him and I don't think he's all that dangerous."

"Are you sure? Isis, there are a lot of—"

"Dangers out there," Isis finished the lecture she had heard a million times over. "Yeah, Electra, I understand. If I run into him again, I'll point him out to the others and you can deal with him however you see fit. Okay?"

Electra nodded in agreement, deciding to change the topic. "You want to learn how to Appear now?"

Isis hopped up to her feet. "Sure."

"All right, we'll try a short distance first," Electra started, glancing around. "How about the boxing ring?"

"Fine by me," Isis replied. She was eager to do something that had nothing to do with mysterious men. Anything to take her mind off the weirdness that was her new life.

"Okay, you'll feel a little weird the first time. Your temperature will go up and you'll feel a tingle throughout your body, similar to an electric shock but not painful at all, and it will be very bright. First, close your eyes and block everything else out," Electra instructed. "Then focus on the ring."

Electra closed her eyes and a bright silver light

consumed her. The air shimmered about her when she disappeared and reappeared in the boxing ring in a split second. She opened her eyes and turned back to Isis.

"Now you try it."

Isis stared at her for a moment, suddenly regretting agreeing to this. After a moment, she closed her eyes and concentrated, blocking out everything else around her. She heard a strange noise, almost like glass being broken but much less harsh. The noise was pleasant and had an almost musical quality to it. A strange tingling traveled throughout her body and it suddenly looked like she had walked into the sun as brightness consumed her. Isis became incredibly warm and felt her short hair whip about around her. When the light dimmed, she cautiously opened one eye.

"Oh, are you absolutely fucking kidding me?" she muttered under her breath, opening her eyes. Isis looked around, and realized she was definitely not in the boxing ring.

To her left there was a large green forest, welcoming and beautiful. To her right there were many hills with a bright light shining behind them. She could hear water behind her and golden grass surrounded her. Isis was never one to panic, but she had never thought it possible to stumble into another dimension. She turned around a couple times, taking in her surroundings.

Where am I? Isis wondered.

CHAPTER TEN

There was nobody with Isis. She was completely alone...or at least she hoped she was completely alone. Running a slender hand through her short dark hair, Isis turned around again. Her surroundings were completely alien to her and Isis knew she wasn't on Earth anymore. *God, I hope there's some kind of guardian version of GPS, because I am so lost,* Isis thought as she swallowed. She instantly regretted tossing her phone before attempting to learn Appearing.

Isis dropped her arm. "Perfect. Just spectacular."

So far, she hadn't seen anything that looked threatening, which she assumed was a good sign. There were no gigantic fanged beasts or anything of the sort, nothing that looked remotely predatory. Isis looked at the ground beneath her feet, squinting as she carefully knelt on one knee. Running her fingers over the smooth silver, she found it was cool to the touch. It was a path of some kind, but it wasn't made of stone or gravel or any other material that paths on Earth were usually made of. Staring at her reflection in the shiny surface, Isis rubbed her fingers together. The air was much purer than anything she had ever experienced. It was refreshing to her lungs and her body was reveling in it.

Isis turned her face to the pale blue sky. The colors were much more vivid than on Earth. The sun warmed her face and a cool breeze played with her hair. If she hadn't been so hopelessly lost, Isis might have even enjoyed the beautiful place. She looked behind her and saw a large body of water in the distance. She squinted when she noticed movement. When she saw the movement was people, Isis started heading in that direction, hoping they'd be friendly. As she got closer, Isis noticed they were dancing on the surface of the water and froze, staring at the bizarre sight.

"Nope," she said, turning around and walking in the opposite direction. Glancing back toward the forest, Isis noticed a large round rock nearby, just inside the trees. She moved over to it, looking around for any other signs of life. When she saw none, Isis sighed and leaned her weight against the huge rock. She crossed her arms in front of her chest, intending to take a moment to get her bearings and then figure out what to do.

A scraping noise above her brought Isis' attention upwards. She was expecting to see some sort of woodland creature, smallish in size. The noise had been so quiet that she felt it could only be some kind of rodent. Isis was taken by surprise when she found herself face-to-face with the golden eyes of an adult mountain lion. She cursed her own inattentiveness and forced herself not to jerk away. Sudden movements around big cats were never a good idea.

The place was so blissfully perfect that she had let her guard down and hadn't even considered that there might be predators in the forests.

The large cat licked its chops and flicked the tip of its tail. Its tan coat sparkled in the dappled sunlight. Its large pink nose twitched and its rounded ears were perked. It seemed like the big cat didn't even blink as it continued to stare at her.

"Hey, there's no chance you're a shape shifter, is there?" Isis asked as she began to carefully back away. The cat roared, exposing enormous jaws.

"Yeah, didn't think so," Isis said as she continued to back away from the rock, making sure not to take her eyes off the animal. She was careful not to look directly into the mountain lion's eyes. Apex predators didn't take too kindly to being stared in the eyes.

The mountain lion crept down the side of the rock with its enormous front paws, every movement graceful and controlled. It pushed off the rough surface with its hind legs and landed on the ground, never taking its eyes off of Isis as it continued to stalk toward her. Isis noticed it had gray markings around its enormous paws, which looked bigger than her face.

Of all the possible ways to die, Isis thought. The mountain lion's eyes drifted to her throat and it paused for a moment. It tilted its head, as though it heard something she could not. Isis stopped and stood perfectly still, praying to every deity she could think of.

The mountain lion suddenly leapt forward with a loud growl, tackling Isis to the ground. She let out a yelp and used her arms to shield her face, trembling despite her best effort not to. Attempting to bring her legs up to her chest so that she could get in the fetal position, Isis tried to remember the best way to escape a large animal attack. To her shock, she felt a rough tongue run over her arms and the exposed parts of her face. She hesitantly lifted one arm, peering at the enormous animal lying on top of her. The mountain lion attempted to nose its head under her arms and she couldn't believe her ears when it began to purr, rubbing its head all over her face.

"Hey, off! You, off, now! Shoo!"

Isis never thought she would be so happy to hear a voice. The heavy weight of the mountain lion disappeared and her sister's shadow fell over her.

"Isis, are you all right?" Electra asked as she brushed some hair out of her eyes. Isis removed her arms from her face, glancing to the side. The mountain lion was stretching out its lean body a few feet away from them.

"Uh, yeah," Isis said, feeling embarrassed as she pushed herself up on her elbows. "My internal organs all seem to be intact."

Electra offered her a hand, which Isis accepted. She raised her arm to brush the dirt off and paused when she noticed there was none on her. Furrowing her brow, Isis glanced back to the ground. *Oh yeah*, she thought when she saw the silver path.

"That's the Argentine Path," Electra explained, following her sister's gaze. "It was made by the first metal-smiths when the first guardians chose their lands. It runs throughout all the lands of the Meadows and it's the safest way to travel between the different territories."

"Safest?" Isis asked, feeling uneasy again.

"It's not what you think," Electra said, tying her

hair back quickly. "Say a fire guardian or messenger from those lands needs to see or speak with someone from the water lands? They can't exactly swim, can they?"

"Are they actually made of fire?" Isis was stunned at the thought.

Electra shook her head with a smile. "No, but fire is a part of who they are. You're very in touch with nature. What's it like when you have to go into a city or the suburbs?"

"Oh," Isis said. She understood Electra's point, having always had a disdain for cities and suburbs. Growing up, Isis had always preferred the peace and quiet of a woodland setting.

"So this is the Meadows?" Isis asked, glancing around once again.

"Yes, this is home. Well, the place I've always called home anyway," Electra replied, nodding over Isis' shoulder. "The Pearl Castle is this way."

"Pearl Castle?" Isis asked as Electra strode past her.

"Home of the royal line," Electra stated. "That's where Mom and some of our other relatives live. That's where we're most likely to find them."

Isis paused, feeling a sudden hesitance. Electra turned back when she realized her sister wasn't following, noticing Isis standing a few feet behind her. Isis massaged the side of her neck, glancing back toward the forest. She knew she wasn't the most trusting person Electra had ever met and was aware that her twin was often confused by her naturally aloof disposition.

"Isis, you have nothing to worry about," Electra reassured as she put her hands on her hips and watched her twin. "The guardians aren't like what you're used to. We're not human."

"Yeah, Electra, that's really part of the problem. You talk about the human world like it's alien and that's the only world I've known," Isis replied as she folded her arms over her chest. Electra's brow furrowed at the response and she turned her attention off to the side. The wind gently lifted her hair up and she bit her lower lip, a thoughtful look crossing her face. Isis recognized the look as a sign that her sister was pondering something, trying to sympathize with a situation she didn't entirely understand. Electra turned her dark green eyes back to Isis.

"You're right," she admitted with a small shrug. "I can't even begin to understand what this is like for you. I can only tell you what I know. If you want to go back to the mansion, we'll go back. Passion's not going anywhere…although with her, you never quite know what she's going to do."

Electra let out a quiet laugh and shook her head. She noticed Isis' expression and realized she was uncomfortable.

"So, do you want to go back?"

After a moment, Isis shook her head. "No, I'm already here. I Appeared here for some reason, might as well find out why."

Electra smiled and nodded over her shoulder. "This way."

"Uh, are there any more mountain lions?" Isis asked, wondering if it was going to be night soon. "Or other large carnivores I should be aware of?"

"Have you ever killed someone in cold blood?" Electra asked. Isis stared at her, trying to figure out whether or not she was serious. She shook her head in response.

"Then you've got nothing to be worried about," Electra replied as she began walking backward on the silver path. "There are numerous big cats and large predators in the Meadows, but they are just one of the many types of security. Animals are often described as having an extra sense, which is not really accurate. They are just very good at sensing things, including things most people try to keep hidden."

"Does it have to do with their being able to sense abnormal brain chemistry?" Isis asked, recalling a course in zoology that she had taken in college. Her professor had a theory about dogs being able to sense sociopaths. He believed that much like they could smell tumors and other kinds of cancer, they could smell or sense strange brain functions.

Electra nodded. "From what shape shifters have told us about the animal form, it's very likely."

They continued down the silver path, walking side by side. Isis noticed Electra occasionally glancing over at her. She had noticed her twin had the same habit as she did when it came to walking: neither of them liked following others. As they continued walking down the path, Electra turned her attention forward and watched the distance.

"How far is it?" Isis asked, drawing Electra's attention to her.

"You Appeared about an hour away from the castle," Electra answered. "I know you don't mind long walks."

Isis was quiet for a long time, watching as the trees faded from view. She couldn't believe she had Appeared so far away. The sun was high in the sky, indicating it was late afternoon. Isis bit her lower lip, not keen on being in a different world when it was dark. She was uncomfortable enough in the daylight. *Note to self: don't eat anything. Just in case,* she thought, recalling the many myths and folklores she had read throughout her life.

"It's not going to get dark, is it?" Isis finally asked her sister.

"Not for a while yet," Electra replied. "Pity. Our evenings are quite lovely."

Isis went quiet again as they continued toward a small stretch of hills. There was another large boulder just before the hills. Electra squinted and grinned when she spotted someone sitting with her back against the large rock.

"Oh good! I can introduce you to a dear friend of mine," she said, gesturing toward the boulder. She picked up her pace slightly and Isis did the same. They soon reached the boulder, where a young woman in a flame-colored dress was sitting with her hands folded behind her copper-colored hair. The woman lazily opened one eye when they approached, smiling.

"Well, if it isn't my old friend," the woman remarked as she opened her eyes, grinning even more when she saw Isis. "And her doppelganger. She as much of a hellcat as you and Passion?"

"Nice, Phoenix," Electra remarked as she leaned against the boulder. "Isis, this is Phoenix. She's one of the daughters of the head fire guardian, Blaze. Although you wouldn't know it from the amount of time she spends here."

"Hey, you try spending any measurable amount of time with Calida," Phoenix argued in a good-natured tone. "Next in line and my sister acts like our Mother is going to retire tomorrow."

"Phoenix is the youngest, most reckless daughter," Electra explained with a smile. Phoenix chuckled as she leaned forward a little to get a better look at Isis.

"Hmm, I like her already," Phoenix stated, turning her eyes to Isis. "You've got that Passion-type aura."

"Speaking of which, is she around?" Electra asked with a laugh, waving off Isis' questioning look.

"Yeah, I think she's somewhere in the Pearl Castle. By the way, remind me to fill you in on Donovan's new apprentice. You are going to laugh so hard," Phoenix said with a wink. Electra looked floored at the sentence whereas Isis was just confused. She was beginning to get used to the feeling and it didn't bother her as much as it once had.

"No way! He finally found an apprentice?"

"Ah, no, he didn't *find* an apprentice. The High Council *assigned* him one," Phoenix replied, her eyes sparkling with laughter.

"The things I miss," Electra commented with a shake of her head. "I'll see you later, Phoenix."

"Yep," Phoenix said as she leaned back against the rocks, giving a wave of her hand by way of parting. Isis and Electra walked for a few more minutes before Electra spoke again.

"The aura she was referring to…that's a way of saying that you're going to irritate most of the older guardian men," she explained as she hooked her thumbs in the belt loops of her jeans.

"Why? What did I do?" Isis asked, a little exasperated. Electra chuckled as they continued on their way.

"Don't get too upset. They're mad at Mom for breaking just about every rule laid down by our ancestors," Electra explained, her smile growing. "She's a sexually liberated single mother who prefers the Earth and the protectors to the Meadows and the guardians. Most of the older men on the High Council are old-fashioned traditionalists, not the best combination. Don't worry, they're not all alike. Phoenix mentioned Donovan. He's very progressive, albeit a little bitter at times. He and Mom have been close for ages, long before us. Alister is another more progressive guardian so to speak and even Death is fairly open-minded."

Isis stopped in her tracks. "Death?"

"Yeah, he's kind of the grim reaper of the guardian world. He keeps death in check," Electra said as if it were the most normal thing in the world.

"There's an afterlife?" Isis asked, thoroughly confused. Electra shrugged her shoulders as she turned around again.

"That's not for the living to know," she replied, waiting for her sister. "Life is an adventure to be lived in stages. You can't flip to the back of the book to find out the ending. Why would you want to?"

"Okay," Isis said with a shake of her head, approaching her sister again. They continued on their way to the Pearl Castle. Walking through the Meadows was like walking through some ancient myth or story. Golden grass stretched as far as Isis could see and the occasional animal could be spotted in the distance, bounding through the fields. When they reached the top of a small hill, Electra stopped and pointed to the north.

"That's the Pearl Castle," she said. Isis stared in amazement at the enormous castle, which was easily the biggest structure she had ever seen. It even rivalled the protectors' mansion. The sprawling castle stretched almost as far as the eye could see. It was made of brick with hints of gold in it, which sparkled in the sun. There was a coat of arms of some kind painted on the wooden doors and also on a few of the numerous flags that sat atop the towers and spires. It looked like something out of a fairytale. Electra smiled as she followed Isis' gaze. After a moment, she began to make her way down the small hill.

"Um, is there anything I should know?" Isis asked as she kept up with her sister. "Is there some kind of…I don't know, gesture or custom I need to learn or tradition or ritual I should partake in or something like that?"

Electra thought for a moment. "Um, no, there's nothing special you need to do or learn. Whatever you do, stay out of everyone's way. Things are kind of crazy on the first two floors. The third and fourth are the living quarters, so they're pretty calm."

As they approached the doors of the castle, Isis noticed two armored guards standing still as stone. They each held an impressive spear and shield, their silver armor glistening in the sunlight. Electra nodded to the guards when they saluted her and moved in unison to push open the enormous doors. Isis fell a couple steps behind Electra, marveling at the grand hall they walked into. The sheer amount of noise made her feel a little uneasy and she moved a bit closer to Electra, staying behind her.

Everyone was dressed in brightly colored clothing, mostly tunics or dresses. Sandals whispered across the floor. The clothing was the finest Isis had ever seen and she had to remind herself that guardians were not deities, even though they certainly looked like they were. Being surrounded by a rainbow of color, Isis suddenly felt self-conscious of her own drab clothing. She squinted when she noticed a lot of the people rushing around seemed to glow or glisten in the light. That was…weird.

"What's the rush?" Isis asked, carefully avoiding getting in anyone's way. A man in a green tunic nimbly danced around her as he continued rushing to wherever he was headed.

"The world never sleeps," Electra replied, nodding to the guardians and messengers she knew as she continued to walk through her home.

"It's like this twenty-four seven?" Isis flattened herself against the wall when a flustered-looking woman in a pastel pink dress darted past her.

Electra nodded, not affected by the rush. "Pretty much."

The two reached a wide winding flight of stairs, jogging up two flights. Every floor in the castle was marble with red carpeting down the middle. Large portraits of beautiful women in elegant dresses decorated the walls, watching the inhabitants with their painted eyes. Isis and Electra continued down the hall. Isis couldn't believe how much it was like a museum of medieval artifacts. Besides the portraits, there were also crests and tapestries and even a few maps. All were remarkably well preserved and showed little to no signs of aging. The hallway entrances and windows were rounded. Isis frowned when she noticed there were almost no corners in the castle. Everything was rounded, giving the aura of grace and elegance. The air was as light and pleasant as it was throughout the lands.

The third floor was wonderfully peaceful,

compared to the first two levels. Electra continued moving ahead, obviously comfortable in the magnificent hallways.

"Electra," a feminine voice called from behind them. Electra turned on her heel, beaming.

"Grandmother," Electra greeted as she ran into the woman's outstretched arms and embraced her.

Isis turned and couldn't help but stare at the woman behind them. She was dressed in a rose-colored dress that was much longer than the one Phoenix had been wearing. She looked somewhat similar to Electra but her hair was black and just barely brushed her chin. Her expressive eyes were dark blue. Physically, the woman didn't look a day over thirty-five, but her eyes and the way she held herself suggested she was much older. *Right, they're immortal,* Isis remembered. She was still getting used to the notion.

"Isis, this is our grandmother, Artemis," Electra introduced the two. Artemis approached her, smiling warmly. When she walked, she appeared to glide. It was very similar to the way Lilly moved.

"Hello Isis. It is good to finally meet you," she said. Isis had absolutely no idea how to respond to the statement.

"Artemis? Like the goddess?" she asked. Artemis glanced back at Electra, who chuckled and spread her hands.

"I guess you could look at it that way," Artemis replied.

"So probably no relation then?" Isis asked, half-joking. Artemis smiled and shook her head.

"No, guardians are not gods," Artemis answered. "I am not even the first guardian to be named such. If we share names with deities, it is merely a coincidence."

A thought came to Isis. "Am I named after any important guardian?"

Artemis' smiled widened. "You are. Both of you are named after guardians my daughter very much admires. However, I feel you should ask her about the guardian you're named after. She will undoubtedly offer a much more satisfying answer than I."

Isis looked over at Electra, who still had her arm wrapped around her grandmother. She could tell they were close and it was clear Artemis adored Electra.

"Grandmother, do you know where we could find Mom or Adonia?" Electra asked pleasantly. Isis was surprised at her usually reserved sister's change in demeanor. She was a whole different person in the Meadows; one who was much more comfortable and outgoing.

Artemis nodded. "Yes, my dear, they're in Adonia's office."

"Thank you," Electra said, stepping away from Artemis and walking past Isis. "It's this way."

Isis smiled politely and nodded at Artemis before turning to keep up with Electra. They proceeded down the hallway. As Isis continued to admire the beautiful place, she found herself wishing she knew more about architecture.

"Mom and Grandmother don't really get along, which is why Mom tends to spend more time at the mansion with Jet and Lilly," Electra explained as they continued on their way. "Grandmother has never really forgiven Mom for running away all those years ago, but even before that, they had their issues."

"Why?" Isis asked. It seemed like whatever family

she was in had its own kind of dysfunction. *And Steve wonders why I'm cynical,* she thought. She felt a twinge of homesickness when she realized that she hadn't seen Steve in a while and hadn't talked to him in at least a month. Even then it was just to give him an alibi. Electra shrugged in response to Isis' question.

"Grandmother is somewhat of a traditionalist and their personalities just clash more often than not," she answered. "They still fight. By the way, if you're ever here when they're in the midst of an argument, steer clear. Things have been known to spontaneously combust around them. I can't even count the number of times I've almost been burned that way."

Isis stared at Electra in shock. There had been a time when she would have laughed at the ludicrous idea of spontaneous combustion. After all that she had seen since discovering her heritage, Isis was ready to believe just about anything. She continued down the hall with Electra.

They reached a set of large doors. There were golden vines carved into the wood that glistened in the sunlight. The levers were made of the same gold material and were spotless. Isis couldn't believe how clean everything was. There weren't even dust particles dancing in the beams of light. Electra gave two short rapid knocks on the door.

"Yes?" a melodic voice drifted out from the room.

"It's Electra. Isis is with me," Electra called out. Isis glanced around the hallway, suddenly finding the walls incredibly interesting.

"Come in," the voice invited. Electra glanced back to Isis, asking with a simple glance whether or not she was ready. Isis hesitated for a moment before nodding once. Electra pushed the door open, stepping aside so Isis could enter. Isis let out a short breath, and stepped inside.

The room had a floor that looked like it was made of clouds and a huge picture window behind a large desk that looked out over the lands. The two women in the office were looking toward the door. One had been leaning over the desk, studying what appeared to be some sort of parchment. She wore a sleeveless orchid-colored dress and her red hair fell below her shoulders. The woman smiled at Isis, rotating her wrist, gesturing for her to come closer. Her green eyes were kind, expressive, and soft all at once.

The other woman in the office sat on a bench in the window, her long legs stretched out in front of her as she looked outside. Her hair was the color of the sun and it gently brushed the tops of her shoulders. The second woman turned to look at them and Isis saw her eyes were a mossy green color, with a lively spark in them. She wore a dress similar to the first woman but it was bright red and much more risqué, exposing more skin. When she smiled at the two, Isis could see the same kind of hesitance that she currently felt.

"Isis, this is our great-grandmother Adonia, queen of the guardians, and that's her granddaughter, Passion, our mother," Electra introduced as she gestured to the two women. Isis smiled and nodded as she tried to hide her loss for words and uneasiness. She really didn't like situations that required interacting with strangers. And this was definitely not a situation she ever thought she would be in.

"Hello Isis," Adonia greeted warmly. Passion swung her legs down and stood up, smiling kindly at the two women. Isis looked from Passion to Adonia, still not sure what to say. She settled on the statue approach: standing silently in the background, which had gotten her through many unpleasant situations in the past. She realized that she would probably have to speak at some point, but she was going to put it off for as long as possible.

"I'm sure Electra has told you much of our home," Adonia continued, smiling at her great granddaughters. The pride in her voice was evident and Isis could see that Electra was close with her as well.

Isis nodded and continued to look around, feeling completely out of place. The ceiling above them was glass and she could see the clear sky. There was a model of the solar system floating above their heads. Isis squinted, frowning when she noticed there weren't wires holding the small model up. The walls were plain; no books or clocks like in the mansion. There was an aura of serenity in the beautiful room.

"Isis, will you excuse us for a moment?" Adonia asked. "I need to speak with Electra."

Isis' head whipped around and she stared at Electra, shaking her head a little. She wasn't eager to be in a situation where she was alone with a complete stranger, especially one that was deity-like. Even the idea of guardians still made Isis a little nervous.

"Don't worry, it'll only be for a minute," Electra reassured her. "Passion doesn't bite and I'm sure you have some questions for her."

Isis glanced back at Passion, smiled politely for her benefit, and turned her eyes back to her twin. "One minute?"

"One minute," Electra nodded in confirmation.

"Any longer and I'll Appear again. I don't even

care where I wind up," Isis threatened and Electra gave her a very dry look.

"You have my word," she promised.

Isis' shoulders dropped in resignation and she nodded. Adonia stepped around the desk and walked past Electra, who followed her out of the office. Isis watched as the door closed behind them, keeping her eyes on it briefly. She turned back around to face Passion, unsure what to do or say.

Passion sighed, looking out the window again. "I'm sorry. I know how uncomfortable you must be."

"Yeah, well I really don't know what to say or ask. So, I don't think I'll be much of a conversationalist," Isis responded, approaching the desk that Passion stood behind. She folded her body into one of the chairs across from it. Passion strode around the desk and perched on the edge, making sure not to crowd the younger woman. Isis couldn't help but smile a little when she recognized the bad habit she shared with her sister: sitting on desks and tables.

Passion chuckled at the expression on Isis' face. "One of the many things my mother gives me hell about."

"I met her just now, in the hallway," Isis mentioned. "She said I should ask you about my name. Well, the guardian you named me after, I guess is a better way to put it."

Passion's entire face lit up. "Well, you haven't learned much of Meadows history yet, but a long, long time ago there was a war that tore this land apart and could have potentially ended the guardians themselves. There were many heroes that are sung of in ballads and celebrated in stories, but there are also many unsung heroes who fought just as bravely.

"The story that is most cherished among the guardians is that of Selene: her sorrow, her heroism, and her bravery in the face of great evil. However, we often overlook the quiet heroism of her loyal friend, Isis. She lost just as much as Selene did — even more in fact — but continued fighting beside her. Isis was incredibly clever and using alliances, she managed to strike a devastating blow against the traitorous guardians who were attempting to overtake the Meadows. Isis was the only guardian who went to Selene's aid when she chased after the dreaded fire guardian, Pyra. When Pyra struck a fatal blow to Selene, it was Isis who ran to her side and surrounded them with a barrier of magic. She remained with Selene, holding her, even when the night guardian ordered her to leave and save herself. When they were surrounded by Pyra and Chaos' forces, and the unquenchable flames were closing in, Isis refused to leave Selene's side. In the face of certain death, she stood firm and never flinched. She refused to leave her gravely wounded friend's side and I greatly admire the amount of courage and love she had. There is much more to the tale and Electra can show you the best accounts, if you're interested."

Isis stared at her, engrossed in the story. "Is she still around?"

Passion smiled and shook her head. "No. She retired many years ago. I never met her, but Adonia did in her youth. Nothing was ever expected of Isis, as she was a mere under-guardian. However, when Selene was allowed to return to life, she could find no peace in the Meadows and named Isis as queen of the lands of night before leaving. She ruled for many years, a great queen among the night guardians."

"Huh, so...okay, wow," Isis said, not really sure what else to say. She made a mental note to look up that story, which sounded like something she would enjoy reading.

"How have your lessons been coming?" Passion asked as she tucked some strands of hair behind her ear with one slender finger.

Isis shrugged. "Okay, I guess. Remington tells me I'm learning much quicker than he expected, but it doesn't feel like it."

"Remington is very wise, so I'm sure you are progressing rather well," Passion said, looking off to the side. "I'm sorry. I really tried to keep you out of this world. I had hoped you would have a normal happy life."

Isis snorted, trying not to be cynical. "It doesn't exist."

Passion let out a quiet, melancholy laugh. "You've been spending too much time with Jet."

A question surfaced in Isis' mind, but she was avoiding it. Still, her curious nature always got the better of her. She began to tap her fingertips on the armrests of her chair, trying to figure out how to ask the question. Her serene surroundings weren't helping her nerves much.

"Do you mind if I ask you something?" Isis began when she finally steeled her resolve.

"Not at all. You can ask me anything you like and I will do my best to answer," Passion replied.

"Do you regret having children?" Isis asked, watching Passion's face for any tells. Passion seemed a fairly unconventional mother, but Isis was only going by human standards and she knew that probably wasn't all that accurate when it came to guardians. From what little she had gleaned from Remington, Jet, and Lilly, her birth had been fairly traumatic and the aftermath had been difficult for Passion. It was part of why Isis was still very wary about the guardians — they struck her as extremely cold and distant, based on what she had read.

Passion shifted her weight and smoothed the front of her dress with one slender hand.

"I have many regrets, Isis. Many, many, *many* regrets," she started, looking back to the young woman. "But having children will never be one of them."

Isis nodded and crossed one leg over the other, pressing her hands together over her knee. She felt a little more relaxed and less antsy.

"I never thought to ask Electra, but do you think our father knew about us?" she asked cautiously. A somewhat bitter expression crossed Passion's face for a split second before she shook her head.

"No. Roan was long gone by the time you two were born. He was declared presumed dead about a month after your birth."

Isis rested her weight against the armrest. "Will you have any more children?"

Passion laughed. "I'm afraid not. Part of my sentence was that I couldn't have any more children or get married."

Isis was stunned. She hadn't been told of Passion's full punishment, but she had not expected it to be so severe.

"That's a little harsh," she commented.

"It's actually rather lenient. They could have had me thrown in the dungeons or taken away my position and banished me from the Meadows,"

Passion replied. Isis was surprised to hear no bitterness in her voice. She sounded like a woman who had accepted her situation and didn't dwell on what she could not change. *Your mother is a wise woman and almost no one gives her credit for it. You will probably never meet a stronger woman than Passion,* Jet had told her shortly after she had been brought to the mansion.

"You're second in line to rule the guardians, right?" Isis asked, remembering what Electra had told her.

"Yes. Electra and you are third depending on which of you wants the title and position. I'm sure you could even rule together if you desired."

"Electra can have it," Isis laughed and shook her head. "I'm not a ruler."

Passion smiled warmly. "You'd be surprised what you're capable of."

CHAPTER ELEVEN

"You lost it!? How could you have lost it!?" a furious shriek echoed throughout the halls of the manor and even the grotesque gargoyle-type sculptures seemed to shiver in fear at the icy bite of the voice. The few residents all melted into the shadows, hiding from their enraged mistress.

Adara's yellow eyes flashed in anger. Gia smirked as she filed her nails, enjoying her nemesis being shamed. Onyx merely stood in the hallway, not offering any excuses. Her light brown eyes followed Adara and her face remained emotionless.

"Someone interfered and I didn't know whether or not it was an agent of our new client. Erring on the side of caution seemed to be the wiser course of action," Onyx explained. "I have since been assured that the mysterious man is not connected with Grenich and will take care of him should our paths cross again."

"Please explain to me how you don't even know when someone's entered a *windowed* room," Adara continued as she paced in front of the woman. "You are supposed to be one of the top assassins, and you don't even know when someone's approaching you!?"

"I'll get that damn flashdrive," Onyx stated with a nonchalant shrug, a hint of irritation creeping into her tone.

"How?" Adara spat at the assassin, twisting around to look at her. She had hated Onyx before the whole debacle at the museum. She just about loathed her now. *I am surrounded by incompetence,* Adara thought. *They're worse than humans.*

"It won't undo the feeling of betrayal, Onyx," Gia taunted. Adara turned around and glared at her daughter, who was even more of a disappointment than Onyx. Gia swallowed and re-focused on filing her perfect nails in the shape of claws, avoiding her mother's gaze.

"You're going to help her find it," Adara snapped, turning her back to her daughter and looking at Onyx. "I don't want to see either of you again unless you have that flashdrive!"

"There is no way I'm working with her," Gia whined.

"Did you not learn how useless your daughter is last night? Her only job was to act as a lookout and she still screwed that up. You're really going to saddle me with her again?" Onyx asked. If there was one thing assassins hated — other than thieves — it was being forced to work with someone else. It was even worse if they had nothing but contempt for the assigned partner.

"Stop!" Adara shouted. "This constant questioning tells me you both need to be reminded whom you work for. So, I'm ordering you to work together, though god knows you'll probably just continue failing."

"And what happens when new management takes over this territory?" Onyx asked.

"Don't test me, Onyx."

Adara turned and stormed up the main stairs toward her bedroom. Stepping into the large room, Adara realized she wasn't alone and drew the knife she always carried on her, her eyes traveling around the space. The room was decorated from floor to ceiling in various shades of gold, one of her favorite colors. A large blood red chair sat in the far corner. The satin sheets on her bed were pale gold in color, standing out from the drab color of the floor and walls. Everything was done extravagantly, fit for a queen.

Adara closed the door behind her, creeping further into the room. She turned around and felt her jaw drop open when she saw the man sitting in a chair in the corner of the room, someone whom she hadn't seen in many years.

He had piercing gray eyes and sharp features. His dark hair was always short, almost in a crew cut. He was wearing a long greenish brown leather trench coat with a dark-colored hoodie beneath it. The man always had an intensely serious look on his face and no one ever really knew what he was thinking. Sitting in the chair, twisting the ring on his pinky finger, he didn't look up or acknowledge her presence in any way.

"Blackjack," Adara breathed in surprise. The name was from his years on pirate ships — a moniker he had picked up along the way. He drifted in and out of towns, leaving a path of death and destruction in his wake. After Roan and Draco were out of the picture, Blackjack had taken the title of most accomplished and feared assassin in the world.

"I suppose this is the part where I ask what you're doing in town," Adara commented. Blackjack smirked and shook his head as he folded his hands in his lap.

"No, this is where *I* ask what the hell you're doing," he corrected with his trademark coolness. Blackjack was the most unflappable man Adara had ever met. She sheathed her knife and crossed her arms over her chest.

"This is my territory," Adara stated. "What I do is none of your concern."

Blackjack clicked his tongue at her, shaking his head as he twisted the ring he wore on his pinky. It was gold with a small glass in the center that contained a single drop of blood. Whose blood it was, nobody knew.

"Actually, that's not entirely accurate, since I've taken on a new client. I believe you know him," Blackjack replied, his eyes flicking up briefly to Adara's face. She swallowed, glancing to where she knew he kept a concealed firearm. Blackjack only ever carried three weapons on him: two guns and a military knife. He never formed attachments to weapons, like most assassins did, and changed the weapons he carried based on the times.

"Are you implying you're going to challenge my position? I really don't think that would go well for you," she mentioned. "I didn't figure you for the type to put down roots anyway."

"Times change, so do shape shifters," he responded. "I have no interest in challenging you. If I desire this territory, I'll just take it."

Blackjack rose to his feet, moving toward the door. "Where are you going?"

Blackjack paused. "He got tired of your incompetence, so now I have to do the job that you can't while making sure you don't become a nuisance. Stay out of my way and make sure your people do the same, or you'll have him to answer to."

Adara watched as he opened the door and left her room. She glanced around, trying to figure out how he got in. The room was strangely colder than it usually was.

~~*~*~*

"Hey stranger."

Isis glanced over her shoulder and smiled at Steve when he stepped around the bench, taking a seat next to her. He was wearing his usual everyday clothes: a regular red and white shirt, torn jeans, and old sneakers.

"Please don't dress up on my account," Isis remarked, giving his clothes a pointed look.

"I'm sorry, your majesty. I forgot that you were a fashionista," Steve laughed as he stretched his arms across the back of the bench. Isis snickered and gazed out across the park. It was a beautiful day. The sun beamed down on the vibrant green grass. The statue of the town's founder, or "some random guy" as Isis called him, stood watch over the vast open space. They sat on a green bench in front of the path that encircled the small lake, where people enjoyed fishing or racing model boats. There were some people fishing on the other side. Isis watched as two college-age women roller-bladed past them.

"So, where've you been?" Steve asked. "I was beginning to get worried when you didn't call and there wasn't an APB on you. Then some of the guys started talking about there being a new crime photographer for the paper."

"Quit my job," Isis explained. "I've decided to take the road less traveled."

Steve stared at her, but didn't seem entirely taken by surprise. Isis twisted her body toward him, resting one arm on the back of the bench, waiting for whatever lecture he would try giving her. *If he only knew the absolute lunacy my life has become,* she thought.

"Have you thought about what you're going to do for money?" Steve asked. "Are you going to leave town again?"

Isis stared at him for a moment, suspicious. "Why aren't you more surprised?"

Steve smiled. "Isis, please. For as long as I've known you, you've had a restless personality. You're not the type to stay in one place for very long and you were never happy with that job. Hell, I'm surprised you kept it as long as you did."

"Right," Isis said skeptically. "I haven't decided yet what I'm going to do."

"Shae's probably going to pitch a fit," Steve warned, amusement clear in his voice. Isis frowned as she stared at her friend. She was getting a very strange vibe off Steve.

"What's new on the force?" she asked, deciding to change the subject. Steve shrugged and glanced down the gravel path when a cool breeze swept over them.

"Nothing much," he responded. "Things have become mercifully boring again. Are we going to lunch or what?"

Isis stared at him. "What's the rush? Are you on the clock or something?"

"Nah, I've just been sitting for too long and I'm getting hungry," Steve said as he stood up. He put his hands in his pockets and nodded over his shoulder. Isis stood up, following her friend.

"The squad hates the new photographer almost as much as they hated you," Steve jested. "I never thought that was possible."

"I'm touched," Isis quipped. She glanced over her shoulder when she thought she heard a twig snap. There was a brown rabbit a few feet behind them, nibbling on some kind of vegetation. His large round eyes fell on Isis and he briefly stopped chewing the leaf in his mouth. Isis turned her eyes back to the path ahead, trying not to be paranoid. Since finding out about shape shifters, she found she was looking at wildlife in a whole different light.

"What's wrong?" Steve asked as he glanced behind them.

"Nothing," Isis replied. "I thought I heard a twig snapping or something."

"What's this I hear about you moving out?" Steve inquired.

"Yeah, I'm going on the road for a while. Until I find some place that feels like home," Isis explained, wishing that she could do that. Jet had been adamant about keeping her friends and family in the dark. She was only to tell them enough to prevent any suspicion or further questioning. For the most part, she was fine with the order but she had fought him about Steve. Isis never lied to Steve and she hated to start.

"Are you working for the CIA?" Steve teased. Isis rolled her eyes over to him, giving him one of her trademark dry looks.

"Yeah, me working for the government," Isis laughed. "That'll be the day."

"Don't sell yourself short, Isis. I always thought you'd make a fantastic covert operative," Steve remarked. "Kicking the shit out of random bad guys *and* getting paid for it."

"And I'm sure my issues with authority wouldn't be a detriment at all," Isis pointed out as the two shared a laugh.

Another twig snapped, causing both Steve and Isis to turn around. Isis pulled her baton out of the scabbard clipped to the back of her jeans and flicked it toward the ground, pressing the button to expand it to its full length.

"I don't suppose you've got your gun on you," Isis murmured under her breath.

"It was an animal, Isis," he said. "We're in a park. For godsakes, put the baton away. There are people around."

Isis quickly hid the weapon behind her back when a group of joggers went by them, smiling politely. The minute the group passed, her smile disappeared. Isis pressed the button and leaned on the baton, collapsing it again. She slid it back in the scabbard, glancing over at Steve, who looked nothing short of exasperated.

"What have I told you about weapons?" he began.

"I don't know, Steve. Whenever you start lecturing me, it just becomes noise," Isis replied. She stepped past him to continue down the path. Steve shook his head and followed.

"You're positive that you're not working deep undercover for the CIA?" he asked. Isis smiled and playfully pushed him with her shoulder. Steve laughed and shook his head, glancing behind them.

"I really have missed you the past couple months," he said, sobering. Isis grinned as she looked up at him.

"I know. Me too," she admitted. Steve stopped and gasped, causing her to go rigid as she looked around. She expected to see a huge tree of a guy or something equally intimidating. Instead she was greeted with the sight of nothing and she looked back to her friend.

"My god, Isis. Did you actually admit to *caring* about someone?" Steve asked, trying to keep a straight face. Her eyes narrowed as she glared at him.

"You are such an asshole sometimes," she grumbled, but smiled despite herself. He just laughed and continued down the path.

"Where do you want to get lunch?" he asked, nearly groaning when she shrugged. Isis couldn't help but smile, knowing how much her indecision could get on her friend's nerves. They finally stepped out of the park and were greeted with the overwhelming sounds of traffic: blaring horns, screeching sirens and alarms, roaring engines. They both cringed; neither one particularly enjoyed the overwhelming noise in cities and towns.

"What else have I missed while I was away?" Isis asked, pulling her sunglasses from the top of her head and slipping them over her eyes. "Anything juicy?"

"No more disappearing bodies if that's what you're asking about," Steve replied. "We do have a couple of bodies, possible work of a serial killer."

"Really?"

"I don't need to tell you that bit of information

doesn't leave the two of us."

"Yes, Steve. I know not to go blabbing about possible serial killers," Isis said with a shake of her head. Steve was so tightly wound at times and she sometimes wondered how he slept at night.

"It's Loman's case, but he wanted a fresh set of eyes on it," Steve explained. "Same method, but no connection between the victims other than they were both women."

"Ah, mommy issues," Isis remarked, her dark sense of humor rearing its head. Her sense of humor was morbid at times and always had been. Steve got it, Shae got it, but most people didn't.

Steve stopped and gently grabbed Isis' elbow. "I don't have to remind you to be careful, do I?"

"Got it, Steve. No taking candy or rides from strangers. Again, queer woman here. I'm well aware of how dangerous the world is, especially when it comes to men with a sense of entitlement," Isis reminded him. Steve had always been overprotective of her and it did get on her nerves. She glanced down to her right hip when she felt her phone vibrate, groaning when she saw the number. *Of course it would be him,* she thought, massaging her brow.

"Steve, I'm going to have to take a rain check on lunch," Isis said. Steve looked at her in surprise, tilting his head.

"I'm sorry, it's just..." Isis paused and tried to think of a lie, but she couldn't. "I'll make it up to you, okay? I promise."

"Sure," Steve replied, although she could tell he still had questions. *So much for not arousing suspicion,* Isis thought as she turned around and hurried toward where she had parked. She could feel Steve's eyes on her back the whole way.

~~*~*~*

Jet flipped through a police file that an informant of his, Detective Loman, had faxed over. Loman was a police informant who also had some valuable FBI contacts. He always had reliable information and trusted protectors — Jet in particular — completely. The Loman family was one of the few human families who knew all about shape shifters and guardians. The knowledge was passed down through the generations, parent to child. It had been that way since any shape shifter could remember, and would most likely remain that way for generations to come.

Jet glanced at the photo of a murder victim. Whenever Loman found something that suggested any kind of supernatural interference he would send it to Jet. The victim had been stabbed, nothing new, but what worried Jet was the trademark that was etched in his mind. He hadn't seen it since he was a boy, but he would remember it for as long as he lived. An ace and king of spades had been rammed into the victim's eyes. Blackjack was in town. *Of all the things I really don't need right now,* he thought as he ran a hand over his face. If anyone could successfully challenge Adara, it would be Blackjack.

The sound of a door shutting drew Jet out of his dark memories and he glanced up. Isis stood in front of the door, looking nothing short of livid. Her hands were on her hips and her body was rigid.

"How am I supposed to avoid suspicion when I'm always running off?" she almost demanded. He leaned back in his chair, amusement dancing across his face despite her angry tone. *She would most likely maim me if I told her that she sounds exactly like her mother,* he thought. Unlike Passion, there was still a certain amount of deference in Isis' voice. That was probably on account of her entire life being turned upside down fairly recently.

"Isis, I warned you that you might be called at any time," Jet replied calmly. "Not just whenever it's convenient."

Isis scowled as she flopped down in a chair and crossed her arms over her chest. Her eyes traveled around the room before settling on Jet again.

"Where are the other three?" she asked.

"I met with them a little earlier. You were a bit harder to track down," Jet explained as he stood up from the chair and moved around the desk, holding the file in his hand. "It actually works out better this way, since you're the newest to this world. I must warn you that what I'm about to show you is very graphic."

Isis leaned forward and grabbed the folder from him, flipping it open. Jet was rather disturbed when she had no visible reaction to the gruesome pictures. She paged through them as she would a book before looking back to him, expectantly.

"That's it? So some sicko has a thing for cards," Isis said, handing the file back to Jet. His felt his mouth drop open as he stared at her, unsure how to respond. She fidgeted a little in her chair and rubbed the bridge of her nose.

"I studied photojournalism," she reminded him. "I've seen all kinds of gory and disturbing photos, many worse than that. It's difficult to shock me."

"Oh," Jet responded, still bothered by her

indifference. "What you're looking at is the work of an assassin by the name of Blackjack. With Roan and Draco out of the picture, he is the top assassin that we know of. The last we heard, he was somewhere in South America. Why he came here, I don't know. It's possible he's the cause of the all the unrest among the assassins, perhaps making a play for Adara's territory or…"

"Or…?" Isis repeated when Jet trailed off, waiting for him to finish. Jet rubbed the back of his neck, considering his next words. The sun on his back suddenly felt uncomfortably hot. He glanced at Isis, lowering his hand again.

"Or he could be after the four of you," he finished. Isis stared at him, waiting for him to continue. When he didn't, she shrugged and spread her hands.

"Isn't every assassin out there after us?" Isis pointed out.

"This one's different," Jet explained. "Isis, he has been around for a *very* long time, certainly longer than me. I don't want the four of you going after him."

"Don't hunt the wacko with a playing card fetish. Got it," Isis summarized, her tone still annoyed. "Can I go?"

Jet nodded and she stood up and left the study. She hadn't been gone for more than five minutes when Lilly hurried into the study, uncharacteristically flustered.

"Lilly, what's wrong?" he asked, unable to conceal the concern in his voice as she closed the door behind her. Lilly was almost never rattled. To see her in such a state was worrying. Jet stood from his chair and approached her.

"I received word from Ivy," Lilly explained, grasping his hands within her own. "Isis' protector has been brought to the Meadows, badly injured."

"Steve?" Jet asked. "What happened?"

"I do not know, but Ivy suggested it might have been Blackjack," Lilly didn't need to say anything more. Jet ran a hand over his mouth. So Blackjack was targeting the Four, probably Isis in particular. The Deverell family had always been a thorn in the assassin's side and Jet knew a few of Roan's brothers delighted in needling various assassins.

"Is he all right?"

"Amethyst believes he will be," Lilly responded. "She was with him in the healing wing when I left."

"I'll head there right away," Jet said as he took a step back. He paused only when Lilly stepped forward and placed a hand on his chest, halting him from disappearing.

"What do we tell Isis?"

Jet thought for a moment. Steve came from a family of protectors, but Isis didn't know. To her, he was just a friend that she had known for most of her life.

"We don't tell her anything for the time being," Jet replied. "If he's going to be okay, then it's not our place to tell her."

"I'm going with you to the Meadows," Lilly said and Jet nodded, already assuming that she would. Lilly was co-leader of the protectors, his partner, and she had the same duties as he did. Jet turned back to the desk, picking up the phone and pressing a few buttons. He waited for Remington to pick up the line in his quarters.

"Yes?" the rich Irish brogue filtered through the

receiver.

"Lilly and I have to run to the Meadows. Steve was in an altercation. I need you to keep the Four here for the time being," Jet spoke hurriedly.

"Easier said than done, but I'll do my best," Remington responded. Jet hung up the phone and turned back to Lilly. The two vanished in a flash of dark blue light.

~~*~*~*

The healing wing of the Pearl Castle was set up for comfort, as were most areas in the enormous castle. There were rarely patients in the healing wing, since the Meadows was the perfect environment. Guardians never got sick and there were not many dangers in their world that posed a serious risk.

There were numerous beds with clean sheets and a pillow at the head of each one. A large curtain wrapped around each bed, providing the patient with a measure of privacy. Various messengers and apprentices milled about the room, most of them passing the time reading books of all shapes and sizes. It was their job to keep the wing immaculate and care for the few patients they had, which wasn't a difficult job.

Lilly and Jet entered the peaceful room and were greeted with the sounds of a hushed argument. They exchanged a look as they moved down the row of beds until they reached the center of the room. Steve stood across the bed from Amethyst, who looked irritated. Her strawberry blonde hair was done up in a neat bun and she was wearing a silky violet dress, which matched her eyes and nails. Aside from watching over the gemstone for which she was named, Amethyst was the head healer in the Meadows. She had been born with a unique gift to mend hurt. Most guardians had some healing capabilities, but Amethyst was one of the greatest healers the Meadows had ever seen.

"Lie down," she commanded. Her voice was so stern that Jet almost obeyed the order. He glanced over his shoulder when a messenger passed behind him. They were obviously giving the guardian and the young protector as much space as possible in the hopes of avoiding the argument.

"No," Steve replied just as resolutely and Lilly stared at him, surprised by his defiance. They had known Steve for a long time as he came from a long line of protectors. He was extremely loyal to the guardians and had been brought up to treat them as respected elders. Neither protector leader had ever heard him actually refuse an order before.

"Steve?" Jet spoke, interrupting the argument. Steve turned to him and Amethyst threw up her hands in defeat.

"He's your problem now," Amethyst grumbled as she passed by. "My recommendation is that he rest for at least a couple hours, but what do I know? I've only been a healer for centuries, longer than any of you have been alive."

Jet watched Amethyst leave. She was one of the oldest guardians in the Meadows and wasn't the most approachable, but she was good at her job. Jet turned his eyes back to Steve and could only wonder what kind of quarrel he had missed. Steve was paler than normal, but otherwise looked fine.

"Blackjack was waiting for me in my apartment,"

Steve explained, reading the question on Jet's face. "The bastard stabbed me in the back when I was closing my door. We have to get back, figure out how to track him down before he does any real damage."

"Steve, I really think you should lie down for a bit," Jet said. "Amethyst said—"

"I know what she said," Steve snapped, shifting his weight a little. Jet didn't miss the small grimace that passed across the younger protector's face. The guardians were able to heal a lot of damage, but more severe wounds would ache for a couple days afterward.

"Do you know what he was after?" Lilly asked. Steve turned his attention to her and rubbed his arm, fidgeting a little. Both protector leaders could see he didn't like being kept in the Meadows.

"Well, he asked me where the guardian's daughter was," he replied, placing his hands on his hips. "I'm guessing he meant Isis, since she's the only daughter of a guardian in the immediate area. Nemesis showed up before he could finish me off."

It wasn't the first time Jet had been grateful for the protection spell that Adonia had placed on the apartment building when Isis first moved in. It alerted Nemesis, one of the guardian warriors, if there was a supernatural threat on the premises. There was no doubt in his mind that it was the only reason Steve had survived. *I guess the question is why the spell apparently protects Steve but not Isis,* Jet thought.

"Can we talk about this later, please? I've got a really bad feeling," Steve said as he shifted his weight, glancing around at the tan brick walls. "You know how trouble seems to find Isis wherever she goes."

Jet rubbed his bottom lip, wondering if Blackjack

was truly after just Isis. Aside from being the daughter of a guardian, he couldn't really think of much else that would make her so valuable. She was a beginner, still learning the ropes. It felt like there was a big part of the picture they were missing.

"You don't have to worry, Isis is at the mansion," Lilly reassured the anxious young protector. Jet almost cringed when he heard his cell phone beep. He took it out of his pocket, turned away, and looked at the screen. *Isis went on an errand and Shae wants to know if Steve is okay. —Remington*

Jet pinched the bridge of his nose in exasperation. Passion's daughter was going to be the death of him. There was a soft shuffling of feet as another messenger in a pale dress moved past them.

"Jet?" Lilly asked, running her hand up his arm.

"What?" Steve asked, craning his neck as he tried to see his phone. "What is it?"

Jet switched it off, slipped it back into his pocket, and shook his head. "It's nothing. Lie down and rest."

"Isis left the mansion, didn't she?" Steve asked, though his tone indicated that he already knew the answer.

"No," Jet lied before turning to Lilly. "Will you stay with him for a while and make sure he follows Amethyst's orders? I have to go back home and take care of something."

Lilly smiled a little, but he could see the worry in her sapphire eyes, and nodded her golden head once. Jet kissed her hand and then took a few steps back, disappearing again in a pillar of dark blue light.

~~*~*~*

By the time Isis reached her apartment, night was already falling. She had been worried about being followed since this was something she wanted to do alone. Stopping at Steve's door, Isis briefly considered knocking before changing her mind and continuing on to the stairway. When she finally reached her own hallway, Isis was shocked to find she actually missed the place. She never thought it would be possible to miss an apartment building, especially since she always complained about how suffocating it was with all the other people who lived there. *I'm going soft in my old age,* she thought with a quiet laugh.

Isis reached her door and took out her keys, twisting open all the locks. She closed the door behind her, glancing up. The hinges didn't squeak anymore, but whoever replaced the door hadn't included a chain lock. She twisted the deadbolt, not pleased that it was the only lock.

Turning, Isis strode through her mostly empty apartment. She had already packed her things with Jade and Shae's help and moved most of it to her room in the mansion. But there was one thing she had purposely left behind, something she didn't want anyone else to know about. Isis switched on the lights and moved to the small hall leading to her bedroom.

Once she was in the bedroom, Isis moved straight for the closet. She opened the door, switched on the light, and knelt on the ground. Easily finding the two loose floorboards, she pried them up. Inside, she had stuffed the flashdrive containing the pictures of the warehouse where the body had been, as well as a notebook of her theories. She hadn't decided yet what to do with them, but whatever she did, Isis wanted to do it alone. A faint stirring of curiosity told her that she wasn't done investigating the matter yet.

The sound of a familiar melody drifted in from the main room, causing the hairs on the back of her neck to stand up. Isis stuffed the notebook in her bag and the flashdrive into the pocket of her jeans before moving toward the main room. She recognized the CD: *Desire* by Bob Dylan. Steve had given it to her a while back. The track playing was *Isis*. She swallowed as she reached the entrance of the main room.

It was empty, which made her very uneasy. Isis walked over to the stereo system, keeping her guard up. She reached for the controls when the system suddenly shut off. Isis dropped her arm and noticed a lamp flicker on in the kitchen. Turning her head, Isis saw a strange man sitting at her kitchen table. He smiled and waved the remote to the stereo system. A large gun with a cylindrical suppressor screwed in the muzzle lay on the table in front of him. *Well shit,* Isis thought as she tried to figure out what to do.

The man wore a greenish brown leather trench coat with a dark hoodie beneath it. His hair was short and dark. Rubbing his large hands together, his cold gray eyes fixed on her, like a snake that had spotted a mouse.

"You've got quite eclectic taste in music," he observed as he put the stereo remote down on the table, near the gun. Isis didn't respond. Even sitting, she could see the man had a very solid build, so it would probably be impossible to knock him over. Glancing down to the gun, the man's fingers touched the weapon in an almost gentle caress.

"Do you know who I am, child?" he asked.

"An intruder, who is also an *incredibly* condescending asshole," Isis replied with a shrug.

"That's all I really need to know."

He smirked, his eyes remaining on the gun. "Hmm, bit of an arrogant attitude, quite an ill-advised trait. I am — or was depending on what you believe — a friend of your father's. You know of him, right? Roan?"

Isis didn't respond, trying to figure out if she could possibly make it to the door before he could fire the gun. The approaching night had coated her apartment in shadows, which might provide decent cover. *Except he's probably not human,* Isis realized. The intruder had the upper hand when it came to weapons. He had a gun and she had a baton. The odds were not in her favor. The man stood, grabbing the gun but didn't point it at her, obviously not done toying with her. Isis took a cautious step back.

"You should know I don't put much stock in biological relations or the importance placed on genetics, so you can stop trying with that bullshit," Isis mentioned.

"I'm sure you've heard of me as well, but I'll introduce myself anyway," the man continued, ignoring her. "I'm known as Blackjack and you have something that my employer wants."

As soon as he finished speaking, the lamp went out and the apartment was plunged into darkness. Isis didn't question her luck and dove to the ground. A single muffled shot rang out, shattering the lamp just above her. She covered her head as sharp bits of plaster and glass rained down on her. Thinking quickly, Isis started crawling, ignoring the few cuts she got from the shards that now decorated the floor. Pressing her back against the couch, she turned her face to the side and tried to keep track of where he was. *Should have borrowed a sword or staff or some kind of weapon from the mansion,* she thought, kicking herself for not thinking to do so.

"Oh Isis," Blackjack sang, sounding too close for comfort. "You can't hide forever. I can see just as well in the dark as you and this isn't the biggest area I've ever had to cover. Come out now and I won't torture you. You have my word."

Isis controlled her breathing as she glanced around, noticing the baseball bat nearby. Something heavy fell in the kitchen, drawing both Blackjack's and Isis' attention.

"Oh, you're a quick one, aren't you?" Blackjack stated with sadistic amusement, making his way toward the noise and away from her. "You probably get that from your fa—"

The sound of something solid hitting flesh made Isis cringe. For a moment, she flashbacked to the night she had almost been strangled in her kitchen and a tremor went through her. Isis shook her head and lunged for the bat, knowing it was her only hope.

Just when her fingers brushed against the smooth wood, Isis was physically lifted to her feet. She struggled against the strong grip, scratching and punching at whomever gripped her. If she was going to die, Isis was at least going to leave her killer with a few scars.

"Stop, stop," a smoky voice whispered. His breath smelled faintly of nicotine. Isis went rigid, remembering the voice from the museum ball.

"You!" Isis exclaimed. "Where's the flashdrive!?"

"Really? *That's* what you're concerned about right now?" The shadowy figure let out a tired sigh. "Just get out of here before you get yourself killed. He won't be out for long."

Isis thought about it for a moment before deciding to take his suggestion. She wasn't a fool: either the man was telling the truth or he was on the assassin's side, in which case she had two enemies to be concerned about. Isis ran out of her apartment, surprised that he didn't try to stop her. The building became a blur as she ran down the stairs and flew out the exit. The cool night breezes felt nice on her face once she was outside.

The sound of squealing tires drew her attention to the right. A small blue car sped around the corner and pulled to a sharp stop in front of her, smoke sliding out from under the tires. The passenger door was pushed open and Isis stared at the driver.

"Get in," Coop ordered.

CHAPTER TWELVE

The small car tore down a quiet road in the dead of night, going well over the speed limit. The driver was flawless in his handling of the car as he continued down the rarely used road. The stars twinkled in the clear sky. A thin filmy gray mist lazily drifted around the road, creating an eerie atmosphere. The trees rustled quietly, nocturnal creatures roamed about the ground unseen.

"Where are we going?" Isis asked, her hand resting on the pocket that held her baton. She was waiting for the right moment to strike.

Coop glanced in the rearview mirror. "Back to the mansion. It is a longer route, but a safer one. It's near impossible to tail someone down these roads — too easy to get turned around and lost."

"Who the hell are you?" Isis snapped, bringing Coop's attention to her. He looked back to the road, steering the wheel a little to the left. He glanced at her again and Isis stared at him, wondering what his deal was.

"You have a very expressive face," Coop mentioned and Isis stared at him, astounded. She blinked a couple times, closed her eyes and opened her mouth as she tried to figure out how to respond.

"*What?*" she squeaked.

"Your face…it's expressive," Coop tried again, sounding very uncomfortable. *I think that's an attempt at a compliment,* Isis thought.

"Well, you can't have it!"

Coop frowned and turned his eyes back to her. "I know that. Why do you think I'd want to mutilate you?"

"I don't know, maybe because you talk like a fucking Martian," Isis stated, stunned. "Oh my god, this is how I die, with a crazy stalker who has no idea how to interact with people."

"I am not insane," Coop said, as he checked the rearview mirror again. Isis glanced behind the car seeing nothing but an empty road behind them.

"You're apparently paranoid, you talk like some kind of space alien or robot, and you're wearing sunglasses at ten o'clock at night. You were wearing sunglasses in that club when we first met. Do you ever take those damn things off?"

Coop took off his sunglasses and looked at her. "Satisfied?"

"Fuck no! Who the hell are you?"

"Someone who just saved you. You don't have to be defensive," Coop replied, remaining calm and collected. "Please try to calm down."

"Word of advice, buddy: don't *ever* tell someone to calm down," Isis snapped. "I want to see some ID."

"I don't have any," Coop said as he slid his sunglasses back on, glancing at the rearview mirror again.

"Really not helping your case, dude," Isis shot back, slipping her phone out of her pocket. Holding it at her side, she reached up and pressed the lights over the rearview mirror.

Coop shook his head as he reached up to switch off the lights. "I was unaware I was on trial."

"I'm sure all stalkers say the exact same thing," Isis muttered, inwardly smiling as she put her phone on her other side. She had gotten a few pictures of the mysterious man. Biting her lower lip, she considered sending them to Shae.

"I haven't been stalking you."

"No? Than how come it seems like wherever I turn, you're there?" Isis demanded, composing a text message.

"Maybe you're stalking me," Coop offered with a small shrug.

"That's original," Isis scoffed, sending the text and slipping the phone back in her pocket.

Coop steered over to the side of the road and stepped on the brake. After shifting into park, he took a cell phone out of one of the inner pockets of his jacket. He pulled off his sunglasses and tucked them into one of his side pockets.

"I have a weapon," Isis warned, watching Coop. As much as she hated to admit it, she didn't sense any malice from the strange man. All she saw was indifference and perhaps a little sadness. There were few things Isis was sure of, but she was fairly certain that it was unlikely Coop was a threat. It was just a gut feeling.

Coop didn't react to her threat as he got out of the car, shut the door, and walked a few feet away. They had stopped in an open field, curling mists adding to the already perfect atmosphere for something out of a horror movie. Just one more thing to add to the list of wonderful elements of the evening that Isis was creating in her mind. She half-expected a werewolf to come charging out of the shadows and attack the car.

Once Coop was a short distance away, Isis immediately began going through the car, searching for anything suspicious or something that would tell her who the man was. She was sure she would be in so much trouble if she ever made it back to the mansion.

Outside, Isis could hear an owl hooting in the distance and the crickets were holding their own private little symphony. Every now and again the trees and grass would rustle in a stray breeze. Isis didn't mind any of the sounds and found them to be soothing as she continued searching the car, hoping to happen across a better weapon than the baton she had with her. The car was completely bare and even had that new car smell. Shifting over to the driver's seat, Isis could have kicked herself for never learning how to hotwire a damn car.

"It's me."

Isis glanced up when she heard Coop's voice. He had left the driver's side window partly open. She perked up her ears, eavesdropping on his quiet conversation.

"You were correct in your concern. The assassin was after her, but we got there in time," he said in his normal indifferent tone. "Well, she's being difficult, which is to be expected."

Coop paused for a moment, listening to what the person on the other line was saying. "That was not my doing. She's a rookie. You had me approach her in a club even when I warned you that was a bad strategy. In case you hadn't noticed, exp…We're not experienced in non-manipulative interactions. Please don't shush me. Yes, she's in the car now. I imagine that she is eavesdropping. It is not my fault. You asked me to help him and even though that wasn't part of our original bargain, I did so. What else do you expect of me? I'm adaptable, but I was modified for battle and survival, not retrieval missions. Not most of the time anyway."

Coop was silent for a few more moments. Isis could hear the barely audible murmur of the person on the other end of the line. The mysterious man rubbed his brow, his shoulders dropping ever so slightly, and Isis could tell he had lost the argument with whomever he was speaking with.

"I will fulfill my end of the bargain and retrieve the assassin, as you asked, but after that my debt to you will be paid and I'll be on my way. Now I need to drop the protector off at the mansion," Coop said before going quiet again. "To the best of my knowledge she has not. Give me some credit. I will see you in an hour or so."

Coop hung up the phone and stood for a moment with his hands on his hips, just staring off into the distance. Isis wondered if he was going to hurl the phone across the field as she shifted back over to the passenger side, not taking her eyes off him. She watched as he tucked the phone into one of his inner jacket pockets before he turned and strode back toward the car, sinking into the driver's side. He closed his door, not sparing Isis a glance. Reaching forward, he turned the key in the ignition and twisted in his seat, putting his arm behind Isis' seat and looking behind them as he backed out of the field onto the quiet road. He spun the wheel, sat back, and shifted into gear. For a long while, neither spoke.

"Who were you talking to?" Isis finally broke the silence.

"No one of concern," Coop answered in a flat tone that said the matter was closed. Isis sat back, observing the surroundings as they sped by. They soon turned onto the hidden road and Isis couldn't help but wonder how Coop knew where it was.

"I can only take you up to the gate," Coop mentioned. "I would appreciate it if you kept my involvement in this a secret."

"What do I tell—?"

"Say whoever it was wore a mask and dropped you off at the gate. If you have to, add in a gun or knife or some other weapon," Coop responded before Isis had a chance to finish asking the question.

Isis licked her lips. "You implied you knew something about the symbol…?"

Coop raised an eyebrow. "Would you believe anything I told you at the moment? Without any kind of evidence that could back up what I revealed to you?"

Isis hesitated, thinking. "No."

"Then I fail to see the point in telling you what I know," he said as he turned the steering wheel and pulled up to the large gate. Once they reached the gate, Coop shifted into park and gestured at her door, motioning for her to be on her way. Isis reached for the door handle and Coop turned his gaze back to the street ahead.

"Thank you," Isis muttered. She rarely thanked

anyone, but she felt she owed it to the strange man. He just continued looking at the road, giving no indication that he had heard her. She went to the gate, opening the box to reveal the handprint scanner.

"Stay out of trouble," Coop said just loud enough for her to hear. Isis rolled her eyes and twisted around a little, raising her eyebrow. He offered her a hint of a smile and shifted into drive, disappearing down the hidden road.

~~*~*~*

Jet paced around the indoor swimming pool, thinking over everything Isis had told him the previous night. He had decided to forego the inevitable lecture for the moment. She already knew that he was angry with her for doing something so incredibly reckless. However, he was more concerned with the altercation she'd had with Blackjack. He couldn't figure out how the assassin had managed to hide in the apartment without the guardians knowing. That was the second time the protection spell hadn't worked when it should have. Another strange part of the story had been Isis' discovery that the pictures she'd gone back for were missing again. What was going on?

The sound of rippling water echoed around the large room. The clean liquid reflected wavy aqua-colored reflections on the soft gray brick walls. Jet's footsteps echoed as he continued to pace up and down at the front of the pool. Droplets of sweat formed at his temple, but Jet paid them no attention. He brushed a hand through his black hair, glancing to where the four women were swimming before looking back down again and continuing to pace.

Isis, Jade, Alex, and Shae continued swimming laps, moving through the water. Isis reached the end of the pool where Jet was walking back and forth and noticed his expression. She put her elbows up on deck and watched him. *Here comes the Inquisition,* she thought as she brushed a dark strand of wet hair behind her ear.

"You've never seen his face?" Jet asked, looking over at her to briefly make eye contact.

"Nope," Isis said with a slight shake of her head, water sprinkling out of her dark locks at the slight movement. Shae popped up next to her, water beading off her skin at the sudden exit.

"I think it's a secret admirer," she teased.

Isis rolled her eyes. "And I suppose in your twisted mind being abducted was some kind of foreplay? Thanks for answering your text by the way."

"Uh, check your damn phone, Ice Queen. The picture didn't go through," Shae replied, grinning.

"Secret admirer?" Jet asked, frowning as he looked between the two women. Alex and Jade had begun to race while Jet was speaking with Shae and Isis. They reached the wall, smoothly rolled forward, changed their direction, and tore off toward the opposite wall again, making almost no noise or splash.

"Yeah, you know? Someone who likes you but doesn't tell you," Shae explained before turning back toward Isis. She shook her head and looked up at Jet, trying to read his expression, frustrated when she found she could not. Jet was good when it came to hiding what he was thinking and Isis still forgot that shape shifters stopped aging at a certain point in their lives. Jet and Lilly were a lot older than her even though they physically didn't look it. Isis could only hope that he didn't bring their short conversation up to Electra. If he did, she would have to figure out some other story to cover for the strange call her twin had overheard and she could only keep so many alibis and stories straight at once.

Jet walked toward the glass door, opened it, and walked up the stairs that led up to the mansion's main floor. The glass door clicked shut.

Isis swam freestyle to the edge of the pool and hopped out, lost in thought. Shae, Jade, and Alex watched as she grabbed a towel, wrapped it around her waist, and sauntered back to the shower room.

"What's up with her?" Alex asked, running a hand down her face to brush off the excess water. Both Jade and Shae shrugged, neither knowing what was on Isis' mind lately.

~~*~*~*

Isis sat in the open fields of the Meadows, allowing the calm environment to wash over her. A cool breeze brushed through the field of golden grass that stretched out before her. Behind her, Isis could hear the gentle murmur of water from Ocean's lands. The calming sounds of the distant woodlands drifted to her ears. One of the mountain lions that guarded the Meadows was lying against a nearby tree. The large cat's presence no longer bothered Isis. She had become accustomed to many of the odd things concerning shape shifters and guardians.

After a few moments, Isis heard footsteps as someone moved through the grass. She slowly opened her eyes, watching as her twin approached her, pausing when she reached Isis.

"How bad was he?" Isis asked, more curious than upset.

Electra sat next to her, following her gaze across the field. "I heard you met Blackjack."

"He mentioned Roan," Isis said as she leaned back so that she rested on her elbows. "Piqued my curiosity about him. Figured I might as well try asking you, seeing as how you're the most likely to give me a straight answer and not tip-toe around anything."

Electra was quiet for a moment, licking her lips as a thoughtful expression crossed her face.

"He was bad, Isis," she finally answered, folding her long legs under her. "One of the worst. His name still strikes fear in many hearts and you'd be hard pressed to find a shape shifter who would willingly say his name aloud. He had a reputation for throwing his victims off high places, but Roan knew many different ways to kill…and torture."

Wonderful, I'm genetically related to a goddamn supervillain, Isis thought, thinking about her next question.

"What happened to him? Nobody's given me an answer about that yet."

Electra shrugged. "That's because nobody really knows. He just disappeared. At least that's what I've been told."

"Is it possible he's alive?"

"Possible, but unlikely," Electra responded, shaking her head. "Assassins don't often meet good ends."

~~*~*~*

Passion hurried to the large meeting room of the Pearl Castle, late as usual. Trying to tie her moderately sweaty hair back, hoping to at least look somewhat presentable, she allowed herself a small secretive smile as her thoughts drifted back to her lover, who was still asleep in her room. What she wouldn't give to be curled up beside her, snuggling beneath the warm covers. Passion couldn't care less about what went on in the meetings and only made an appearance because she was required to or when her grandmother requested she attend. Discussing dull matters that were of little to no importance was not high on her list of priorities.

Reaching the door, Passion pulled it open. Adonia was sitting at the head of the table and smiled in greeting to her granddaughter. The main guardian women were all there with their apprentices and heirs sitting behind them. All eyes turned toward Passion when she entered the room. *Late again,* Passion thought, ignoring the disapproving look Artemis shot her. She made her way to the empty seat next to Electra and sat down.

"Good of you to finally make an appearance," Electra teased and Passion swatted at her playfully with a quiet laugh.

"As I was saying, Aneurin will be arriving tomorrow," Adonia began.

Passion closed her eyes and put her head back, not bothering to hide her annoyance. Aneurin was a guardian Passion didn't particularly care for. Most of the guardian men didn't do anything aside from nitpick anything and everything the guardian women did. Aneurin was especially harsh to Passion and she couldn't stand him. He always found a way to follow her around when he visited. He looked over her shoulder constantly and made little noises of disapproval, which drove her crazy. The fact that he'd been the main proponent of her sentence, part of which involved giving up Isis, made her loathe him even more. Aneurin had made it clear to her on numerous occasions that had it been his decision, she would have been banished from the Meadows.

"Mom, don't make a scene," she heard Electra whisper. She nodded to her daughter, assuring her that she wouldn't lose her temper. Passion turned her attention forward again, held her tongue, and continued listening to Adonia.

"He has a few things he wants to go over. Mostly issues about Blackjack and the mysterious figure that has been popping up all over," Adonia continued. "Passion, I should warn you: he may want to speak with Electra and possibly Isis."

Passion's whole body went rigid and she stared at Adonia in disbelief. "He wants to interrogate my daughters?"

"Passion, relax. It's not an interrogation," Artemis spoke up.

"He'll turn it into one. You know how he is," Passion insisted. Electra crossed her arms over her chest. The meeting had barely even begun and already her mother was getting worked up. That was never a good sign.

"Passion, you know I won't let him," Adonia tried to assure her.

"Why is it always Aneurin? Why can't Alister conduct these random observations?" Passion asked, trying her best to keep her tone respectful. She had promised Electra that she would keep her temper under control, but this was almost too much.

Alister was one of the guardian men who respected the work the guardian women did. Whenever he was observing, he stayed out of the way and was able to finish his business causing little interruption. Though guardian women were a strictly matriarchal society and kept almost no records of their male relatives, it was well known that Alister was Passion's father.

"Alister is not available," Adonia answered.

"If Aneurin gets near my daughters…" Passion warned, her eyes briefly turning bright red.

"Don't threaten your elders, Passion. Settle down," Artemis scolded.

"Oh right. I forgot. I'm to act as an obedient subject who is just supposed to blindly follow authority," Passion replied. "Why don't you just throw me in the dungeons and get it over with, Mother."

"That's enough from both of you!" Adonia slammed her hands on the smooth surface of the table as she stood from her chair. Passion continued glaring at Artemis, who returned the fierce stare. They were both stubborn, especially when they thought they were right, which they almost always did. The room went silent as all eyes turned to the guardian queen. It was incredibly rare that she raised her voice. Even Artemis and Passion remained quiet.

"I'm tempted to throw you both in the dungeons if only for a night. Your bickering is endless and I know I'm not the only one who is tired of it," Adonia continued, looking between the two of them. "Artemis, leave the past in the past. Passion, not many agreed with your sentence, your mother least of all, so stop holding a grudge. Can I count on you both to at least act civil toward each other tomorrow?"

Passion and Artemis looked back at her and nodded.

"Good. Does anyone else have any concerns?" Adonia looked around the table, nodding when one woman raised her hand. "Ocean, go ahead."

Ocean stood from her seat and looked to Adonia. She was dressed in her regular royal blue dress that perfectly matched her sparkling eyes. She had wavy light brown hair that was pulled back in a bun with two dolphin-shaped barrettes holding it neatly in place. Her skin had a slight shimmer to it, like all guardians. Her motions were as graceful and smooth as the water she watched over.

"How long is Aneurin staying?"

"He will be here two days," Adonia replied. Ocean nodded and took her seat again.

"Is he bringing anyone else with him?" Ivy asked. Ivy was the lead guardian of plants and therefore always wore green. She wore a dress the color of moss and her eyes were the color of grass. She had long red hair that she tied back in a tight ponytail.

"Yes. Merrick will be assisting," Adonia answered, sitting back even further.

"Oh, come *on*," Passion grumbled, sitting back in a huff.

"Passion," Adonia tried to soothe her granddaughter.

"Did he just get bored and decide it would be as good a time as any to annoy me?" Passion asked, crossing her arms over her chest. "I mean, Merrick *and* him? That is awfully convenient. It is well known that the male water guardians hate me more than any other guardian."

Passion glanced toward Ocean. "Apologies, Ocean, but your masculine counterparts are terrible individuals."

Ocean shrugged, not offering any defense or disagreeing with Passion's statement.

"Passion, do you just not like anybody?" Calida spoke up from the seat behind her mother, Blaze. Phoenix sent an icy glare at her older sister while Electra just ran a hand over her face and tilted her chair back. Calida wasn't rebellious like most of the younger guardians. Electra and Phoenix looked up to Passion, whereas Calida saw the feisty guardian as a rule breaker and therefore a bad example to the younger generations.

"All Merrick does is make snide comments about how much of a whore he thinks I am. When he's not too busy talking shit about Jet and Lilly, that is," Passion said, ignoring the young fire guardian. The guardians remained quiet, already used to Passion's colorful protests. It was just business as usual.

"Perhaps if you conducted yourself more appropriately," Artemis began, interrupted by Passion's laughter.

"Ah yes, I forgot our people's long and distinguished history of placing the blame solely on the victim," Passion remarked. "The problem isn't that Merrick is an awful person. It's my fault for wearing a dress with a V-neck and taking multiple lovers."

Phoenix snorted, earning her a warning glare from her mother. Electra sighed, knowing that her mother and grandmother would probably continue baiting each other with little barbs until it became a serious fight.

"Mother," Electra murmured as she covered her face with her hands.

"That's a bit of an over generalization, don't you think?" Artemis remarked coolly.

"I don't know the polite way to say 'being a wanton whore,'" Passion responded, matching her mother's icy tone.

"Don't use that language in here," Artemis reprimanded.

"I don't see why not. It's what you were implying," Passion shot back.

"Okay, meeting dismissed," Adonia stated before the usual argument could ensue. It was going to be a very long couple of days.

~~*~*~*

Isis struck a punching bag, her fists smacking against the firm red surface. She was sweating buckets but still had energy to burn. As she was just about to start practicing kicking, Isis heard movement behind her. She turned around and watched as a silver light formed in the center of the room. In seconds, her sister stood before her.

"Electra, what's up?" Isis asked as she unwound the tape from her knuckles, striding over to the benches where she kept a towel and a water bottle.

"I came to give you a heads up," Electra replied as she followed her sister.

"End of the world?" Isis quipped with a grin as she placed the tape on the smooth bench.

"Worse," Electra responded. "A guardian man is coming for an evaluation, assessment, whatever you want to call it."

"Oh?" Isis said, unscrewing the cap off her water bottle. "The guardian men? Haven't met any of them yet. They're the ones who dislike the two of us for existing, right?"

"A lot of them," Electra agreed as she sat on the bench, stretching her long legs in front of her. "They're probably going to want to question the both of us. You have to be on your best behavior, which is *much* more difficult than it sounds."

"Don't tell them to go fuck themselves, got it," Isis jested as she screwed the cap back on the water bottle. Electra gave her an unamused look. Isis shrugged, spreading her hands in front of her.

"I know how to behave, Electra," Isis reassured her, feeling more than a little insulted. Electra leaned forward.

"I hate it when they do their 'observations,'" she spat out the word as though it left an awful taste in her mouth.

"You said they weren't all the same," Isis mentioned as she sat down next to her twin. "I remember you mentioning Alister and Donovan in particular."

"Donovan is part of the High Council, but he tends to be as hands off as he possibly can be, and Alister is busy," Electra replied. "It's being done by Aneurin and a water guardian, Merrick."

Isis leaned back, cringing when the frigid bricks touched her bare shoulders. She wasn't thrilled with the idea of meeting more guardians, particularly ones who already didn't like her. She hadn't even settled entirely into her new life and already she was going to be questioned by another complete stranger. It seemed like whenever she came to terms with one new aspect of her life, another curveball was thrown at her. The grilling was just another stress that Isis didn't need.

"I'll get you if you're summoned. Expect to be," Electra stated as she stood up again.

"Okay," Isis replied, not able to offer much resistance.

Electra disappeared and Shae walked in. Shae made a beeline for her cousin, hopping up on the bench next to Isis. Isis shook her head, recognizing the peppy look in her cousin's eyes. It usually signified the beginning of a headache for Isis.

"Whatcha doin'?" Shae asked playfully. Isis stared at her. Her cousin always sounded like she was fresh out of high school when she was feeling mischievous. Sometimes it was endearing; other times it was just plain irritating. Today happened to be the latter.

"What does it look like?" Isis replied as she wiped the sweat off her face.

"Daydreaming. Getting lost in that pretty head of yours," Shae said as she stretched out across the bench in front of Isis, who rolled her eyes again. Her cousin knew how to get on her nerves. She'd be a rich woman if she were paid for it.

"I was not," Isis argued, as she ran the towel over her face and chest. She glanced up to the window. There were still a few hours of daylight.

"Were too," Shae replied in her sing-song voice.

"All right, I was thinking, not daydreaming. Not about what you assume I was, anyway," Isis admitted. She had given up long ago trying to hide what she was thinking from her cousin. Shae was just too good at reading body language.

Shae snickered. "I'm sorry. I must've missed the day you became telepathic."

"You always think I'm daydreaming about some fairytale romance when the truth is I'm not like you, never have been. You're an extroverted pansexual. I'm an introverted Gray-A, leaning toward aro most of the time. Romance isn't particularly appealing to me," Isis stated. "Please tell me I'm wrong."

Shae turned her head to the side, grinning. "Who said anything about fairytale romances? You've really got to do something about those overdramatic tendencies, Ice Queen."

"So I can get me a man and settle down?" Isis concluded her cousin's thought with a painfully bad southern accent. Shae laughed loudly at her cousin's sourness. She looked at Isis with her sparkling green eyes and Isis couldn't help but snicker at her own statement. She had a sense of humor and was usually able to identify when she was being dramatic.

"You're not averse to all relationships," Shae replied as she sat up. "What about Steve? You guys have been friends since elementary school. I always thought you two would hook up, with how protective you are of each other."

"And then he went and came out as gay—"

"Bi," Shae corrected, waggling a finger at Isis.

"You're right: bi," Isis agreed. "The guy is like my brother anyway."

She almost shuddered at the thought of being romantically linked to Steve. True, he was a great guy, one whom his boyfriend was lucky to have, but she had just never seen him that way and knew Steve felt the same way about her. She still owed him a beating for scaring the hell out of her, though. Isis hadn't been able to get a hold of him on the phone since she'd had the altercation with Blackjack. He had called her earlier that day and left a message to let her know he was all right, just out of town for a couple days. Isis had been so relieved to hear his voice that she had forgotten to call him back to chew him out. She made a mental note to do so later.

"Hmm, if I remember correctly, he left in the middle of the prom because he knew you weren't going and planned to spend the night alone," Shae recalled, bringing Isis back to the present. Isis sighed heavily and rolled her neck. She should've known Shae was going to bring that up.

"Once again, you're rewriting the narrative of what actually happened. He decided to skip out on prom because our stupid high school wouldn't let him go with his boyfriend at the time because the administrators were a bunch of goddamn homophobes," Isis reminded her. "He wound up at my house because we were both bored out of our damn minds. We watched movies while I prepared my photography portfolio."

"Oh yeah," Shae replied. "That entire evening is a bit of a blur."

Isis stared at her. "Because you got wasted and proceeded to make out with half the student body?"

Shae waved her hand dismissively at the question, though a knowing smile danced on her lips. Isis shook her head and stood up, intending to leave the workout room. Shae followed, staring at her cousin. Isis turned her neck just before they reached the stairs and looked at her expectantly.

"You're hiding something," Shae said as she continued to scrutinize Isis. Isis smiled and shook her head.

"No, Shae. I'm really not," she replied. She didn't give Shae a chance to respond as she turned and jogged up the stairs. Her mind drifted briefly back to Coop, but she had already decided that some things were better left secret.

CHAPTER THIRTEEN

In the lower levels of the Pearl Castle in the Meadows, there were many doors. Most led to various sections of the dungeons — which were mostly empty, but there was one that led to a small hallway. Down the small hallway there were doors leading to different rooms. Each room had two metal chairs and a matching metal table. There was one light that hung from the ceiling, which hummed whenever they were illuminating the dreary rooms. The bricks were painted soft colors and there was a two-way mirror that stretched across one wall. It was in these rooms that interrogations took place. Aneurin loved using the rooms whenever he came for an observation.

In the second room, two figures sat. One wore a dark blue tunic with gold trim, signifying he was someone important. The other wore a crimson dress made of the finest guardian silk. Her honey-colored hair was tied back in a tight ponytail, and her arms were folded in front of her on the table. The woman sat still, watching as the man sorted through some parchment. They both smiled politely whenever they'd meet each other's eyes, but there was always something off about the expression. To any casual observer, it would soon become apparent that the two didn't like each other, despite the civility. To the schooled eye, it would be rather clear that the two couldn't stand each other.

Passion bit the inside of her cheek, forcing the polite smile to remain on her face. Aneurin watched her with his soft blue eyes, tapping a fancy glass pen on the table. He was getting under her skin and he knew it. Running a hand through his dark hair, the guardian man continued to smile at her. They had already gotten the pleasantries out of the way and now he would try to go in for the kill, but he was going would take his time and toy with her for a bit first. He wanted her to understand who was in charge.

"So, you see how trying to prevent your daughter's destiny looks a little suspicious," he finished in his usual cordial tone, baiting Passion. She cleared her throat and kept the courteous expression on her face, though it almost slipped. Already her face was starting to ache from the constant smiling and Passion was beginning to wonder how much longer she could hold the expression.

"If you don't mind my asking, exactly what does this have to do with my job?" she asked, making sure she maintained a deferential tone. For Passion, that was a very hard thing to do. She was so used to rebelling against his snide attitude and frequent insinuations. The interrogation room had a hostile air to it. The bricks soaked up anger and hatred, and it would ooze out when there was tension. The light illuminated the guardian glow in both Passion and Aneurin's skin.

"Of course," Aneurin responded with an understanding nod. "It is well within your rights as a guardian to ask me such a question."

Passion almost flinched when he said the word "guardian." Aneurin always managed to say it with a subtle revulsion in his voice. He *hated* that she still held that title after what she had done and made sure that she knew it. Passion forced herself to remain calm and civil. If she let Aneurin tear her apart, he might not have time to question Electra and Isis. She would do anything to spare her daughters his passive aggressive bullying. They didn't deserve it and Passion would do anything in her power to protect them from it.

"I just have to make sure your loyalties are in the right place," Aneurin answered as he tapped the end of his pen on the parchment laid in front of him.

"I see," Passion replied. "In that case, yes. I do see where one might draw that conclusion, but I assure you my loyalties have always and will always remain with my home and my people."

Aneurin let out a quiet laugh. "There was a time when a question like that would've sent you into quite a temperamental fit."

Passion smiled and laughed behind her clenched teeth, not trusting herself to speak. She rubbed the back of her neck. Her back and neck were killing her; she was so tense.

"Yes, your younger years," Aneurin continued, spotting the tautness in her posture. "My, how you must miss them. All those exciting…indiscretions."

Why doesn't he just call me a slut or a harlot or whatever and get it over with? Passion thought as she played with her fingers, doing her best not to fidget.

"Those days are behind me," she stated, keeping her mask of pleasant obedience in place. "I'm a mother now. New set of priorities."

"Plenty of guardians still court their spouse after they decide not to have any more children," Aneurin stopped abruptly and put a hand over his mouth, putting on an impressive horrified face. "Oh, Passion, I do apologize. I forgot. Please forgive me."

Passion bit her cheek so hard that she tasted blood. *How could he forget? The sentence was mostly his damn idea,* she thought as her smile fell. She cleared her throat again and shook her head.

"It was a long time ago," she responded, her voice soft.

"Quite and I'm certain you have found other lovers for when you desired intimate company."

"Could I possibly get some water?"

"In a minute," Aneurin stated as he looked back to the parchment in front of him. Passion glanced over to the mirror, knowing she wouldn't see a drop of water while she was in that room. Aneurin had a funny way of forgetting simple requests during questionings. She began to tap the chair arm with her fingernails, longing to smack the irritating grin off his face. Aneurin always smiled, but something about it was always so cold. Especially when directed at Passion.

Aneurin shuffled a few more sheets of parchment, as if he were actually doing something besides taunting her. "You do seem to get into an awful lot of arguments with your mother, Lady Artemis."

Passion was unable to prevent a bitter laugh from

escaping her lips. She hated being in this room. She was a guardian. Guardians needed to be with nature to be happy and content. Passion had heard stories about guardians dying because they were cut off from open air for too long. *That would be my luck: I'd die in here, with him, and he'd say I died of guilt or shame or something along those lines,* she thought as she ran her hands over the smooth arm rests.

"What are those arguments about?" Aneurin asked, bringing Passion out of her thoughts. She started to tap the metal chair arm again, as she struggled to keep her fiery temper under control. She couldn't lose it here, not with him. Passion refused to give Aneurin the satisfaction. Besides her daughters, she also had her pride. A narrow-minded parasite like Aneurin shouldn't be able to get under her skin with his childish taunts and insinuations.

"My mother and I have always had our differences," Passion answered, already feeling drained. "Most mothers and daughters do. Electra and I have disagreements too. I'm sure Artemis and Adonia have some as well."

"I'm sure you're right," Aneurin was obviously humoring her, talking down to her, a surefire way to get on both Passion and Electra's nerves. "So how are your daughters?"

"They're fine," Passion replied, smiling a little.

"On our side?" Aneurin asked, not looking at the guardian across from him.

Passion's eyes flashed and her smile dropped. "Just because Roan is their father doesn't make them an enemy or mean they're at risk of becoming one."

"Passion, I would *never* imply such a thing," Aneurin said, another one of his infuriating smiles splitting his lips. He had found her weak spot.

"I know exactly what you were implying," Passion growled. She'd had it with his games.

"I don't believe an evil father necessarily means they'd be evil as well. Just like I'm sure having you for a mother doesn't mean they'll be so…adventurous, shall we say," Aneurin stated, leaning back in his chair. A smug grin split his features and his eyes dared her to say something.

Passion bit her tongue as she clutched the arms of the chair. Her knuckles turned white from the intensity of her grasp. She swallowed and relaxed her grasp, exhaling as she forced herself to settle down. Eventually, she was able to sit back in the chair and fold her hands in her lap. Aneurin looked somewhat impressed.

"Well, this has been illuminating," he said, marking something on the parchment in front of him. "Thank you, Passion. You may leave now."

Passion got up, forcing her stiff legs not to shake at the sudden weight. Her whole body ached and she made a mental note to go for a swim. She strode toward the door and her hand just settled on the lever when Aneurin's voice stopped her.

"Passion?"

She froze, not bothering to turn around, knowing he would speak again.

"Let's remember the chain of command, shall we?" he stated. From the low sound of his voice, he wasn't even looking at her. She lowered her head before pushing the lever down and pulling the door open. There were so many smart comebacks she could think of, but she bit her tongue again.

Aneurin smiled as he placed the parchment back in

his satchel. He had found the interview rather entertaining, as they usually were. He pulled out a new sheet of parchment, studying the sketch at the top of the parchment.

"Merrick," Aneurin called out to the head water guardian who had accompanied him. The man stepped into the open doorway, his small eyes fixing on the guardian king. Aneurin looked up from the parchment.

"Would you mind sending a messenger to summon Electra?"

"Right away, sir," he said with a nod.

Two minutes later Electra swaggered into the cold room. She wore her normal attire: jeans with an ordinary cranberry-colored backless top, something a human or shape shifter would wear. Her black shoes had a small heel on them, which clicked with each step she took. She never dressed properly and Aneurin couldn't do anything about it, since she didn't have an official title or apprenticeship yet. He let out a quiet sigh of disappointment. He never thought he'd come across a guardian more detrimental to guardian traditions than Passion. That was before Electra had been born.

"Please, have a seat," Aneurin gestured to the chair that was across the table from him.

Electra grabbed the chair and slid it around. She straddled it backward, resting her hands on the chair's head, looking at him with her piercing hazel eyes. They were green with little flecks of gold.

"Electra, I haven't seen you in a while," Aneurin began, looking pointedly at the way Electra was sitting on the chair. Electra, being her mother's daughter, ignored him.

"You should visit more often," she replied with a smile. She always acted civil and showed a modicum of respect, if only to appease him. Still, she remained rebellious to show him that he didn't own her. Her mother had trained her well, as had Jet and Lilly's children. It had been two years since his last assessment and Electra hadn't noticeably changed in that time.

"I see you still insist on dressing so," Aneurin gestured at her, "commonly."

"I seem to remember Mom turning your face red last time. Shame she didn't do it again, I really liked the color on you," Electra responded as she crossed her wrists.

"So much for pleasantries," Aneurin remarked as he scribbled a note on the parchment in front of him. "You're so much like your mother."

Electra shrugged, smiling wider. "Thank you for the compliment."

"I guess it can be taken that way," Aneurin agreed with a nod. "Of course, you wouldn't want to repeat her mistakes, would you?"

Electra's smile melted away and her eyes flashed. Aneurin folded his hands on top of the page in front of him and smiled sympathetically at the young guardian.

"I understand you've finally met your sister and have been teaching the young woman," he continued.

"Yes. Jade and Remington have been helping me," Electra responded, suspicion clouding her eyes. She had hoped to keep her sister out of this. After all, her twin was more shape shifter than guardian since she lived on Earth with the protectors. But she was a daughter of the Meadows since her mother was a guardian; therefore she was considered one as well.

"I see. You two are getting along than?"

"We're sisters — more than that we're twins," Electra frowned, confusion reflecting on her face.

"And you were both lied to," Aneurin added. "Kept in the dark for no reason other than your mother couldn't face up to her past…indiscretions."

"I highly doubt it was that simple," Electra responded, a hint of bitterness in her voice. Aneurin raised his eyebrow, deducting that there was still tension between Electra and Passion. She hadn't yet forgiven her mother for keeping her in the dark, even if she recognized that Passion hadn't done it for malicious or selfish reasons.

"You'd be surprised," Aneurin was quick to retort. "I assume you told your sister about your father."

Electra gritted her teeth. "I have."

Aneurin leaned forward as though he were about to share a secret. "Wasn't so difficult, was it?"

"For me, no. But I wasn't the one forced to abandon her solely because some old-fashioned guardians with perhaps more power than is wise think punishment more important than compassion and understanding," Electra replied, leaning forward a little. "I mean honestly, what did you hope to accomplish with that sentence?"

"I know it may be hard for you to understand, but our laws are in place for a reason," Aneurin answered. Electra clenched her fists, not responding.

"Your eyes tell me that I've upset you," Aneurin commented as he tapped the end of his pen on the parchment in a slow rhythmic pattern. Electra closed her eyes briefly and let out a slow breath, remaining calm and collected. When she was angry, her eyes often turned a stormy gray color. When she opened her eyes again, they were back to the hazel color they had been when she entered. A courteous smile found its way back onto her face and her hands relaxed.

"Not at all," she replied in a remarkably composed voice.

"Good," he said. "I'd hate for you to be upset with me over a misunderstanding. Would you mind fetching your sister for me? I wish to meet her."

Electra opened her mouth to protest, but thought better of it. No matter how Aneurin made it sound, he didn't make requests. He granted her the courtesy of asking, but if she refused then he would send someone else. Electra rose from the chair and turned to leave the interrogation room.

"Electra," Aneurin stated, his eyes never leaving her back. Electra turned and waited for him to speak.

"Before I forget, would you mind going over the rules of courtship? I think it would be very beneficial for the younger guardians to have a little…refresher," he stated with another pleasant smile. "That'll be all."

Electra clenched her jaw, annoyed by the insinuation. After a moment, she shook her head and disappeared from the room in a flash of silver light.

~~*~*~*

Isis walked into what looked like a typical interrogation room, mentally groaning. She didn't think any place in the Meadows could be so dreary. The room had a cold feeling to it, even though the air was perfect — as it always was in the guardians' home world.

A man sat in one of the chairs flipping through a

few papers. He had dark hair and light-blue eyes. The way he was dressed reminded Isis of an ancient deity: a fancy blue tunic with golden trim around the neck and sleeves. He looked up at her and did a double take. Isis tilted her head, unsure what the problem was.

"Forgive me," the man said with a friendly laugh. "You're the spitting image of your sister."

Isis frowned. "Yes, I think that's the definition of *identical* twins."

The man's smile didn't fade, but his eyes hardened momentarily. "Matching sense of humor too, I see."

God dammit, Isis thought, angry with herself for the small slip. How did she do that? Sometimes it felt as though she were born on everyone's bad side. Even the guardian man she had passed on her way into the room glared at her as though she had spat on him. No matter, she'd given Electra her word that she'd behave and that was precisely what Isis planned to do.

"Please have a seat," the man gestured to the chair across from him.

Isis sat in the smooth chair placed in front of the clean table. He smiled at her, but to Isis it looked like a smirk. She smiled back, sure that her grin probably looked just as phony.

"So, Isis, at last we properly meet. The last time I saw you was shortly after your birth, right before Jet brought you to Earth. I'm Aneurin, leader of the guardian men," he introduced himself as he looked down to the parchment in front of him, his eyes going back and forth as he skimmed the small amount of writing on it. "I've heard a lot about you over the years."

"All good I hope," Isis jested, hoping to come off

as endearing. When Electra had arrived to retrieve her, she had been furious. In the short time she had known Electra, Isis had never seen her sister so angry and was actually a little frightened of her. Isis assumed that it was the man in front of her who had infuriated Electra. She had warned her about the man Isis was about to see. Apparently, he was the most passive aggressive twit that Isis would ever meet.

"Mostly," Aneurin responded without any trace of humor, but still in a conversational tone. "Your great-grandmother tells me you have a clear understanding of the rules and laws of the guardians."

"Uh, yeah, mostly," Isis said, answering what she perceived to be a question. "I'm sure there's a lot more I have to learn though."

Despite her confidant tone, Isis was feeling more than a little uncomfortable and would rather have been just about anywhere else. She had never liked meeting strangers one on one, and the environment wasn't helping at all.

"I understand Electra has told you about the lineage on your paternal side?" Aneurin asked as he glanced at the parchment in front of him again. *I've just met him and he already has some kind of file on me? That can't be good,* Isis thought as she looked at the parchment in front of Aneurin. On the bright side, it was just one sheet. That was a comfort, a small one, granted, but still…

"She has and I've heard some things about Roan from Jet, Lilly, and Remington too," Isis responded. "Would you mind my asking what this is about?"

Aneurin clicked his tongue and scribbled something down on the parchment. "You've inherited your mother's impatience, I see."

"I'm sorry," Isis responded. She hated the sound of someone clicking their tongue, especially when it was directed at her. It was one of the most condescending sounds and it usually meant that someone was about to talk down to her, which was one of her many pet peeves.

"No, no, it is probably my fault. I do tend to go on and on. When you've lived as long as I have, it's difficult not to do," Aneurin responded in a mildly boastful tone. Isis scrunched up her nose a little and squinted at him, running her tongue over the backs of her teeth.

"I see that a mysterious figure has been following you around. Do you have any theories about the identity of this *shadow*?" Aneurin asked, his tone changing a little at the word "shadow." Isis decided to ignore it for the time being.

"No, I don't," she replied, brushing some hair behind her ear. "Maybe you have one?"

"Do you really think this *shadow* exists?" Aneurin asked with mild concern. Isis squinted again, staring at the guardian in bewilderment.

"I…don't understand the question. Are you implying that I was hallucinating or something?" Isis asked, trying not to jump to conclusions. The room seemed to shrink a few inches, taking on an almost claustrophobic atmosphere.

Aneurin shook his head as he continued to smile. "I'm not implying anything. It's just you're the only one who has actually seen this figure and even you really haven't seen him. It is a valid question, Isis."

"Wait, what?" She had to be misunderstanding something. If he was asking what she thought he was, then he was probably one of the most obnoxious people Isis had ever met.

"Isis, I understand you've had a pretty difficult life. You grew up human in a family that was, quite frankly, human. You've always been a bit of an outsider, which is to be expected considering you were being raised as a species that you were not, something we try to prevent."

"Excuse me, sir, but I resent that implication. I had a pretty decent life. Those ordinary humans you speak of with such disdain took me in and loved me as their daughter. So, I'd thank you not to look down on them," Isis interrupted. She had issues with members of her extended family, but she would be damned if she let this…man talk shit about her nuclear family. That was crossing a line.

"Could this shadow possibly be a figment of your imagination, maybe like an imaginary friend?" he kept needling her, ignoring her interruption. Isis' jaw dropped open and she stared at him for a moment, not sure how to respond. After a moment, she raised her hand, gathering her thoughts.

"Whoa, whoa, hang on. If it was a figment of my imagination, how do you explain the missing flashdrive?"

"Well, sometimes people take things and they don't know they do—"

"You think *I* took it?" Isis asked in disbelief, trying to keep her voice down. She was shocked at the guardian's insinuations. Isis had been insulted plenty of times in her life, even accused of things she hadn't done, but his accusations were just plain bizarre. He thought she'd taken something that could technically be considered a tool of war, if what she'd heard about it was true.

"I don't think you meant to," Aneurin replied and Isis narrowed her eyes. She really didn't like how close his tone was to pity. He began to tap his pen on the table again, which made her ire rise even more.

"We're going to be here for a while, aren't we?" Isis finally asked with a sigh. Aneurin smiled as he watched her.

"Just that much more time to get to know each other," he replied. She tilted her chair back and crossed her arms over her chest. She was nothing if not resilient and could hold out for as long as he could.

"Well then, let's explore this 'theory' of yours," Isis said, making quote marks with her fingers around the word "theory." "I'm absolutely *fascinated* by it. And while we're on the topic, I would *love* some clarification of this Key prophecy, since I hear only members of the High Council have actually read it."

~~*~*~*

"She's been gone an awfully long time."

Jade gave Alex a warning look and shook her head, cautioning her to tread very carefully. Alex shrugged and held up the target bag for Jade to kick. They were in the boxing ring in the training room. Electra was sitting on the benches against the wall and Shae was sitting next to her, peeling an orange. The sun was setting, casting dark orange squares on the floor. The bright lights above them had been turned on an hour ago.

"I wouldn't worry too much about it," Shae commented, gently bumping Electra with her shoulder. "My cousin has a temper, but she's also very talented when it comes to difficult authority figures."

"This is the same woman who was fired from three jobs for issues with authority," Alex pointed out, stumbling back a few steps when Jade kicked the target with much more force than was necessary.

"Hey, only two of those firings were technically her fault. The third was a totally unfair firing: that was her boss playing politics," Shae argued. "Isis was a good photojournalist and she was fired because she did her job."

"I appreciate your attempting to reassure me, but Isis has never encountered a guardian on a power trip," Electra said, raising her arm so she could play with the light from the setting sun.

Jade shrugged. "Aneurin's probably just—"

"Tormenting her," Electra interrupted, pulling her legs up so that she could sit cross-legged on the relatively narrow surface.

"Has a lot of questions," Jade finished her thought, glancing over to Electra. "It's the first time he's seen her and he just wants to…feel her out, for lack of a better term."

Alex's face scrunched up. "Ooh, there is *no* way you could phrase that without it sounding wrong."

Jade laughed and spun around, striking the target bag with impressive accuracy. Shae leaned against Electra, resting her chin on the young guardian's shoulder.

"Would you feel better if I called Isis?" she asked with her usual mischievous smile. "She never remembers to turn her phone on silent and I downloaded some…well, let's just call them risqué ringtones."

No sooner had she finished speaking then a bright

silver light began to form off to the side. There was a quiet sound, similar to breaking glass but not as harsh, and within a few seconds Isis was standing there. To everyone's great surprise, she didn't look infuriated or murderous.

"I'm never going to get used to that," she muttered to herself, glancing around the room. She noticed the four other women in the room, staring at her in varying states of surprise. Isis twisted to look behind her and then turned her attention to them again, spreading her hands with an expectant expression.

"Dammit, Isis. I was just about to call you," Shae said, snapping her fingers in disappointment. "I had the most perfect ringtone set up and everything."

"You didn't," Isis pulled out her phone, unlocking the screen. "For fucks sake, Shae. That's not funny. I hate it when you do shit like that."

"Isis, what happened? You were gone for a long time," Electra mentioned.

"He asked me questions and I answered them," Isis mumbled, still focusing on her phone.

"That's it?" Jade questioned. She and Alex were standing at the ropes of the boxing ring, both focused on Isis.

"Uh huh," Isis responded, swiping a couple things on her phone before slipping it back into her pocket.

"No insinuations? No insults?" Electra asked as she stood up. Isis stared at her, noticing how confused her twin seemed to be. Turning her attention to Shae, Isis shook her head.

"Contrary to what my cousin would have you believe, I do know how to handle difficult personalities," she replied. "I have dealt with passive aggressive people for most of my life. Someone like Aneurin is a cake walk."

Shae shook her head, laughing, "Just like the holidays, right Ice Queen?"

"Basically," Isis replied and Shae hopped to her feet, approaching Isis and draping an arm over her shoulders. Isis rolled her eyes and noticed that the other three women looked nothing short of impressed. If Aneurin was the most difficult person she would have to deal with in this new world she found herself in, then Isis felt she was probably in good shape.

"I'll kill him," an angered voice interrupted the laid-back environment in the workout space. "If he upset her, I swear, I'll wring his neck."

The women all glanced to the stairs where the loud voice originated. There was a quiet muttering before Passion and Jet stepped into view. Passion's dark green eyes fell on Isis and softened a little.

"Are you all right?" she asked.

"Apparently, our Isis here is incapable of being rattled," Jade mentioned, amusement clear in her voice. "Would've loved to have seen Aneurin's face during that questioning."

"What happened?" Jet asked, looking between the four women.

"We're getting a fascinating look at the inner-workings of human bred resilience," Alex remarked with her typical dryness, yelping when Jade elbowed her roughly in the ribs. Isis snickered and glanced over her shoulder, noticing that even Alex looked a little impressed.

"Right, well," Jet began, rubbing his hands together. "Lilly and I have another task for the four of you, so if you could go up to the office. I'll be up shortly; I just need to have a word with Passion and Electra while they're here."

Both Jade and Alex hopped out of the boxing ring, heading for the stairs. They were followed by Shae and Isis. Isis smiled politely at Passion when she passed her to go up the steps, wondering what sort of errand Jet was going to send them on this time. *God, I hope it's something not involving assassins,* she thought.

~~*~*~*

The Four sat around Jet's office, patiently waiting for his arrival. Jade was stretched out across the chaise lounge. Alex rested her weight on the side of it, watching the two chairs in front of Jet's desk. Shae sat in the one on the right and Isis sat next to her in the one on the left, focusing on her phone again.

"You'll never find all the secrets," Shae teased in a sing-song voice and Alex snorted. Isis glared at her cousin.

"Sometimes, I really hate you," she grumbled, turning her attention back to the phone.

Shae started giggling, putting a hand over her face. Jet strode into the office, looking much less stressed than he had in days, and sat behind the large desk.

"I got word from one of our contacts today at the local Nature Museum that they just discovered a new plant and it could possibly pose a threat to the Meadows. It's some kind of hybrid whose blossoms can wreak havoc with animals' senses of smell. There is a backroom that is sort of like a greenhouse. All you have to do is destroy the plant and any research on it, which should be relatively easy," Jet explained.

"Our contact is working late, so you should be able to get in and out fairly easily."

"How did humans get this thing?" Shae asked.

"We don't know," Jet answered with a frown. "The flower was thought to be extinct. Passion doesn't think the guardians even have a specimen."

"When do we go?" Jade asked, taking her usual unspoken role as the levelheaded leader of the Four.

"Midnight," Jet answered.

~~*~*~*

Midnight fell on the town, blanketing everything in darkness. A few streetlamps lit the street with a dirty yellow light. The only ones still awake were the club rats and the shape shifters. Being a nocturnal species, shape shifters often wandered about while most humans slept. Almost everything was closed beside the nightclubs. The few large buildings in the town were dark, slumbering giants in the night.

"You know, I'm sort of bummed we never get to use any kind of, like," Isis paused and rotated her wrist a couple times, "knockout gas or something like that."

Jade frowned and looked back at her as they continued down the dark hall. "Really?"

Isis shrugged and spread her hands. "Just saying. This kind of ruins the whole spy mystique if people just let us in the damn door. Where's the race against the clock to retrieve top secret nuclear codes? Where's the danger?"

"Says the woman who was almost killed by an assassin on our first mission," Alex pointed out and Shae let out a laugh, covering her mouth. Her eyes still sparkled with mirth. Jade shook her head and led the other three forward down the dark hall.

In the Nature Museum, a few guards patrolled past the exhibits. There was an evolutionary exhibit, which was filled with all kinds of animal models. Strange looking animals were shown evolving into normal looking species. Some animals looked fierce, teeth bared and yellow eyes wide. Others looked peaceful, sitting in front of a cave with small offspring hopping around playfully.

"Ooh," Shae started smacking Isis' arm, pointing at an exhibit across the hall with a stegosaurus. "We should all shift into dinosaurs!"

"That's a *terrible* idea," Isis was quick to protest.

"Not possible to take on the forms of extinct species," Alex reminded her as they emerged into the large main area. She went over to the front desk, hopping behind it, and pulled out the walkie-talkie the woman in the lab coat — Dr. Bell according to her nametag — had given her. Isis leaned on the desk, watching her teammate work.

"How long are the cameras out?" Alex pressed the button on the walkie-talkie.

"The security system will be off for as long as it takes me to finish setting up the new exhibit," Dr. Bell replied. "So, three hours, give or take."

Alex nodded to the other three women. "You heard her. Good luck."

Shae smiled and waggled her fingers. "Don't get into too much trouble. Isis, try not to get strangled this time."

Isis laughed sarcastically, flipping her off and cracking Shae up even more. Jade and Isis then shifted into sleek cats, Jade was tortoiseshell and Isis was all black. The two cats took off down the hallway, heading toward the small laboratory. Once they reached a large door marked "Botany Lab," which was decorated with vines painted on the door, Isis shifted back into human form. Testing the door, she gritted her teeth and prayed they wouldn't set off any kind of flashing alarm.

Jade shifted back into her human form and cautiously stepped inside the door, which lead to another hallway. After a moment, she nodded and gestured for Isis to follow her.

"Okay the botany lab is down the hall, second door on your right. I'll be in the room where they keep all the research. Be as quick as possible," Jade instructed. Isis nodded and raced off down the hall in the direction of the botany lab. She soon came upon the door and pressed down the lever, smiling when she found it unlocked, and opened the door.

Isis entered a room that looked like a jungle. Vines hung down from various containers. Bright lights were suspended over tables of plants of all shapes and sizes. The air was humid and Isis began to sweat. She could hear something bubbling nearby and noticed the brightly lit aquariums with different kinds of aquatic plants in them.

Isis reached into her pocket and pulled out the picture of the flower, studying it for a moment. It was a pale blue color with golden yellow inside; a rather pretty blossom. She pushed aside vines that hung down from the hanging plants. The leaves brushed through her soft hair, feeling uncomfortably similar to small fingers. Looking around the room, it took Isis a moment to locate what she was looking for. Isis took a clear plastic vial she had secured around her wrist with a rubber band. As she was about to tilt the vial, something caught her attention and Isis paused.

"Huh," she muttered, pressing the button in her ear piece. "Hey guys?"

"Yeah?" Jade's voice crackled through the static in her ear. Isis bit her lower lip, studying the plant in front of her. She drummed her gloved fingers on the metal surface of the shelves.

"How many flowers are supposed to be on this plant?" she asked, leaning forward to look behind the container. Despite the abundance of plants, the lab was remarkably clean. There wasn't a stray speck of dirt anywhere.

"Three. Why?" Jade responded.

"There are only two on it," Isis responded.

"What? You must have the wrong plant."

"No, trust me, this is the right plant," Isis replied as she caught another whiff of the pungent odor that was unique to the flower. She could see why an animal's sense of smell would be knocked out by the rancid scent. Isis was about to heave if she had to smell the damn thing any longer. It was awful, definitely not a flower for perfume.

"Just destroy it," Jade replied after a moment. "We'll tell Jet and Lilly about it when we get back."

"Fine by me," Isis said as she emptied the vial on top of the plant. The plant immediately shriveled into dust.

"I'm coming back," Isis reported, slipping the vial back on her wrist using the rubber band. She closed her eyes and allowed her body to form back into a black cat and ran out. She didn't notice the sharp green eyes watching her every move from the shadows.

~~*~*~*

They were halfway back to the mansion before anyone spoke.

"You're sure you checked all the refrigeration units?" Jade asked Isis. Isis glanced over to her from the passenger seat.

"Yes, Jade. I did everything you instructed, to the letter. It wasn't in the refrigeration units or at any of the lab areas. It was just…gone," she paused, thinking for a moment. "That seems to happen to me a lot, actually."

"How do you mean?" Alex asked.

"Well, first there was the body that vanished into—"

"Shit!" Jade yelled as she skidded to a rough halt. The four women inside the car were thrown forward and then back by the sudden stop. Isis looked out the window and was shocked to see the front of the dark blue car was just inches from a woman's slender legs. The woman stood confidently, a small smile playing on her lips, and she appeared completely unbothered at almost being run over. The small silver sequined hourglass on her shirt glistened in the headlights. The mysterious woman had short black hair, falling just shy of her chin. Most of her features were obscured by the bright glow from the headlights.

"Are you out of your goddamn mind, Sly?" Jade shouted. Sly smirked and leaned down on the car's hood, drumming her fingernails once.

"Come now, Jade, is that any way to greet a lover?" Sly teased with a suggestive edge in her voice. She trailed her fingers along the hood as she approached the driver's side. She leaned down, her dark emerald-colored eyes wandering over the other women in the car. They settled on Isis and Sly tilted her head ever so slightly, pursing her lips.

"The daughter of Passion," she observed, her eyes running over Isis. "The other one. Jade, dear, aren't you going to introduce us?"

"Isis, this is Sly. She'll likely be a huge pain in your ass," Jade stated, her eyes never leaving Sly's. Sly gave the woman a very dry look. Isis looked back out the windshield, smiling. She'd heard stories about Sly and had looked forward to meeting the protectors' elusive contact.

"Nice to meet you," Isis said, giving a small wave. Sly grinned, amused.

"She's *adorable*, isn't she?" she mentioned, turning her attention back to Jade. The elder protector raised an eyebrow as she held Sly's gaze.

"Did you want a ride to the mansion?" she asked and Sly laughed with a shake of her head.

"Weather's still warm and I promised Alpha I'd spend the night with her. Maybe over the weekend though," Sly answered. "I assume you're coming from the Nature Museum."

Jade nodded once. Sly reached into her shirt and produced a small folded bit of paper, holding it between her index and middle finger.

"You might want to take a minor detour and head over to the house of the guy who's the head of research. I happened to be passing by, heard some rather suspicious noises inside," she explained, offering the paper to Jade, who took it with a look of skepticism. "Word is that Blackjack is back on the prowl and challenging Adara for leadership. A job like this would probably be right up his alley, especially if he's making a play for this territory. Call the Monroes and verify the information if you must. I know how much protectors enjoy wasting time with bureaucratic nonsense."

Sly stepped away from the window, sauntering around the front of the car. She paused at the passenger's side, glancing at Isis again.

"Au revoir," Sly said as she melted back into the night. Jade shifted into gear and handed the paper to Isis.

"Call the mansion and verify that," she instructed. "I'm going to head in that general direction."

Isis nodded and pulled out her cell phone, dialing the number she had memorized a while ago.

~~*~*~*

The small brick house was completely dark. It sat between two similar looking houses in a suburban area and pretty much all the houses looked the same. All the neighboring homes had at least one light on outside.

The Four sat in the car across the street, watching the quiet house. Jet had verified Sly's information and agreed that it warranted a look. No one had been expecting the peaceful scene before them.

"There's a for sale sign on the front lawn," Isis pointed out. She didn't like the scene at all. The hair on the back of her neck had been standing on end ever since they turned onto the street. Something wasn't right and Isis was sure she wasn't alone in feeling that way.

"There are some Tasers in a box under my seat,"

Jade said. "Isis, you've got your baton."

"Yeah, that'll do a lot against an experienced assassin trying to start a coup," Isis grumbled.

Jade ignored her as she reached over and opened the glove box, pulling out a Berretta. Isis' eyes widened at the sight of the gun and when she twisted around, she saw Alex retrieving the Tasers. Twisting back, Isis stared at Jade. The older protector was checking to make sure the gun was loaded and she looked over at Isis.

"What?" Jade asked.

"We can't just go in there armed," Isis hissed, glancing to the house. "Best case scenario: he calls the police. People aren't exactly crazy about armed strangers barging into their house."

"Isis, I doubt he's even home. We're just going to knock on the door and I'd rather be prepared," Jade explained as she turned back to the other two in the car. "You two go around back and try to remain inconspicuous. Last thing we need is to catch the attention of a neighborhood watch. I don't need to remind you that if there is an assassin on the premises, we're not to engage unless someone's life is in danger."

Alex and Shae nodded. Shae opened the door on her side and the two slipped out, venturing down the street in the opposite direction. Jade turned back to Isis, who still felt unsure.

"We have to check this out. Come on," Jade murmured as she opened the door on her side. Isis hesitated for a moment and then opened her door, stepping out into the night. She moved around the front of the car and fell into step with Jade as they crossed the quiet street. Isis caught glimpses of domestic scenes in the surrounding houses: a woman reading beside the window, a child moving a toy car along the sill, a couple talking in a hallway. It made the small house they were approaching stand out even more. Even the sale sign seemed too still.

Jade and Isis jogged up the two stone steps to the dark-colored front door. Jade pressed the doorbell and waited while Isis stood against the thin iron railing, leaning back to peer into one of the windows. The blinds had been drawn, blocking any view of the inside of the house. Isis straightened up again when Jade rang the bell a second time. They could hear a faint echo of the bell inside. When there was no response, Jade's hand went behind her back, her fingertips brushing over the butt of the gun. She raised her free hand and knocked, two quick raps.

"Are we sure this is the right address?" Isis whispered.

"According to Jet, yeah," Jade answered, frowning. Isis let out a breath and rubbed her arms, shifting her weight. Something wasn't right with this picture. The guy had been living here for over ten years and Jet had said nothing about the house being on the market.

Jade tested the knob and it turned easily. The door was unlocked. Isis exchanged a glance with the older protector. That was just unheard of, even in the suburbs. Jade pushed the door and it creaked as it swung open. Isis stepped behind Jade as the older shape shifter moved inside the house.

The house was stripped bare. There was no furniture or appliances and it was freezing cold, which was unusual for a warmer evening. Ancient cobwebs were everywhere, trapping nothing besides dust.

There wasn't any trace of insects or animals. It looked like the house had been abandoned for years. Oddly enough, the structure of the home was sound from what they could see. The walls looked untouched and so did the windows. If it weren't for the dust and cobwebs, Isis would've thought the house had just been built.

Isis swallowed as she moved over toward the entrance to what was probably a hallway. She heard Jade mutter some words that she didn't catch and she glanced back to her teammate, who was crouching on the floor. Her fingers brushed over a suspicious stain, which looked a lot like blood from what Isis could see.

"What is that?" she whispered. Jade shook her head.

"Can't say for sure, but it looks and smells like blood," Jade answered, pulling her hand back and studying the room, her eyes slowly traveling over the space. "Well, this is really not reassuring."

Isis was about to respond when suddenly, the back door banged shut. She glanced back and just caught a glimpse of a shadowy figure.

"Jade!" Isis yelled as she took off down the hall in pursuit. She didn't bother to look to see if Jade was following. Isis reached the door, flung it open, and ran out across the short backyard, vaulting her slender body over the chain link fence and into the dark alleyway behind the small house. She glanced right and left at the surrounding garages. Turning right and speeding down the curved alley, Isis darted out across the street and into another alley.

The street lamps hummed above her and the soft night breeze brushed past her face. As she rounded another bend, Isis could see Shae and Alex up ahead at the other end of the alley. Shae had her hands on her knees and was panting while Alex held her Taser aimed at the stranger they had cornered. A tall man stood in front of them with his hands up. Isis glanced behind her when she heard the sound of a car screeching to a halt at the end of the alley. Jade shifted into park as Isis continued toward her two other teammates.

"I didn't do anything. How did you even know to be here?" the man asked in a tone that was oddly detached but at the same time irritated. He was obviously less than thrilled to be there.

"If you didn't do anything, why were you running away from the house?" Alex demanded. The man didn't reply, just crossed his arms over his chest. Shae glanced to Isis as she finally reached them. Isis stared at Shae and Alex, who both appeared out of breath.

"Who's this?" Jade asked as she ran up to them.

"We don't know," Alex replied, her eyes never leaving the man. "He's not exactly cooperative."

Isis turned her attention to the mysterious man and felt her eyes widen. The man looked at her and ran a hand over his face.

"Great," he muttered.

"Coop!?"

CHAPTER FOURTEEN

Shae and Alex did a double take, looking between Coop and Isis, confused. They had been intent on catching the man, who was unbelievably fast and agile. They weren't sure if they were supposed to recognize him. Coop put his hands down, crossed them over his chest, and leaned back against the garage behind him.

"Isis, how do you know this man?" Jade asked, her tone indicating that it wasn't a request. Isis licked her lips and turned her eyes to her teammate, already knowing she was in a world of trouble. *Really should have told someone about him,* she thought as she tried to figure out how to respond to Jade's question.

"His name is Coop. We've run into each other a couple times," Isis replied, glancing back to Coop. "Always at awfully convenient times."

Coop shrugged. "Is it a crime to be in the right place at the right time?"

"Yeah, it usually is," Isis replied as she glared at him. He was looking around the alley, not concerned about what was going on.

"Oh, oh, Isis. Honey, no," Shae said, trying to hide the amusement in her voice. "You are going to be in *so* much trouble."

"Did you call Jet?" Jade finally spoke, looking at Coop. Isis also watched the strange man, who stood very rigidly. His eyes were traveling all around the alley, not looking at the women surrounding him. It was odd, he seemed to be on edge even though he still appeared confident. There was something bizarre about the man.

"Yes. Is the scientist all right?" Alex asked, looking over to Isis and Jade.

"Didn't find any trace of him, did you?" Coop interrupted, his tone becoming softer. "House was empty, looked abandoned, am I right?"

"And how exactly would you know that?" Shae asked curiously. Coop pinched the bridge of his nose, as if he were getting a massive headache.

"Mainly because every shape shifter has heard the stories of bodies vanishing without a trace," he responded, looking to Shae.

"One problem, though," Alex remarked. "The scientist was human. The few incidents that you're talking about have always involved a shape shifter disappearing."

"The incidents that you know of," Coop corrected.

"What the hell are you doing here anyway?" Isis suddenly asked. "I got the distinct impression you were leaving town."

"I was going to after I finished a job for a friend," Coop answered, shifting his weight. "I got a little sidetracked when...Dr. Hoffman promised to give me some valuable information that I desperately needed, so I stopped here first and I wound up getting pulled into this mess. May I go now? I'm certain that your time would be better spent elsewhere."

Isis looked Coop up and down. Even though it was dark, she could see that he had been in some sort of scuffle. There was dirt on his face and clothes, which were ripped in a few places. It looked as though he'd been crawling through shrubbery or something.

"Okay, I understand how this looks," Coop's voice drew Isis out of her thoughts. "But you're just going to have to take my word for it. I didn't come here for malicious purposes and I didn't harm Dr. Hoffman."

"Interesting how you assume the man was harmed in some way," Jade remarked. Coop turned his eyes in her direction.

"Do you really think he just abandoned a lucrative career and position?" he asked, sounding as close to sarcastic as Isis had ever heard him sound.

"You know, you once offered to explain that strange symbol I found. Ever plan on following up on that?" Isis asked, her tone getting sharper. She was frustrated with the mysterious man and his way of talking without ever actually saying anything.

"If I did, you would assume I was lying," Coop replied in his normal evasive manner.

"If you want to leave, then tell us what exactly you know," Isis demanded.

Coop stared at her, refusing to answer the question. Shae shifted her weight, blowing some hair out of her face, while Alex and Jade exchanged a brief look.

"Fine, be difficult. The protectors can deal with

you. I'm done," Isis said, turning to ask Jade a question.

"If you want to condemn an innocent man, that's your prerogative," Coop replied. Isis' mouth dropped open and she turned her attention back to Coop, who just watched her. Shae snorted and turned around, covering her mouth as her shoulders shook.

"You are *unbelievable*," Isis hissed, seething. "You haven't given me one reason to trust you and yet you still expect me to just take your word and let you go."

"I did save your life twice," Coop pointed out with a shrug. Jade stepped forward and raised a hand, turning her eyes to Isis.

"You have a lot of explaining to do when we get back to the mansion," Jade warned her younger teammate before turning to Coop. "You're coming with us."

Coop's shoulders slumped a little and he nodded, offering no resistance when Shae and Alex took their respective places in front and behind him. Isis fell into step behind Jade.

"I really didn't think it was that big a deal," Isis offered, cringing at the glare Jade leveled at her.

"*A lot* of explaining to do," Jade reiterated as she stepped around the car and sank behind the door that she hadn't even bothered to close when she'd leapt out. *Great,* Isis thought as she opened the passenger's door and took her seat.

~~*~*~*

The ride back to the mansion was filled with an uncomfortable silence. The only time it was broken was when Alex called the mansion to tell the Monroes what had happened. After the call, none of the five occupants spoke another word and barely even moved. The walk to the main hall was equally grim.

Jet was waiting in the main room, along with Passion and Electra. Jet grabbed Coop's shoulder and disappeared. The other women also left the room to do various things, leaving Passion and Electra alone with Isis.

Isis stared at the space where Coop had stood. She didn't know what to think at the moment — everything had happened too fast for her to fully comprehend. She still wasn't sure what to feel regarding Coop: anger, gratitude, or both. There was a sadness about him, and it made her feel some sympathy for him, which pissed her off. Isis also worried about just how much trouble she was going to be in for not being upfront about a possible threat.

"Where will Jet take him?" she finally asked, not looking at the guardians.

Passion answered, "To the dungeons in the Meadows. Lilly's going to meet them in the Pearl Castle."

Isis looked at Passion, horrified. "You're not going to torture him, are you?"

"No, Isis. The guardians would never torture anybody. He will be questioned though," Electra explained. "The term dungeon has a much different connotation on Earth. Trust me, in the Meadows prisoners are treated with dignity and respect. The guardians, for our many faults, have always been firmly against torture."

"Oh," Isis said, glancing back to where Coop had been. "Just...be easy on him. I know he's infuriatingly vague, but I think he has been through some shit.

Maybe he has PTSD or something, I don't know."

"Isis, who is he?" Electra asked.

"Remember that call I got a while back?" Isis began. "Right before you taught me how to Appear?"

"The—" Electra stopped and her eyes widened. "That's the guy?"

"What guy?" Passion asked, concerned, as she glanced between the two of them. Electra was staring at Isis, who seemed to shrink in size.

"Yeah," Isis said, running her hands over face, deciding to come clean. "Look, he's probably harmless. I met him at a club and he's…kind of… turned up a few times."

Electra shook her head, muttering something under her breath. Isis put her hands in her pockets and shifted her weight, knowing that her twin was disappointed in her. Looking back on it, it had been one of her less than stellar ideas. She should have tried to dig up more information on Coop. At the very least, she should have told her teammates about the strange man. Despite everything that had happened, Isis didn't believe Coop was the culprit in the sudden disappearance of the scientist or anyone else for that matter.

"Isis, why didn't you tell Jet and Lilly?" Passion asked and Isis could hear the disappointment in her voice.

"He didn't strike me as dangerous and I really think he has some answers about all the weird occurrences that have been happening. I thought I could get some information out of him," Isis replied, realizing how lame the answer sounded. "It's hard to explain, but if anything, I genuinely believe he's a victim in all of this somehow."

"You still should have told Jet and Lilly," Electra commented evenly. Isis bit the inside of her check in frustration and pinched the bridge of her nose, closing her eyes as she tried to not lose her temper. She could understand their anger and disappointment, but they were just brushing off her explanation without listening.

"There's really not much I can do about it now, is there?" she replied, attempting to keep the anger out of her tone. "So I guess I'll be sitting in the cell right next to his."

"No, Isis," Passion responded as she glanced between the two young women. "I'll smooth it over with the Monroes, and Adonia as well, but I want your word that from this point on, you'll report any kind of suspicious coincidences to Jet or Lilly."

Isis let out a bitter laugh. "Trust me, after this, I'll report anyone I meet."

"I doubt you have to go that far," Electra said with a small smile. "Is there anything else we should know about Coop?"

Isis was quiet for a moment as she looked at the two women, rubbing the back of her neck as she thought about the question. The lighting in the room was bright without being harsh, helping to relax the tension she was carrying in her shoulders.

"There was one thing he told me, when we first met," Isis began hesitantly. "He said that there were people after us that not even Jet, Lilly, or the guardians knew about. And he mentioned that there was going to be some kind of change in leadership in the assassins soon, which I know is a concern. But something about the way he phrased it; it sounded like there was someone behind it, someone who wasn't an assassin."

Passion looked over to Electra, her mouth partly open as though she wanted to say something. Electra shook her head once. Isis arched an eyebrow as she watched them, waiting for an explanation.

"What was that?" she asked. The two looked back at her, neither offering an explanation. Her eyes widened.

"Oh my god. You know what he's talking about," Isis stated in disbelief.

"Not entirely, Isis. It's more just stories and…" Electra began.

"What about how it all ties in with the vanishing body?" Isis interrupted, glancing over to Passion and back to Electra, looking for any sign they knew more than they were letting on.

"Whenever you have unsolved mysteries, it's a breeding ground for various rumors, most of them utterly ridiculous," Passion explained. "There've always been stories about places that might hire assassins and manipulate their hierarchies, but there has never been any evidence to suggest any merit of truth to them. And believe me, we've looked."

She glanced over toward the window, shuddering a little. The guardian rested a hand at the base of her throat.

"Well, I'd like to read up on some of those rumors and stories," Isis mentioned and Electra nodded.

"I'll dig up some books in the Meadows library. Jet and Lilly probably have a few books in the library here that would also be worthwhile," she agreed.

"There's one other thing I'm unclear on," Isis said, placing her hands on her hips. "Everyone says Roan disappeared. Was he wiped from existence like the body from the warehouse?"

Passion looked over at Electra and then at Isis, shaking her head. "Not exactly."

For the first time, Electra appeared just as confused as Isis as she turned her attention to the older guardian.

"Is there something else that has been kept from me, Mother?" Electra asked. Both Passion and Isis turned their attention to her, picking up on the trace of bitterness in her voice.

Passion glanced at her reflection in the window, debating about how to answer the question. After a moment, she swallowed and rubbed the side of her neck. Her shoulders dropped a little and she gestured to the entertainment room off to the side.

"The two of you are going to want to sit down," Passion began as she followed them into the room. "It's a somewhat lengthy story and not a pleasant one."

She moved over to a large chair and sat down, folding her legs up under her. Isis glanced over to Electra, who shrugged and moved over to the couch. Isis followed and sat next to her. Passion interlaced her fingers in front of her and leaned against one of the arms of the chair.

"You should know that only one other guardian knows the whole story of what happened the night Roan disappeared," Passion started, turning her eyes to her feet for a moment. "If the High Council had known the entirety of what happened, I probably would have been banished."

Isis frowned. "Should you be telling us? Couldn't some guardian, I don't know, overhear us?"

Electra stared at Isis in confusion. "Why would

they be listening?"

"I got the impression they were omniscient," Isis replied with a shrug. Electra chuckled and shook her head. Even Passion appeared amused.

"I'm sure some would like to be," Electra replied. "But no, they can't just hear everything going on here. Really, Isis, they're not gods. They have no reason to eavesdrop on the mansion. God, omniscience would be an absolute nightmare."

Isis shrugged and leaned back, watching Passion. Electra folded one leg up under her, watching her mother with a similar expression. Isis noticed a certain amount of stiffness in her twin's posture. Over the months, Isis had come to learn just how sheltered her twin's life had been. Living a relatively ordinary life had given Isis a chance to build up a suit of armor. Lying was a trivial thing to her. She was used to being lied to, which had led to her developing a certain amount of cynicism, but Electra had been raised in the Meadows. Nobody had a reason to lie in her beloved home.

"The night Roan disappeared," Passion began, running her fingers through her wavy hair, "he had gotten in a fight with another assassin over who knows what, territory most likely. He somehow managed to drag himself back to the apartment we shared. Fate often has a funny sense of humor. An incredibly twisted kind of humor, granted, but funny in its own way. After witnessing Roan for what he really was, I returned to the Meadows but I just happened to be in the apartment to get a few things I had left behind. When I heard a noise outside, I went to the front door, opened it, and there he was. He had lost so much blood that he couldn't even stand up.

He looked up at me and there was so much pain in his eyes. He didn't have much time left and I couldn't get a healer because guardians can't heal people who have taken a life in cold blood and I wasn't supposed to be there anyway."

Passion frowned, looking off to some distant point. "Healing abilities don't run in the royal line, so I couldn't have done it. Still, Roan was suffering and I can't bear to see anyone suffer, regardless of their past actions. So I did what I could — I helped him over to the couch and tried to stop the bleeding. As soon as I got him to the couch, he started insisting that I leave and go back to the Meadows. He kept saying he didn't want me to get in trouble with the guardians. When I refused to leave him, he told me he was sorry and that he loved me. I reassured him as best I could. A few minutes later he was gone."

Passion went quiet, rubbing her hands together and swallowing. "I didn't know what to do, so I did the only thing I could think of. I appeared back in the Pearl Castle. What happened next was pure luck. Donovan, one of my lovers, happened to be there. He had come to meet with Adonia and Artemis about some unrelated matter. He saw me Appear, covered in blood and shaking, and approached me to make sure I was all right. I remember that I could barely form coherent sentences, but I somehow managed to tell him everything that had happened. He was shocked, but he calmed me down and we returned to the apartment so I could show him Roan's body."

Passion looked to her hands again, which still moved in slow methodical circles. "When we arrived, the body was gone and hasn't been seen since. Donovan and I agreed to never discuss what had happened. We both would have faced consequences if the High Council found out that we'd returned to the apartment."

"I don't think I've met Donovan," Isis mentioned, glancing over to Electra. She shook her head.

"He's a night guardian and one who delights in needling the members of the High Council. For as progressive as he is, Donovan is a notorious cynic," she said with a shake of her head.

"Donovan has been on the High Council for a long time, Electra," Passion stated with a quiet sigh. "The amount of politics he regularly has to play is enough to turn anyone into a cynic."

"I can understand that," Isis said with a small shrug. "Kind of."

Electra glanced back at her sister, who offered her a small smile. Isis looked back to Passion and leaned forward. It was a quiet evening in the mansion, but none of the three noticed.

"I don't understand what is so horrible about what you did," Isis said. "Was it going back to the apartment or helping Roan?"

Passion leaned back a little. "It's complicated and due a lot to archaic ways of thinking. Many older guardians still hold a very black-and-white view of evil, which they almost see as a kind of virus. They would view my helping Roan as conspiring with an assassin. There's also a very strict rule that states we're not supposed to be on Earth without a protector escort."

"So, they would've preferred you left a man to bleed to death on your doorstep?" Isis asked, taken aback at the thought. Humans had plenty of inhumane and unjust laws, but at least they attempted to protect good Samaritans most of the time.

"Unfortunately, when someone has committed as many crimes as Roan did, the members of the High Council have zero tolerance. I should've called Jet and Lilly and let them handle the situation," Passion explained. Her tone told Isis that she didn't agree with the sentiment at all.

Isis shook her head, looking between the two women. "I'm sorry, but I really don't see how leaving someone to bleed to death is any less evil than murder. Do the guardians really believe that murder justifies murder?"

"No, but they do think it justifies apathy," Electra responded, unable to keep the resentment from her voice. "Remember, Roan wasn't exactly a victim of injustice. He didn't care about anybody. If the price were right, he probably would have killed his own mother. He killed at least fifteen innocents, including one of his own brothers, without a second thought. His body count is probably higher, but assassins are very good at covering their tracks."

Isis stared at Electra for a moment, before looking back to Passion. "Roan had brothers? Please tell me they're not assassins."

I really need to get some kind of family tree or something, she thought as she waited for a response. Electra shifted her weight and lowered her leg back to the floor, rolling her neck to work out the kinks.

"Roan had five brothers; all are protectors. He actually came from a fairly prestigious family. He was the son of Dayton, a legendary protector. In fact, his portrait is upstairs. The Deverells all take after him and their mothers," Passion responded with a slight smile. Even Electra grinned at the mention of the

Deverells.

"Do they have names?" Isis asked, leaning back in the couch. She wasn't sure she wanted to know about any more blood relations. *Twisted little bunch they are,* Isis thought with morbid amusement. Electra had already explained to her that guardian women only traced their lineage through the mother's line and the men traced theirs through the father's. The High Council kept track of family lines to avoid any incestuous relationships and nonbinary guardians chose which family line they wanted to be counted among.

"Ajax, Malone, Devin, Nero, and Orion," Electra answered. "They were kind of my father figures as I grew up, though I can't really remember Orion."

"Why? What happened to Orion?" Isis asked.

Electra and Passion exchanged another quick look, which irritated Isis. The two seemed to have a secret unspoken language, which they only used when debating whether or not to tell Isis something.

"Orion was the brother Roan killed. He was the eldest of the six," Electra finally answered. Isis looked up at the ceiling, contemplating how weird her life had become.

"So, what about the surviving four?" she asked, keeping her eyes on the ceiling. Isis wanted to find all the skeletons in her biological family's closet in one swoop if she could so she wouldn't be blindsided later.

"They never stay in one place too long. Assassins have placed a high price on the Deverell family," Passion answered. "They travel around the world and report back to Jet and Lilly about any strange occurrences or feuds that might require their attention. Last I heard, they were in Greece, but that was a few years ago. You'll meet them eventually."

Passion got to her feet. "I'm going to check and see how the interrogation is going. Don't worry, Isis. I'll smooth things over with Jet and Lilly."

"Thanks," Isis said, although she doubted Passion could smooth things over completely. It wasn't that she didn't have faith in the guardian, but her own track record spoke for itself. She got on people's bad sides, especially those in a position of authority. Even in her youth — Isis hadn't been a juvenile delinquent, but there were plenty of adults who probably hoped to never meet her again.

Isis watched as Passion disappeared in a brilliant flash of gold light. Electra twisted her body around so that she was facing her twin. She rested her head against her fist and Isis stared up at the ceiling again.

"You okay?" Electra asked. Isis shrugged in response.

"Yeah. Why wouldn't I be?"

"Just finding out all that stuff and this whole thing with Coop," Electra responded. "It's got to be kind of confusing."

"Electra, a few months ago, I was a human only child with a job I hated. Now I'm some sort of mythical creature living in a mansion — which is actually more like a castle — who will probably be expected to save the world or something at some point," Isis explained, sounding a little amused. "Very few things can shock or confuse me anymore."

Electra smiled and shook her head. Isis continued to look up at the immaculate ceiling, resting her hands on her brow. The shape shifters in charge of cleaning were miracle workers. Isis was still impressed by how the mansion could be so clean and still feel so cozy. It truly was home for the shape shifters who lived there.

"Do you really think Coop is a threat?" Isis asked, turning her eyes over to her twin. Electra shrugged.

"I don't know. It's possible he has some kind of malicious intentions, but I also know that people sometimes surprise us," she answered.

Isis stood up and stretched, feeling the need for solitude. "I'm going to take a walk and get some fresh air."

"All right," Electra got up. "I'm going back to the Meadows. I'll tell you when I hear anything."

Electra disappeared in a flash of silver light. As soon as she had vanished, Isis walked the short distance to the main hall and the large front door. Opening the door, she stepped out into the night. For a while, she just walked the grounds, enjoying the pleasant evening. The warm temperature and the darkness were soothing. Isis closed her eyes and inhaled the sweet air. The mansion's isolation protected it from the unpleasant smell of cars and industry. She had actually grown rather fond of the mansion.

Isis soon found herself at the mansion's front gates and heard a soft whistling in the distance. It was odd that someone would be out walking, so late at night and so close to the hidden property. Something about the whistled tune was almost hypnotic, though. Without thinking, Isis opened the gate and began walking down the winding road. Rubbing her arms as a cool breeze wrapped about her, Isis decided to walk just to the end of the street to see if she could find the source of the sound. Her mind was racing with the evening's events and she needed a few minutes to clear it.

Isis was so absorbed in thought and the whistling, which seemed to make the world melt away, that she didn't notice when she stepped onto the main street. She also failed to notice the man fall into step just behind her. Before Isis had a chance to struggle, a strong hand wrapped around her mouth, pulling her back as a needle was plunged into her neck. She felt a warm liquid coursing through her veins and her vision became hazy. Soon, her legs started to wobble as if they couldn't support her weight anymore. *Fuck, I'm an idiot,* she thought as she tried to force her body to wake up and put up a fight.

"We meet again, daughter of the Meadows," she heard a chilling steely voice breathe in her ear before she succumbed to darkness. The assassin smiled, switched the small recorder off, and lifted the limp woman up, bringing her to a car that was parked a short distance away. After putting her in the trunk, Blackjack returned to the driver's side and got into the car. The engine soon roared to life, settling down to a quiet purr. Blackjack pulled away from the curb and drove off into the night.

As the car sped away, a dark figure stepped out of the shadows and walked down the street, turning onto the mostly hidden road. He reached the mansion's gate and approached the security box, looking up to where he knew there was a security monitor. Drawing a large Glock from a holster hidden beneath his hoodie, he shot out the camera. For good measure, he fired two shots into the security box containing the hand scanner. A silent alarm would be flashing in the mansion's security room, alerting the inhabitants to an intruder. Soon, someone would be out to investigate. Now he had to point them in the right direction.

The figure placed the gun back in its holster and took a deck of cards out of one of the inner pockets of the jacket. Sliding the cards out, he swiftly sorted through them and pulled out the ace and king of spades. Drawing a large Bowie knife, he moved to a nearby tree illuminated by the light near the gate. Plunging the blade through the cards and nailing them to the tree, he then jogged back down the hidden road, pursuing Blackjack.

CHAPTER FIFTEEN

When Isis came to, the first thing she noticed was that she couldn't see. She could just barely make out pinpricks of light piercing some kind of rough fabric, possibly burlap. The next thing she was aware of was the feeling of being dragged down some hard surface. Isis immediately began to struggle against whomever or whatever was holding her, kicking and scratching with everything she had. Somewhere in the distance, she could hear arguing. It sounded like a woman shouting at a much calmer voice, which spoke in a clipped tone. Someone wasn't happy and the person they were unhappy with didn't care.

Isis was tossed into some kind of cell as the hood was yanked off her head. Muddied water splashed up to her stomach as she fell to her knees in a chamber partly filled with the liquid. Isis got to her feet and slammed her body against the heavy iron door, pounding it with the flat of her palm.

"Asshole!" she yelled, giving the door one last kick for good measure. There was a sliding panel on the upper part of the door where she assumed her jailers could look down on their prisoner. Another sliding panel at the base of the heavy door was likely for food to be slid through. Isis put her hands on her hips and blocked out the awful stench of rot and decay as she forced herself to calm down so she could figure out what to do. Feeling her pockets, Isis found they had been emptied. Looking up, Isis saw a light bulb but nothing else. No windows or other openings that she could potentially escape through. An idea began to take form in her mind as she remembered her guardian heritage.

Dumbasses, Isis thought as she closed her eyes and thought of the mansion. Time passed, but she didn't feel warmer or see the usual flash of light nor did she hear the soft sound similar to glass breaking. She opened her eyes and looked around to find herself in the exact same cell.

"For fucks sake," she grumbled in frustration.

"No guardian magic in this place," a rough but amused voice murmured. Isis rolled her eyes over to the panel and saw a pair of cloudy blue eyes studying her. They were a little too rounded, like a rodent's eyes, and the flesh around them was as chalky as a corpse.

"Great, my jailer is a goddamn cliché," Isis muttered under her breath.

"Poor little mouse is trapped in the spider's web," the unpleasant voice taunted. "But she won't be here for long. He's coming to retrieve her."

"It's fly, jackass," Isis snapped in annoyance. "Spiders catch flies. Jesus. If you're going to threaten or intimidate me, could you at least make an effort to get your goddamn metaphors right?"

The eyes had a momentarily puzzled look in them before the panel was slammed shut. Isis glanced down to her damp jeans. They had ripped when she'd fallen and her knees were badly scraped. She scowled, irritated by the possibility of getting an infection or tetanus. There was an uncomfortable looking slab of stone jutting out of the wall to the side, likely meant to be a bed, and the gray walls were completely smooth. The water most likely deterred vermin from making their home in the small space. It didn't look like anything could live in the space for very long. There were no cobwebs and the sloshing water kept any kind of silence at bay.

Isis glanced back up to the sliding panel when she heard it swish open. A pair of yellow eyes appeared at the top. The flesh was a healthier shade than the man with the cloudy blue eyes and the eyeliner led Isis to believe her new visitor was a woman. Her eyes were filled with hatred — probably directed at anyone who crossed her path. The unnatural glow behind her shone in Isis' face.

"Where is it?" the woman growled at her.

"You're *really* going to have to be more specific. I'm not telepathic," Isis replied, using irritation to cover her bewilderment.

"Bravado won't protect you, daughter of the Meadows," the woman spat at her. "You're in assassin territory now, a place even protectors won't venture into."

Well shit, Isis thought as she continued watching the woman. "How's the change in management going?"

The gold eyes widened, fury flashing across them. The panel slammed shut again, leaving her in dim lighting. Isis glanced up when the light bulb above her flickered. Leaning against the back wall in the small cell, she tried to figure out just how the hell to get out of there. No answer was forthcoming, only the quiet splash of dirty water. As Isis walked around the cell, thinking about what to do, she began to hear quiet popping sounds, which filled her with dread, followed by muffled shouting and footsteps rushing around. It sounded like gunshots somewhere overhead and Isis knew she didn't want to be trapped with assassins during some kind of gunfight.

~~*~*~*

The dungeons of the Meadows were not the same sort of prisons found on Earth. There were different levels, all designed in a similar way, with most prisoners being kept in the uppermost level. The walls were painted a neutral color, to help prisoners feel at ease. Large windows across from the cells enabled the prisoners to see outside and bright lights illuminated everything in the nighttime hours. The cells themselves were fairly well-sized. Each cell had a desk and a bed and the floors were tiled. There were three walls of brick and one of guardian glass, a material exactly like ordinary glass except for one difference: guardian glass was unbreakable. The door could only be opened by the guards. In the middle of the door was a slit where meals were passed through. It was designed to be a comfortable living space. The guardians were strictly against any form of cruelty and they always had been.

Jet and Lilly stood in front of one cell, watching the prisoner behind the glass. Coop leaned against the desk in his cell. He had already told them his story at least four different times and judging from their stillness, he was about to give it yet again. Why couldn't normals ever just accept simple truths? No, they had to poke and prod every little detail, no matter how insignificant. Coop kept his gaze forward on the opposite wall, keeping the protectors in his peripheral vision.

Coop was beginning to feel a small amount of aggravation. Or was it frustration? It had been so long since he had experienced any kind of genuine emotion that he sometimes couldn't remember what it was like. The protectors didn't know how lucky they were. Living in blissful ignorance, unaware of the horrendous things happening almost right under their noses. It was a luxury Coop knew he would never experience and sometimes he felt some resentment because of it.

"Coop, did you kill the scientist?" Jet asked after a moment. At least he finally accepted that the man was most likely dead. No more beating that particular dead horse with a stick.

"No," Coop replied, glancing over at Lilly. She had been silent since she had arrived, observing him. Her expression was neutral.

"Who did?" Jet pressed.

"Nobody you would know," Coop answered. Jet dragged a hand down his face, his expression reflecting frustration. Coop was certain he had already gotten under his skin, most normals disliked vague responses. This was especially true of normals in positions of leadership.

"Coop, we have to catch—"

"Even if I did tell you, you would not believe me.

You live in a world much different than the one I'm accustomed to. If I'm being honest, I don't even know how to begin explaining the situation to you and I have no desire to bring even more danger into your lives."

"What does that mean?"

"It means you are wasting time asking me these pointless questions. I won't tell you anything, and I have been conditioned to withstand all known forms of torture. So, you wouldn't be able to pry an answer out of me even if you did believe in making use of enhanced interrogation techniques," Coop stated.

Lilly dropped her arms to her sides, clasping her hands in front of her. "What if we started with a simple question, one that wouldn't implicate you in any possible crime? Who are you?"

"Someone who has places to go and is growing weary of answering the same questions," Coop answered, crossing his arms over his chest.

"You make helping you very difficult," Jet commented. Coop turned his attention to Jet, sizing him up.

"Helping me? I don't need your help. If anything, you need mine," he said, looking between the two protectors. Despite doing his best to sound sincere, Coop knew he couldn't entirely change his natural flat tone.

"So why don't we try to help each other?" Lilly offered. Coop shook his head, almost chuckling at the notion. The protectors were very noble, he'd give them that.

"If only it were so simple."

Jet laughed. "You remind me of one of our informants. She enjoys being an enigma and acts as though she can take on the world by herself."

"I assume you're speaking of Sly."

Jet's eyes widened in astonishment and he turned his gaze to Lilly, who looked just as surprised as her husband. Coop looked between them, reading the stunned expressions.

"We have some…mutual contacts," he explained. Lilly's eyebrow rose at the answer and she turned her attention back to Coop.

"Mutual contacts?" she asked.

"Okay Coop, enough with the roundabout answers," Jet said. Coop looked to the side when he heard hurried footsteps. Someone was coming down the hall.

"Sorry, but we're about to be interrupted," he said without taking his attention off the hall. Jet opened his mouth to say something, but then the large door to the corridor of cells was thrown open. Electra ran down the hall to the protectors, her long hair bouncing as she jogged over to them. Her eyes were wide and her expression reflected concern, perhaps even fear.

"Jet, Lilly! Shae and Jade just called for me. Isis is missing. The ace and king of spades were found on the mansion's grounds, just outside the gates," she explained, a little breathless.

"She's in trouble and you're shocked?" Coop asked, ignoring the hostile glare Electra aimed at him. "I was under the impression that was a fairly common occurrence."

"Adara or Blackjack might think she has the Key," Jet mentioned, glancing at Lilly.

Lilly shook her head. "I think it more likely they think her valuable due to her guardian blood. Either way, she's probably not in the best—"

"I think you're both incorrect," Coop mentioned, rubbing the back of his neck. "There are people interested in replacing the leader of the assassins in your territory and appointing their own puppet in her place. Targeting a member of the Four would be an excellent show of strength. I didn't think he'd make a play this soon, but this would definitely be a move he'd make."

Noticing they were all staring at him with varying degrees of suspicion, Coop shifted his weight a little. "Look, if that is the case, and I am not often wrong about these things, then Isis is in a very, *very* dangerous situation. She's going to need help getting out of it and I am willing to help you, but not without a price."

"How did I know that was coming," Electra snarled, her furious gaze fixing on the man in the cell. Coop glanced at her before turning his attention back to Jet and Lilly.

"I don't want money or any kind of favor. I only want to leave town and be left alone. Plus, I do owe Isis and if there is a takeover of assassins happening, it is being orchestrated by someone whom I have unfinished business with."

"Coop, you haven't given us any reason to trust you and now you're asking us to let you go on nothing more than your word? Why should we even consider such a proposition?" Lilly pointed out.

"And what makes you think you'd be any use to us or her anyway?" Electra inquired, her fists still clenched at her sides. "If there's some kind of assassin battle happening, what use is a single ordinary shape shifter?"

"I am not an ordinary shape shifter. Trust me, I'd be *very* useful in this rescue," Coop replied. The three people in front of him looked at him with skepticism. Coop sighed, his shoulders dropping in defeat, and he rubbed his eyes. He'd have to tell them something if he wanted to get out of there. *Or show them,* he thought as he looked over to the glass wall, an idea taking shape in his mind. It was something he loathed doing, but he couldn't think of any alternative.

Coop turned so that he stood in front of the glass wall, a little less than an arm's length away, and made a flat palm on the glass, as if he planned to press right through it. He took a deep breath in through his nose and let it out through his mouth as he focused entirely on the wall. Drawing his hand back, Coop curled it into a fist and prepared himself.

"I wouldn't do that if I were you," Electra warned. "That glass is—"

Coop let his fist fly, striking the glass so hard that Jet, Lilly, and Electra winced. Coop was completely unaffected. By all rights, his hand should have shattered under the force with which he had hit the unbreakable glass. Even more surprising, there was a relatively large crack in the glass where he'd struck it. Coop drew back his fist again, let it fly, and it burst through the glass. Lilly let out a cry of surprise and covered her mouth with her hands, her eyes widening.

Coop snaked his hand out of the hole and reached over to the box, pressing his hand against it. After a moment, there was a pleasant beep and a clicking sound. In a movement faster than the eye could see, Coop pulled his hand back into the safety of the cell as the door slid open with a swooshing noise. The mysterious shape shifter stood at attention in the open cell, waiting for their reaction.

Jet, Lilly, and Electra still stood against the wall across from the cell, just staring at the hole in the unbreakable glass. Jet and Electra's mouths opened in the shape of an "O" and Lilly still had her hands over her mouth.

"I believe time is of the essence," Coop reminded them after a moment.

"Your hand isn't bleeding," Electra snapped, the statement sounding more like an accusation.

"No, it was but it healed almost instantly. Glass won't leave any lasting damage, not even guardian glass," Coop replied, wiggling his fingers behind his back. He really didn't enjoy doing things like that. It revealed a little too much of what he was and it led to too many uncomfortable questions.

"*How?*" Jet finally found his voice again. "How did you do that? Why didn't you do that before?"

"How did you open the cell door?" Lilly asked, dropping her hands from her mouth. "Only the guards can do that."

"It was unnecessary to reveal my abilities before. I had to show you that I'm very useful to you at the moment and that seemed the best way," Coop answered. "And I can open anything...well almost. Think of me as a kind of living lock pick, among other things."

"Enough with the riddles, Coop — give us a clear answer!" Electra's shout startled Jet and even Lilly looked over at her. Coop turned his eyes to her, remaining at attention.

"All I can tell you, all I will tell you, is that I have been modified and trained extensively to be a superior soldier," Coop answered as he turned his attention forward again.

"By whom?" Jet asked.

Coop shook his head once. "Better if you don't know. You really don't have time for that at the moment. Not if you want her sister back in one piece."

Jet bit his lower lip and looked over at Lilly, who nodded in agreement after a moment. Coop couldn't help but be impressed with how the two were able to communicate without words, something most normals weren't able to do with such ease. Turning his attention to the windows behind them, he noticed it was dark. The night would offer a decent advantage, certainly one he could work with.

"Could you get Alex, Jade, and Shae into Adara's manor?" Jet asked Coop, ignoring the icy look Electra sent in his direction.

Coop lifted his shoulders in a small shrug. "If you wish to use that strategy, yes I could. However, you would have a better chance of success if I went alone."

"No!" Jet and Lilly stated at the same time.

"As you wish. But I will walk away without a second thought if I even sense one of them pointing a weapon at me," he warned. He knew how irrational normals could get when it came to loyalty, particularly to friends and family.

"Fine, you're free to go for the moment," Jet said, turning to speak with his wife in a hushed tone. Coop stepped out of the cell, waiting for Jet or Lilly to Appear with him.

He was grabbed by Electra, who slammed him against one of the smooth walls. His body tensed up for a moment as he fought the overwhelming instinct to break the young guardian's arm. Though he could've slipped away from her, Coop allowed her to feel as though she was in control for the moment. He admired her strength and skill. Even though he didn't completely understand why, Coop was a little envious of the fact that she loved her family. He was envious of most families, another privilege that had been denied to him. A violent shake brought Coop out of his thoughts.

"If anything happens to my sister, I will hold you personally responsible," she threatened, leaning in closer. "You do *not* want me to hold you responsible, Coop. I will hunt you to the ends of the Earth and I *will* make you suffer."

"I won't let anything happen to Isis," Coop promised. *Her eyes haven't changed color,* he noticed, knowing that was a clear sign of how angry she was.

Electra let him go, shoving him toward the protectors. Jet grabbed his shoulder and they Appeared at the mansion in a flash of light. Jade, Alex, and Shae were pacing around the main room. All of them stared when the three Appeared in the hall and then threw questioning glances at Jet and Lilly when they saw Coop.

"Coop is going to take you to the manor and he'll get you in," Jet explained, holding up a hand to prevent any questions or protests.

"According to him, there's likely a hostile takeover happening," Lilly continued. "We have seen this territory change hands between assassins before, as has Jade, and it is always an incredibly violent affair."

"Wait, are you telling us that Isis is in the middle of a damn assassin coup?" Shae asked, her wide eyes darting between Jet and Lilly. The other two women had similar expressions of concern.

"Unfortunately, that may be the case. Even if she's not, any kind of extraction is likely to be dangerous, so take a few weapons and exercise caution. One of you needs to keep an eye on Coop. Lilly and I will call on some of our allies and hopefully get you some backup."

The three women nodded and hurried to prepare for what would undoubtedly be a very dangerous mission. Coop turned his head to the side when he overheard Jet mention the assassin leader's name, eavesdropping on the conversation he was having with Lilly.

"She might be open to a temporary truce," he mentioned. "If only to remain in power."

"It's a risky proposition, one many protectors would not agree with," Lilly replied. "But if it could keep things stable for the time being, perhaps it is worth a try."

"You can't stop what is happening," Coop mentioned, interrupting their conversation. "The assassin invited a very powerful threat into her territory, unaware of the danger. And he will not leave until he has control of this state."

Coop swallowed and turned his gaze to the towering doors a few feet away. "I've seen too many people underestimate this man. And they have all paid a very steep price as a result."

Hopefully Isis has enough sense to stay out of the thick of whatever fighting is going on, Coop thought, tapping the ground with his heel as he focused on the tile.

~~*~*~*

Isis stood with her back against one of the walls near the door to her cell. She had pressed herself flat against the rough cold stone and was waiting. Her entire body was rigid and in one scraped hand, she held a broken light bulb. The cell was completely dark and it had taken a while for her eyes to adjust to the darkness.

She had used the cramped conditions to her advantage and climbed up the walls using nothing more than her long legs and arms. Once she had reached the ceiling of the cell, Isis proceeded to unscrew the light bulb. When she'd done that, she put the narrow end of the bulb in her mouth and carefully climbed back down. That had been the most difficult part of the entire ordeal. Somehow, she made it all the way down without falling or getting a mouthful of glass. Back on the ground, she coughed and broke the bulb against one of the walls. Now at least she had a weapon. It was a pitiful excuse for one, but a weapon was a weapon.

The sounds overhead had been intensifying and now sounded like an actual battle. She could hear mutterings and hissing in the hall, which made her even more nervous. Isis knew she had to be out of the cell before whatever was happening in the upper levels spilled to the lower ones. Prisoners of war didn't often fare well during hostile takeovers.

"She's in the last cell. Help yourselves," a faint deep voice spoke from somewhere outside. It was followed by the scraping sound of footsteps, coming closer and closer...

When she heard the panel slid open again, Isis sank even deeper into the shadows, tensing up as she waited for her opportunity. *Please, please, please, please,* she begged to whatever guardian might be listening.

Luck was on her side for once. The panel slid shut again, followed by the clanking sound of turning gears and a lock being opened. When the cell door began to open, Isis put one foot on the stone step that led to the door. She grasped the wall with her free hand, waiting.

A gangly figure stepped into the open door and Isis didn't even pause to see what he looked like. She swung the sharp broken bulb at his face, using her forward momentum to put extra force into the swing. There was the sickening sound of glass digging into flesh, followed by screams of agony as Isis tackled him to the floor. Blinking a few times as her vision adjusted to the sudden brightness, Isis scrambled to her feet and started to dash for where she hoped the exit was. Something hot and round was jammed into her back and a jolt of powerful electricity surged through her body, causing her to stumble and hit the floor again with a cry, her limbs twitching.

Turning to look over her shoulder, Isis stared up at the strange jailer, who had gotten back to his feet. He looked like a living corpse with his pasty skin. He wore a dark butcher's smock over yellow clothing. There wasn't a trace of hair on his skull, not even eyebrows or eyelashes. The broken bulb was jutting gruesomely out of his right eye socket. His good eye was wide and filled with rage. In his right hand, he held what looked like a long silver baton with a round end. There was bright red button under his gloved thumb. He pressed it and the end crackled with blue electricity. He began to advance on Isis even as she scooted away from him.

A loud blast made Isis curl up and cover her head

for protection. She felt small bits of rock and dust rain down on her. The man let out a roar and Isis heard something thrown, followed by a scream. Looking up, she noticed the jailer glaring down the hall. He turned his eye back to her and started to advance on her again.

In a split second, Isis decided to change her strategy and lashed out at the man when he got within kicking range. Her kick found its target and dislocated his kneecap. He howled in pain as he crashed to the ground and Isis followed through with a kick to the chin that snapped his head back, knocking him out cold. When she moved to find out if the man had any weapons on him, a hail of bullets sprayed from the opposite end of the hall, making her duck behind the safety of a wall again. Isis was almost grateful for the strange architecture and layout of the house, which provided a fair amount of coverage. She gritted her teeth, trying to figure out what to do, her eyes falling on the prone man. There was a sheath with an impressive-looking knife attached to his shin.

"This is so stupid, this is so stupid," she grumbled, shaking her head. "God, this is a stupid plan. I'm gonna die, I'm gonna die. I am *so* gonna die."

Isis dove at the body, forward rolling on the prone man, narrowly avoiding the bullets from the guards at the far end of the hall. Isis quickly snatched the knife, never stopping, and hid behind the nearest wall, avoiding the second hail of bullets. It wasn't a gun, but it was better than a broken bulb.

Screams and gruesome popping sounds echoed from where the bullets had come from. Isis tried to steady her breathing as she adjusted her grip on the knife. She wished she had more experience fighting with knives. *One problem at a time, Isis,* she reminded herself as she kept her back pressed against the wall. Heavy footsteps were coming down the hall. Isis glanced around, looking for any kind of useful feature that she might be able to utilize. There were three heavy iron doors along the wall on each side of her and the bricks between them looked quite old. There was a large opening in front of her and one behind her.

The sudden sound of a distant explosion, followed by a tremor underfoot, made Isis crouch down. She swallowed as she tightened her grip on the knife and peered around the corner of the wall, finding herself face-to-face with the eyes of another strange man, identical to the first one she'd taken out except that he was much broader.

Isis swung the knife with a yell and managed to slice the man's arm open. He laughed as he swung at her and Isis ducked under the clumsy swing, spinning so that she was behind him. Slicing the knife down his back, she jumped back when he turned and lunged for her, barely managing to avoid his enormous hands. Isis froze when she saw the patch sewn on one of his sleeves, which bore the same symbol she had seen in the warehouse. The momentary distraction proved to be a costly mistake when Isis found herself lifted clear off the ground and tossed down the hall. Isis slammed into a wall, the breath rushing out of her body, and lost her grip on the knife. She blinked rapidly and struggled to get her breath back, forcing herself back to her feet. To the right, the loud report of gunfire continued. All around her were the broken bodies of dead assassins, which she assumed was the handiwork of the lumbering giant who was her current problem.

Suddenly, bright yellow lights started flashing throughout the hallway and Isis cringed when a harsh noise echoed throughout the space, some sort of alarm, as best she could tell. *Well that can't be good,* Isis thought as she rose unsteadily to her feet. Every breath caused stabbing pain and Isis couldn't help but wince, supporting herself against the wall. Noticing the glint of the knife she had dropped, Isis dove for it. Spotting movement out of the corner of her eye, Isis gasped and hid behind a nearby pillar just as a group of armed man descended the stairway. She could hear bullets striking the stone of the pillar and closed her eyes, turning her face away from the dust the deadly projectiles created.

If I manage to get out of this alive, Shae will never let me hear the end of it, Isis thought as she tried to figure out what to do.

~~*~*~*

Shae had never been in the middle of an all-out gunfight before. When they reached the valley where the Obsidian Manor was located, they could already see the flashes of guns being fired in the distance. Jade must have noticed how uneasy Shae was because she assigned the younger protector to keep an eye on Coop while she and Alex helped their allies create a window to hopefully attempt an extraction.

That plan had gone to shit almost immediately. The entire scene was all-out chaos. There were strange men in uniforms firing with wild abandon. They learned the hard way that there were also a good number of snipers and marksmen. Coop had told them earlier to avoid anyone wearing a strange symbol, which he had hastily sketched on a scrap of paper Alex provided him with. *They will mostly rely on the assassins to do the killing, but if they see me or realize the protectors are interfering, they will take a more active part in the fighting. Believe me, they won't run out of ammunition and they will kill you,* he had warned.

Shae stayed on Coop's heels as he led her down the second floor hall. Pausing at a body in the hallway, Coop knelt down and retrieved the firearm the woman still clutched. Checking the magazine, he handed it to Shae. Grabbing the second gun in the holster on her waist, Coop again checked the mag, barely even noticing the bullets hitting the wall nearby. Shae found cover to duck behind, wincing at the sheer amount of noise. She couldn't hear anything other than yells and gunfire. Though she wouldn't admit it, Coop scared her by how unaffected he was by the violence that surrounded them. Shae was a highly trained protector operative, but even she sought cover when bullets were flying. Coop might as well have been taking a pleasant stroll through a park. He turned his attention to the far end of the hall and fired a couple shots. Shae heard a thump before he turned his attention to her again, nodding over his shoulder.

They turned down another hall and Coop suddenly raised his hand, signaling to stop. He tilted his head a little and his nostrils twitched.

"There is an armed assassin in the room down this hall, second door on the right," he explained. "The scent is...familiar."

Shae swallowed and followed close behind Coop. Right before they reached the door, it started to open.

Coop rammed his shoulder into it, knocking back the person behind the door. Shae heard the weapon clatter to the ground as Coop moved into the room. She raised her gun and moved into the doorway, freezing for a moment when she recognized Blackjack. Blood was flowing from his broken nose as Coop landed another punch to his face. Before the assassin could retaliate, Coop leapt up and brought his elbow down hard on Blackjack's skull, knocking him out and possibly killing him. Shae felt her mouth drop open, stunned by what she had just witnessed. Coop moved faster than anyone Shae had ever seen — so fast that he was little more than a blur. She stared at his back, jolting a little when he twisted around, his eyes traveling up to some point above her head.

"There's an alarm going off," he mentioned, gesturing to where he was looking. Shae stepped inside the room and noticed a flashing yellow light above the doorway. Turning her eyes back to Coop, she noticed he had a thoughtful expression on his face.

"How the hell did you do that?" Shae asked, glancing over her shoulder to make sure they had no unwanted company. "Blackjack is one of the most renowned assassins. He's been around for ages."

"Still a normal," Coop replied as he continued to look around.

"A what?" Shae squinted, confused by his response. Coop was already searching Blackjack, retrieving his weapons.

"Nothing. He's good, dangerously so, but I've been trained to handle adversaries like him in much greater numbers," Coop stated, his tone telling Shae that she wouldn't get any further explanation from him. "And he's still alive."

Coop stood up again, pointing his gun at the unconscious assassin. Shae quickly strode forward and put her hand on his wrist, noticing he flinched a little as if he weren't used to contact. She shook her head when he turned his eyes to her.

"No," she said in a firm voice and Coop stared at her, puzzled.

"I don't understand," he said, glancing back at Blackjack's prone form. "If I do not kill him, he will wake up and he will be angry. This man has very powerful backers, powerful enough to fund all this carnage. He's the one they want controlling this particular territory. Those are *not* adversaries you want to deal with. This is the most logical solution."

"I don't care! You can't just shoot him in cold blood," Shae protested.

"You don't think he would do the same to you or Isis or anyone else you care about?" Coop asked.

"I know he would and that's why I'm different from him," Shae explained. "I don't kill unless there is absolutely no other alternative."

"When he wakes up—"

"Coop, if you kill him, won't his employers just find another assassin to be in charge of this territory?" Shae asked, deciding to try a different tactic. "And won't they be just as bad?"

Coop studied her, his brow furrowing. "Yes…that is likely."

"So, killing him doesn't make much sense," Shae replied, turning as she pressed a button on her earpiece. "Jade, Coop knocked out Blackjack in one of the bedrooms on the second floor. Can you send someone to take care of it?"

"Maybe, if we can. There are a lot of guards," Jade responded, pausing. "A lot of them have that symbol Coop mentioned on the ride over."

"We'll be out to help once we've retrieved my wayward cousin," Shae said, switching her earpiece off again. She nodded to Coop and gestured at the open door. He hesitated and Shae could tell he didn't like leaving a loose end. After a moment, he moved out into the hallway.

They were about to turn the corner when Coop suddenly pushed Shae back and made her stand flat against the wall behind him. She was about to ask what the hell he was doing when multiple bullets struck the wall, sending slivers of plaster and wood flying everywhere.

"You have a mirror?" Coop asked, yelling over the constant noise. Shae reached into the pocket of her jeans, retrieving a small compact she always carried, and passed it to him. Coop opened it and held it out in front of him, using it to see around the corner. More bullets hit the wall and Shae heard glass shattering.

"Uh, sorry about the mirror," Coop said as he tossed the shattered remains of the small compact. Shae shrugged as she checked to make sure the safety was off on her gun.

"It was cheap, easy to replace," she replied with a small grin. "What did you see?"

"There are at least ten guards on the stairs, probably about seven on the opposite end of the hall. They've got us pinned down," Coop reported, glancing to the side. "They managed to create a crude but effective kill box."

"Well there's a window at the end of the hall behind us, but I don't think the drop would be a pleasant one," Shae mentioned. "And we'd probably have more guards waiting for us down there anyway."

Coop was looking to the hall and Shae found his expression to be unsettling. It looked like he was contemplating doing something incredibly stupid.

"They'll be keeping Isis in the lowest level and chances are the hostiles down there are a different breed, not something protectors can handle," he said as though speaking to himself. He suddenly turned to Shae, his dark eyes intense.

"I can get down there, past the kill box, but it will be easier with cover fire," he explained. "I do not wish to ask you to take any unneeded risk. There are at least two marksmen out there, so you would have to be quick and not be exposed for any longer than necessary."

"What?" Shae asked, bewildered when Coop started to strip off his bulletproof vest. "That's suicide. You'll be killed before you reach the stairway!"

"I don't intend to use the stairway," Coop replied, tossing the vest to the side. He tensed up and bent a little at the knees, his eyes focused on the small section of railing they could see from where they stood.

Shae followed his gaze and her mouth dropped open. "That's a straight drop to solid stone, not to mention the epicenter of the fucking firefight between a bunch of assassins. How is breaking your legs and getting riddled with bullets going to help Isis?"

"My bones are stronger than yours. And I've been

trained to survive in the middle of firefights," Coop explained, not glancing at Shae. "I've free fallen further distances than that and fought way more opponents. Just lay down that cover fire when I tell you."

"Coop, no!"

"Now!" Coop shouted before taking off.

"Would you just — for fucks sake!" Shae spun out from behind the wall when Coop bolted, firing a few shots. Coop sailed over the railing, plummeting out of Shae's sight and she waited, listening for the inevitable crash and shout of pain. Men were so damn impulsive at times, especially shape shifter men. A bullet grazed her upper arm and she gasped, swinging back behind the cover of the wall. Most of the gunmen appeared to be more focused on Coop and she could only hope he somehow managed to avoid their bullets.

Shae closed her eyes and turned away from the wall as more bullets hit it. There was the sound of shouting, gunfire, and thumping as the fight continued to rage on.

"Jade, I've got a situation on the second floor," Shae said into her earpiece. "I'm pinned down and running out of ammo and oh yeah, Coop just went over the damn railing!"

~~*~*~*

Isis watched the shadow growing on the floor near her, indicating someone was closing in on her hiding place. Pressing her back against the cold pillar even more, she tightened her grip on the knife and waited. The muzzle of a high-powered rifle soon came into view, followed by a gloved hand. Isis felt her insides clench up and she tried to steady her breathing. She didn't want to kill anyone, but she was aware that she probably wouldn't have a choice.

Just as the round helmet started to appear from around the pillar, there was a loud shot and Isis jumped back when a spray of blood shot out of the back of the guard's neck. There were more rapid shots, followed by the sound of bodies dropping to the ground.

"Enough of this childish game," she heard the woman's voice from earlier echo throughout the large space followed by another couple shots. "This is an impulsive and sloppy move on his part and if he thinks I will not retaliate, he has severely underestimated me."

Peering out from behind the pillar, Isis spotted a taller woman reloading a shotgun. She wore a sidearm on her right side and a blade on her left.

"And have those goddamn protectors taken care of! I'm going to put down the hybrid," the woman yelled to someone behind her, who scurried off to do her bidding. Isis felt hope swell in her chest at the mention of protectors.

The woman finished reloading the gun and moved to the hall leading to the cells, disappearing from Isis' sight. Once her footsteps faded away, Isis peeked out from behind the pillar again. Creeping toward the wide stairs leading to the upper level, Isis glanced down the hall but didn't see the woman. She bolted for the stairs as fast as she could go and had just put her foot on the first step when the butt of a shotgun slammed under her chin, knocking her down. Isis let out a cry and writhed on the dirt floor, wondering why the hell anyone would have a dirt floor in their damn basement. The tall woman stood over her, the shotgun resting on one shoulder.

"One of the advantages of living in a place as large as this for as long as I have is I know all the nooks and crannies, all the little secret passageways," the woman said as she advanced on Isis. "We haven't properly met. My name is Adara, I'm the leader of the assassins in this state and unfortunately for you, you're about to be added to my killed marks list."

"Charming," Isis grumbled, pushing herself up on her elbows. "Doesn't seem like I'm your biggest problem at the moment, lady."

"No, but killing you would definitely help end the ruckus upstairs," Adara agreed, lowering her shotgun so that she held it in front of her, moving closer to Isis. "You see, a man I worked for thinks he can simply depose me because of some silly little flashdrive, which I understand you're in possession of."

"Not this shit *again*," Isis groaned with a roll of her eyes. "I don't fucking have it!"

"Oh, I believe you, but my former client doesn't. At first, I was planning to hand you over to him so that he could torture you for an answer you don't have. However, since he has chosen to be so aggressive, I've decided it's in my best interest to shoot you in the face so that whatever information you have dies with you," Adara finished, pumping the foregrip of the shotgun. "Nothing personal."

Isis lashed out and kicked the woman in the stomach. She arched backward and struck Adara under the chin with her foot. Landing neatly, Isis spun on the balls of her feet and took off in the opposite direction, trying to think of a plan as she fled back to the hall of cells. A round hitting a wall dangerously near her made her stop and raise her hands. Isis closed her eyes and waited for the end. *I can't fucking believe this is how I'm going to die,* she thought with no small amount of irritation.

"I changed my mind. It is personal," she heard Adara's angry voice behind her. *Figures,* Isis thought, nodding a little. It seemed fitting that she would die as a result of getting on the bad side of a goddamn assassin. *Steve will definitely make sure that goes in my obituary,* she mused, feeling a pang of sadness at the thought of never seeing her friend again. Isis let out a yelp and stiffened when the shotgun went off again, the shell embedding in the wall above her.

"Uh, your aim is a little off," she mentioned, turning around and staring at the scene that greeted her. Coop slammed the woman against one of the heavy iron doors and tossed her to the ground, standing above her with his foot on the shotgun she had held only a moment ago.

"You must be one of their little toys," Adara said, staring at him. "What a pesky little runaway you are, but you ought to bring a nice price."

"You're a fool if you think you can trade me or that one for your life," Coop responded, nodding toward Isis. "They have sent in the troops, instated a new assassin in the position you have held for many years. Your life, and the lives of those loyal to you, are forfeit. You have nothing."

Isis stared between the two, not following the conversation at all. She watched as Adara got to her feet, drawing the blade she wore. Coop kicked the shotgun toward Isis, and lunged at the assassin. Isis retrieved the shotgun as the two fought, trying to figure out how to work the damn thing. Looking up, she watched as Coop moved with an unnatural ease and speed, dodging the precise sweeps of the knife. Adara was a skilled fighter, but she couldn't land a blow on Coop. When she thrust the knife forward, he latched onto her wrist and pulled her over his hip, throwing her to the ground. Maneuvering into a painful-looking joint lock, he forced her to drop the knife. She let out a growl of frustration, thrashing about in an attempt to break his hold, but Coop didn't react.

"I have an offer if you are interested. One that would allow you to keep your life," Coop said, his grip not loosening. Adara scowled, still attempting to break his hold while Isis looked to the strange man, wondering how he managed to get away from the Meadows.

"I'm listening," Adara got out between gritted teeth.

"They wouldn't be so threatened by you if you weren't valuable in some way. My allies and I believe that you were the lover of one of the higher ups, possibly one of his sons. We also believe you know the location of a laboratory, one of the main ones, among other things. Are we correct in that theory?"

Adara was quiet for a moment. "And if you were?"

"We want to know where it is. You tell us the location, anything else you know, and help us catch your former lover, and we'll allow you to go on your way," Coop finished. Isis stared at him, her mouth dropping open. There was something different in his eyes, something like hope or relief.

"Oh, I don't think so," Isis immediately protested.

"Stay out of this, protector! Don't make me use

you as bait," Coop warned before addressing Adara again. "Do we have a deal? The information and your ex for your life?"

Fury blazed in Adara's eyes. "Fine."

Coop released her, flipping back to his feet. "We'll have to get past the protectors and you're not to harm that one, the guardian's daughter."

Adara's eyes flicked briefly to Isis, but she turned her attention back to Coop, smiling. "Lead the way."

Isis raised the shotgun, aiming it at Coop and Adara. "Um, hello? She's a freaking assassin and she was going to kill me. I'm not just going to—"

She didn't get another word out as Coop moved in a blur, disarming her before she even had a chance to react, knocking her to the ground again. Even in the darkness, she could see his eyes blazing as they fixed on her.

"I do not have time for your simplistic black and white morality," he snapped, sounding close to angry. "I promised Jet and Lilly I would help to extract you safely. I have done that. You can come with us, reunite with your team, and leave. Or you can stay down here and wait for the guards or assassins, who will kill you without a second thought."

Isis narrowed her eyes at him as she stood up again. "You're a despicable man."

"Undoubtedly," he replied. "Stay behind her. There's a secret passage that will take us outside. The fighting is sparser out there. You're less likely to get shot."

"Well, I've already been stabbed in the back, so what's a little bullet wound?" Isis stated, moving to stand behind Adara, wishing she had a weapon of some kind. Coop stared at her, his brow furrowing a little.

"I was unaware you were wounded. Are you—?"

"It's a figure of speech, you ass!"

Coop looked puzzled but moved to stand in front of the assassin. They started to move toward the staircase leading to the main part of the manor.

"You won't escape him, daughter of the Meadows," Adara mentioned, turning her head a little. "Someone has their eyes on you. I almost feel pity for you. Me they just want to kill, but you…oh, if only you knew what's waiting for you."

"If only you knew how much I *really* don't care," Isis replied, wanting to get out of the creepy manor. She didn't need to be subjected to some assassin's vague threats. As they approached the stairway, Isis felt very uneasy. It was too quiet. Something was wrong.

"Coop…?"

They reached the stairway and immediately, bullets rained down on them. Isis gasped when blood splattered in her eyes, temporarily blinding her. For a split second, she thought she had been shot. When she realized she hadn't, Isis threw herself backward, attempting to find cover so she could get the blood out of her eyes. Her hand brushed against something wet and spongey causing Isis to gag, her mind conjuring up unpleasant images about what she had touched.

She heard a crunch, clattering, and three shots. Wiping the blood out of her eyes and off her face as best she could, Isis blinked a few times to clear her vision. A shadow fell over her and Isis twisted, striking out with a strong kick. She managed to hit the guard's knee, causing him to lose his balance, and was about to follow through with a kick to the helmeted head when she heard a thwack noise. The man stiffened and toppled over, revealing the grip of a knife embedded in the back of his neck up to the hilt.

"No, no, no!"

She turned her attention from the dead man to where Coop was looking at Adara's body. Isis swallowed as she got back to her feet, looking around for any more guards as she approached him. Looking down at the body, Isis could tell the woman was dead. She had been shot in the head a couple times and half her skull was missing.

Coop had a hand on his forehead, a defeated look on his face. "Every time. Every time I get close to an answer or a lead, they always snatch it away. They toy with me, they constantly toy with me and I can't take it anymore."

Isis looked over at him, hearing a hint of frustration in his flat tone. Her eyes widened when she saw he had been shot in the stomach and the shoulder. It looked like a bullet had grazed his neck and temple as well. Blood was pumping heavily from his wounds and she couldn't believe he was still standing, let alone walking.

"Coop, you've been shot!" Isis exclaimed as she looked around for anything to bind the wounds with.

"I am aware," he replied, moving over to the steps and slumping down on them. Dropping his face into his hands, he let out a long breath.

"We have to find something to slow the blee — what the fucking hell!?"

Isis stumbled back when the wounds started to rapidly disappear, the skin healing almost instantly. Coop didn't appear to notice as his gaze traveled back to the assassin's body. Folding his hands together, he rested them against his lips. To Isis, he looked like a beaten man and she couldn't help but feel some sort of sympathy for him. Isis approached him again and cautiously reached out, putting a hand on his shoulder.

Coop jerked back at the touch, raising his hand as if to ward off a blow, and she pulled her hand back. He looked back at the body. Isis bit her lower lip and sat next to him. For a moment, they sat in silence, listening to the fighting above them. It sounded like it was gradually letting up.

"I think...I think I'm tired," Coop finally spoke. "I do not know for certain, but it feels like what I've read about tiredness."

He ran a bloody hand over his dark hair, closing his eyes. "It is frustrating to constantly fight when you know it's unlikely any good will come from it. You fight and you fight, but you still lose. I don't understand how normals do it."

Isis shrugged, brushing some hair behind her ear, grimacing at the ache in her body. "I don't know if it will make you feel any better, but...you did manage to save my skin tonight, even if you were kind of a dick about it."

Coop let out a quiet huff of laughter, glancing over his shoulder. "The fighting is letting up; it will be over soon. The guards are starting to withdraw. They've completed their mission; they have no reason to stay. Your teammates will be looking for you. And me too, I suppose."

"I guess I owe you a drink," Isis mentioned, looking up to the heavy door leading to the main floor. It was getting a lot quieter.

Coop shook his head. "I don't consume alcohol. I'm either going to be in the dungeons in the Meadows or else out of town anyway."

"Ah," Isis said, raising an eyebrow. "Things to do, places to go, people to save? That kind of thing?"

Coop smiled faintly, a sad reminiscing kind of smile. "In a way. There are some shape shifters out there who need help and I'm one of the only ones who can do that."

"Shape shifters?"

"I wish I could tell you more, but there is no time and these walls have many ears."

"Go," Isis whispered, looking up the stairs. The sounds of gunfire had almost completely ceased and even the alarms had gone silent. She glanced back to him when she felt his eyes on her. He was staring at her with a questioning expression.

"I do not understand."

"Of course you don't, you're from Mars," Isis teased with a grin. "You saved me and now I saved you, so that makes us even. I'm going to leave and as far as I'm concerned, you escaped after…helping me out. But if our paths cross again, don't expect me to stick my neck out for you."

Isis stood and hurried up the stairs, shutting the door behind her. Coop stared after her for a moment, trying to understand the gesture. She was the second member of her family to set him free. Coop looked down to his hands, swallowing as his mind drifted back to his dark past, losing track of time for the first time in ages. It wasn't often he had a moment to rest and he wanted to savor it for however long it would last.

"I've said it once, I'll say it again: you're a stupid,

stupid man."

Coop shook his head. "How could you have possibly known I'd be here?"

Dane strode out from one of the dark corners, likely leading to some sort of secret passage. Sauntering over to the stairs, he pulled himself up and over the railing, sinking down on the steps next to Coop, glancing around the space at the bodies. He rolled his eyes back to Coop, an almost mischievous look creeping onto his face.

"Never can leave the past in the past, can you?" he observed. "Bloodbaths follow us wherever we go."

Coop grunted in response, leaning back on the steps. The smells in the air were starting to bother him, but he disregarded it.

"A nice normal saves you, offers to buy you a drink, and you just let her vanish into the night," Dane clicked his tongue and shook his head in mock disappointment. Coop turned his eyes back to Dane.

"We're not allowed that luxury. The Corporation saw to that long ago, the one you insist on returning to despite being offered a way out," he pointed out. Dane leaned back on the steps, his smile slipping only a little.

"Don't lash out at me because you can't repress what you are, my friend. I've warned you about that how many times now?" Dane began, interlacing his fingers as he put them behind his head.

"Right," Coop replied. He had forgotten about most of what the Corporation did to shape shifters, which he was thankful for. When someone escaped from hell, reminiscing about the place wasn't exactly high on the list of things to do.

"You know, you could come back with me. I'll

help you catch the guardian's daughter—"

"Leave it alone, Dane," Coop warned and Dane lifted his shoulders in a nonchalant shrug.

"Figured I'd offer, in case you had actually come to your senses," Dane said, straightening up so that he rested on his elbows. "Off to save the world then?"

"Not the world, just you and the others," Coop replied, as his eyes travelled over the blood splattered walls. "You deserve to be free, Dane, whether you believe it or not."

"We don't need saving, Coop. You're wasting your time," Dane muttered, his tone becoming much darker. He stood up again, sticking his hands in his pockets as he began walking up the stairs. "Your attempt at selflessness is going to get you captured and something tells me the welcome home party won't be a pleasant experience."

Coop shook his head and looked down to his thumbs, tapping them together. He had given up on giving Dane hope a long time ago. It was impossible to give hope to someone who didn't believe in it. Still, no one could blame Dane for being the pessimist he was. Few knew what he went through day in and day out, what he had gone through from the day he'd been born. The fact that Dane retained his sarcastic personality was a miracle in and of itself.

"You didn't answer my question," Coop said, stopping Dane in his tracks. "How did you know I would be here?"

Dane twisted around, looking over his shoulder. "I didn't. I heard some rather interesting whispers around the barracks, something about a shift in power among assassins, and I was intrigued. When I got here, I noticed the protectors were getting involved and I know how much you enjoy fighting hopeless battles alongside the underdog. Figured I'd make sure you didn't get in over your head."

"Were you...were you *worried* about me?" Coop asked, almost not believing what he heard. Dane froze for a moment, his indifferent demeanor slipping for a split second before the walls went right back up.

"Don't flatter yourself," he scoffed as he continued up the stairs. "Watch your back, Coop."

With that, Dane was gone, heading back to the hellish prison where he lived. Coop grinned a little, vowing that he would free Dane and the others and soon. He would prove to them that hope and freedom existed, even if it was the last thing he did.

With that silent vow, Coop stood and moved up the stairs, disappearing into the night.

~~*~*~*

Isis woke up in a comfortable bed in the healing wing of the Pearl Castle. Clean sheets were drawn up to her shoulders and the room was peaceful. She was on her side, fully healed thanks to Amethyst, and in clean clothes. Her eyes fluttered open and she smiled as she breathed in the pure air. The morning birds chirped outside. The bright sun beamed down upon her, casting shadows of the window upon her bed and the clean tiled floor. A cool breeze drifted in from an open window and Isis closed her eyes again, basking in the perfect atmosphere that was the polar opposite of the hell she had escaped the previous night.

"You stubborn reckless woman!"

Isis jumped up in shock, not realizing how close

she was to the edge of the bed. She fell backward, entangled in the covers as she wound up in an undignified heap on the floor.

"God dammit, Steve!" Isis yelled as she straightened up again, tossing the covers back onto the bed. "What the hell is wrong with you?"

"What's wrong with me!?" Steve shouted, exasperated. "You're the one who doesn't seem to realize the purpose of gates!"

"Yeah, well, learn how to answer your damn phone, jackass!" Isis shot back, unable to think of a good retort. She glared at her friend, though part of her wondered why he was there in the first place. The Meadows was supposed to be inaccessible to all but the guardians and a few select shape shifters.

"Hey!"

Both Steve and Isis turned at the sound of a new voice. Electra stood a few feet away with her hands on her hips. There was a flash of faded pink as a messenger rushed past the young guardian.

"We can hear you two out in the main hall," she scolded.

"She started it," Steve protested, pointing at Isis.

"Real mature, Steve," Isis replied, irritated. Electra rolled her eyes and shook her head.

Isis smoothed the front of her jeans, glancing at her friend again. She was wearing her clothes from last night, and it made her a little self-conscious to be around guardians who were all dressed in finery. Usually Isis couldn't sleep in street clothes, but she had been so exhausted last night that she hadn't even noticed what she was wearing. She had barely had enough energy to tell Amethyst where she had been wounded. Noticing that Steve was wearing a regular plain blue t-shirt and black jeans — his normal weekend off-hours attire — Isis felt a lot less self-conscious.

"What *is* he doing here anyway? He's human," Isis grumbled, stretching one arm across her chest. The guardian healers really were remarkable; Isis didn't even feel any lingering ache from last night's fight. She was certain she had at least broken a couple ribs. Steve and Electra exchanged an uncomfortable look.

"Steve is…well, he's actually a shape shifter, from a long line of protectors," Electra explained, her tone careful. "He was assigned to protect you. It's a long, complicated story."

"Oh good, another one of those," Isis commented as she sat back on the bed and slipped on her black shoes.

"Are you mad?" Steve asked, looking at her with his big brown doe-eyes. Isis closed her eyes and rubbed the side of her face.

"No, I'm not mad," she replied after a moment, turning her eyes back to her friend. "After everything that has happened over the past couple months, I'm actually not even really that surprised to be honest."

She got up and started to leave the room.

"Where are you going?" Electra asked, drawing Isis' attention back to her.

"Are the other three here?" she asked. Electra nodded. Isis shrugged and replied, "Then I'm off to find them and hopefully chill out for a few minutes until we have to save the world again."

"Have fun," Electra said with a small smile. Isis returned the smile and nodded, slipping out of the healing rooms, eager to find her three friends, teammates, whatever they could be called. *I think I could actually get used to this strange new life,* she thought with a soft laugh.

~~*~*~*

Jet, Lilly, and Adonia watched Isis rejoin the other three from Adonia's office in the castle. Jet and Lilly turned when they heard a knock on the door.

"Enter," Adonia called out and the door opened. A messenger gestured for Sly to enter and she sauntered into the office, giving Jet and Lilly a crafty smile. Approaching the large desk, she folded herself into one of the chairs, crossing one long leg over the other.

"Good day to all of you. How does this fine morning find you?" she teased, mocking the formality frequently favored by guardian leaders. Lilly smiled a little, crossing her arms over her chest, while Jet studied her.

"Did you find anything?" he asked after a moment. Sly whistled, laying her hands over her knee.

"I did, though I do not think it will put your minds at ease. There's a spot near the forest I frequent, an old campsite that isn't used anymore. It's a favorite meeting spot for local assassins, due to its remoteness. You can talk about all sorts of unsavory business and not worry about being overheard. They also leave notes for each other, which you really can't decipher unless you're also an assassin. Boring stuff mostly: so-and-so is covering this job, vague threats, warnings, things like that. Anyway, after hearing about the ruckus last night, I figured there might be some sort of note or message to recognize the new regime, some attempt to get on ole Blackjack's good side."

"Was there?" Lilly asked and Sly nodded.

"I found Gia strung up by her ankles in the old oak tree, disemboweled, throat slit from ear-to-ear. They had branded her too," Sly raised her hands up. "An odd symbol was burned into her palms, one I've seen here and there. The same one I believe young Isis stumbled upon before she came to the mansion."

Sly dropped her hands again, raising an eyebrow as she waited for their response. Lilly turned her wide eyes to Jet and he could see the same dread he felt in her gaze. Assassins were known to be brutal when taking over territories, but they didn't often target each other. If they did, they tended to make the kills quick.

"Not sure about you, but I think that message is pretty loud and clear," Sly mentioned. "We're now in the era of Blackjack and whoever is backing him."

"Were you able to find any trace of Coop?" Lilly asked and Sly shook her head in response.

"The guy has disappeared off the face of the Earth. In fact, I can't find a shred of evidence that he ever even existed. Your man of mystery knows how to hide his tracks," she reported. "Did you get any leads on the mystery shadow watching out for Isis?"

"No," Jet replied, looking back out the window, glancing over at Adonia. "I guess we're still in the dark and that greatly concerns me."

For a long while Adonia was silent, watching her great granddaughter converse with Jade, Alex, and Shae. The heavenly appearance of her office helped calm everyone's nerves. She turned from the window.

"I feel as though our questions will be answered, probably very soon," she said. "I only hope that we are prepared for the answers we receive."

Jet and Lilly exchanged a look and watched Adonia stride out of her office, closing the door behind her.

"You protectors are such a *fun* bunch," Sly quipped, scrunching up her nose a little. "I do agree with her: it would appear someone is making a name for themselves and I don't think they are the type who would be content to stay behind the scenes for very long."

She slapped her hands on the arm rests and pushed herself out of the chair. "This has been a treat, but if you don't mind, I think I'd like to find my lover and spend some time with her."

Sly left the room, shutting the door behind her, and Jet turned his attention back to the window. Lilly moved closer to him, resting her head on his shoulder and he gently kissed the top of her golden hair.

"I worry about her too," she whispered, placing a hand on his chest. "They are a good team and they will do great things."

Jet smiled and rested his cheek against his wife's soft hair, trusting her wisdom as he always had. Whatever the future held for them, they would get through it.

~~*~*~*

In a small dark room, hidden away from all eyes, one man sat hunched over files on a small desk. Studying the gruesome images from the woods, he sighed and rubbed the bridge of his nose. It was going to be another incredibly long day. The door opened, drawing his attention, and he almost groaned when he recognized the lean man in the hoodie who entered. His brother, his ally, his foe.

"Where oh where to begin," his brother began, pushing his hood back. "Your piss poor plan to retrieve Adara utterly failed, which of course means we didn't get the valuable information on the Grenich Corporation that she probably had. Said corporation now has complete control of the assassins in this territory as a result, meaning the protectors are in even *more* danger. *And* if all that weren't bad enough, Coop has left town and is now who knows where. So, we also don't have an experiment helping us anymore. Bravo, brother. Bra-fucking-vo."

His brother clapped slowly and the man narrowed his eyes as he glared at him, not appreciating his sarcasm.

"Coop is a free man and therefore allowed to do whatever he wants. If he believes he can do more good for them elsewhere, more power to him," the man muttered. "Shouldn't you be wearing a mask or something?"

"Took it off before I opened the door," his brother replied, pulling a small portion of the mask he used to conceal the lower part of his face out of his collar to show the other man. He leaned forward, resting his knuckles on the desk. "Look, if you stay on the defensive, you'll never accomplish anything. You sure as hell won't do any good, hiding in dank corners like a little mouse."

"And what, pray tell, is your solution? Just keep shooting until you run out of bullets? Sorry, this isn't the Wild West," the man scolded, not attempting to hide the harshness in his tone.

His brother leaned forward even closer, anger blazing in his eyes. "If you don't do something soon, they will get her. He's already using assassins, like

Blackjack, as pawns. They completely upended the assassin hierarchy in this state practically overnight. That doesn't concern you at all?"

The man shook his head and turned his attention back to the file in front of him, trying to figure out if he should do anything in response. It was much too soon and he didn't have near enough resources, but the temptation was there. The man studied a picture of the woman's slit throat. The Corporation heads would never be so bold and the man was certain one of their sons was behind the gruesome act.

His brother snatched the picture away from him, slapping it back on the desk. "They almost have you in a checkmate and I won't let you play this game with her. If Carding gets her, so help me, I'll—"

"You'll what?" the man challenged, closing the file and putting it off to the side for the moment. "Kill me? Please. You couldn't do it then and you can't do it now. Your threats are empty and mean absolutely nothing to me. You've already taken away everything that ever mattered in my life. Need I remind you again that it's *your* goddamn fault we're in this situation in the first place? You certainly helped the Corporation for long enough. So, don't come in here, throwing a temper tantrum, and making demands."

"I know you don't believe in change—"

"Oh no, see that's where you're mistaken. I believe most people can change. I don't believe *you* could ever change. There's a big difference."

His brother faltered, the man knew which sensitive parts to strike when dealing with him. He slumped in the chair across from the desk, anger and hurt swimming in his eyes.

"You're never going to forgive me, are you?" he

whispered. The man was quiet, watching his brother.

"Can you blame me?"

His brother didn't respond and turned his eyes to the floor. For a moment, the man's coldness slipped. He wanted to forgive his brother — so much that it hurt sometimes — but he just couldn't. Not after all he had done, not after all he had taken from him. Some things were simply unforgivable.

"So what's our next step?" his brother asked, looking up and returning to his "work as usual" mode. Now the first man smiled. He opened one of the plain green drawers, which his brother insisted on describing as vomit-colored. He pushed aside a small flashdrive and a couple plain photographs from an old abandoned warehouse, which had once captured the scene of a murder. He pulled out a single rancid-smelling flower, rolling it lazily between his thumb and his index finger. His brother stared at him, a faint trace of horror in his bright green eyes. He shook his head a little.

"No. Not yet, it's too soon," he protested. The man tossed the flower to his brother, who easily caught it.

"Here I thought you'd be happy with the next step. You're going to be reunited with the love of your life."

His brother shot him a look of skepticism. "Oh yeah. I'm sure she'll be positively *thrilled* to see me."

"Nobody ever said redemption was easy," the man paused, "or free."

The younger man put his feet up on the desk, smiling at the irritated eye roll it elicited from his older brother. "So, what's the plan? I just appear in the Meadows and let them take me to the dungeons?"

The man nodded, twisting his chair. His eyes never left his brother.

"And how exactly is this going to help us accomplish our goal?"

"Everything is on a need-to-know basis. Trust me. You owe me that much."

"Fine," his brother relented and stood from his chair. "I'm going for a drink. I'll Appear there—"

"When I tell you to," the man interrupted. "Enjoy your last days of freedom. It's going to be a *long* time before you get any more of them."

His brother snorted. "Freedom, please. You and I both know that's a fantasy, a fairy tale told to humans so they can sleep better at night."

"As much as I'd enjoy getting into this pessimistic philosophical chat, I've got work to do," the man stated as he turned back to his files. The last thing he wanted to deal with was one of his brother's childish nihilistic moods. He was neither in the mood nor had the patience for it.

"I'll await your call then." His brother turned to leave, but hesitated, stating darkly, "He's not going to lay a hand on her. He's not going to turn her into one of those mindless drones in that prison he calls a state of the art laboratory."

"No, he won't. We won't let him," the man reassured his brother, looking up to meet his gaze. "If all goes well, no other shape shifters will suffer at his hands."

His brother twisted and looked at him, nodding once. It was an indication that he trusted the man's word. He slunk out the door, leaving the man alone with his work. The man sighed and turned back to his files.

"Another day, another fight with a ruthless, power-hungry lunatic with too much money and influence," the man muttered to himself as he ran his hands over his scruffy face. *Just a regular day in the secretive hell on Earth. Oh Isis, I hope my brother and I can spare you this grief.*

To Be Continued

ACKNOWLEDGMENTS

Thank you so much to my friends and family, who are continually supportive of me. Thank you to my parents for their endless patience, love, and support. Thank you to my brother, Michael, and Mom for being great proofreaders. Thank you to my amazing godmother, Leandra Torres (Aunt Punkey), a woman who I very much admire and who is always there with an encouraging word.

Thank you to my amazing editor, Rose Anne Roper. Thank you to my cover artist, Najla Qamber. Thank you to my always awesome beta reader, Taia Hartman.

Thank you so much to Snowy Wings Publishing for helping me achieve a dream and providing support, as well as helping immensely with marketing. I must give a very special thank you to my good friend, Lyssa Chiavari, who invited me to join Snowy Wings and for being one of the absolute best people in the world. It is truly an honor to know you and call you a friend.

Thank you so much to all the wonderful professors in my life, who have taught me and continue to teach me to this day. Thank you so much, Alex and Jess Hall for your continued knowledge of all things concerning mythology. It is an honor to know you both. Thank you, Marco Benassi and Alexander Bolyanatz, for never giving up on me and providing advice when needed. Thank you Ángela Rebellón (the best ASL teacher there is). Thank you to all the professors and teachers who I've thanked in previous novels. If you enjoyed this novel, it is thanks to them. Any success I've experienced is thanks in large part to the dedicated professors and teachers I've had the privilege to learn from.

Thank you so much to all the incredible asexual artists who I have met through Asexual Artists. Thank you to my dear friends, Joel Cornah, Darcie Little Badger, and T. Hueston. You put such beautiful art into the world and it inspires me so very much. I love you all.

Thank you so much to my family and friends for providing me with the support I need to continue on the rocky path that is writing. Thank you, Billy Payne, for coming to my first reading and making the experience a lot less terrifying. Thank you Robyn Byrd, Emily Kittell-Queller (extra special thanks to you and your housemates for being a safe haven on the holidays), Julie Denninger-Greensly, Ryan Prior, Leigh Hellman, and anyone else who I'm forgetting (and will undoubtedly feel just awful about later). Your love, kind words, encouragement, and support make a world of difference in my life.

A special thank you to Becca (who gave me the most wonderful compliment a writer can ever hope to hear) and Susan Sandahl, who continue to be active on my author page and are some of the most awesome people I've ever had the pleasure of meeting. You're both my favorite readers and I apologize for the ridiculously long wait.

Again, I must thank all my readers. Thank you for your kind words and gestures. Thank you for getting lost in the crazy world I created. Thank you for continuing to be so generous with your time. I cannot begin to express my gratitude to you all. You continue to humble me and I hope this book lived up to your expectations. Thank you all, so very, very much.

.

ABOUT THE AUTHOR

Lauren Jankowski, an openly aromantic asexual feminist activist and author from Illinois, has been an avid reader and a genre feminist for most of her life. She holds a degree in Women and Genders Studies from Beloit College. In 2015, she founded "Asexual Artists," a Tumblr and WordPress site dedicated to highlighting the contributions of asexual identifying individuals to the arts.

She has been writing fiction since high school, when she noticed a lack of strong women in the popular genre books. When she's not writing or researching, she enjoys reading (particularly anything relating to ancient myths) or playing with her pets. She participates in activism for asexual visibility and feminist causes. She hopes to bring more strong heroines to literature, including badass asexual women.

Her ongoing fantasy series is *The Shape Shifter Chronicles*, which is published through Snowy Wings Publishing.